WAR
AND HIS
QUEEN

USA Today & Wall Street Journal Bestselling Author
AMO JONES

War and His Queen
Copyright 2024 Amo Jones (Villainous Pen Publishing)

All rights reserved. No part of this publication may be reproduced, distributed, or transmitted in any form or by any means, including photocopying, recording, translating, or other electronic or mechanical methods, without prior written permission of the publisher, except in the case of brief quotations embodied in reviews and certain other non-commercial uses permitted by copyright law.

This book is a work of fiction. All names, characters, locations, and incidents are products of the author's imagination. Any resemblance to actual persons, things, living or dead, locales, or events is entirely coincidental.

Editor: Sarah Plocher
First proofread: Virginia Tesi Carey
Final proofread: Rumi Khan
Formatting: Champagne Book Design
Cover design: Jay Aheer
Photographer: Michelle Lancaster

The Elite Kings Club left a trail of fear behind every person who whispered their names throughout the centuries that they'd existed. They were the product of every nightmare you were told as a child, only now, they don't go bump in the night. They race modified cars, throw parties to conceal their morbid games, and leave behind the kind of chaos that can never be tamed.

They were from an ancient bloodline of the three Founding Fathers, and it was almost time for them to plunge deeper into the depths of hell. Now that they were all on their motherland, and even closer to an island with history as dark as it was ruthless, no one had a say in the carnage of what was to come. And in this case, with War and Halen. Until now, they were nothing but exactly as they appeared on the outside.

He was a brother's best friend, and a boy Halen had never not known.

She was the daughter of one of the most feared families known to man, and the only girl who ever kindled his rage. They'd push and pull until it tore them apart…if only to feel the shell of their bodies close.

Halen knew crossing that line with him was dangerous ground, yet she yielded her weapon and did it anyway. But history was being challenged, and the Kings were about to learn that not all enemies are discovered on a battlefield.

Some are the ghosts of what was left behind.

TRIGGER LIST AND AUTHOR NOTE

If you don't want to read the triggers,
please still read the author note.

*This book will not be the darkest book in the *Carpe Noctem* series. Compared to upcoming books in the series, I would consider this slightly above middle ground.

Explicit language
Questionable sex scenes (dark)
Gun play
Dubious consent
Non-con (reread this one please)
Murder (a lot of it)
Characters who don't give a fuck about redemption (if a few shades darker than morally gray is not for you, please don't read this book)
Sexual abuse (on page and off)
Extremely graphic violence and torture scenes
Lust murder (please reread)
Human pawns used as their weapons for their battleground; nothing more and nothing less (no one else is important to each other but each other)
Excessive drug and alcohol use on page (Pablo Escobar, hit me up—also joking)
Self-harm discussed

Before going into this book please understand that these characters do not hold back.

This book is for the messy folk. The ones who love the toxicity of a violently bonded couple. They're sadistic in their mind games and do everything in their power to break the other, but if anyone else dares, they'll fuck them up. This is an "I can destroy you as much as I want but if anyone else even so much as breathes at you wrong, I'll rip their fucking lungs out and hang them as an ornament on my wall" type book. From both sides…

In saying that (haha…) this is a book of fiction. No, I am not these things, do what they do, believe in the same things they do, nor do these characters represent who I am as a woman or a human. They can be (at times) a terrifying figment of my imagination. Using my artistic flair for chaos, I allow them to control every step of the way when executing their stories.

I do not advise anyone to partake in any of the activities you find inside (please don't. I don't look good in orange). This book is recommended for people over the age of 18. Please heed the triggers and this note carefully. I have warned you. If you're new to dark romance and are not familiar with the content that may lay ahead, you can continue, of course, but know that this series will not be a kind first date. It will tear through your virtue and leave you there to bleed out.

I mean, War and Halen won't be a terrible first date, but if you're starting from Priest and his Anarchist, or Stella and her Outlaws, I would back up and start with *War and His Queen*.

If you're still reading and yelling at me to shut the fuck up already so you can get to the good shit.…

Leave your morals here and flip the page…

To my readers.
Yes, the men I write do want to fuck you just like that...

WAR

AND HIS

QUEEN

HALEN

OUR PARENTS WOULD TELL STORIES ABOUT THE DAYS when they were in high school in the Hamptons instead of Riverside. I can't think of anything worse than going to school in the fucking Hamptons. Nothing against the place, but having to exist with the mundane who know nothing of the world I was born into sounds like a fucking liability.

I draw in a deep breath. I've been waiting thirty fucking minutes. Only they would make me wait at all—and for what? It better be a good reason. I am tired as hell. Me and the girls sat up all night last night planning what we were going to do. How it was going to be done and what kind of carnage we could create with the time that we have left before the ritual.

Digging through my handbag, something pinches my thumb and I suck it between my lips as the clovers from my bracelet shine against the sun. "These assholes better hurry up."

Elaborate patterns line the gold archway to the front door of Hayes Castle. I wish I was joking. Our home is an excessive portrayal of modern-day regency, presenting a deceptive image of perfection and gold.

Leaning against the entryway table next to the bifurcated staircase, I hear cars pulling up outside. Doors open and close, and then heavy footsteps pound against the marble porch. Finally, both doors part open, and there, standing in front of me, is my twin brother.

"Don't fucking look at me like that, Halen. This is the first time we're not all waiting on you."

"First of all…" I take a step toward him, before he widens the door further, revealing War and Vaden out on the driveway. "Wait, why are you all here and not already there?"

War lifts his arm to rest on the door of my car, flashing me a wide smirk. Aside from being painfully annoying all my life, he has made it his mission for as long as I can remember to make everything difficult for me. He also has a perverse way of getting off on my demise.

"Get in the car, Halen."

With a raised brow, my mouth snaps closed. "Uhm, I wasn't talking to you."

His tongue glides over his lower lip. "Oh, you weren't? Hmmm… let me see where I can find the fucks I can give you. Maybe they're beneath my nine-inch cock. Get in the car."

"Shut the fuck up. Both of you." Priest—aka said twin brother—turns his back to me and I watch as he makes his way back down to his ride. He opens the front door, and I trace the lines of his flared guards. Priest's S15 is the best you'd ever see. Dumped almost on its ass and rolling with deep black rims. We all have different cars, but they all stick with the same theme. Even our Euros do.

Black. Even the number plates that we don't have to display.

"Pap is away, you know!" I call out, flipping Priest off behind his back and shoulder barging past War on my way down.

"Wanna try that again?" War calls out from behind his GTR. The fact that he *stole* the R32 body that I wanted to build when we were fourteen, and worked it to push over eight hundred horse, meant that not only did I need to import the R34 from Japan, but I threw in a Hakosuka for shits and gigs. Vaden then made a mad dash for the S14, before War was an absolute asshole and took a damn RX4. War's 32 is pretty, though. Gloss black with a wide body kit and bronze deep-dish rims. And that's not even mentioning what's under the hood. We're just one massive family with a Godzilla complex. Which only meant River grabbed the Honda NSX and Stella the RX7 Batty. Priest has a collection too long to detail.

I can almost feel the daggers Vaden is shooting at War. "We're laughing until we're not and Priest shoots you between the eyes."

"My aim is better!" I call out, sliding into my 34. I push the start button and breathe out a sigh as she purrs beneath me like a well-groomed beast.

There's a knock on my window. I flutter my lashes up at my twin and crank it down. Our similarities end with our hair color. Where my eyes are green like Mom's, his are honey hazel and rimmed black. How he stands at six-six and me five-four I will never know. The math is not mathing.

"Yes, brother?"

"Don't look at me like that." He flicks my forehead with his finger. "You ain't racing at Devil's Cockpit." My smile falls. "I mean it, Halen. You're not. I need you to hang back with the girls for tonight."

"What!" I snap. "Do I look like a babysitter to you?" It doesn't help that I'm the oldest girl, even if not by much. The others don't need a damn babysitter. Except for maybe Stella.

"You look like you'll be whatever I want you to be." He leans down, tossing a mask onto the passenger seat. "It's Friday the thirteenth."

"I don't want—" He stalks off once again. My window closes as I open my Spotify playlist. I need backup.

I tap my best friend's number, checking my lipstick in the rearview mirror before directing my car out of the circular driveway. Riverside is a smaller town, with a population of 13,534. The population is important, because anytime it drops, we make sure it's from natural causes. If anyone steps into our town and inflicts harm, they answer to our Fathers, and soon… to us.

"I'm ready, but hear me out…"

I slump against my chair, narrowing my eyes even though I know she can't see me. No one relied on me to take care of others, but I liked to anyway. It's like I was birthed with a natural flair to protect my family, so I'd never complain, but if they thought I was *babysitting*, then maybe they wouldn't find out about what we really do.

Sometimes, and I mean mostly every day, we needed a fucking break. To be away from the glamour and gold, and just… exist. Do whatever the fuck we want without our brothers looking down on us like pesky house cats that hadn't been fed in two hours.

"I don't want to hear you out, Evie!" Evelyn Paige has been in my life since we were two years old. Mother said we reminded her of her and her best friend Tate. I wasn't so sure if that was true. I love Aunty Tay, but the bitch is as crazy as Mom. I swear, we all watch as they enable each other through bad decisions. Now it's shopping, holidays, and petty revenge. I can't imagine what they would have been like as teenagers.

Evie is not that. Not even close.

"You better be ready!" I tap the indicator to turn down her street. It's a little after ten, so it's quiet when I pull my car up to the curb outside her house, the RB engine rumbling beneath my butt.

I open a new text to her, tucking my long chocolate brown hair behind my ear. When she doesn't answer, I peer up at her house.

All homes in Riverside are somewhere on the scale of *big money energy*, and Evie's dad's pockets were one of the steepest in our town. Her parents owned a billion-dollar umbrella company and decided to raise their only daughter here. To be given the right to buy in Riverside, you have to get council approval, and that council is the Elite Kings. So, her family either has history tied to one of the ten Founding Families, or they came in by jumping into Dad's. Considering his Forbes ranking, I'd say it could be a combination of both.

The light on their patio switches on and a glimmer of chestnut hair glows under the light. Evelyn Paige was anything but basic. She always went all out with her outfits, even when we'd be chilling.

She leisurely descends the wide porch wearing a beige matching set that includes a short skirt, a little crop top, knee-high beige boots that have a relaxed fit around her legs, and a long trench coat. She has her hair in a tight, low bun and is wearing white-rimmed sunglasses that cover her amber eyes.

The passenger door opens, and she slides in, moving the discarded mask onto the floor.

"You look hot, bitch, but are those my shoes?" She leans over the center to scan my outfit. Tassel-ripped, high-waisted, wide-bottom jeans with knee tears over the thighs, paired with Air 1s. I kept the top simple with a tied white crop top that tucks beneath my boobs.

"No." I hesitate, sliding into first gear. Shit. They could be. Since we all share a similar style, in a way that none of us are consistent, I don't know who leaves what in my room.

"I have your Dolce shoes, anyway." She shrugs, tapping the mirror down to check her lipstick. "Figure you won't need them since you have them in every other color, and besides—" I glare at her from over my arm. And besides what? "—you know pink isn't your color."

She has a point. "True."

"What's the plan tonight?"

I tap my finger against the steering wheel, looking between the road and the LED dash that illuminates the time.

"Hales…" Her voice breaks through my thoughts and she shifts in her seat to face me. "I know that fucking look. What are you thinking?"

"The Kings are doing their usual tonight and being bossy with it." I'm not sure if I'm thinking at all, since I'm pretty sure if I get caught doing what I'm about to suggest we do, that it will end in one or two ways. The first? Priest will lock me in my room like fucking Rapunzel and won't let me out for weeks, or… War. War's wrath isn't something I particularly want to witness.

I pump the brakes when we reach a red light, my eyes flicking between the two signs in front of us. One points to the Riverside town center, and the other to the highway that leads straight to Chevalier Hill.

"I mean…" Evie teases as she removes her sunglasses. Her eyes glisten with mischief as she looks between me and the sign, rubbing her hands over her dark brown thighs. "This would absolutely piss your brother off."

"He's not the one I'm trying to piss off." I squeeze the steering wheel.

Evie pauses, raising a perfectly laminated brow. She knows who I'm referring to. "What did he do now?"

I push the clutch and drive it into first. They'll be spilling through these streets any minute now and when they do, I don't want to be here.

I punch in the clutch and tap the accelerator with my other foot. Just as I hit a high RPM, I release the clutch and slam that same foot down on the brakes until my back tires lose traction and smoke veils the windows of the car. Evie and I both breathe in the familiar smell of hot asphalt and burnt rubber as if it's our signature perfume.

Dropping it into second, I release the brakes and floor us forward. I'd never go to Chevalier Hill, but it would be fun to see how far we can actually go until someone, or something, stops us.

First stop: pick up the girls.

Love was nothing more than a mask used to forgive someone for all the wrongs they did. Love didn't exist. Obsession did.

My fingers touched the top of the water as my eyes closed. Birds chirped around the crashing waterfall as I dug my toes deeper into the sand. I'd waited for this moment. The elated minutes that passed when I knew I shouldn't be here.

I opened my eyes and looked over my shoulder. Where the hell did River go? Our towels were sprawled out over the sand as the sound of Metallica played through the air. I loved it here.

Water continued to swallow my body as I moved deeper and deeper out. As soon as the bite of cold evaporated, I dipped beneath the water, holding my nose. My skin no longer prickled like a furnace as I pushed up from the sandy ground, surfacing back to the top. I swiped my eyes clean as ink bled down my hands from my mascara, and I spun around to face the shoreline once again, hoping to find River, only to collide with a hard body. My hand flew and landed against his chest. I knew who it was. Even without his telling tattoos, I'd know. The vehemence that followed him everywhere was trailed by a tongue of flames that always seemed to taste me anytime he was near. One of these days he was going to swallow me whole.

Stop, Halen. Think. Not that. Not now.

"War..." I shoved myself away from him, but his hand snapped around my back, forcing me close. As if he knew that I didn't want him to be near, but more I needed him to. In darkness, even the violent burn of hatred could lead you home. "What the fuck are you doing?" I managed to writhe my way around in his arms, and just when I thought he was going to let me swim to the shoreline, his hand was on my belly, pressing me back again.

His fingers sprawled out over my skin. "Stop fucking talking." I bit down on my bottom lip as my breath caught in my throat. I didn't fucking want to stop talking. I wanted to be angry at him for touching me. I wanted to let that fire burn until it turned us both to ash.

He brushed his lips against the side of my neck and fear pebbled over my flesh. Fear, anger, hatred—they were all cooked with the same ingredients used to fuel the one emotion that was abused as much as it was chased. "You want this. Stop fucking playing." His fingertips skimmed the line of my bikini and my thighs clenched together. "I don't know why. All I'd do is break you open and tear out every single thing that makes you *good*."

I pushed away from him and this time instead of him holding me in place, he let go. I swam through the water, annoyed with myself for not fighting hard enough. Why did I let that happen?

Fuck War.

And fuck the casualties that he always seems to take down with him.

"You good?" Stella peered at me over her Prada glasses, holding two red Solo cups in each hand. Her midnight black hair was braided into two fancy fishtails on either side of her head. "What'd he do?"

"Nothing." I swiped one of the cups from her. If there was one thing that I was good at doing, that was ignoring War.

Well… no, that was only a half-truth.

Passing the people drinking near the swing that swoops out to the water, I followed the trail through the clearing, stepping over broken twigs and flowers. Devil's Cockpit starts from the bed of water on the other side near the skid pad, but you can also cut through this track to get to the private sandy cove.

I hadn't quite reached the end when I felt the invisible touch of eyes from behind. Maybe it was the silence because of the separation between where I stood and where I had to go, or maybe it was the way the wind curled around my ankles and that familiar weight of dread filled my stomach.

My fingers prickled as I spun around, only to be met with nothing. Nothing but the empty pathway that I just walked. Before I could overthink, I continued through the track. That same weight fell to the ground when a shadow stepped out from behind a tree.

He was tall and lanky, and had a red-and-white spiral earring hooked from his lobe.

His head tilted to the side and my mouth watered.

He was way too old to be here.

"You lost?" My feet carried me to where he stood, as the wind tossed around the loose strands of my hair.

I tucked a lock behind my ear. "I'm Halen, I—" I paused. *Oh no.* He didn't answer.

I sidestepped away from him, but my arm brushed his in passing. Blinding pain gripped around my throat as I fell to my knees. I couldn't breathe. The world began to crumble around me.

The track.

The sand.

The laughter and sounds of shredding tires.

Everything dissolved around me as he grabbed me by my throat and hauled me to my feet. The world as I knew it was no longer.

The world as I knew it was bleak.

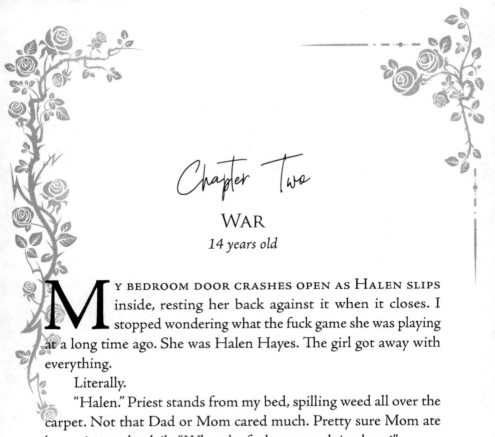

Chapter Two

WAR

14 years old

MY BEDROOM DOOR CRASHES OPEN AS HALEN SLIPS inside, resting her back against it when it closes. I stopped wondering what the fuck game she was playing at a long time ago. She was Halen Hayes. The girl got away with everything.

Literally.

"Halen." Priest stands from my bed, spilling weed all over the carpet. Not that Dad or Mom cared much. Pretty sure Mom ate brownies on the daily. "What the fuck are you doing here?"

Even with J. Cole and Joyner Lucas beating through the walls, it does nothing to distract Priest.

"Ah… like I'm not coming if you guys are throwing a party!" She flicks her long brown hair over her shoulder, narrowing her eyes on all of us. She settles on me, because she always fucking does.

My eyes fall to the cup she's holding in her hand. "You drunk?"

"Hmmm?" She straightens her shoulders a little too tightly, as if trying to appear sober. "No. Unfortunately."

Vaden watches her closely, his eyes darkening. "She's off her face."

"Aw, Vade…" She drops her bottom lip. "We could bet your R35 that I'm not."

Priest points at his twin with a rolled J between his fingers. "Go downstairs. Now. I'm taking you home."

"You can't. You're drunk." I push up from my bed, holding her stare. "I'll take her." We'd been avoiding each other since her thirteenth birthday. Pretty sure she made an extra effort to stay away from me after that.

Priest tucks the joint behind his ear, closing the distance between the two of them. He lowers himself to her eye level, which is more than a whole foot shorter. "You were supposed to be at home."

She challenges him. "I was. And then I decided that I wanted to get drunk. Lucky for me, you guys make that easy."

"I'll drop her on the way to Emma's." The party is small right now because the night is young. It's barely nine p.m. and she is clearly already off her shit. In a couple hours, the house will be filled with drunk fuckboys, and well... Dad said no blood on the carpet.

I wait for him to answer, careful around the subject of Halen. Priest didn't give much of a shit about anything, but when it came to his sister, he folded. Not always, because she liked to use his patience as a fucking jump rope. He leaves her alone but make no mistake, he's always watching her. They were called the Shadow Twins growing up. She was daylight, he was darkness, and everywhere she went, he would be there. Priest was her veil, and if anyone tried lifting that shit, he'd slit your fucking throat and wear your organs as jewelry.

Priest ignores her, keeping his eyes fixed on mine. "Lock her in her room when you get there."

"Errr—I'm right here!" she snaps, taking another step closer to Priest. I grab her by the arm, opening the door with my other and hauling her ass down the hallway.

"War!" she growls, hitting my hand away, which only makes me squeeze harder. I don't release her until we're down the stairs, out the front door, and I'm throwing her into the passenger seat of my RX4.

"You really gonna handle that?" Vaden asks from the shadows

on the patio as I slam her door closed. He flicks his cigarette onto the concrete. "Or do we need to go over how we don't shit where we eat?" He raises a single dark brow at me, taking a careful step out of the shadows. The glow of the garden lights details his face, flaunting one blue eye and one brown. "Or how we all took an oath between us that we wouldn't fuck around with each other."

I flip him off, reaching for the door handle on the driver's side. "You don't have to tell me shit." That oath was bullshit. We all knew it. It was made for *me* by *me*. They all simply agreed.

Priest knew why I did it. He was too smart not to.

I swing the door closed and pump the clutch. The rotary engine pulses beneath me like a song I could play on repeat, but Halen reaches for the radio anyway. Tension snaps between us, but she wouldn't be able to stay quiet for long. It isn't until we're down the long driveway that she turns the music off and shifts her body around to face me. I knew she was going to say some dumb shit, but I wasn't expecting…

"I need you to fuck me."

I slam on the brakes and she flies forward, one hand on the dash. "What the fuck, Halen?"

Her emerald eyes widen on me as her fingers rake through her hair to pile it on top of her head. "It's a simple request, War." She shrugs, her long hair now tied in a high pony. "Please? I need to—" She pauses a moment, her eyes drifting off in the distance before her head shakes and she's back on me. "—scrub my V-card and I'd rather not fuck any peasants from school."

My mouth opens and then closes. I've never been speechless, but of course it was her who was the first to do it.

"Stop fucking talking." I turn back to the road, shifting into first gear. I'm about to release the clutch when her fingers wrap around my chin and she's forcing my attention back onto her. Halen and I have always been a no go. Brotherhood oath aside, I'd never do it. It's why I put the fucking thing in place to begin with. I didn't do it for anyone else but myself. Then there's Priest.

And Bishop fucking Hayes as her daddy. Yeah, you've got a better chance of getting laid in a fucking nunnery than me *ever* hitting that.

"War, I'm serious." My eyes drop to her lips. They're on the puffy side. Always looking like she's been kissed way too fucking much. They suit her diamond-cut face. Thick lashes surround emerald green eyes, and her cheekbones are high and sharp—until she smiles. She'd always been cute. If cute meant she could also break your nose with her right hook. *True fucking story.* But tonight was the first night I recognized just how much her features had changed. Somewhere between the little girl I'd known all my life and this woman she was growing into, was whoever this person was looking back at me, asking me to fuck her.

Fuck.

I would be lying to myself if I said she wasn't hot. But that didn't take away the fact that she was a Hayes.

Fuck. That.

Her lashes fan out over her cheeks as she searches my eyes. I don't even care that I've stopped in the middle of the road and that there is a chance we could be spotted since everyone knew who owned our cars in this town, even our exotic rides.

"Halo…"

I don't even get to finish my sentence before she's sliding over the center, gripping me from the back of my neck and lowering herself onto my lap.

My hand comes to her throat out of instinct, but instead of it helping my situation, all it does is show the tattoos on my hand against her virgin fucking skin.

She blushes, and just when I think she's going to panic and tell me to let her go, the corner of her mouth curves up and her teeth catch her bottom lip. "Okay, then let's play."

"Fuck me…" I growl, my patience waning. If this is all it's going to take for me to question everything, then shit. I need to distract myself. Distance. I need more distance.

"I'm trying!" She rolls her eyes. I catch her hips when she thrusts against me, shoving her back into her chair.

Her head hits the window. "Ow!"

"Stay the fuck there. I mean it."

"Fine!" She whacks down the mirror, fixing her lipstick. "But don't say I didn't come to you first."

Now

That was almost six years ago and as much as neither her nor I have ever spoken about it again, I kind of want to every time she's around, just to torment her. Have we stayed away from each other since? Yeah. It was easy enough to do, until we were all together. Which is almost every fucking day. I don't think any of us have gone longer than a week from being apart.

So we did what we had to. People in Riverside wouldn't so much as breathe near any of those girls without us knowing about it. It's hard to try and get with a girl whose family is part of the most feared criminal organization known to man. Organization is probably putting it lightly. It's a order. A way of life. Generation through generation, we have controlled all sectors of power in the world. Dubbed the modern-day illuminati from conspiracists throughout the years. They're almost right. Only they're not.

It's kept the weak away from the girls. If you're not up to stepping up against us, then you don't deserve to have them on their knees. It's a win-win.

"Yo!" I whistle out to Vaden as he slides into his jacked-up R35. I toss the *Scream* mask at him and he catches it in midair as I open the driver's door to my R32. I gutted the fucking thing from the ground up, dumped it on its ass, and dressed it up with deep-dish rims. Currently, it's pushing eight hundred horse, which is nothing if you compare it to Vaden's new Hennessey Venom, but it's still the fastest JDM we have and I didn't pay a couple mill for it.

The mask hangs off Vaden's finger. "The fuck? What's with the cheesy cliché? The only mask that touches this face is my million-dollar Calvaria."

"Put the fucking thing on." Priest opens the door to his 180SX. He pauses, looking down at my Jason mask. "Time to play with the children."

Chapter Three

HALEN

I REV THE ENGINE LOUDLY OUTSIDE THE VITIOSIS MANOR, after Evie and I went home quickly to switch out cars. The Hakosuka is *the* favorite child. Painted ivory with blacked-out badges, she's the perfect ride or die. Early on, we had to change the engine because older GTRs didn't come with the RB. But now, she's a weapon.

When she takes too long, I slide my ass up onto the car door through the window. The Vitiosis manor offers direct mountain views due to its secluded location. It incorporates modern-day gothic architecture, featuring glass windows, sleek black paneling, and Marquina marble stoneware. Our parents started developing Elite Boulevard, which now extends across the entire land behind Riverside, during their pregnancies.

Down Elite Boulevard, is Hayes, Vitiosis, and Malum Lane. The first house you come across is Hayes Castle, situated between Malum and Vitiosis. Brantley and Saint, Stella and Vaden's parents, decided to build theirs at a safe distance from civilization. All of the Kings have been building their own houses for years now, and last I checked, Priest's was almost ready. We hadn't seen any of them because each house is hidden from view, branching off from our parents' land.

Naturally.

The chandelier hanging from the ceiling casts a flickering light over the patio. Their laughter fills the air as they stumble out the door, their tangled locks a chaotic mix of blonde and raven. Stella has her midnight hair in a ponytail, braided down her back, while River's sandy waves have been ironed flat.

River chose a sleek strapless minidress in black with side slits and thigh-high strapped heels, while Stella opted for a glossy, form-fitting black strapless minidress and coordinating thigh-high boots.

"I said not to make me wait!" I raise a brow at my other two sisters, before sliding back into the car and winding my window up.

While Stella piles in and slams the door closed, River leans forward, her arm brushing against mine. "First of all," her hair falls to one side, "you and I both know that we had to all wait for the pack of demons to go play with their toys."

"I feel like they're getting worse with age." Evie tosses the bag of coke to River. Since Stella is a couple years younger than us, we mostly try to keep her away from trouble. But she's eighteen, and as much as we've tried to shelter her from a lot of shit growing up, she's a King. She's going to want to play...

...and she does.

Evie turns to me. "Well, where to? New York? Please! I wonder if I can find that one—"

Suppressing a laugh, I steer us around the circular driveway that takes us down the mountain and back onto Elite Boulevard. "Have you not been on Snapchat?"

Evie shakes her head slowly as Stella leans forward and turns the music up. "Fight the Feeling" by Rod Wave plays through the subwoofers. "No!" she yells, just as her phone lights up. I watch as the two little lines that appear between her brows slowly disappear and the corner of her mouth twitches. "Oh, perfect."

I turn the music down a smidge. "Yup." My eyes meet the girls in the back. "I've been thinking. We could start something similar to Devil's Cockpit, but without them being annoying." I pause, thinking over my next words. Whatever they do on Perdita is in a whole different genre of playtime. Perdita is our mother island, and is a short three-hour flight off the coast of Riverside. The island itself is occupied by our own people, and civilians who are connected to the ten Founding Families who prefer to live in a lawless society. It's run by a bitch I hate, and weaponized by a bunch of boys who have been bred on the island for hundreds of years. The Lost Boys. Only they aren't boys. They're as calm as Red Riding Hood, but as hungry as the wolf.

Stella peeks up from the back after scrolling through the private Snapchat. "You started something in Bayonet Falls? That place is abandoned, isn't it? Since the war between *they who shall not be named* and us." I choke on my laugh at Stella's poor attempt of trying to not bring up the Gentlemen.

"Yeah, but that's why it's a perfect place to have them."

"By them, you mean races? Actually, a good idea. It's between Riverside and Chevalier Hill, so it's not fucking with the treaty, and—"

She raises her index finger, flashing her ten-carat radiant diamond ring. Our fathers ice us out with every birthday, drowning us in diamonds. I'm sure there's a hidden meaning behind why, and I'm certain it has to do with intimidation.

"—most importantly, we can do whatever the fuck we want." The sweet smoke of zaza fills the air as Stella hands it to Evie. "You know they think we're all virgins."

My teeth catch my lip to stop my smile. "Only because we allow them to."

I guide us through the forested landscape of Vitiosis Drive. Riverside may have over thirteen thousand residents, but everyone, including people who don't live here, know who we are.

Us girls came up with a loophole when we were young to keep the boys from finding out about anything we do. We would drive into the city and hit parties there. It was a four-hour drive there and four-hour drive home, but we usually left on a Friday and came home on a Saturday.

Playing with lies was easy, since we were all in it for each other.

Deep down, I knew none of us wanted to be caught, yet it granted us freedom. Freedom to be around people that didn't know us, our parents, or our families. At least not personally, and if they did figure us out, it was easy to say that rumors were just that—rumors.

Of course, we don't kill people.

No, my pop wasn't the president of the United States of America for two whole terms while also helping run a secret order.

No, we don't gather and drink each other's blood during a ritual to take over when it's our time.

The Elite Kings were notoriously known amongst circles that we wanted to stay *away* from. We wanted normalcy. To snort coke off each other's tits and make out with random guys. That would never happen in Riverside, or anywhere north toward New York. So, we went in the opposite direction, hovering around smaller city folks who are too busy and uptight that they don't care about what's going on around them. The straight-laced kind.

Evie didn't need to be with us since she wasn't a King, but she knew enough without knowing too much. She was the popular girl at school. Everyone wanted to be her friend because that's how Evie made you feel. Wanted. Cherished and loved. She was the humanity to our family, and I think her father was that to Dad too.

River's flash to her phone is popping off in the back, before she directs it toward me and Evie. I flip my middle finger up, and Evie sticks her tongue out to the side.

Lost in a fit of laughter, I turn back to the road and hit the volume up.

The moment we pass the farewell sign as we leave Riverside, I drop it into third and floor it. The deeper you drive on this highway, the clearer it is how very little people come down it. It would have been years since cars drove this road, since the only place it leads to is an abandoned town, and the one town that we have a treaty to never set foot in. The simplistic straight road with bumps of hills and nothing surrounding us but woodlands on either side.

I'm laughing at River and Stella lip-synching "Low Life" for whatever TikTok trend is happening right now, when something runs out in front of my car. My skin prickles and I scream, slamming on the brakes so fast the tires skid to a halt.

Evie hits the radio off as seconds pass in silence, and I turn, checking them briefly. "You're all okay?"

Stella has her hand over her chest. "Yes, but what the fuck was that?" It didn't help that there are no streetlights or road lights, so all that we could see was directly ahead of us through the headlights.

"I don't know…" I whisper, leaning back in my chair. "I'll check."

I move to open the door, but Evie's hand comes to my arm to stop me. "Be for fucking real right now. This is how everyone dies in *every* movie."

"This isn't a movie. It's Riverside. Which means it's worse." I open my door and my Jordans hit the pavement. I walk around the front of my car, where headlights beam toward the endless road of darkness. Someone is curved to the side, clutching his stomach. "Shit." I drop beside him, squeezing his arm to roll him onto his back.

Wearing nothing but a pair of ripped jeans and boots, there's a deep gash over his ribs where blood weeps from. He's clearly unconscious. I pause when I notice the *Scream* mask.

"Jesus… did we hit him?" Evie asks, her eyes wide on his body.

I scan the front of my car. "If we did, he would have done damage. Old cars like this wouldn't take to it very well. No. I think he ran out for help." I push up, pointing to his body. "Stay here with him. I need to call my dad." I run back to my car and lean in through the door.

River clears her throat from the back seat, flicking her nails. "You and I both know what this is."

"I know. But Evie is here, and I don't want to have to have that conversation with her. Ever."

"I think it's about time." Stella sighs, resting her head on the window. "You kept our world from her long enough, and she knows the Elite Kings Club exists and that our families are crooked. This is just a *hey, yeah, so on top of that, we also*—"

"—Halen! He's moving!"

"Well, at least he's not dead," River mumbles. I know they're right. I know that beneath it all, I've kept Evie away from the drama of our world, not because I didn't trust her, but because I didn't want to put her in danger. Maybe doing that was placing her in the direct line of it. Priest has been on my ass for years about telling her everything so we don't have to tiptoe around her. She is with me eighty percent of the time. It makes things difficult.

A loud howl vibrates through the trees in the forest on either side of the road as I make my way back to them. Evie jumps, turning from left to right. "What the fuck was that?"

"A werewolf?" I joke, leaning back down to the guy on the road. Abs ripple over his torso, his skin naked of tattoos. I tear off my jacket, ignoring the cold bite that leaves teeth marks over my skin, and rest it against the wound on his ribs. He groans beneath the mask, so I slowly peel it off.

Jesus. Please don't know this guy. Please tell me these idiots haven't finally taken their shit too far and they've actually killed someone on land. Though he is moving…

"Hey…" I slap the guy's face, around his high cheekbones and larger set lips. There's a bump in his nose from being hit one too many times, and a dusting of a beard over his jaw.

His eyes peel open, resting on me. "Damn…"

I raise a brow. "Okay, playa. Where'd you come from?"

He coughs, keeping his hand on his tanned stomach as he tries to lift himself off the road.

"Hey! Stay there." I force him back down with a shove.

He clears his throat. "I—I must be lost."

I bring his face back to mine by his chin. "I'm Halen. Halen Hayes."

His face pales. "I'm lost." Clearly. What the fuck is going on?

I peer up at Evie, who cocks her head to the side, looking

between me and the guy. There have been two times in my life where Evie has found herself in a position to ask questions. She always chooses not to. I'll wait for the day when she finally does, and then I'll allow her to decide what she wants to do. I can handle that later. Right now, I need to find my fucking brother.

"I'm going to need you to get up. Are you hurt anywhere else besides your ribs?"

"No. I don't think so."

I place my hand under his head. "Ev? Help?"

"Ah…" She shuffles on her shoes, looking back to the car. "This a good idea? Halen, we don't know him, and I get that you're this big dog and your families are all untouchable, for whatever reason, but they're not here right now and he could be a killer!"

The guy chokes on his laugh. "That's fucking rich."

"Okay, buddy. Shut the fuck up and get up." I jerk him forcefully, and he finally lets me move him off the road, shuffling onto his feet. I wrap his arm over my shoulder and direct him to the passenger side of the car. "Ev, get in the back with the girls."

"Halen…"

"Evie!" I widen my eyes at her, opening the passenger door with the hand I'm not holding the bleeding stranger with.

"Fine." She moves past us both, jumping into the back seat. I lean down and move the passenger chair back farther, dumping the boy down and leaving his mask on his lap. I shut his door and round the front of the car, pausing when I reach my side. Laughter and more howls tear through the forest, and for a moment, I think I see shadows move behind the trees.

I roll my eyes, sliding into the driver's seat and turning the key over. "Sadists."

"What's going on?" Evie leans forward, and with her literally breathing down my neck, I know there's no way out.

"This was our brothers."

"Yeah, I know they do that weird—whatever—thing it's called every Friday night."

That's about as far as her knowledge will go, the same as everyone else who attends. The poor idiot bleeding out in my passenger seat included.

"But isn't it just, like, a hunting game or something?"

"Or something…" River snickers.

The more time passes, the more we are all on edge about the ritual. I know the boys are more involved in the world than we are right now, but that wasn't by choice. I tried to fight for more position, but it didn't work. Mom broke the way for girls, or as we used to be rudely named, Swans, but the way paved is clearly only for the men of the EKC.

Am I mad? Not really. Our time will come, but in the meantime, their hobbies have become reckless. It's only a matter of time before it lands in the Fathers' hands, or they become a worldwide issue.

The guy beside me shuffles around to face me, his body sliding down the seat.

"If you get blood on my custom Recaro seats, oh lost one, I might have to finish what my dear brother started."

"Oh this?" He gestures down to his side, lifting my jacket from his wound. "Wasn't Priest."

"Of course, it wasn't." I bat my lashes down at him. "My brother doesn't let the evidence run free." I turn back to the road, rolling my eyes when I see the Welcome to Riverside sign. This was a game. The high of a chase. They all love the chase, but this one has War all over it.

Just as we pass the sign, I hook a sharp right and drive us down the familiar road. Void of lights and asphalt, we jolt in our seats through the bumps. It's nothing but a narrow dirt road in the middle of a forest.

"Fuck. Can you slow it?" The guy beside me groans, shuffling further up his seat, and I press the accelerator more, smirking.

He blanches. "Or not."

It feels like the road goes on forever, until we reach the clearance and see the wide field. The water rushes fiercely down the mountain and into the renowned water hole below, the natural pool surrounded by large trees. A bonfire rages nearby in the darkness, where cars are parked and lined around the edge, marking the start of Devil's Cockpit track.

People spill out around the space, drinking and laughing amongst each other, but I ignore them all and drive directly forward, breaking up a circle of jocks.

When they see my car, none of them complain.

"I can't believe you're bringing me here. What a setup…"

"Hey." I leave the engine idling and remove my belt. "No one told you to jump out in front of my car and ruin our night." I reach for my phone and open Snapchat, sending out a message in the group chat that was for the meetup in Bayonet Falls.

"For help—" He glares at me, but the corner of his mouth curves in a smirk. "I did it for help." I hate to admit it, but he's a little cute. If the whole wounded puppy thing did it for me.

Or maybe it could. Since War decided to have his little toy land directly on my lap, why not wind that bitch up and let it dance?

"Ew. I can't believe our weekend is ruined," River complains, tapping on the passenger seat. "Hurry up, asshole. Get out so we can leave."

"You know, you guys are all quite charming. Anyone ever tell you that?" He reaches for the door, and my eye twitches when I realize he'll leave blood there.

"Yes," I answer sweetly. "My daddy does every night when he tucks me into bed."

He laughs but stumbles out. I shove my side open and follow behind him, rounding the front of the car. Devil's Cockpit is the Riverside meetup, where everyone who attends Riverside Elite University and Riverside Prep comes every weekend.

This is the starting point, which then carries on through the back of Riverside against the cliffs that drop out to the ocean, before looping around once you hit the fence line of Elite Kings Estate and coming back to Devil's Cockpit. This isn't your average track. It's rough. If you're not skilled enough, you die. Point blank.

It's more their little game that they participate in behind the guise of the races and partying that no one knows about. It's all a decoy for what's really going on deep in the forest. I don't know much about it since we never spent time around here. In fact, we made it our mission to be as far away from Riverside as possible when we could, much less during weekends.

Until their subject jumped out in front of my car.

"Halen!" Connor, one of the varsity players who attends Riverside Elite, nudges his head up at me, while lifting his red Solo cup. I smile but it doesn't reach my eyes. He's only ever bold enough to say hello to me when he's drunk. Bunch of fucking idiots. All of them. All too afraid of the Kings to actually talk to any of us.

I can't say I blame them.

My headlights beam onto where chopped logs are splayed out behind the fire. War, Priest, and Vaden are all sitting there with an array of girls around—or on—them.

Priest empties his drink and shoves the girl off his lap. Stumbling, she lets out a yelp before hitting the ground.

"How embarrassing," Evie mutters below her breath. "I'm getting a drink."

"Don't even fucking start." I glare at my brother as he gets closer.

People separate farther away from us, stumbling and dancing amongst each other. The music is loud enough that people can't hear our conversation, but me and Priest fighting is nothing anyone hasn't seen before. I love my brother. Even when we're fighting. Even more so when we're fighting because at least he's showing *something*. I have to keep him here, in his humanity. Even if that involves rage.

"Why did you bring him back here?"

"Where the fuck else was I supposed to take him?"

"Fuck." Priest grabs the guy by his arm, forcing him over to where War and Vaden are.

I turn slowly to face the girls, annoyed. Evie's hiding her laugh behind her hand.

"Are you laughing?"

Her hand slips. "Yes?"

"We should have just left him," River complains, following Priest. Stella looks between the both of us, coming up to my side and hooking her arm in mine.

"I didn't dress for this kind of vibe."

"I'll postpone Bayonet Falls." I widen my eyes at her, and we all follow Priest. My phone's vibrating in my pocket but I know that if I take it out now, the questions will start. When I say I can't breathe without one of them knowing how many breaths I've taken a day, I mean it. It's almost like when you have strict parents, but all it does is make kids disobey—kind of like that. Except we've been smart about it for years and they don't know anything.

Fire crackles through the air, its flames stretching out into the vacant night, as the Milky Way dusts the sky in a decoration of stars and the full moon.

Priest shoves the guy down onto the ground. "Shut the fuck up and you might actually live to see your teammates." He looks towards War, but I resist the urge to follow his gaze.

War is a ho. All of them are, with the exception of Vaden. Priest is selective with who he sleeps with, in a sense that he usually just hovers around one or two girls and bounces between them both, but War has a collection. Tillie told me he got it from Nate, and you know what? I can totally picture that.

"Why is Emma on War's lap like she fucking belongs there?" Evie whispers into my ear.

I don't care enough, nor do I want to give him the satisfaction of me seeing it. Over the years, we've all been good girls around the families. We've acted as we should in public and kept our messiness behind doors. While the rest of them freely engage in promiscuity and drugs, acting like they own everything.

I've hated it.

River has hated it.

Stella doesn't really care about it.

And if Dad ever finds out the kind of bullshit that they've been doing behind these parties and races, I'm pretty sure he's going to lose it.

Priest is nothing like our dad and a little more like our pop. Mom said it's what scares Dad the most about him completely taking the gavel.

But I think they're both wrong. I think he's more like the first Hayes that founded the EKC. That's not what should be worrying them yet. They should be more worried that all three of them are like unhinged hyenas, and since they don't have to play with the big dogs yet, they're killing time by risking exposure on our own streets, all for shits and giggles.

"Priest?" I glare at my brother through the waves of heat. "Leave him alone."

War chokes on his laugh, and much to my annoyance, my eyes shift to him just as he's moving Emma around to straddle his lap. His tatted hands land on her ass cheeks as he leans forward and drags his tongue from the side of her neck, and across her jaw, all while keeping his eyes locked on mine. My stomach explodes into a ball of fire and all the anger that I've kept hidden threatens to surface. Years. Years of us all acting like placid little Kings that sit in the shadows of these assholes. He's never done this, though. The small number of times that we've been here, War hasn't paraded his conquests around in front of me. I don't know if that was on purpose, or whether this one is for—whatever reason—but now I kind of want to punch him.

Straight in the face. It wouldn't be my first time.

Pop Smoke starts playing loudly and I move from the spot I'm at to where the wounded boy is, lowering myself down to kneel in front of him. "Let me have a look?"

His brown eyes come to mine. It's the first time that I've

realized he's probably a little older than us. If I do my calculations right, that is not good. "You got anything to numb the pain?"

My focus drops to his lips and my mouth twitches. I reach into the back pocket of my jeans.

Step one, boys. We do drugs. Just like you do.

I flash the ball in front of me and he shuffles up to rest his back against the log, one leg stretching out and the other bent. He rests his other arm on his knee, caging me in between his legs. I can feel the heat of the flames against my back. It does enough to keep me warm, since he ruined my jacket.

"Halen? Back the fuck up." War's icy tone sends shivers down my spine. *Oh? You did see me here?* Bet you fucking do now.

I turn slightly, hiding my smile from behind my shoulder. "How about no?"

Priest empties the rest of his drink in the fire, coming directly for me. He leans down to snatch the bag from my fingers, but I close it in my palm.

"Priest, I'm the same fucking age as you. Fuck you and go sit down."

He glares down at me. "I'm taking you home."

"No. You're not. Because I'm not fourteen anymore—none of us are—and since we've spent the better half of our lives partying in towns away from Riverside just to make you lot comfortable, I'm telling you right now—" I pause, hating that I'm sitting so low and he's towering over me. He's tall enough as it is without me being in this position, but I kind of like the way I'm resting against the wounded puppy. I'm almost sure he's allowing me to do it. *Who is he and why does he have balls bigger than every other boy in this town?*

"What?" he snarls, turning over his shoulder slightly until he finds River and Stella. I know I've got him, because there are rules, and as ruthless as the Kings are, we follow our rules. One of them just so happens to be keeping our family drama out of the public eye. All it takes is the right person to see a crack in our perfectly constructed castle and they'll slither in and try to demolish the foundation.

Priest glares down at me. "We will talk about this later." He turns back to where he came from, not another word said. It's not like they're completely stupid. They've seen us drunk and act a fool. Before me and the girls decided to dance our way around them, we were always their problem. Getting drunk at their parties, dancing around their friends, but soon enough it was as annoying for us as it was for them because they'd just end up ruining our night.

I turn back to the puppy, finding him already tracing the lines of my jaw and face. Why is it the longer I look at him, the hotter he gets? It doesn't help that he's exactly my type. I happen to fall for the pretty damaged ones.

Whether that damage is self-inflicted or not.

"What do you say?" I wiggle the bag in front of his face, catching movement in my periphery. Both River and Stella drop to the log he's leaning on. Goosebumps shiver down my spine.

I'm cold. I need another jacket.

I pop open the little bag, keeping my eyes on his as I tap the powder onto the crease where my thumb and finger connects. Bringing it up to his nose, he holds my stare as he leans down and takes the hit, clearing his nostril on his way back.

"Stella…" Vaden growls from somewhere behind me.

Stella finishes taking her hair out of her braid, winking at me and flicking it over her shoulder as her eyes sway up to her brother. They both have heterochromia, only flipped opposite.

With a wide smile, she snatches the bag off me.

The guy grabs my wrist and I watch as his tongue laps up the residue on my hand, keeping his eyes on mine. My breathing hitches and I lean down, catching his chin with my fingers and moving slightly to the side so War can see the movement.

Hovering my lips over his, I whisper, "Kiss me."

I accentuate the 'me' on purpose. I'm sure War doesn't remember shit about that night years ago, but just in case he does, and because I'm feeling petty as hell, I climb on his lap.

His hand lands on the back of my ass as he pulls me into him. His lips are on mine in an instant and my mouth parts for him enough for me to be able to smirk.

He moves his hand from my ass to his stomach and I feel him twitch against my lips. I rest my hand over his, lifting it from his wound. It's not as bad as I thought. More a deep graze.

I arch a brow at him. "A little dramatic, don't you think?"

"Halen." The agitation in War's tone isn't missed. By anyone, I'm sure, which makes no sense since he has always made it very clear—all two times—that in no way ever do I affect him the way he does me.

I roll my eyes, glaring at him from over my shoulder. "What?"

"Get off the fucking ground."

"He's cute, though…" I bat my lashes between War and Priest. I leave Vaden out of it because for the most part, he isn't as bad as the other two. Vaden somewhat allows Stella to do what she wants. He just makes sure to keep a close eye on her. Why I couldn't get him as a brother, I will never know. "Can I keep him?" If they want to see me as a problem, I'll be a fucking problem.

Orange hues from the fire cast shadows over War's jaw. A very clenched jaw.

With his lip curled in a snarl, my stomach coils like hot wire when his eyes darken on mine.

What the fuck is his problem?

He flips the hoodie of his jersey over his head to shade his scowl.

I still remember the day Dad sat down with me and told me about boys. Well, he tried. And I loved him for it because his message was a lot different than Mom's. Where she was the stricter parent, Dad was chill. He was good. He told me to stay away from boys until I was twenty-five because if Priest turned out to be a flop, I'd get to take the gavel. Obviously, my brother didn't turn into a flop.

If anything, he will yield the gavel the same way Pop did. I was only eight or nine at the time, so the thought of boys was a major ick, but as time went on… War changed. I can't remember ever not having a crush on him. Would I ever tell him? Hell no. Did I get drunk one night and try to fuck him? Yes. Thankfully, he kept that to himself. Most likely to protect their little brotherhood.

I try not to think about when exactly War turned from being a friend, someone I could always rely on, to this. Probably around the time I asked him to fuck me.

"Jesus…" Evie hands me a drink over my shoulder. "You really just left the kiddie pool and dove headfirst into the adult section."

I take the Solo cup from her, pushing up from the wounded puppy's chest while bringing the rim to my lips.

"I did." I stay near the girls. "Because I'm over it and I know Dad will be on my side when it comes to this—Mom too. They just don't know how bad it has been, and also, if he continues to make it an issue, I'll let our parents know about his little game that they play on the weekends." I take a sip of the alcohol, letting the cheap vodka slide down my throat. "Maybe give an insight as to why some people go missing."

"Well," River lowers herself down onto a log, tipping her head back to swallow her drink, "I hate to say it, but I'm pretty sure no one is going to come near us here anyway, even if we did hang around more."

Stella recoils. "Psh… They won't be able to help themselves."

A hand rests on my hip and I turn over my shoulder when the wounded puppy's fingers graze my exposed belly, where the band of my skirt is. He keeps his eyes on mine as his hand finds my pocket. He takes out my phone, lifting it to my face to unlock it, and starts punching in his name and number. He slides it inside the front of my shirt when he finishes, his fingers crawling to the back of my neck to spin me around. He lowers his lips to mine. This time I let his tongue slide inside, turning my head to give him more access.

He pulls back, a smirk on his face. "I'll text you." Then he walks off and I touch my back pocket, feeling the mask he'd left stuffed inside.

I bite down on my lower lip and watch as his back muscles ripple when he makes his way to a waiting blacked-out Range Rover.

"Okay!" I swing my attention back to the three of them. "Who is that, and I'm definitely keeping him."

"Keeping him, huh?" War, now suddenly free of Emma so it's just our "family" around this side, glares at me. He leans forward and it's the first time I've noticed how angry he is. War has always been beautiful, even as a child. His baby features hardened over the years into a jawline sharp enough to slice your heart open, and cheekbones carved from a Greek god. His feather brown hair is kept shorter, just enough to be able to run your fingers through, but his eyes—they're what you can't see past. They're the kind that burn your brain if you look too long, which is why people don't.

Me included.

He's one hundred percent a pretty boy, and he knows it. "Maybe try your first time with someone a little softer. Caden isn't it…"

"Caden, huh?" I tilt my head to the side as Evie replaces my empty cup with a freshly poured one. "And who said it would be my first time?"

His body stills, and I watch the exact moment a dark shadow creeps over his face. I didn't know much about the three of them and what they do on Perdita. They leave, and then every time they come back, they're all on edge. The way War is staring at me right now is exactly what they're like fresh off the plane.

"Halen, stop being a fucking brat." Priest kicks dust into the fire. "We've got to head out for a bit. Can you behave while we're gone?"

"I'm not a child!" I scold him. Either he's realized there's a lot that he doesn't know, or he has finally given up. I'm not his child. I'm his sister, and as much as I know he will do anything and everything to protect me and destroy anyone who so much as looks at me the wrong way, he needs to know that I don't need his help.

We came from the same womb. Even though he doesn't like hearing it, I can hold my own.

"Yeah, fuck no…" War shakes his head, leaning back and breaking eye contact. "We ain't leaving them here."

Priest ignores him as Vaden clears his throat. "We have to. They'll be fine."

War's jaw tenses, annoyance once again flashing over his features. He stares at me like one would an enemy. This has everything to do with me and nothing at all to do with River.

Chapter Four

WAR

I STARE BACK THROUGH THE CRACKS OF THE TREES, WATCHING as Halen moves around the party like she fucking owns it. Everyone seems to be smart enough to keep their distance, and now I know what Priest meant by leaving them here. They would be safe enough. And they clearly are.

Priest places a wet handle in the palm of my hand and I look down at it. I can't see shit, but when I realize it's the bone-carved Malum knife, I don't have to. Blood drips down from the blade when he follows my view. We all have a family knife, where its handle is carved from the bone of our original ancestor.

"I told you not to worry. No one's gonna touch River."

Yeah… River. Because that's who I was pissed about…

I swipe the edge of the knife against my jeans and shove it into my back pocket. "You gonna handle Caden?"

"Oh yeah?" Priest snickers, turning his attention fully on me. "And how am I gonna do that? Start a war?"

I bite back my anger. "Worth it."

Priest holds my stare. "You're starting to care too much."

"He fucking paraded her around on purpose, to show that he could because the timer was up."

Priest moves the branch away so we can see the girls clearer. "Let him have it. The only reason why Halen did it was because she doesn't know who he is."

"And who's gonna tell them?"

Vaden steps up behind me. "Why we standing here creepin'?"

"Because this asshole was." Priest finally turns and we follow behind him as he disappears farther into the forest.

One of these days, we were going to get caught. We just have to hope that when we do, it's after the ritual and we've taken the place of our fathers.

∞

I pull into the driveway of the Castle, resting my head against the back of the chair.

"Just crash here." Priest rolls out of the car as the sun rises up from behind the sharp ceilings of their mansion. The royals have nothing on the Hayes. "War... you need to fucking sleep."

I turn the car off and stumble out. Bloodstains litter my jeans and hoodie as we climb the one hundred steps it takes to get to the front door. The halls echo as they widen.

Bishop is leaning against the stairwell when we enter, sipping his coffee. He's suited already, the buttons undone to expose his tattoos. Bishop is everything you'd expect a ruthless leader of a macabre, prestigious order to be as a father. I'd heard he's different than his dad. Since Hector and Priest are like two unhinged maniacs, I'd say something skipped a generation.

"Busy night?" Bishop gestures to both of us. His hair's damp, and his tie rests casually around his neck.

"How are you awake?" Priest shuts the door, scrubbing his eyes with the back of his hand.

"I hardly sleep. Your mom and I are heading to Brazil this weekend to prepare for the ritual."

"Yeah, okay. Anything else?"

He looks between the two of us, running his hand through his beard. "Do I need to be worried about this here?"

"No, sir..." Priest answers flatly.

I shake my head and flash him a grin. "Nah, Unc. Nothing to stress about."

"War. Who your father is, is exactly why I'm worried about *this*." He gestures to our clothes. No doubt the blood.

I sidestep him and follow Priest up the stairs.

"Did you at least clean? Or do I need to call it in?" He doesn't turn when he asks the questions.

"Yeah, Dad... we did."

"I need names, Priest. We cross-check. If anything is left behind, I can call in the Skull Keeper."

"I'll send them to you, B," I answer Bishop as we hit the top of the stairs. We take a right, down Priest's side of the second level. "You need to cut your old man some slack. He has a point. Vaden having to go off and decompress is enough to prove that. A bunch of fucked-up individuals."

"Hell no. Pop said they never gave him a break when they were young." He stumbles into his room, and I stand at the threshold. This level is for the twins. Half for Priest, and the other for Halen. Their bedrooms take up the whole space of this level, so that's enough to know how big they are. Bishop and Madison stay on a different level and whole other side of the house. Madison's logic when she built this was to keep them as far away as possible, since she knew what she was in for. Smart. Gotta give her that. And since their house is a literal fucking castle, whenever we throw parties on this side of the house, they never know.

Not that they care.

My heart rattles my rib cage the longer I stand here. Finally giving in, I turn toward Halen's side of the hallway, her door directly at the end.

What the fuck was she playing at last night, and why did it piss me off so much? Over the years, especially after her little fuck-me antics when she was fourteen, I'd squashed every thought I'd have that would surface about her. But it was hard to deny... I mean... they all *were* attractive young girls.

Except River. Distant cousin aside on Stella's part.

Halen was a brat, though. She always got what she wanted. Except *me* that night.

I chuckle. She hated that...

"I'm gonna crash in the Lighthouse." Priest was already out by the time I closed his door, and I make my way back through the house and to the entrance. Crossing the garden to the tower that stands off the side of the Castle, I tap the elevator button and step inside. It reaches the top and dings open as I stumble through the familiar space.

Encased with windows that overlook Riverside, I punch buttons on the control screen until blinds drop to cover the glass.

My brain fades in and out as fatigue takes over.

I barely hit the California king when I'm lights out.

Something tugs on my jeans, jerking me from my sleep. I fly off the bed, fatigue gone.

Halen stands with her hands on her hips, her hair tied in a high pony and her tight little body on display. She's in a sports bra and gym shorts that curve just over the swell of her ass. Sweat drips over her body and— "Are your fucking nipples pierced?"

"What?" She looks down at her tits.

I instinctively step forward without realizing.

She counters it by stepping backward. "Stop!"

Nah, hell no. I am not stopping. What the fuck is she playing at and why do I feel like she's been existing behind smoke and mirrors all this fucking time?

I reach for her arm, but she jerks away again.

"Halen..." It's an unintentional growl.

"War..." she parrots with the same tone, her bright green eyes wide. "Don't touch me."

"What?" It's like a slap in the face. She and I have always been a little closer than me and the other girls—even River. No one knew it, but Halen was the one I'd talk to late at night if I needed some-one. But that all changed.

Sometimes I forget that.

"I mean because you have blood all over you!" she scolds, drop-ping to her knees in front of me to tug my jeans down.

I spread my arms wide, working my jaw. What the fuck is she doing? Or what the fuck am I doing? She's done shit like this be-fore—especially when I sleep in the Lighthouse. Halen would make it her mission to come in and make sure we weren't doing dumb shit.

I groan, wrapping her ponytail around my fist and forcing her head back so she's looking up at me from below. This position isn't helping either.

"You can't drop to your knees and pull off my jeans, Halen."

"Why?" She bats her eyelashes up at me and I fight with ev-erything inside to not force her onto the bed and fuck all the rebel-lion out of her. "Because you're afraid Priest will walk in and think we're doing something else?" She pushes up to stand but I force her back down by her hair, tightening my grip.

"I don't give a fuck what it looks like to your brother, Halo. If I wanted to fuck you, I would have fucked you six years ago when you were rubbing your shit all over my cock and begging me to."

"Fuck you." She whacks my hand away and this time I let her up because if there's anything hotter than Halen, it's angry Halen.

Her shoulders straighten, her eyes on mine. "And yes, I do have my nipples pierced, amongst other things—" My brain short-circuits but before I can interrupt her rant, she keeps going. "—and I wouldn't fuck you either, War. That's like… incest."

"Mmmhmm. Sure thing, baby girl." She stops when she hits the door, her hand on the button to the elevator.

The muscles on either side of her spine tense and I watch as she slowly turns over her shoulder.

"War…" She crosses her arms in front of herself, pushing her fat tits higher. Fuck. "You're not the only person I asked to fuck me that night—" My smirk falls. "—only difference between you and him?" The bitch has the audacity to look smug as she steps backward into the elevator. "Is he actually had the balls to follow through."

Rage burns through me and I launch forward but she palms the button to close the doors. It's the longest thirty seconds ever by the time they reopen and take me down. She's running through the front door just as I hit outside. I jog across the field, through the front doors, and take the stairs two at a time. I just get close enough to grab her when she slams her door in my face and the sound of her lock clinking vibrates through the wood.

I squeeze the handle anyway, jiggling it roughly. Little fucking bitch.

"You need to get on more," Priest calls out from behind me and my rage hovers in the back of my brain. I acted impulsively and now she thinks I give a fuck.

One night of them kicking it with us for less than thirty minutes and I've lost all fucking control.

I turn to face him. "Huh, tell your sister that."

Priest's eyes fall over my shoulder. "What's she doing now?" He opens his bedroom door and I make my way into his room, unbuckling my jeans and kicking them off.

"The usual. What the fuck is going on with the girls?"

His room is about as big as a penthouse apartment. The bed is stuffed in the corner, and a floating fireplace dangles from the ceiling in the middle of the room.

There's a fuck ton of random shit. Like a pool table, a Jacuzzi out on the patio behind the floor-to-ceiling glass sliding doors, and a fuck off one-hundred-inch TV that comes down from the opposite side so that if you're in the Jacuzzi on the patio, you can watch it. The bathroom takes up the space on the other side of the room, complete with a black marble finish.

I tap the touch screen and turn on the rainforest shower.

"Don't know. I'm guessing they're acting out." Priest leans against the entry, crossing his arms in front of himself. "Or maybe they're not bullshitting, and they've played us all along and really have been living some fucking double life we don't know about."

I shuffle out of my briefs, holding my cock before slipping beneath the hot water. "Yeah, well, whatever it is, we gonna handle that?"

"Can't." Priest stares at me in the mirror, biting down on his toothbrush. "We actually can't. Halen is right, they're the same rank as us and are technically Kings. We can't fucking do shit about it." He leans over to spit, and I tap the soap dispenser until foam curls into the palm of my hand.

"So, that's it?"

Priest shrugs. "Yeah, I mean she's twenty. I should have probably laid off her a long time ago. Make no mistake, if anyone hurts them or does them wrong, we know the drill." I turn the shower off and step out, water dripping over the heated tiles. Wrapping the towel around my waist, Priest's eyes fall to my discarded clothes. "She ask about that?"

"About what?" I ignore the bloody clothes, flashing him a smirk. "Naw, bro. She knows better than to ask questions."

A door opens and then closes. "If you're walking back in here for more bullshit, Halen, my dick is out this time."

Priest shoves me backward slightly and I laugh, knowing damn well Halen is fucking toast for the rest of the day. This is her pattern. She stirs shit, and then bounces. It's always been that way with her.

"I've seen your dick more than I've seen my own at this point," Vaden calls from the room, and I make my way back out, drying my hair with another towel. Vaden's eyes come to mine. The Vitiosis duo have always been a fascination to people who see them. Aside from their—I'll just admit it—attractive looks, they both share an, I guess, abnormality. Vaden's right eye is ice blue, his left is brown, and Stella the same, only opposite sides, and where Stella's brown eye is, it's a fifth covered. It's eighty percent brown and twenty percent blue, where her other eye is completely blue.

Brantley told us stories as kids, saying that it was because half his soul was doomed. Tried to scare Vaden as a kid, only nothing could scare him.

Not one single fucking thing.

Good for us; too bad for our enemies.

I shove on a pair of jeans from Priest's dresser, running my hand through my hair. "We're actually fucking leaving them here when we leave next week."

The door opens and Aire enters, flipping his cap backward with Samson not far behind him. Aire falls onto the leather sofa, blowing out a deep breath. "Fuck. Not sure I asked for this kind of life. Not gonna lie."

Priest's eyes come to mine, before flying to him. "Well, shit. You can always leave?"

Aire moves forward, looking between Priest and I. "Fuck no! I'm just sayin'. Why is my last name the one that is in finance? Why couldn't my King lineage be Nate fucking Malum, or Bishop motherfucking Hayes, or fuck! Brantley Vitiosis. Y'all are iconic. This fuck and I are just—"

"Bro, shut the fuck up with your whining." I roll my eyes, reaching for the canister with weed inside of it. I pop it open and sprinkle a decent amount in a blunt paper. "You think our life is fucking easy because of who our dads are? Naw, bruh. You've got it twisted. We're burning time right now, but once that gavel is in our hand, it's on."

"I didn't say easier," Aire brushes me off. "I just meant none of you go to college. We still fucking have to."

I chuckle, licking the blunt paper. It's not his fault. I mean, he, and Samson have never been directly inside, even though they are in the technical sense Kings. Chase Divitae—Latin for wealth—is Aire's father, and Cash Ditio—Latin for power—is Samson's. Our duties aren't quite on par with theirs. Through high school we were all tight. But after… the famous divide had already begun. Dad's generation had all founding names. Through the years, they thinned out to the final three once they all branched off to their respectful callings. Hayes, Malum, and Vitiosis are always the only three who go forward to the table.

"When do you guys head back?" Samson asks, watching as I light the end of the joint and take a hit. I hand it to him while blowing out a thick cloud. "This Friday. But since Halen and the girls have decided to throw diva…"

"Mmm, I was gonna talk to you about that. It's everywhere that she had her tongue down someone's throat at Devil's Cockpit. Whuddup with that?" Samson passes it to Vaden, lowering down on the bed opposite me. Samson is definitely the opposite of Aire— in a good way.

"He got loose." Vaden cuts down the conversation before it can get far. They know not to ask questions.

Aire shrugs, changing the subject. "So where were the girls even going?"

I freeze. My eyes fly to Priest and Vaden. That was something we hadn't even asked ourselves amongst all the drama… and blood.

Aire continues, not picking up on the shift in atmosphere. I've had to stop Priest from killing him multiple times through the years because he's so fucking stupid. I'm not stopping him anymore. "I'd heard of them making appearances in as far as NYC."

"You heard and didn't think to tell us about this?" In fact, I might just kill him myself. Unfortunately, I can't just switch off to not giving a fuck so quickly like Priest can. I always react with emotion, usually aggression. Not that Priest isn't unhinged, because he is, and usually I'm the logical one when it comes to what counts, but not when it comes to the girls. We've been watching over them all their lives. That shit doesn't switch off automatically, at least not for me. Vaden? Eh. He's a cold motherfucker anyway. Priest? Not enough involvement with the EKC for him to care. If Halen is getting in the way of anything to do with the club, he'll scratch her out. Blood or not, the Elite Kings Club and keeping the engine steamed is all this fucker cares about really—outside of Halen.

"We haven't been catching up as much—" Aire bites, but not

enough to piss me right off. He's smart. He knows I'd fucking lay him out.

I lean back against my chair, flicking the Zippo between my fingers. "They won't be doing that anymore, since they were so careless with telling us. It means they have a new place to act a fool."

There's a knock on the door and Samson throws the joint on my lap as it opens.

Bishop and my old man stand on the threshold, casting a quick glance around the room. I pluck the half-smoked blunt from my lap, glaring at little bitch Samson before placing it between my lips. I squint around the veil of smoke as my pap's eyes land on me.

Drawing in a long hit, I flash him a smirk as I blow smoke rings. "Sup, Daddy."

"Shithead."

I pucker my lips in a kiss, kicking my leg up to rest on the edge of the bed. "What can we help you elders with?"

"Yeah?" My dad mirrors my smirk, his eyes darkening. "Why don't you ask your mommy if I fuck like an elder?"

I flip him off.

Priest leans against the poker table, shoving his hands inside his pockets. He and Bishop are tight. Kind of like brothers, only somehow worse. I don't think any of our dads really were dads. They all had to put the family first and then be a father second.

A King doesn't need love. We just need loyalty.

"What is it and why do I think I'm not going to like this shit?"

"Because you're not." Bishop turns over his shoulder, checking Dad before coming back to me. "Meet in the Cave in an hour." The Cave is where they conduct all their meetings. Going forward, pretty sure ours will be the Lighthouse.

"You're calling a meet?" Vaden asks, leaning back on his elbow.

"Yeah. Bran will be there—" He pauses, looking around the room. The corner of his mouth twitches. "As will your sisters."

"What?" I lean forward and dub out the blunt.

"Son…" Dad stares at me. Doesn't help we're already around the same height. "See you in an hour."

I'm still glaring at the door after they leave when Priest taps my leg with his. "What the fuck is your problem with them coming in? You knew it was gonna happen. Makes sense it's now since we're so close to the ritual."

"I don't know. I thought when they were older."

"They are older," Vaden interrupts, flicking the army knife between his fingers. "Honestly, I thought it would be done before now."

"Nah." Priest disappears in the closet. "Mom wanted to give Halen and the girls a normal high school life. I think when they got close to starting college, she bled Dad out for more time, but at the end of the day, they're Kings. Mom fought for a chance with the Silver Swans and now that she has one, she has to come to the party."

I shuffle on a shirt and a pair of Jordans, heading out of the room. "I'll meet you down there." I slam the door closed and keep my eyes locked on Halen's room. My fingers flex in my palm when I think back to the last conversation we had.

Who the fuck has she fucked and why the fuck does it bother me so damn much?

HALEN

I STARE BLANKLY AT MY DAD'S OFFICE DOOR...

Noises bang around and the lump in my throat grows bigger the longer time goes on. What will he do? What will they do? Does he know? I am not sure. The house smells of freshly baked cookies and I take the steps away from the Cave so I won't be tempted to force myself into his space and tell him all of the things that have been eating me up since, but I collide with a hard body.

I spin around, my hand flying out to whoever it is, when it lands on a tatted chest. My panic turns into a frown. "You basically live here."

War flashes me a dimpled smirk. I hate when he does that because it is hard to hate him. He is a constant reminder of everything I was born into and love.

I love War.

I love Vaden.

I love all of them, even when they are annoying and cruel.

"Are you asking me to move in?" He raises a perfectly curved brow. "You know I'm your mom's favorite." I shove him out of my way but his hand catches mine before I can take another step. "How's your hangover? Remember anything from Friday night?" The lump in my throat grows as I try to swallow everything I've fought hard to forget.

Only I am sure that one day, it is going to choke me.

I fold my arms in front of myself, ignoring the way my cheeks burn. Well, I am doing terrible at this. "No. Nothing important anyway. Why?"

His eyes narrow. I know what

he's asking me. It's obvious, but aside from him being a complete asshole for mentioning it, I am not surprised. "Really?"

I shrug, stepping backward to go back to the kitchen. I need to see my mom. I just… need her. And anyway, not that we have a no-partying rule in the house, but I did come home drunk enough for her to stay up all night to watch me sleep. They left for a forty-eight-hour trip to Europe the next morning, so I didn't get a chance to see her after.

"Halen?" War calls out, and I pause my steps but don't turn. "What will you do without us at college?"

"Oh God, I don't know, War." I turn and start walking backward. "Whatever we want?"

As soon as he's gone, my face falls. Mom reaches into the oven, dropping a baking tray on top of the stove and tossing the dishcloth on the counter. "Fuck. Maybe I'm not a baker."

"Correct!" A plastic smile melts onto my face. I vow to never re-move it. "But it's okay, because dad is."

I stare at the patterns on the walls as I wait. Satin black paint is licked over the ceilings and walls, and a single chandelier spirals down the center of the room before blooming into a ray of crystals. I've never been in the Cave before. It was always for EKC meetings. This was my norm. I knew my dad wasn't a good man.

I knew my uncles weren't either.

Hell, I wouldn't even cross Tillie, War's mom. I'd heard stories about her too. But being in here feels different. Like all the stories I had heard over the years weren't only true, because I knew they were, but that they felt… right. Justified.

Dad makes his way to me, leaning back against the table while fisting the edge. It's just us in here for now, but I know that isn't going to be for long. For one, he called this meeting.

"Baby girl…" His hand rests on my cheek and I exhale a nervous breath. I love my dad. He is the rock of not just our family, but the order as a whole. People look up to him, worship him. I'm worried about what that means for Priest once he takes the gavel, and they shift that power that to him. What will he do with it? He's sensible and will always make the right choices for the EKC, but my brother is soulless. What happens when he has to make the hard choices and other lives are on the line?

Jesus.

I knew what our family meant and the covenant behind it. I knew that Dad was, in short, an underground god. He made the rules and everyone followed.

Every. Single. Person.

We didn't need to call it a mafia because it wasn't. We were the order of the Elite Kings Club and that in itself held more weight than any other term you'd find in the dictionary under *bad motherfuckers*. Our history is pure. Our lineage unwavering. We never procreated with anyone outside of our world, but even if we did, they had a connection to it.

"Look at me."

Dad startles me out of my reverie, and my eyes travel up his black suit, past the tattoos on his chest, and continue until I meet his gaze. He'd always kept his beard short, but recently he's been growing it out longer. Thicker. It only makes him look scarier.

He touches the side of my head, brushing my hair behind my ear. "War is going to give you shit about this. Maybe even your brother."

"I don't care." I blink past his words. "I deserve to be here. We deserve to be here."

"You do. You all do." He nods, smiling just enough for the wrinkle lines around his eyes to deepen. Evie goes on and on about the dads and how hot they are. I've had to stop myself from slapping her on more than one occasion. People have spread ridiculous rumors about her and Priest, but really, the truth is that we can't trust her around our dads. She's not interested in our brothers. "They don't know about you girls training. We need to keep it that way for now. I don't want to bombard your brother with too much too fast. Save it for after the ritual."

"It's not so much Priest than it is War…" I roll my eyes and relax into the chair. "He's got this weird complex about us being around because of River."

Dad raises a brow.

"What?" I scowl. He's always doing this. Open sentences and cryptic comments. I don't know how Mom tolerates it.

"You think that's why War is the way he is?"

Dad pushes off the table and saunters his way to the front.

"What's that supposed to mean?" I ask as he continues to pour a finger of whiskey into an empty glass.

He brings it to his lips, keeping his eyes on mine. "It means the apple doesn't fall far from the fucking tree." He shoots his drink back and I watch as the amber liquid disappears down his throat. Before I can ask him once again to explain, the door opens and the other fathers pile in. Nate takes the spot to Dad's right, Brantley opposite, and before I say anything more, someone else walks in.

Uncle Eli.

My smile widens and I shoot up from my chair, flying across the room.

He catches me with a hug. "Hey, princess," he whispers into my hair, kissing my head.

"You never come around as much anymore!" I scold, and I fight with myself to not jut out my lip.

His arms tighten around me. "I know. You know you can always come to Spain—" He pauses a moment. "—shit."

"I get it." I step back from him, still giddy. "You guys have all branched out and are doing God's work. I haven't seen Lilith or Luna for so long!"

He chuckles deeply, directing me back to my chair and taking the one beside me. Uncle Eli was the fun one. For years, he'd play games with me, take me out with Luna when we were little.

"Okay, hold up!" Nate calls out, his hands raised. More people are coming through the door, but I already know who it will be. "Why don't I get a hug like that? The fuck! I thought I was the favorite uncle?"

"You still are." I roll my eyes with a smile, winking at Eli and Brantley. "So. Lilith and Luna? How are they?" I ask, lowering down onto the chair. Luna is Eli's daughter that he had with one of the baddest chicks I know, aside from my mother and Tills. She is wild. Not wild like Aunty Tate, who took me to pierce my nipples when I was sixteen, but still wild. Eli, from one of the Founding Families, is also in a throuple with Kyrin and Lilith, who are part of an adult-style circus called Midnight Mayhem.

I hadn't seen Luna since we were little. When they all separated and decided Midnight Mayhem would no longer be a traveling circus, but homebound, all of them spread throughout the world to go international. Eli, Kyrin, and Lilith chose L'embruix, a village snuggled in the valleys of Spain. I'd seen photos and it looked haunting, yet somewhat romantic.

"They're good. Luna—" Eli pauses and turns to face Bishop. A look passes between the two of them and if I didn't know better, I would have missed whatever it was.

But I did. Enough to know that there's something going on.

A hard thigh brushes against mine and my breath catches. I don't have to look to know who it is. I don't know why it has started to bother me more than usual. War and I were the closest out of us all through our childhood, to the point where we would finish each other's sentences.

I know where it all turned around and went to shit, and it had nothing to do with War's taste in girls. Girls who are *nothing* like me. Not that he has actually kept any around long enough for me to compare.

"It's time to start implementing plans that have been years in the making. As you all know, we have been working to make things more accommodating for the future Swans." I roll my eyes at the name. How fucked up was Pop and the generations before him to have not just pushed the girls who were born into the EKC away, but to have them, well… killed. Mom tried to explain it more than once. I just wasn't into reliving what she had.

"So, it's done?" Priest holds Dad's stare, and minutes pass over the table. There's no debate. If you're smart, you wouldn't sit at this table to fight.

Dad leans back in his chair, a cigar rolling between his finger and thumb.

A dark smile plays across his lips. "Yes. So play nice. You know your sister is a good shot."

Forgiveness wasn't a currency I'd ever spend. If you crossed me, I'd simply make you pay.

Church bells rang in the distance as I shaded my eyes from the sun. The familiar sculpt of the building peeked out through the green trees and bushes.

I took a step forward, but a hand came to my belly. It was a ghost of a touch. Physically unfamiliar, spiritually everything I'd ever known.

The words that came from his mouth scribbled poetry over my skin. "Halo…"

I pulled away from him and before I could think twice, I ran. *How could he? Why was he?*

I ran so fast that I didn't realize when the soft blades of grass beneath the soles of my feet turned to shards of gravel that cut through my skin.

I didn't stop when I flew through the doors to the building, tears streaming down my face and clothes drenched in water. Four people stood at the bottom of the staircase to the main room, all dressed in black. They slowly turned, just as the door slammed closed behind me.

My hands shook as I dipped them into the stoup and crossed myself with water that was anything but holy. This wasn't a church. This was hell.

Their faces were covered by black hoods, but I knew who they were. My bottom lip trembled and my heart fractured in my chest.

"I don't want—" Someone grabbed me from the back of my throat before forcing my face into the stoup. I desperately tried to push away, break free. My lungs burned every time I took in water, but it was no use. Nothing was of use.

My muscles gave way before I did.

They could take me. All of me.

Chapter Six

WAR

IF THERE WAS ONE THING THAT I WAS THANKFUL FOR WHEN it came to the girls, it was that they weren't interested in expanding their circle any further than what we had. Evie didn't count. She was family.

River bounces down the steps that lead into the lounge, where I'm smoking a blunt and sipping on whiskey. The way it slides down my throat like honey means it's expensive.

She raises a brow, flicking her long blonde hair over her shoulder. "Should I be worried about this party tonight?"

"Worried how?" I ask, biting down on the trunk. I narrow my eyes at her cheekily and she crosses her arms in front of herself, cocking her hip. River has been an actual pain in my ass since the day she took her first breath in this world. I mean, deep down, I was happy for the olds, but at the same time, like why couldn't they give me a brother? Or anything. Anything easier than River.

Even as those words filter through my mind, I wince. I couldn't imagine my life without her. Whether she's a pain in the ass or not, River is as loyal as a fucking golden retriever… who just so happens to have a Doberman and pit bull as best friends.

She flops down onto the single leather sofa near the fireplace. Flames lick up the back of the stone as River swings her legs back and forward restlessly.

"You take your meds today?"

She doesn't answer. That's a no.

"That skirt is rather short, little

sis…" I flick ash into the metal tray on the coffee table. All of our parents smoke chronic, which makes it easy for us because we've never had to hide the fact that we do. Not that we would hide it anyway. Just saves the argument.

"So is my patience with you today, big brother, so please, if you have something to say—say it."

Straight to the point. Good.

"What did Halen mean about you guys going out of Riverside to party?" I try not to make it obvious why I'm asking. I mean, I am asking for all of us… not just for me.

"It's true." River plays with her nails, staring up at me from behind dark-lined eyes. She looks like Dad when she does that. I should tell her. Ruin her day. "We've been doing it since we were in high school." She swings around. "So. Where's the alcohol?"

Her heels clink down the way she came when she disappears in search for alcohol, just as Vaden leans against the wall on the opposite side.

His tall frame towers over the bar, and I watch as he stares Stella up and down when she passes him, her black hair flowing down her back like fucking silk. The music is loud, but no one has arrived. After Bishop announced that the girls were coming in, we all knew better than to challenge him, even though I know he expected me to. Priest was right. That didn't mean I had to like it, or that I was going to get used to it quickly.

"They all leave?" I ask Vaden, but eye Stella as she quirks a brow down at me. Fuck. This is already fucking weird.

Exhaust pipes idle outside and headlights beam through the windows that overlook the garden out the back. The heady sound of Japanese imports and American muscle shake the glass that separates us from the pool area.

"Yep. Last-minute shit for the ritual." Vaden shoots back a finger of whiskey, turning his head. The single cross tattoo on the side of his neck catches my eye and I grin.

Vaden takes the steps down to the sofa as the lighting in here dims, enough for us to be able to keep a watchful eye on the masses that are rolling in through the back. "I found a new tattoo artist. Did I tell you?" He rolls up a dollar bill that's beside the dust of coke, throwing his Philipp Plein hoodie over his head and bringing his eyes to mine. He says his eyes are different because when he was conceived, his soul was in a tug-of-war with which side it wanted to pick. The dark—his dad—or the light—his mom. It couldn't decide, so it took both. Over the years, his blue eye has started to bleed dark…

"Oh yeah? Is he hot?" River asks suggestively, wriggling her eyebrows while lighting the end of a joint. She hands it to me.

I hold it between my lips.

"She," Vaden corrects. "And not my type."

"No one is your type, oh unsaved one." Halen leans down, planting a kiss to his cheek. She ignores me on her way to the other side of the lounge. She's most likely going to ignore me for as long as she can, and that's fine. I can do this song and dance with Halen Hayes until my fucking legs give out.

"I brought a snack."

My smile falls to a scowl. I pinch the blunt between my fingers and aim it toward her, flicking it onto her lap. "Leave."

She plucks it, unfazed. "Fuck you, War."

I hold her stare. "You already tried."

She freezes, the blunt just a whisper away from her lips. She's the first to break away, desperate to change the subject when Priest lowers onto the single sofa that sits in front of the glass doors that lead to the backyard. You can see everything from here. People gathering out back, cars driving through the paddock gates and parking in a line. The pool illuminates blood red, where a DJ is setting up from his deck in the corner. Every group from Riverside University is here. All of them. It's funny, because none of us attended the school, but we didn't have to attend the bullshit system to be feared. They aren't stupid.

Clearly.

Except for whoever Halen's little toy is.

"What do you think, War?" River leans her head on the armchair, until her long blonde locks touch the floor. She blows smoke rings from between her lips. "Should we do a drag train tonight? Maybe take the peasants out to our new destination?"

I shrug, watching as Vaden strolls past River. He holds her gaze while dragging his finger across her throat as he moves toward the bar on the other side of the room.

"You're lucky about that no fuck oath, Vaden…" River watches after him. "Cousin or not." We all fall silent and she rolls her eyes. "I'm kidding. It was just kind of hot." I know she isn't. Not that any of us would do as our ancestors did and happily fuck around with each other, but we sit in limbo of *we don't fucking dig up old shit*. In fear that there is DNA crossed way back then. Vaden and Stella are our cousins, though, through my mother being their mom's half-sister. They never grew up together. Saint is also Bishop's half-sister. About as close as Halen and I will ever get to incest, since her dad shares a half-sister with my mom, without either of them sharing the same parent or blood.

Yeah. I know.

And no.

"Jesus… this how you girls act when we're not around?" I point to both River and Halen, but I hold Halen's stare. My sister perfected the art of lying to me as soon as she knew how to talk, but Halen… she can lie all she wants through those pretty little lips. Her soul tells mine tales that I bet she would kill to keep hidden.

"Worse," Halen teases, crossing her leg over the other. She's wearing a vintage band shirt that hangs slightly off her shoulder, little black shorts, black thigh-high boots, and a leather harness strapped around her thigh. Her tits swell out of the small tear down her chest.

My eyes fall to the soft curve of her breasts. "How?"

She pushes up to the front of the sofa, snatching her phone

off the coffee table. "We can do a train. I know *just* where we can go. Where's Stella?"

My eyes fly over her shoulder and land on the raven-haired vixen walking her way up through the masses. She snatches a drink off some dude and sinks it in one go, tossing the cup into one of the many trash cans we have set up.

I watch as Halen opens a new message on her phone, blinking, before shoving it back into her pocket. People usually get crazy when we have parties, but no one comes into the house. Not ever. Only us and who we invite in. A guy tried once, and I shot him on the spot. Wish I could say I was joking. He healed. It's fine.

Stella strolls back through the doors, sitting opposite Priest. "What'd I miss?"

We're not surprised when she shows up wearing a tight strapless gray top, a short denim skirt, denim thigh-high boots, and crystal tassel chains. The girls all have a similar style, in the sense that they don't ever follow any rules. One day they'll be in heels, the next it will be Jordans or Uggs.

Except for River. River is pretty consistent with her aesthetic.

I kick my boot up on the coffee table, allowing my eyes to rest on the swarm of people outside. On any other day, I'd probably grab one just to sit on my dick and look pretty, but right now, I don't want to. I can't even say why.

"Nothing. Halen wants to start a train." Vaden gestures to where she sits.

"Oh, are you driving, Hale?" Stella asks, turning her focus to Halen.

"I don't know. Maybe."

"Hmmm…" I push up from the chair and swipe a bottle of whiskey on my way out the doors. "I ain't driving anywhere."

Music fucks my senses as I push through bodies. The parties get old, especially with time, but they're still a perfect distraction for us. Especially a few days before we're set to fly out.

I lift the bottle to my lips, swirling the liquid around my mouth until it hits the back of my throat. Halen catches my eye through the window, where they're all still seated inside, and I reach out to catch the first set of hands that land in mine.

Warm. Nothing like the ice queen inside.

I tug her into my chest, raising my finger to the side of her jaw. I don't even know her name, but she's pretty. She'll do. "I'm bored."

"We can't have that." Her fingers trail up my chest before curling to the back of my head. She pulls me down until her lips brush my ear. "And I have a friend."

I bury my hand in her hair and tug her in close, until my teeth sink into her bottom lip. "Then I'm no longer bored."

"Hey, bitches!" Halen stands outside, one hand on her hip and the other twirling her keys. "Who wants to burn rubber?"

I shift backward. Yeah, timing is not suspicious at all.

"She's bossy," the girl in front of me says.

"Ah—" the other girl murmurs, snatching the keys off her flirty little friend. "She's Halen fucking Hayes. You do as you're told."

The corner of my mouth slowly lifts in a wicked smirk. *That you do.*

I watch as the dark clouds roll over the thick trees in the distance, coming to a stop where we are in the town center. Perdita isn't a place for the mundane. It's an island completely owned by the Elite Kings.

It's a weapon.

Historically, Perdita has always been run by one of the Founding Families: the Stuprum bloodline.

My mother's bloodline.

Only when it was time for her to reign, she declined the crown and handed it down to another, who was the one who ran it to this day. When you wear the crown of Perdita, you become Katsia. It can get confusing as fuck when you flick through our family grimoires, especially now, since the old Katsia wasn't the next Katsia-in-line's biological mom, but that didn't matter to the old one—for whatever reason. She cared about the girl enough to crown and love her as much as a Katsia could love. People don't know this as it is classified information, but even the old Katsia wasn't of pure bloodline, since my mother was the last living Stuprum and they whacked off all the others, including Mom's sister.

"Boys," *Hector Hayes announces through an ashtray for a throat. He'd done two terms of presidency. He may have kept America happy—well, sixty percent—but most people hate him. And those that hate him? They still fear him.*

Bishop isn't like Hector. He rules the Kings down a path of destruction, sure, but he has a moral compass.

"I hate that flight." *Priest stretches out his arms, clicking his neck. We stand out the front of an iron gate with tips as sharp as swords. The house itself is modern, designed with glass windows as walls which display the main street of town behind us. High towered ceilings and corpulent overgrown shrubs manicure the footpath. Flowers grow through the foliage, but they lack vibrancy. Almost withered.*

"What did you think, Vaden?" *Hector lifts his eyes to V who stands beside me.*

Vaden stares back at Hector. "I think I'm ready."

Hector smirks wide, his cheeks creasing as he slowly turns back to the gate. He looks up to a camera that's pointing down and twirls his finger in the air. "If you haven't figured it out, I'll be doing your training. Teaching you the fundamentals of a King. Most you know, some you don't, others you will soon find out, and those I don't show you, already live within you. You just need to rip the layers of humanity off to reveal the roots before you water the seed."

"Samson and Aire? They won't be part of this either?"

"Their duties and training will be completed elsewhere." *Hector pushes open the high-wire gate, straightening his suit. He takes a moment to look between all of us.* "Your fathers didn't have this opportunity. They were thrust into this life by my choice and the sins of their own fathers. You're all privileged in that aspect, where none of yours screwed up." *He pauses, his eyes narrowing on Vaden.* "Yours didn't force you to have sex with another girl while recording it and then try to kill everyone around you. Yours," *he points to War.* "Well, to be fair,*

Nate's old man wasn't horrible compared to both me and Brantley's Dad, and your—" He finally settles on Priest, and none of us miss the pride in his eyes.

Priest is about as expressionless as a fucking blank wall begging to be graffitied, but the corner of his mouth moves up a little. Hector winks at him. "Well, yours didn't try to kill your girl, among other things, to say the least."

"Don't worry, Pop..." Priest steps closer to his grandfather. We all watch in silence as he grabs Hector by the back of the head and pulls him in for a hug. "I won't let you down, ever."

I bite the inside of my cheek. Well, goddamn. This is going to be an EKC Hector two point oh.

"No more killing Swans..." I sneer at Hector in passing, hiding my snicker. He can think I'm joking, and if I didn't see the love he has for Halen, I would probably be skeptical around the subject. But if anyone comes near any of those girls, they'll have to go through all of us first. As much as Priest loves his pop and he's EKC first, his sister is more than a sister to him. She's his soulmate. She's his other half. It's why he's so unfazed by her.

If the Kingdom falls, anyone left standing would be eradicated.

"Come on..." The gate slams closed. "Someone here wants to meet you."

We had started training when we were five years old. For years, it was the simple things. I have a feeling it is only going to go up from there.

50 Cent's "Just a Lil Bit" plays through one of the cars parked up near the water hole, and I lean back on the hood of my R32, one leg perched on the bonnet and the other laid flat. I think we all silently agreed to give the girls until the ritual before we thrust them right into the belly of the fire. They think they can handle it, and shit, maybe they can. Halen, most definitely. And Stella, because she's a fucking menace. But River? I'm not so sure. She puts on a hard front, but we all know she keeps everything bottled.

"So?"

Candy? Cassandra? Fuck…

"What do you say?" She drags her long nail down my chest, stopping at the tattoo that sits below my collarbone. We had long since driven out to Devil's Cockpit, after following Halen here. I got the feeling this wasn't the final destination, though.

"What?" I try to hold the bottle of beer to my lips, but my head spins from all of the alcohol and weed. I definitely can't fucking drive from here.

"Give me your fucking keys." Priest shoves his hand into my jeans pocket and I lose my feet, tipping sideways.

In front of the cascading waterfalls, modified cars line the empty patch of land. Engines overpower all other sounds except for the thudding of distant music. There has to be fifty odd cars parked. Most JDM, others exotic. We have our fancy bullshit cars too, we just never drive them unless we have to. Priest with his McLaren, me with the LaFerrari, and Vaden with his Phantom.

"No one drives my car."

He rolls his eyes and pockets them. He and I both know I can't say shit right now.

"So that's a yes?" the annoying voice yaps off again from below.

I catch her with a thumb beneath her chin, forcing her eyes up to mine. I don't hold them long enough to care, because I don't.

"Shut the fuck up."

Her little mouth opens, and then closes, before she turns in my grip and backs her ass up against my shit. Candy. Her name is Candy and I'm pretty sure she's been here before. By here, I don't mean Devil's Cockpit. Tonight isn't for racing, more for cars to just burn rubber and show off.

Beside me, Vaden chuckles with a soft laugh, lighting his joint and inhaling deeply. "You'll make her cry."

She doesn't say a word.

Halen's car is almost as familiar as her touch. Not that I've felt it, well, at all since that night I shoved her off my lap, but I know everything there is to know about Halen, and her car is no different.

The RB engine purrs like a kitten as she rolls her Hakosuka to a halt in front of mine, Priest's, and Vaden's. I stay perched on the hood, with Priest to the left leaning against his, and Vaden on the opposite side of mine. Girls hover far enough away from Priest to not get too close, but close enough so that he knows they're all interested. Not that he needs to know that. The fucker picks and drops as he pleases, without making any of them feel comfortable enough to rub against his shit without permission.

Shit. Maybe that's where I've got it wrong.

I shove Candy out of my way with a kick of my knee and she pretends like she didn't notice and walks off to find her friends. How the fuck did she end up hanging off me anyway?

A car door slams closed, and I look up from the bottle dangling between my fingers. Long tanned legs that shouldn't be on a girl who is five-something-short, long toffee brown hair, and a face that could honestly put every single fucking model out of business, Halen is every fucking thing I should not want.

I don't want.

But I'm... no. I'm drunk. And I'll blame it on the fuck-me boots she's wearing.

Surprise, surprise.

She looks around my body when another car door closes.

"Aw, Halo, what's the matter?" I call out to her, tilting my head.

Priest kicks off his car, walking off with someone into the crowd.

Finally, another body rounds hers, an arm hooking around her torso, pulling her into his chest.

My smirk falls as does the bottle I'm holding between my fingers. Just as it splatters against the concrete, I push up from my car, anger boiling through my veins.

She knew exactly what the fuck she was doing bringing whoever this fucker is here.

A hand squeezes my arm, stopping me, and I turn over my shoulder to find Vaden staring between us both. Evie, her annoying little best friend who is more like family than our own actual family, jumps in front of her, snapping a photo of them both, and I fall back against my car, allowing the anger inside of me to turn to liquid metal.

Vaden whistles low. "Might wanna tighten that shit up if you don't want Priest to think you're considering breaking that promise."

My jaw clenches so hard I swear my teeth crack. "You and I both know that was specifically for me and Halen, since I'm sure the rest of you aren't into incest."

Vaden's dead expression slowly turns into a deep grin. His white teeth flash against his pale skin, the dimples in both his cheeks deepening. Vaden doesn't smile often, but when he does, it balances on the line of perfection and fucking creepy. Can't decide which it is more.

"You just worked that out? Unless you do end up fucking Stella."

"I'm not gonna fuck Stella!" I rear back my head, insulted.

"What's wrong with Stella?" Vaden blinks, all smiles gone. When I search his eyes, he shoves me playfully. "Incest is not your thing either. Got it."

"Good, because I was about to break it down into one hundred different ways on why your statement pissed me off. Starting with missionary."

The music becomes louder as another car pulls into the concrete slab behind us. The distinct sound of tires shredding tread screams around a winding engine.

I shift over my shoulder to see a '74 Beamer's ass looping around in a cloud of smoke, and just as I'm about to look away, a pair of emerald eyes catch mine from behind the mist. My chest contracts as she holds my stare, almost daringly. My fucking cheeks heat as she keeps the same, blank expression on her face, for the entire time of the skid. She's the first to break when the fuckboy behind her turns her in his grip and back against him.

"Why the fuck is he here?" I ask, popping the trunk to get

another bottle. I slam it closed and Vaden is instantly in my face. I ignore his glaring. "Who the fuck is he? Did she drag him off the side of the street?"

"You wanna be drinking more?"

I bite down on the beer cap, twisting it off. This is the second time I've ever seen her with another guy, and I gotta admit, both times I've not handled it well.

"Not drinking enough." I make my way to the sandy edge of the water, lifting the beer to my lips. I tilt my head up to the sky above, as stars flicker against the dark atmosphere. Kind of a subtle reminder of what's to come, what we've still got to be wary of, and the new laws of our time. The smell of burnt rubber evaporates around me, and for the first time in a long fucking time, I breathe out a deep sigh.

"Are you okay?"

My lip twitches at the sound of her voice. "Am I okay?" I don't bother to look down to her.

"I'm not going to like much of what I'm about to find out about the Elite Kings, am I..." She finally lands beside me.

I angle my gaze down to her. "You can handle anything."

That I am fucking sure of.

She crosses her arms and shifts, peering up at me through dark lashes. It feels a lot like being punched in the gut anytime we lock eyes lately. Not sure what the fuck is happening. "How do you know what I can handle?"

"Halo..." I tease, using her nickname. "You're a fucking Hayes."

"Mmm..." she muses, tucking the loose strands of her hair behind her ear. Her piercings glimmer from the full moon. "I'm not my brother, War."

"Thank fuck for that," I mumble around my bottle. "The world could only handle one of him."

She chuckles, turning her back to the water and gazing out at the commotion going on behind me. It's perfect because I can take in every sharp detail of her face. Every feature shaved from some mystical wand.

"How old were you?" she asks, and the question leaves her mouth as a whisper. I don't understand what she's saying. With Halen, it could be anything. Her eyes shoot to mine and hold me hostage. "How old?"

It sinks in.

My brows rise slightly. "Ah." I clear my throat. "Thirteen." Would she piece that together? Maybe not.

She sucks in a deep breath, closing her eyes and then opening them back onto me. Smoke cradles her beauty delicately, as her face radiates against the taillights. She's completely in her element.

"I was fourteen."

The bottle slips from my fingers once again, and before I can snatch her backward and ask her what the fuck she means, and whether I mistook her question, she's too far in the crowd to not make it obvious.

HALEN

H E WOULD SURELY LET GO OF MY MOMENTARY SLIPUP. I shouldn't have said that to him. I don't even know why I did.

"Why do you taste so good?" The stray bites at the nape of my neck from behind and I curl forward, recoiling away from him. "How long do we have to stay here?"

"What?" I turn in his grip. "The night has only just started."

His eyes cross together as his hands find my hips. I don't know why I'm even entertaining him. I mean, sure, Caden was fun, and I'm annoyed he never did text me back, but this one leaves me bored. I shouldn't be surprised. It's what happens when I pick up a literal stray. *Honestly, do I not learn…*

In my defense, by stray, I mean Instagram, but same, same. I know he attends Riverside Elite, but I don't know what his parents do or how he came about living here.

"Hey, Halen!" Girls walk past and I wave at them. I'm trying to be more like Evie.

I told her I'd try. We'll see how long that lasts…

A loud clap sounds out when my ass cheek stings like wildfire. "Baby…" Evie takes my hand and shuffles beneath my arm, pulling me in close. "Where the fuck have you been and why are you kissing some boy that I don't know?"

I snicker, unlatching his arm from around my body to put some distance between us.

"Are you fucking drunk too?" I search her sharp cheekbones and soft lips.

My phone vibrates in my hand, and I swipe to open the message.

If you don't want anyone to get hurt, I'd get them to leave.

I read over the words.

And then read them again.

Looking up from my phone, I focus on what's going on around me. The smoke is still thick in the air from whoever it was that was just on the platform, and the crowd of people are all cheering.

I type out a message.

What are you talking about?

Shoving my phone into my back pocket, I round the driver's side to my car and reach through the wound-down window to take the keys from the leather seat.

The music suddenly gets louder, the crowd in a state of chaos as people chant and cheer.

I can't breathe or see. I've never panicked before. I've never had to, but the text War sent sends a shiver down my spine.

The current song continues playing as a robotic voice comes through the speakers. "Hello, train wrecks…" My stomach sinks.

A chorus of screams echoes through the crowd in excitement. Idiots. Alcohol, cocaine, and Molly equates to idiots.

Us included sometimes.

My back straightens as I spin back around to find Evie, but she's gone.

My phone vibrates again, and I read over Vaden's text. **She's safe.**

Before I can cuss them all out, Instastray grabs me by my arm and forces his lips to mine. "God damn."

Mine fall open in shock, but my blood thickens through my ears. I need to find my best friend. I know he said that she's safe, but

I have to make sure. They'd never hurt her, but what if she didn't get out in time?

"You're going to blink, and someone will be gone—who did it?" the voice declares.

I shove the stray away as my eyes search around the place in a panic. Swiping my phone unlocked, I hit dial on Evie's name as the familiar sound of tires tearing up the asphalt screeches over Slipknot's "Wait and Bleed."

Of fucking course.

Priest has his dumped-out 180SX on the skid pad, smoke building around his tires. His window is down, a hoodie shadowing his face, but when his eyes land on mine, they flash with cadaverous indifference.

If eyes are the window to your soul, then Priest Hayes simply doesn't have one.

"What have you done?" I whisper as my heart beats to a precarious tune. Drunk people cheer him, and the music once again becomes louder.

My phone lights up and I tap the message. **We said she's fucking fine.** That time it's War.

"Dude!" someone calls out from behind me, and I turn back to face him.

Instastray stumbles forward, clutching his stomach. I try to adjust my vision through the smoke, when blood spills from between his fingers as he slumps forward, collapsing into my arms. Unable to hold him up, we both topple to the ground.

Moving his hands out of the way, dread fills me.

I don't question it, because I know.

I hold his blue eyes, placing his hand back over the wound. This one is deep. So much deeper than Caden's. This wasn't a warning cut; this one was made with intent.

"I'm sorry." I stare blankly down at him. Blood sets to slime on my hands, but I stay there, silent.

Someone screams, and people start running, scrambling. Chaos erupts as doors close in the distance and tires skid to leave.

The music continues to play, the smoke unrelenting.

Instastray coughs loudly and blood sprays over my face. I hold him until he stops moving, and then I slowly lay him flat on the ground, standing on shaky legs. I already know everyone would have left. That there would no doubt be police, and parents asking questions about tonight. Questions that will always be taken care of.

The music stops, and I swear all I can hear is the loud beating of my heart.

"I want to know why the fuck you all decided it would be a great idea to start this!" I yell out into the veil of smoke, knowing they can hear me.

Heavy footsteps thud behind me. I don't have to turn to know who it is. Call it twin sensitivity, but I know when my brother is nearby. Or when he has caused chaos.

"You already know why this happened. You all want to be Kings? Then you'll play like a King."

My mouth closes and I grind my teeth. I peer up to my brother. "I am a King, Priest." I tilt my head at him. Priest has been following in Grandpa's footsteps since he knew how to walk. Could it be possible that he's influenced by the notorious Mad King?

Priest shrugs. "Sorry, sis. You know the rules. Evie is home. Now you can go too."

"So, why?" I ask, my arms flying around the place. "What has this boy done to any of you?"

"Mmm…" War breaks through the smoke, swiping the blade over his shoulder. "We can start with the obvious if you want, Halo. Like for one?" He's so close I can feel the heat from his body penetrating mine. He presses the blade to my lips and flattens it until they're glossed with blood. "Ask me."

"War…" Priest warns, but War doesn't back down. His jaw locked on me.

"Go on." His eyes flash a menacing shade of rebellion. "Ask me."

"Why." I angle my head up to him but he's way too fucking tall and large. "Why'd you kill him?" I bring my hand up to his chest to push him away but end up resting it there instead. I'm aware of everyone around us right now, but I can't seem to care.

He presses his thumb against my lip.

My eyes narrow. "Are you fucking joking?"

This time I do shove him away.

He laughs, his head tilting back enough for me to see blood splatter all over the tattoo on the side of his neck.

His eyes come back to mine, and I hate how they always look lazy. High. "Am I? Why don't you kiss someone again and test that?"

He breaks the tension with a single step back.

Fucking. Lockjaw.

When I find Priest, he's staring right at me already. It's deep enough to leave a scar. Shit.

My fingers fly over the screen of my phone to distract myself, and hopefully Priest. I don't know how War can get away with killing someone, yet I'm the one getting fucking glared at. "I've dialed it in. They'll fix all of this."

"Fix?" My brother finally speaks, but his tone is flat. It's not when he's angry that you have to be worried.

It's when he's like this. Calm. Collected.

Lethal.

I watch as his jaw sets when he and Vaden share a look.

"Okay, what the fuck is happening?"

"Get in the car, Halen." War jerks his head over my shoulder. "And go home."

I stare between him and my car, where River is waiting in the passenger seat and Stella in the back.

He doesn't let up. "You wanna fight me on this? Do it later. For now? Get the fuck out of here."

"War," Priest warns, this time stepping forward and placing his body between us. "Do I need to start asking the questions?"

A tear threatens to fall as I blink past it. "It's nothing." I hold War's stare. "Don't worry. It's *nothing*."

Priest freezes, but I don't wait for them to stop their bickering before I do exactly as I'm told and go back to my car.

Vaden's leaning against my door, a burning cigarette in his mouth.

"Move."

He holds my stare. One black, one blue.

"Don't fucking start."

My brows knit together when he finally moves and I slide into the driver's seat, ignoring the way my hands feel against the steering wheel. I fire it up and reverse us out, pushing into first and burning rubber to get us out of there.

"You wanna talk about that?" River asks quietly from beside me.

I shake my head. "No. I'm good."

"I mean, he was cute..." Stella adds from the back seat.

"He was." I clear my throat.

"—for a Rebel..." Stella adds casually.

I squeeze the steering wheel. "How... how do you know?" I didn't even know. The Rebels are a lowline bunch who were connected to one of the families that rebelled against the Kings years and years ago—not even during our lifetime. They're not a threat to us at all. Their families and anyone connected to them have been slowly dropping off the face of the earth for years now. First I've heard of one of them being around—ever.

Stella doesn't answer for a moment. "Because I know men."

We all fall silent.

Thick trees pass our windows on the way up the drive, and I park us at the front, cutting the engine. The silence is loud, and the blood had long since set on my hands. Every now and then I get a whiff of metal and my stomach rolls. It's not that I'm precious about death. Far from it. It's that I wasn't prepared.

"Halen," River whispers, but I don't know what to tell her or Stella. On top of that, I need to check in on Evie. They'd never hurt her. Priest and Evie were good friends at one point. So close I actually accused them both of sleeping together behind my back. I regret it now, because since that outburst they've never been the same with one another.

"You know that you can talk with us." River's voice is gentle.

"I know." The handle is in my hand as I push it open. "We'll talk later. Go home to your beds and sleep." I quickly make my way out of the car before they can stop me.

I can count how many times we've slept alone over the years, and it's a total of three.

I swing the front door open onto our family driver, Creed, standing in the foyer.

He uses his thumb to swipe below his lip. "Halen." He checks over me. "After you shower, discard your clothes outside your room."

I nod, smiling at him before jogging up the stairs. Right now, my batteries are on low. What I feared was happening with my brother is coming to fruition, and I know I can't stop him.

Do I want to stop him?

I slip inside my bedroom and shut my door, breathing out a long sigh as soon as I'm in the confinement of something familiar.

Ivory walls, beige furnishings.

I count everything in my head. A California king bed is made directly opposite the door, to the right of that, a small leather sofa and makeup vanity, and to the right again, a marble fitted bathroom that overflows into a two-story loft style closet. There are rows of clothes, and a large jewelry safe that's built into the center. It wasn't big enough to house my Fabergé eggs, so they're displayed in a glass cabinet above my bed. Dad buys me a new one for every birthday.

Twenty. That's how many I have.

I patter my way into the bathroom, stripping off my shirt and reaching behind myself for my bra.

What the fuck are they playing at?

I mean, sure, we've all played a little hide-and-seek through the forest, but murder? So plain in sight? The boys are smart. Way smarter than anyone else I know, so I know that what they did to-night wasn't a reckless murder because someone decided to kiss me. It had to have something to do with the fact that he was part of the Rebels. But they're not even one of the three organizations that have tried to challenge us over the years. I—

My hand instinctively moves to my mouth to suppress the bile in my throat.

After steadying my breath, I give up on my bra, leaning over the bathroom sink and squeezing the edge. My head hangs low as I try to block out the noise, and a bead of sweat rolls down the bridge of my nose.

I hadn't realized how hard I was squeezing my eyes closed until I open them.

A hand grazes the base of my spine and I stiffen. Lifting my head, I meet War's eyes in the oval mirror. His hair is a mess and all over the place, his neck tattoo obscured by blood. It's a simple tattoo. The EKC skull logo beneath a city.

We both look like we just stepped off a Tarantino set.

My tongue's tied.

Words aren't enough to fill the space that has always been be-tween us. Did we both hold an unspoken rule? Not possible... it couldn't. He was always clear about how he felt, but then lately...

His knuckles graze my spine as he slowly unclasps my bra.

I wince.

Why is he touching me? And why the fuck is he in my room? All the questions I want to ask him, all of which I *don't*.

I let my bra fall to the sink in front of me as he finds me once again in the mirror. His eyes are weak, his lips glistening as if he'd run his tongue over them one too many times. I lose myself in the abysmal cobalt eyes that are lined by ebony lashes. War is beauti-ful. Almost too pretty if it wasn't for the fact that his soul had been touched by the Devil. In another life, he'd definitely be some cheesy Instagram model.

"Why'd you kill the stray?" The words leave my mouth in a

whisper. I know I'm asking a question he has already answered, but I need to know. When it's just us.

He removes his hand from my back and a cool shiver breaks out over my skin. "I already told you."

I slowly turn and he makes no effort to pull away. Whatever he's got going through his head tonight, it snorted his whole bag of coke. He's always on edge, but tonight it has been something... more.

I lift my hand up to his chest to push him away slightly, but it rests there instead. I bend my head to scan his tattoos, before looking up into his eyes, mine crossing because he's so close. With red splatter all over his white shirt and face, my hand continues up to touch his hair, feeling the brittle strands from dried blood.

"Halen?" His soft lips swell around the edges, and when he says the next words, they curve up slightly. "If you ask me to fuck you again, I'm not saying no."

My heart skips a beat as my eyes fly straight back to his, but it's hard with his height. "What?"

He strokes the side of my neck with his palm, drawing his finger down just below my ear. *"Even with blood on my hands."*

Liquid metal touches my tongue and I release my lip from my teeth. "I forgot about that."

He doesn't move. "No, you didn't."

He steps back and I hate that the physical distance is minuscule compared to the one I feel inside. His touch burns but I'd turn to ash if it meant he didn't leave.

His eyes glass over before he swipes the bottom of his lip with his thumb. "He won't be the last, Halen."

Chapter Eight

WAR

MY FINGER BEATS AGAINST MY THIGH AS I KEEP MY eyes locked on the tarmac outside my window.

"Nah, because I know that y'all aren't leaving without me!" Baylee announces, widening his arms and waltzing through the cabin doors.

I let out a deep chuckle, fighting an eye roll. "Who the fuck let you on?"

"Well." He sits opposite me as Priest and Vaden shuffle in behind him. "The old man was talking with Uncle B, so I magically appeared in his car when he was too far to turn around—" His hand flies out to touch the stewardess as she pushes a cart of Dom Perignon. "Can we have two of those, please?" He tilts his head and bites down on his lower lip. "Well, damn. Aren't you just cute."

She blushes, pouring the bubbles into his glass and handing us one each. "You say that every time, Baylee. It still doesn't work." Alaina brushes past us both.

I chuckle into my champagne.

"One day she's gonna break." He adjusts his Rolex on his wrist, holding my stare. Baylee is Bishop's nephew and Priest and Halen's first cousin. His dad, Abel, lives outside of the EKC culture, but that doesn't stop Baylee from making sure he's on as many runs as possible with us. "What's the damage this time?"

"Damage?" I ask, raising a brow. I shrug. "Same, same."

"Well, don't worry. Y'all know

that you don't have to tell me nothing. You do you and I'mma do me. Fuck, I love Perdita."

I ignore him when I turn to face Priest, who's in the spot directly beside my aisle.

He turns his head slowly, his cognac eyes meeting mine lazily. The corner of my mouth tips up slightly.

A silent conversation passes between us that neither of us want to touch on. Priest doesn't tolerate anyone he doesn't want to, and his cousin is no exception.

"Hey, cous," Baylee teases with a full-tooth smile.

"Baylee…" Priest answers, closing his eyes while tossing a hoodie over his head. I'm about to stretch my legs out wide, ready for takeoff, when I hear heels clink up the metal stairs.

What?

She lifts her dark sunglasses up over her head, her eyes falling on her brother. "Sorry I'm late."

He shrugs. "Wouldn't expect you any other way."

She ignores me as she makes her way down the aisle. I kick out my leg, when Baylee's foot connects with mine, and I'm met with a curved brow.

"You always manage to squeeze your ass into the plane before we leave." I reach into my pocket and open a new message.

"Yeah, and?" Baylee leans forward, tapping my phone away and forcing my eyes to his. "Why is the ice queen here?"

I shrug without looking at her. I'm done being the only one asking questions. Do I feel a certain way about her taking on more of a role within our world? Fuck yes. It has never been done in the history of the EKC ever, and I'm not so sure I want it to be her who is the one testing it out. Why couldn't there have been a generation between ours and our parents?

"She's a King, Baylee. You ain't. So why are you here?"

He leans back against his chair, flashing another smile. "Well, I think you and I both know why I'm here."

I tap out a message to River, reminding her to not throw any parties while we're not there before turning my phone on airplane mode and shuffling my hoodie over my head. The plane takes off and I lean against the window, my knee jiggling beneath my weight.

Baylee has long since crashed, and when I look up to the seats in front of me, Vaden is asleep, his head tilted back and face like stone. I don't even want to see what she's doing. We both know that it'll turn into an argument. Or it won't, and I'll just want to shove her up against a wall and squeeze the life out of her. Am I mad? Yeah, probably, but that doesn't beat the fact that years ago... we were just a couple of kids who told each other secrets...

She grabs me by the hand and drags me toward the withered cathedral. With stained glass windows and a small bell hanging at the front, it was all rusted doom and gloom.

I know what she is doing, even if I pretend that I don't.

"War!" she yells, and every hair on my body stands to life when I find her pulling open the large door. Not only is the church old, but it's haunted. I could have sworn Mom said that it was newly built. Maybe they brought it over from somewhere else.

Probably from Perdita.

Then it would definitely be haunted.

I chase her through the doors, pausing when I see Hector standing at the end of the aisle, his hands in the pockets of his pants and his back turned to us. Halen doesn't flinch, bouncing down the aisle with her leather dress in the breeze and her Docs tied at her feet. Her dark hair is braided into two, and I'm certain that she'll always have her hair long enough to do braids.

"Princess..." Hector greets lowly, his eyes drifting up to meet mine.

The church smells musty. It smells exactly what it looks like.

He holds my stare. "What are you both doing?"

"Err..." Halen turns over her shoulder slightly, until I find my feet catching up to where he stands. "Just with War." She bends to the side. "Is Priest here?"

Hector sits back, reaching inside his suit jacket and taking out a cigar. He places it into his mouth, and I watch as his eyes continue to bounce between Halen and I, almost as though he is trying to figure out what mischief we are up to.

Which is nothing. We aren't doing anything. I am keeping her out of it.

I reach for Halen's hand, and the second my palm meets hers, her little fingers close around me. She stands directly in front, even though I want to push her aside. It is subtle. Kind of like she knows, or has an inkling, that her pop is someone who should be feared. Or maybe everyone knows that. We sure as fuck do.

She wants to protect me anyway.

"Go back out to the car, Halo. I'll be there soon."

She turns, exhaling loudly as she crosses her little arms in front of herself. "But you said we were—"

I don't take my eyes off Hector. "Now, Halo."

She finally storms off, her little feet slapping against the wooden floors. It's not until I hear the old church door slam closed that I finally break the silence.

"I guess I should ask why you're here?"

"Hmm..." Hector pops the button off his coat, lowering himself down onto the pulpit. I want to distract myself some way, maybe the stained glass windows and how the afternoon sun bleeds through the Virgin Mary statue that stands as a reminder of why we should never set foot in the house of God.

It almost feels weird to be here.

"I want to ask you something, son, and I want you to be honest with me." He gestures to the bench seat that was near, so I follow his silent order. My legs are tired anyway from all the fucking running Halen had me doing tonight. I mean for real... why was the girl obsessed with cemeteries? The one in Riverside is even more creepy than any of the ones I'd seen in movies too. What with all the family crypts. Doesn't help that it is smack-dab in the middle of the forest either.

"Sure." I kick my foot out and try to stop myself from thinking of all the reasons why he would want to ask me any questions. I was a King,

but Priest was his grandson, and they were both close as hell. We all knew it. Even Bishop knew, and hated it a little, I think. Bishop wasn't a saint, but he wasn't the Devil.

Because his father was.

Priest… it was undecided how he would go.

"You care about my granddaughter?" I watch as he rolls a fat cigar between his fingers as dried tobacco falls to the ground. "Don't fuck around with your answer."

"It doesn't matter what I feel."

"That's not an answer."

I think over his words, praying to God that he doesn't make me answer even though I damn well know no God lives here. "Yes."

He pauses a moment, until his hand rests on my shoulder. "Good. She'll need that. Especially when it comes to Perdita, or whatever games you lot decide." He turns to me. "Some things, she should not know. For her protection."

The tires touch down on the tarmac. Three hours doesn't feel like long, but it's a fucking lifetime when you can feel daggers being shot at your back for the whole trip. I can't even get my thoughts together.

I shove off my belt and move down the aisle, desperate to get the fuck out of the small confinement of this jet.

Away from her.

Am I'm being unreasonable? Maybe. Fuck knows. All I know is that I tried to keep her away as long as I could. No one can stop it now. Can protect her now. And as much as I know that she can handle herself, I know that the shit she's about to find out will push even her boundaries. The princess that never fucking had any is about to feel what it's like to suddenly have a fucking lot.

The stairs unravel and I take them two at a time, noticing the black cars lined up waiting for us. All black SUVs.

I make my way to the Lambo Urus and throw my bag into the passenger side. I haven't even let the dash light up when Priest knocks on my window, gesturing for me to wind it down. "We don't want any fucking mishaps with her here."

I finally flip the on button and feel the car purr to life beneath me. Not my usual taste. Too flashy for me—for most of us.

I shrug. "It'll be fine. She wanted it, she got it."

Priest holds my stare. "You and I both know that regardless of whether she wanted it or not, that she would have to take it."

I don't answer him when I hit the button on my window. "See you at the crib."

I tap the gear into drive and direct the car down the long road behind the airstrip. Apparently when our parents were our age, it was all bush, so overgrown that they had to plow through gravel and old trees to get to the township. Perdita has changed a lot over the years since they'd been here. They make sure to announce that every time. Not that any of them come here anymore.

None except Hector.

I turn on the radio and lean to the side against the window. Pop Smoke was the greatest steal of our time. The greats always leave first.

I carry on down the road, my eyes shifting to the rearview mirror to see who is behind me, when a sleek black Maserati slides in front of Priest, slipping between the two of us. I can't help the chuckle that leaves me, because despite me not being a fan of her being around, her presence is always effortless.

Chapter Nine

HALEN

I DROP DOWN INTO THIRD GEAR AND SWALLOW THE LAUGH that wants to spill out of my mouth. Trees zip past as the gravel beneath my tires whips up and hits the window. I knew that they'd be pissed I was coming, but at least they're all hiding it.

Except War.

Priest's name flashes over the LCD screen of my dash.

I tap answer. "Yes, brother?"

"How do you know these roads?"

My eyes fly up to the rearview mirror as I drop it down into fourth. "I don't know what you're taking about, our cold-blooded King." I hit the red phone button before he can continue.

Priest has been void of emotions since the day he was born, walking around a mere shell of a boy. Mom thought it was some sort of personality disorder. She went through doctors, physiatrists, therapists—fucking hypnosis. Nothing came back wrong or abnormal. Priest wasn't clinically or officially anything other than who he is. Himself. Which isn't exactly ideal for me since he may be cold, but he's not stupid.

I spin the wheel to the right, slamming on the brakes until the ass swings out and gravel kicks up to the boys behind me. I'm still laughing when I tap the gas, but before I can reach speed, War zips past me with a roar of his engine, and a middle finger pressed against the window.

"Fucker."

Following War down Perdita's

main town square, I watch as the locals wander the streets. They live by a nocturnal body clock, spending their days in bed and nights on the street. We'd protect everyone here for as long as we could. That was a fact.

Lights flicker on as the sun sets over the mountains. I slow the car down and continue to follow War, until he hits his brakes outside high iron gates. The house behind it has pointed cobblestone ceilings and hundreds of windows.

War's door opens and my hand instinctively goes to my handle. His Jordans come into view as he climbs out of the car but gets back inside and closes his door again. The brake lights disappear when his car moves forward. Gates part and I follow him through with a rumble of my engine.

The Perdita mansion is extravagant, and over the years, I can see they've added on extensions. It has nothing on Hayes Castle, but it's still big. Two pointed peaks reach high up to the sky before coming down into twin pillars, fixated to the wraparound patio. The stairs leading up to the front door are marble, illustrated with gold spirals. Before you can get there, you have to pass the two Lost Boys.

Lost Boys are the pickings of boys who have seen the trauma of this world and instead of it scaring them, or hardening them, it broke them. They're boys who were born different. A little more violent than the others, but all without self-control. They came here, where they would be trained and shaped into exactly what they are now.

Soldiers.

After swinging my car slightly in front of War's, I turn it off but keep my focus on the Lost Boys. One stands tall and lean, his youthful skin glossy against the impending moonlight. The other is shorter, but also heavier. His hair is in a high bun, and the AKs strapped to both their chests are there for a reason. To intimidate. Make no mistake, they'll pop anyone their *master* tells them to. Lost Boys are loyal and fierce by the time they come out the other end, but there's a catch.

They have an expiration date.

I push my door open and swing my legs out, raking my hair away from my face. "Hi, boys."

Both Lost Boys cast a lazy glance toward me, before their eyes shoot over my shoulder. I don't have to guess to know who they're looking at. This island may be run by a family that's connected to Tillie, War's mom, but they know exactly who owns it. No one wants any beef with a King, especially this generation, I'm beginning to learn.

Dad was always logical, but Priest is unhinged, War is filled with rage, and Vaden has a heart made of stone. There is no rhyme or reason as to why they do what they do or play the games that they play.

"She knows we're here." War slams the door closed and both Lost Boys look between each other, whispering in Latin, our native tongue.

They separate, allowing us to walk through. I follow behind War, glancing a sneaky gaze at the tall one to my right. Just as I pass him, I brush his chest with my hand. He's cute. They all are, but especially him.

The front door opens and we're instantly in her space. You can smell her everywhere. As soon as you walk in, you're met with a sparse stairwell that eventually breaks into two wings.

I shiver.

Despite the gaudy art hanging on the porcelain walls, the house itself feels like a barren womb deserving of love. She was just the wrong woman to carry it.

The clacking of heels intrudes on the dark melancholy sound of Rachmaninoff, the "Isle of the Dead", that seems to continue to play subtly throughout the house. Creepy, honestly, when you think of what the piece depicts.

In a flurry of white silk and cherry red hair, Katsia Stuprum makes her way down the stairs, her blood red nails a stark contrast to the achromic color palette of the house.

"Afternoon, Kings and—" She pauses for a moment when her Jimmy Choos hit the bottom, her eyes holding mine.

I raise a challenging brow at her. "Still a King."

She blinks, but hides whatever she's thinking behind a vacant smile, allowing her naked body to slip through the crack of her silk robe. "Follow me."

War turns over his shoulder a little, and I know he's looking at me. Or at the very least, he's wanting to say something. Probably to yell at me, since we haven't spoken after what happened last night.

I turn to face Vaden and Priest, only to find them both regarding me already.

"What?"

Vaden shakes his head slowly, rolling his eyes before following War down the long corridor.

Priest doesn't move. His eyes remain on me, his jaw tight. "I'm allowing this to happen, Halen. You may run circles around Dad, but nothing goes without my signing off."

"I know that!" I chide, folding my arms in front of myself. Even though we know it's a shit time for a brother-sister discussion, we also know that we aren't going anywhere until both of us understand the other. "You don't have to say anything."

"Halen, I'm not telling you this because I think you can't take care of yourself. I know you can. This is about you making more of a mess out of a situation because you react out of emotion."

My mouth opens, and then closes.

Part of me doesn't even want to ask what the fuck he's on about. "I'm here for the same reason you all are, Priest."

I step backward, needing distance from him. There weren't many times in my life where I was surprised by my brother. He did what he wanted and made no apologies. He came into this world with a brutal amount of insouciance and carried it like a sixth sense.

"It's not the same, Halen," he challenges.

"We will talk later."

I cut him off by stepping around his body and following the

trail the rest of them left behind. Passing canvas after canvas, my steps slow as they begin to conflate together.

A door swings open at the end of the hall, pulling me out of my haze. As soon as I'm inside, my skin prickles with unease. There's a large spa built inground, with a waterfall flowing from the ceiling. Perfumed steam wanders through the air with crisp notes of pine and lemon. A Venetian-stained desk sits adjacent to a generous-sized bookshelf that curves around to another room. Directly opposite us are large floor-to-ceiling windows that give a direct view to the sharp cliff drop and boundless ocean.

"Did you know," she begins, but I don't take my eyes off the view. "This was the first room that was built in this house?" I can't help but feel like she's directing this at me, but again, I can't seem to release myself from the view. "They built it here to keep an eye on the pirates that would try to come. Do you know what the pirates would do when they would try to settle here in Perdita, Halen?"

I finally pull my eyes from the view and watch as she slowly drops her satin robe, dipping her toe into the velvet water.

"No, Katsia, I don't." I make an effort to not ask shit about her.

I glance at her tits. They're great tits. Kudos to her.

She finally lowers herself into the bath and reaches for a long champagne flute beside her, holding my eyes. "Unimpressive."

"Enough." Priest closes the door behind himself. "That's not why we're here, Katsia. You know that."

"Hmm." Her smirk presses against her glass. The longer I look at her, the more I feel myself heat. I've never liked her much, and I had only met her once. I could take it. Take her, this island, and everything she thinks she sits so royally on.

But then I know I'd cause a scene, a scene that War and Priest would have been expecting me to create. One that they *want* me to create, because then I would prove them right. That I'm not ready.

I look around her space, noting the blank walls. Before I can stop myself, my feet are carrying me to a photo frame where a young girl stands, smiling broadly down the camera lens. Beside her is a young boy. He seems agile, if not for the lashes across his face.

Sweat beads at my temple as I turn back to face Katsia, only I'm met with War's threatening gaze.

My cheeks burn when he lowers it down the length of my body before resting back at my face. Over the past couple weeks, which has been since I've had more presence in this world, he's been more obvious.

I hate Perdita.

I want to go home.

I take a step forward, curling my fingers around the first chair I see and lowering myself down, so I'm directly opposite Katsia. She grins up at me, the congestion melting the makeup off her flawless skin.

"You ready for the shipment?" I ask sweetly, as if I'm unbothered.

I am. Very much so.

But fuck if I'll ever let her know it.

"Not yet." Her head tilts back when she swallows more champagne. "Say, Halen, I've heard so much about you."

"Really?" I answer, and I'm painfully aware of how all the boys are silent. For once. "I've not heard shit about you."

That's a lie. I'm being petty. It has nothing to do with the way she keeps eyeing War either.

Nothing.

War clears his throat and my jaw tightens. I'm not stupid. I know who War is and the kind of girls he has been with over the years. He's the worst of the three. I often wonder why I found him the most attractive out of every other guy at school.

He's nothing like my father, and apparently you seek your daddy in your partners.

He's more like his own.

Vaden places his glass down on the desk. "We'll wait."

I don't want to choose right now to ask what the fuck the shipment is since we got off the plane fast and everything happened too quickly. I knew there was a shipment because of what I overheard with Priest, but I didn't know what.

Priest doesn't move when War opens the door as both he and Vaden exit. I stay seated, eyes locked on her and the way she's following War. Something is definitely there.

"Next time, Katsia?" Priest's words are low as he rounds the bath, kneeling behind her. Her whole body changes. Her shoulders stiffen and her eyes widen as the color of her face turns ashen. It's like watching a deer realize the lion is about to eat. "Send a text to say so." He reaches for the wet strands of her hair, moving them gently off her shoulder, only Priest is anything but gentle and I know that the next thing he's going to do won't be. He grabs her by the back of the neck, forcing her head to the side.

She winces, her fear exploited. "My time is precious, and you are not." He releases her so hard she falls into the middle of the bath, before strolling toward the door, placing a cigarette into his mouth and lighting the end.

Finally, I stand and follow, because what the fuck is happening right now and why do I get the feeling I've been left out of shit that I shouldn't have?

I don't bother to talk to any of them as we make our way back to our cars. I don't even know what to be angry about at this moment. And I'm not sure where my anger is coming from. The fact that I don't know what the *shipment* is and that I thought this was just one of their frequent visits to ensure the island is being run right—which if I looked closer, I don't think it is—or that War and Katsia *clearly* have some kind of… thing.

And now I'm angry that I'm angry at that.

Fuck.

"Halen, meet us at the Hutt."

I open my door and ignore War, slamming it closed behind myself and blowing out a heated breath. I squeeze the steering wheel to numb the prickles of rage burning through me. When it swings open again, I half expect to see War, but instead it's Priest.

He kneels to my eye level. "You wanna start with the diva shit, save it for when we're back in Riverside." I don't bother looking at him, keeping my eyes locked ahead. "I mean it, Halen. Meet us at the Hutt and I will fill you in."

"Will you, though?" I snap, and I hate that it comes out as bitter as it tastes. "Because the way I see it, I've been kept in the dark."

"Yeah?" He raises his brows. "Of course, the fuck you have. You're new here, remember? Back there, you're Halen Hayes, the golden daughter and royalty, but here, you're a fucking King. So *act* like it!" He slams the door in my face and I jolt in my seat.

Agh!

I slam my car into reverse and direct it out of the long driveway, not bothering to wait for any of them. I know where I'm going and I know this island.

I need a drink.

I drive toward the main street, parking my car outside the town square. Reaching for my phone, I hit dial.

"What's wrong, baby?"

"I don't know if I can do this."

"Speak."

I rest my head against my chair, blinking up at the ceiling. "The boys have their ways. I don't know anything, and they're drip-feeding me little bits." I swallow past the swell of my throat.

A door closes in the background. "*Amica*, you need to understand that this is new for them too. They're adapting as much as you girls are, but listen to my words."

I press my phone against my ear.

"You are Halen Hayes. My daughter. A prodigy. You belong there just as much as they do. If they forget that, remind them."

My throat burns when I swallow once more as I rasp, "I hope I make you proud one day."

"I'm always proud of you."

After talking with Dad, I jump out of the car and look both ways before running across the road. The BAR sign flashes from a wooden panel, as I push through the lumber doors. The chatter quietens instantly, but the music continues to flow. I spot a dark area nestled at the end of the bar, passing girls dancing on tables as half-naked men holding serving trays duck and weave between patrons.

One heads straight for me as I slide into the booth. A single low light hangs in the middle of the circular table, offering shades of jacinth. The waiter stops near my table, and I trace the black paint that's smudged over his tight abs, before following up to where it's smeared below his eyes.

"Hmmm… let me guess…" he pries, and I arch a single brow. He's tall and skinny. Kind of has the whole MGK thing going for him. "Vodka?"

I shuffle backward. "Well, that depends."

He laughs, reaching for the bottle in his cart, and lays it down on my table with a shot glass. "I knew your mother."

I sigh. "Of course, you did." Flipping off the lid, I pour clear liquid into the glass, hauling it up to my lips. "Should I be worried?"

"No…" he teases, placing a napkin in front of me. "I was only a child when I met her."

My head tips back as I swallow my shot in one go. Before I can ask him more questions, he's gone.

Shot after shot, I watch as the colors of the room fuse together. Girls dance against each other in lace underwear as the pretty, shirtless waiters at the bar feed them more alcohol. The longer I sit here, the more I have time to think of all the ways I'm epically messing this up. Priest told me not to be emotional, yet here I am. Drinking in a Perdita bar with no one to talk to because everyone here is too afraid to come near me. I wanted to play with the big boys and now I'm acting like a child.

I miss Evie. She'd know what to do right now.

Pushing up from the table, I pause when I see someone seated near the bar staring right at me. He has long, dark hair, a body that towers over the rest, and a ring that glistens against the ambient lighting.

I sway on my feet and try to stand up straight, but the room tilts sideways.

Forcing my eyes back to the strange man, he guzzles his beer down before regarding me flippantly. He stands, sliding his empty beer bottle across the table, and dropping money down before turning to leave.

"Hey…" I go to reach toward the bar to rest on it, when I slip and fall. Arms catch me, but I don't see who it is because everything goes black.

Chapter Ten

WAR

THE COLOGNE OF A KING IS GASOLINE, BURNT RUBBER, and the burning flesh of our enemies.

I tip my head back, raising the beer bottle to my mouth. I hate that I'm distracted tonight, but after yesterday with Halen and Perdita, we came too close.

He knows it.

If it wasn't for us carrying her ass right onto the plane and tucking her into bed when we got home, there would have been a lot of questions that she would have had that would go unanswered.

"You're stressing too much." Priest glowers blankly at the masses of people. Two cars line up. A Bugatti and an Evo. I know which one I've got my money on.

"No, I'm not." I cross my legs at the ankle, resting back against the side of the car.

Desperation dances behind us attached to big tits and asses, but none of us give them any attention.

"He's right." Vaden taps my foot with his. "You're stressing too much."

I shake my head. "Nah, because what if she didn't get drunk? What if she peeked and wanted to know what the fuck was happening. Then what? How would we explain?"

"We wouldn't." Priest shrugs, and sometimes I just want to reach between us and shake the fucking life into him. Whenever we see anything at all inside of him, it's always during times when we shouldn't. Once upon a time, Halen was his anchor of some sorts, but as time has gone on, we've watched that lowly slip. I don't think he'd hurt her—he wouldn't—and he'd absolutely rip anyone apart who even so much as thought of coming near her with any shit intentions, but he's getting worse as time goes on.

Colder.

Distant.

Harder.

My old man once told us that Bishop was always the reasonable one of the three. That he never lost control and was like his grandfather. That ain't Priest.

That ain't any of us, but it's definitely not Priest.

One of the girls waltzes out onto the track, gripping a gun. She does the little shake-her-ass dance before raising her hand into the air and firing. Tires skid against the asphalt as they try to gain traction before zipping forward, the Bugatti hot off the line.

I roll my eyes, bringing the joint to my lips and inhaling. Devil's Cockpit was built when we were kids. Our parents put it in as a place for us to come and do whatever it is that we want. It's a twenty-acre block of land nestled behind the township. Through the years, it had been a BMX track, a dirt bike track, and a playground. Everything was knocked down and rebuilt as the years went on. Once we hit high school, we knew exactly what we wanted.

It's not an easy track, it requires drifting, skills, and a level of carelessness to get your ass away from the cliff's edge near a tight bend also known as Halen's Bend. Since she was the first girl who successfully drifted it, it's only fitting. Besides, the girl can drive.

"Excuse me!" Evie falls onto Vaden's lap, caressing his face, clearly on shrooms. "Why are you so damn beautiful?" Her finger glides all over the hard edges of Vaden's features. "A sculpture emanating every poem ever written from a heartbroken woman. You're a tragedy, Vitiosis. A damn tragedy."

I kick out my leg and hold Priest's eyes. "You're not going to do what you want to do."

"Why not?" Priest leans forward, scooping up the rolled dollar bill and playing with it between his fingers. Beside the fact that the table is frosty as hell, between the weed and tobacco, I know that Priest pulling further and further away has nothing to do with it.

He's always been this way. Cold and distant, with an uncanny kind of macabre. Most likely why Bishop was adamant on bringing in Halen. The levelheaded one. I mean... I say that fucking lightly.

I narrow my eyes. "How about she's your sister?"

He leans back against his chair, spreading his legs wide. The party around us doesn't exist to him. The cars, the girls, the drinks, even the coke. It doesn't. "She wanted this. To be involved in this side of our world. Did I try to protect her from it? Sure. But now that she's here?" He tosses the rolled bill back onto the table and holds my stare. "She has to be treated the same way we would anyone."

Well, fuck. Good thing you said that, huh?

I bite my tongue. Not that I give that much of a fuck about the fact that I'd be obvious, but Priest... All this time, she probably thought I was stopping her from coming in closer because I wanted to protect her from the outside.

All along, it was from her own brother.

"War?" A hand curves over my shoulder, and scarlet painted nails come into view. Too desperate. Too loud. Demanding to be picked.

She leans down behind my ear, bringing a whiff of her perfume. Flowers and antiseptic.

"Can you show me the back seat of your car?"

Jenna Hale had been hanging around our shit since we were in high school, and aside from the fact that she's definitely hot enough to walk a runway, she has never been my type for anything more than what she's good for.

Bending her over the teacher's desk. It just so happened that my teacher was also her daddy and the fucker kept trying to fail me on all my classes. Made sure to clean her up using the handkerchief he kept in his top draw.

I catch Priest's eyes again, his brows slightly lifted as the little bud of ember burns saffron every time he inhales. "You gonna get that?" He doesn't look away from me as his teeth catch the trunk of his smoke. I know what he's waiting for. To see if his suspicions of Halen and I are valid.

I ignore her, but she rounds the chair and rests both of her hands on my shoulders, lowering herself down onto my lap.

I lean my head back against the outdoor sofa, catching her eyes. "What do you want?"

She wriggles on my lap. "I'm bored."

I grab her by the wrist and shove her off me. "Then go fuck someone who wants to fuck you."

She doesn't even huff as she turns and makes her way to where her lame friends are waiting near the line of cars on the other side.

Movement catches my eye at the lone car that rolls up slowly behind ours. Hidden beneath the trees, they probably think they look inconspicuous.

Someone moves inside and my hackles rise as I find myself slowly standing to my feet, staying locked on whoever is in the car.

"What?" Vaden asks but doesn't move from his chair.

My body vibrates as I canter forward, and the rest of the party dissolves around us. Smoke twirls around my feet from someone doing donuts behind the starting line. Usually, the smell of burning rubber would get my dick hard, but right now, all I see is that. *It*. Right there, hovering in the shadows.

Priest creeps up behind me. "That car…"

"Yeah…"

He advances forward and I follow close behind. People part as we continue, crossing the track and burnout pad. Headlights flash, blinding both of us, and Priest picks up his pace.

Fuck.

I jog faster, but the car reverses, before stopping sideways. The tinted windows show nothing, but when it rolls down slightly, we see a slither of a baseball cap.

"Aye!" Priest charges, but whoever it is winds their window up and drives forward, leaving dust and gravel behind.

I pause, looking between Priest and the disappearing car. "You've seen it before?"

Priest bares his teeth, turning back around. "Yeah. But only the other day." I watch as his eyes move around the place, never pausing on one spot for longer than a second. "They're getting bold, and I'm losing patience."

Vaden looks between him and I. "You keep saying that but not doing anything about it."

I lean back on a tree trunk, crossing my ankles at my feet. The night is gristly and bleak, the crescent moon luminescent. Rolling my bottom lip beneath my teeth, I nudge my head. "Let's play a game."

HALEN

SLIDING UP THE HOOD OF MY CAR, I LET MY FEET DANGLE over the edge while pulling up my thigh-high leather boots.

"This is creepy…"

"What is?" I breathe out a sigh, lying back and glaring up at the dark sky. Around the loud music and laughter, there's the celestial sound of squealing tires and hot engines redlining. I could not be in a better place. Despite the hangover from last night.

"You smiling like that…" River tilts her head to the side, standing right beside the car.

I turn my head slowly to her. "Well, I'm happy. For one, my brother has let go of his obsession with keeping me under his thumb, and two? I don't know. Everything is good and as it should be."

River rounds the car, her high heels crunching over the gravel. *Wait.* I push myself up to check—yes. *Her* Valentinos. She slips up beside me, her perfectly styled blonde hair rippling in the wind.

"Have you seen the boys?" she asks but keeps her focus to the front. It wasn't so much a question more than it was a statement.

Or a warning.

I scan the area, but my brain is too slow to keep up with my eyes. Or the other way around. Everything tilts to the side the more I try to strain my eyes. Damn. I only had a hit of a blunt.

"No. Not since they were up there—" I wave my hand at the small stage that's built to the side, where couches and beer bottles are all littered. "—doing whatever!"

"Speaking of…" Evie takes my hand and my skin clings to the hood of the car. "I'm going to go steal their coke."

"Evie." I glare at her, but I'm pretty sure my eyes are over her shoulder and not actually making eye contact. "You don't do coke."

She blinks. "Okay, fine. I just want to piss off Priest."

"You won't piss him off." I let her pull me off the car, reaching backward and hooking my fingers into River's. Part of me is glad Stella didn't come out tonight, but then she doesn't usually. "He doesn't care enough about anything."

"Vaden will…" Evie grabs me by the hand and we all start making our way through the sea of people. They move the closer we get to them. It has always worked for us, until it didn't. Until it became annoying and to the point where we had to leave the town to have any fun.

I jog up the steps, dropping down onto the sofa and placing my heels against the coffee table. I don't think I'll be drinking ever again after last night.

"How was the first week?" Evie asks us both when she sits at Priest's spot. After the last incident, I told her a little more about us… without telling her too much.

A car fires up in the background. I should be wondering where they are, but I'm too focused on Evie to care.

"Fine." That was putting it lightly. Whatever is going on, on this side, I am almost certain they're hiding it from me. I just have to figure out why they're doing it and if it's to protect me, or for another reason.

The music lulls me into a relaxed state as I take a sip of water.

Maybe I shouldn't ignore it the way we have always ignored it…

"Don't you think it's a little fucking sexist that you guys don't have to go to school?" River glares across the room at the boys, twirling her long blonde hair around her finger. "I mean, I'm all for tradition, but I think I'd rather just go back to being a Swan."

Vaden watches River closely, running his finger over his upper lip.

I know he wants to say something to her, tell her she's being annoying. Out of all of us, he and River have the closest brother-sister friendship. Even though she and War are siblings, War is too hard on her. Vaden is the one she calls when she's in trouble because she knows that he isn't going to yell at her and pull the daddy card. Vaden is the calm one. The one we all can count on but the one we also know has hidden demons.

The kind that I'm not sure we really want to know.

The kind that only the boys know.

They keep secrets from us, sure, we all know that, but is it the kind of secrets that will drive a wedge in our dynamics? I'm not so sure. At least… not yet.

"It's not sexist, Riv. Shut up." War takes a swig of his whiskey, ignoring all of us. They think it isn't obvious that the only time we spend together with them is when we're all drinking, like they think it's to keep us from asking questions why we aren't with them when they're not.

I haven't asked any questions. Mainly because I don't want to know.

I push up from the chair, straightening my short miniskirt and Dad's vintage Van Halen band tee. I tied the front and tucked it to display my fishnet tights that cling around my waist. I need more alcohol if I want to get through this night.

Especially since it's the first time we've all been drinking together since the night I shamelessly tried to get War to fuck me. That was a month ago.

I think they knew that we had been absent, but it worked for us as much as it did for them.

We have secrets just like they do.

Ours are more fun. Theirs, I'm sure are lined with the blood of our enemies, or whatever.

I stumble to the patio door of Priest's room that overlooks the party out back. People are dancing, laughing, drinking. It's the usual Saturday night at Hayes Castle.

Pushing the heavy curtains out of the way, I leave the door open, not really caring who is watching, since everyone always is. I lift the glass to my lips, inhaling the smoky notes of whiskey and awaiting the burn to slide down my throat. Lithe plays loudly through the speakers, vibrant lights dangling through the trees.

My phone vibrates in my pocket, but I don't want to pull it out to check.

My life is a series of what-ifs. My loyalty, my family, and my needs.

The sound of the door clicking shut makes goosebumps prickle over my skin.

I follow Jessica as she dances her way through a group of seniors. So desperate and needy, but I like her. I like anyone who is shamelessly themselves.

"Something got your attention, Halo?"

I swallow past the lump in my throat, unable to turn to look at him. I hate that I threw myself at him last month. It will never happen again. In fact, I'd go as far as to say I've revenge fucked my way out of feeling shitty about it.

"Mmmm, not so much," I quip. Fuck the dreaded moment for the whiskey, I'll take it right now.

His arm brushes mine and my eyes flick down to the connection. For as long as I can remember, War and I have always been a duo. He was the apology for my psychotic brother. There was a carnal tug-of-war that always erupted anytime we were near one another, no matter how much we fought it. It was out of our control, so we both did the only thing we could.

Stayed away.

He towers over my five-foot-plus frame, but I never feel too small beside him. He has always made me feel like the most important person in every room. Maybe that's why I read into it too much, and in my drunk stupor, tried to fuck him.

"You wanna talk about last month?"

I grimace, biting down on the anger that surfaces. I love War, but that never took away my pride, and last month, it took a hit.

"No. I'm good."

"Halen…" he rasps, leaning his forearms on the rail. He doesn't look to me, merely keeping his eyes locked on the masses out in the garden. Mom's inspiration for the parterre drawing straight from the Italian Renaissance.

I hate that I find myself tracing the sculpted lines of his jaw. The way it makes every Instagram model look like a solid one. War in any room, turns heads. That's just a fact.

My cheeks heat. Damn whiskey.

"I don't want to talk about it. I was drunk—it's fine. It was handled."

He stills before his head jerks to me. My stomach drops when his baby blue eyes find mine.

"Don't look at me like that," I blurt, forcing myself away from his trance and playing with the bracelet around my wrist.

His fingers come to my chin, forcing my face to his.

I hate it.

His merciless touch both stings and fills me with dread, but then his thumb skims my bottom lip. So dulcet. Like swallowing honey. I hate him in a way that only love can breed.

"Don't do that."

"Do what?" I bend my head to the side, my heart beating so slow it almost flatlines.

He pauses a moment, and just when I think he's not going to say anything, he says the words that leave a shudder down my spine. "Act like I didn't want to fuck you the second you wrapped your legs around my waist."

A tremor prickles over me but I manage to catch myself before I make it obvious. "But you didn't."

His hand slips from my chin and lands on my wrist. "Because I can't."

I shrug, forcing myself out of his grip. "So, I found someone who could."

I leave my empty glass on the railing and him with his thoughts.

I swallow past the familiar whiskey on my way up to the platform. The same whiskey that most likely brought those memories to the surface. After then, we never spoke about it. Not once. I think in the back of my mind, he liked the idea that I was bluffing. That they knew we couldn't fuck anyone in this town because everyone was too scared to.

"I kind of wish we were somewhere else right now." The words leave my lips, but my eyes remain locked on the sky above.

I remember when I was a little girl, Dad told me the story of the Kings and the old tale that the Vitiosis elders believed in. Apparently, Vaden and Stella's original founding mother was a witch.

I believed that.

"Bored?"

I lower down onto a chair, finding my brother directly opposite. The silence that beats between us is loud.

"You do know you have to be on your best behavior and that you can't get into any more trouble this close to the ritual, right?"

Priest slowly lifts his bottle to his mouth. "We know. We just don't care."

Vaden's absence is palpable, and when my eyes bounce around the group, they land on War without trying. He's being more obvious as time goes on. The surreptitious eye contact and brushing of skin. I know it could be a problem going forward, but I'm not so sure Priest cares as much as he used to. It's almost like he's completely let go of the reins.

"I don't have the patience tonight." Mainly because I had to wake up this morning in my bed with no recollection of what happened on Perdita after I blacked out.

"You?" Priest mocks harshly.

The crowd has thinned out even more. Thank God. Whatever the boys are planning, I'm sure the less civilians are here, the better.

"What have you done, brother?"

"I'm not sure I want to tell you, little sis. You know..." He leans forward, resting his elbows on his thighs. "Since you're such a daddy's girl."

My blood turns cold. "I might need a drink."

I shove past Vaden who appears from nowhere, gliding down the steps and to where another group of people are standing.

I lean against the table with bottles of alcohol sprawled out, scanning the group closely. There's us, and then there's them. Whoever *they* are.

Five older guys are dressed in casual clothes, except for the bracelets around their wrists.

One of them shuffles closer to me, his head tilting to the side until his hair grazes the top of his shirt. "Halen?"

"That's me..." I answer, flicking the bottle cap off and swirling the liquid around inside. "Who are you?"

He isn't that great to look at, but the boy exudes confidence, and sometimes, that's all a man needs to get attention.

He leans against the car behind him.

"Maserati?" I raise a brow, and although our conversation is loud enough for the rest of his group to hear, they don't pay us any attention.

"Impressed?"

I hold his stare. "Not even close."

He chuckles loudly, his head tilting back. "Huh. Didn't think the daughter of Bishop Hayes would be impressed by much of anything."

"Oh, you'd be surprised..." I joke, and I'm not flirting. This guy is weird, but if they're here, my brother would know so they must be fine. No one sets foot in any of their parties without their approval.

"I have to admit," his long finger taps against the side panel, "I haven't seen you here before."

"A race?" My head tips back and I fight with myself to not be offended. "You must be new here."

His laughter dies off almost sarcastically. "Ah, if only that were true."

Someone whistles from the side and a shrill of adrenaline rushes through me.

I glance up to my group and notice them all watching my encounter with the new guy.

"You should probably go back there…"

"Is that a threat?" I ask, my patience with him wavering.

"Never."

I swipe my bottle and take slow steps as I make my way back up to the platform. Stopping when I notice everyone watching me, I widen my eyes. "What?"

"Sit the fuck down, Halen." War points to the chair I was just on, disregarding me.

"Who are they?" I point behind me with my thumb, well aware they know who I'm talking about. I know they know who I'm talking about, since they're the reason why they're here.

Priest doesn't move his eyes from me, and I know that whatever he's about to say, I'm not going to like. I never seem to lately. He's my twin and I love him, but I'd be lying if I didn't say there was a void deep inside his cold heart that not even I could warm. One that I don't think anyone could, no matter how close they were to him.

War and Vaden included.

"I'm not sheltering you anymore, Hales." Priest lifts a cigarette to his lips, biting down the trunk and lighting the end. When he does that, he looks like Dad when he was his age. It's creepy.

He jerks his finger toward me, leaning back on his chair. "You all wanted in, so let this be your first night as a King."

I hear a faint growl from behind me, but I don't move. "What's that supposed to mean?"

Goosebumps rise over my flesh, and I step backward on shaky legs. I'm not as sheltered as they think I am, but I am starting to get the feeling that their version and mine are different.

Worlds apart different.

A side of me hates that Dad removed me at a young age and pushed so hard for me to finish school and live a life outside of them, because now I feel like an outcast in a group that has always been family, but another part of me likes it. It means that I get to walk in with fresh eyes. I see through the scope, not just the vision that I'm primed to see.

"It means that I hope you can run in those heels." I turn, just as War blows out smoke rings, before his lip curves up in a cold grin. "Because you're gonna need to be able to do that."

"I can run just fine." I fall onto the sofa, clutching the bottle of whiskey, only Vaden's foot connects with the base and he kicks it out of my hand. "V!"

He shrugs. "Probably won't help you tonight, little one, and after last night, we need a few to recover."

"I don't need help!" I glance sideways.

"Mmmm, whatever this game is, I'm playing!" Evie piles her long hair onto the top of her head.

I choke. "No. You and River can go—"

Priest interrupts this time. "Agreed. They're going."

The heat of War's rage warms me from my side when his long fingers close around my hand, and he places a plastic cup in my palm.

My eyes narrow as I refocus on War's face. His mouth is in a flat line, cold as stone. Will my feelings toward War always be as clouded as they are now? Maybe.

I take a small sip of whatever he gave me anyway and hiss when the poison touches the tip of my tongue.

River and Evie shift together, forming one, as someone blurs toward them. Evie laughs, music plays, and my head turns fuzzy. I don't know how long I sit here. Minutes. Hours.

I push myself up from the sofa but stumble back down. Shit. What the fuck was in that drink?

Fuck love.
And fuck him too.

My eyes watered as I stared up at the small oval carved into the plank above my bed. I traced the lines so many times that it was almost engraved in my head.

Not that it wasn't already.

Not because I did it myself.

A halo. Symbolic for something pure, protected, cared for.

Pulling the blankets up near my chin, I hide beneath them, ignoring the pungency of mold and sawdust. I began to count to five then six in Latin. I'd felt the wane of my anger burn behind my eyes the longer I was here.

I stopped longing for deliverance.

For my best friend.

For the carefully constructed life I'd been fed, only to have this choke me.

I didn't care anymore. I just hated that every time I swallowed, it felt like razor blades were stuck in my throat. I wish they were. I wish it were real blades that cut me open and bled me out until I was nothing but a corpse on the floor.

My eyes closed, even though I knew sleep wouldn't come.

The door opened in the room and my skin prickled. My fingers clamped together beneath the cover, as I scrambled for the black Van Cleef bracelet locked around my wrist.

It would happen again. I guess I should be thankful.

They were okay.

The shadow stood over my bed, and I blinked up at the harsh lines of the silhouette. Afraid to blink because I knew. I knew that sometimes, that was all it took to be over.

But then other times, it would feel like weeks.

The mattress dipped beneath his weight. The umbrella of the top bunk doing nothing to calm my racing heart. He didn't care. He used it as he pleased. He would take everything with an iron fist and make no apologies when he tore it from me.

His head tilted to the side a little, and because of the flickering light from the burning candle on the other side of the room, I allowed myself to follow the hollowness of his high cheekbones and his pillowy lips. Even his side profile was melodic. Girls wrote poetry because of boys like him.

He slid out of his coat and placed it onto the end of the bed. I watched as his long fingers fumbled with his belt. I sighed melodiously as he peeled back the covers and a gust of wind prowled over my naked body.

It's okay. You know what you have to do.

He moved over my body, hovering an inch above me. I didn't breathe. I wished it was that easy to just die.

Slowly, his hips met mine, the tip of his cock resting against my entrance.

I squeezed my eyes closed as my lips parted. "War, please." Dry and hoarse—dead and gone. I couldn't see past the blinding pain as he forced himself inside of me in one thrust.

"Stay with me, Halo..."

HALEN

I FLY UP FROM WHERE I'M LYING WITH LEATHER CLINGING TO my skin like adhesive, and my brain hammers against my skull like I've just woken after drinking for days. I hadn't been drinking. Except for—

I reach up to touch my head, attempting to open my eyes further. Where the fuck am I? Simple black leather seats.

War's GTR.

Loose gravel touches the soles of my feet after I've shoved the door open. We were still on the track, only now I'm looking out over Halen's Bend and the cliff that commands a view of the ocean. When I was a little kid, I loved this spot. I'd pretend that pirates would come to take me away.

Now that's slightly terrifying considering whatever Katsia was yapping on about.

I slam the door closed, observing the once busy party. There's not a single person within view. I round the back of the car and quiver when cold air conflates with my anxiety and leaves its warning as goosebumps over my skin.

I don't know how much time has passed since I was with everyone, and I can feel the claws of sobriety sinking further into my brain the more that time goes on.

What the fuck.

Shoving my hands into my jacket pockets, I try to find my phone but come up empty.

I stomp back to the car and

swing the door open once again, ignoring the faint smell of War's cologne that's still lingering in the air.

Fucker.

He gave me a drink—what the fuck did he slip me?

I'm reaching beneath the driver's seat, my fingers barely touching, when something pierces the side of my belly.

"Oh my fuck!" I shriek, spinning around while holding the new dull ache burning at my side.

He's wearing a blank white mask, a small pocketknife grasped in one hand and a phone in the other. I can't tell if he's proud or scared of what he's just done.

Did he just stab me?

"What did—"

He suddenly stumbles backward, dropping the knife and swiping his bloody hand over his mask, leaving a smudge of red.

His head jerks from left to right as if in a panic, before he bolts off.

"Hey!" I scream, moving as fast as I can out the back of the car while swiping up the knife he dropped. "You motherfucker."

I try to put one foot in front of the other to chase him, crossing the track that I've drifted on so many times before, and heading straight for the forest, but the man pushes through the clearing.

I chase him, knife clasped tightly in my fist and adrenaline pulsing through my veins. I fight the fatigue that's gobbling me whole, and instead feed it my revenge.

I'm going to fucking kill him.

My legs ache as I push forward, jumping over fallen logs and ignoring the leaves slapping across my face. My lungs burn and the tears on my cheeks have long since dried.

I stop, my hand coming to the wound on the side of my stomach. Wincing, I pull away, looking down at my palm that's stained with blood.

My mouth opens, and then closes, as I fall backward into something hard.

My eyes close as the pain spreads, so I apply more pressure and ride through the pain.

They pop open when heavy footsteps get closer.

I shoot up from the ground, the pain now blinding as I turn over my shoulder, holding my breath. I don't know who it is. All I know is some asshole hurt me tonight.

What the fuck is happening?

"Fuck, Halen!" Someone is directly in front of me, and I wince from the salacious heat of his body.

Too close.

I reach out to shove him away, but my nipples harden against my bra. This is a problem when they're both decorated with metal.

"Fuck you. Go away—"

He grabs my hand and forces my back against the tree. "Let me look at it!"

His knuckles graze over the side of my belly and I turn rigid at the impetuous pulse between my legs. It's enough to distract me. "How the fuck did you do this?"

"Someone—" I say through clenched teeth. His features blur together and I'm pretty sure my skin is cold to the touch. "Am I dying?"

He bites on a laugh. It's not one he wants to give me. "Finish your sentence."

I shove him away again, finally over his antics. "You drugged me."

He knocks my hand away, and when I try to shove him again, he snatches my wrist and forces it up above my head. "Fucking chill! The more you panic, the faster you'll lose blood."

"I don't care."

His hand comes to my chin, forcing my face up to his. "I drugged you. You were supposed to stay in the fucking car."

"Why!" I yell, irritation coursing through me.

"Because your brother has gone completely over the edge and

doesn't fucking see you as someone who needs to be protected anymore."

My mouth closes and the knife I'm holding slowly slips from my fingers. "What do you mean?"

War shoves his fingers into his hair and pulls.

He blows out an exasperated breath as his arms drop to his sides. "You're an equal now, and when we complete the ritual, it will only get worse than what it is now. You have to do everything that we do, Halen. You don't get to pick and choose who your loyalty is to. Your old man? He isn't the knight in shining armor you have grown to think he is. Are you ready for that? To see this side of him? This side of—"

"Of who, War?" His name falls from my tongue like velvet, suffocating his rage. They think I don't know who my dad is? I know who he is. I'd heard the stories about him when he was young, and that kind of madness doesn't get put to sleep just because you age and have a couple kids.

Not even for love.

Not even for children. Especially when you're a King.

But that's not what he's afraid I'll see.

With the blanket of darkness around us both, I lower my tone. "Say it." I lean my head against the bark, wincing when the distant throbbing returns on my side.

He means Priest.

Vaden.

Him.

Am I ready to see that? Yes. I know without a doubt that I am.

His hand covers mine and my breath hitches, but when he presses his knee between my thighs, I whimper, collapsing forward until my forehead rests on his chest. "Let me see it properly."

"Fuck you," I gasp, my heart racing.

"You've said that already." His teeth graze the edge of my jaw, forcing my hand away from the wound. His other hand flies over his phone screen, before a flashlight beams onto my skin. A beat of silence stretches between us as his body turns rigid. "I'm gonna fucking kill them all."

I swallow. "You don't even know who did it."

"Don't care. They're all dead."

I shudder. "So this game that you protected me from seeing tonight. Are you going to do this every time?"

His thigh shifts once more and my mouth turns dry when I feel how close he is to me.

"Do what?"

My stomach tightens as my back slightly arches off the tree.

A loud bang explodes through my ears, cutting the tension, and I pull from his grip, shoving my shirt back down. As soon as his hand slips from mine and the connection is broken, I feel the absence. I hate that I feel that shit right down to my soul.

"What the fuck was that?"

He doesn't step away from me, but his shoulders are back, his head snapped slightly to the side. It's as if he's waiting for someone to appear from behind us. When I hear twigs snapping beneath heavy boots, I know that whoever is here isn't welcome. The muscles in War's arm ripple against the moonlight as he slowly turns while forcefully shoving me behind him.

"Tsk, tsk… Well, what happened to the fallen princess?"

I grit my teeth at the snarky comment. I hadn't even risen to *fall* yet. I was barely halfway there, since I apparently have no idea what twisted game the boys actually play during these nights.

"You have about two seconds to run, Raphael," War says tonelessly. "I may have never seen your face, but mark my words, I always know when you're near."

I sidestep away from him to see if I can get a better look at who this guy is, but War's hand flies out to stop me.

"I'm not here for a fight." The guy surrenders and I finally break away from War to see who he is, but he counters my step once more.

Goddamn wall of muscle.

"I've come to warn you all."

"About what?" War hisses. Anger flows from his body in searing waves of lava.

"We don't much like to be pushed out of our turf, War..." he singsongs.

"Motherfucker, you—" War growls, stepping forward. As soon as he does, Raphael steps back, raising his arms. I finally catch a peek. Dressed in white from head to toe, his face is covered by a pastel-colored mask. "You have ten seconds to run before I gut you alive and send you back to your owner in liquid form."

"Ah... the true EKC threats. I've got to admit, they're not nearly as colorful as I would have hoped."

He goes to turn back when War's next words stop him. "Three hundred degrees." Raphael's—or whoever's—shoulders stiffen. "Three hundred degrees, a special little concoction named lye solution, and your ass is simple syrup. Your owner will love that. Add some moisture into his creations..." I shudder as the air blows over my skin.

Raphael shoots off through the forest, and as soon as he's gone the pain in my side returns.

I fall backward, hissing through the sting. Blood seeps between my fingers and War catches me swiftly, sweeping me up by the back of my thighs and lifting me off the ground.

"I'm only letting you carry me because I don't think I can feel my legs." His cologne is a blend of cedar and bergamot. Like walking through the doors of your favorite place. Familiar. *Safe*.

My head falls against his shoulder as everything fades away.

Chapter Thirteen

HALEN

MY VISION BLURS AND ANYTIME I TRY TO FOCUS ON AN object, it only makes it worse. The room blends to a smudged color palette behind a pool of tears as I try to push up from the soft surface I'm lying on.

A hand is on my chest, forcing me back down.

"I thought you said it was just a cut…"

"It was." War's tone is hard.

"If it was just a cut, why is she so fucked up?" Priest hisses from somewhere.

I force my eyes open, reaching up and scrubbing them with the palm of my hands.

"I'm fine!" I grumble, crawling up the bed and leaning against the headboard. "And War drugged me."

I look to my brother. His eyes narrow as they fly between us. I haven't even registered where I am yet. The ground is uneven and slowly the room comes into focus.

I'm on the fucking 747.

Priest closes his eyes for a second, nostrils flaring as the tension leaves his muscles. "Could have been worse and at least it knocked you out for a few hours."

But— "Wait." I shove the white woolen blanket off my body. "Why are we on Riddler?" We only ever use this plane if we're going away for family vacations because of the sheer size of it.

The door behind War closes

and he chuckles, shaking his head while lowering himself down onto the mattress of the bed. I force myself to move away from him because no matter how much I try, I can't not be angry with him. He does too many things to piss me off.

Like for one—whatever happened last night. It isn't the drugging, no. I'm not precious and I don't care. I know that it wasn't the intention to harm me, so it's not that.

My step falters when turbulence shakes the plane. "I know you all. Why are we on Riddler? We only use this for vacations."

The door closes opposite and Vaden slowly lowers himself into the chair in the corner of the room while holding a glass of whiskey. Riddler had been gutted and restructured in design to match our private jet. There are bedrooms upstairs, the biggest one being the room I woke up in.

"Halen, you wanted in, so this is what's going to happen going forward." Priest's monotone voice is one of his many red flags.

"You say it like I had a choice, Priest…" I say softly, and I instantly hate that I sounded so weak. I didn't want to be weak. Especially not in front of the very men that have always made me feel that way because of just how insane they are.

He ignores me. "Correct. So here's what you need to know going forward. All of what happened last night, was a retaliation from a rival group."

"The Gentlemen?" I blurt the first one that comes to mind. Naturally.

Vaden tenses in his chair. "No."

"Who?" I ask, folding my arms in front of myself.

"The same man who cut you was the one who cornered us, Halen. He's what they call a Baker—" White noise pierces through my ears as the room shifts sideways and the pain in my side returns. "Hey!" War's arm is around my back, helping me stand straight. "You good?"

I stare blankly at him, before looking around the room and

resting a little longer on War before going back to my brother. "You all underestimate us."

Priest's eyes narrow. Oh, how the tables have turned.

"Let up on her." War makes his way to the opposite side of the room, opening the curtains and looking out to the puffy clouds in the sky. "Pretty sure she can handle it."

Silence.

War Malum, always there to take my hand. Even if it is to lead me to hell.

"So?" I ask, glaring around at all three of them. "Why are we on Riddler?"

Vaden raises his glass to his lips, his eyes landing on mine. They flash with a dark shadow. "Because we want to play a game."

My mouth slams shut. I ignore the way his answer sends ice down my spine. "Do I even want to ask with who?"

"Did it not cross your mind…" War's tone gets louder as he comes close behind me. "That it could be you?"

I swallow past the lump in my throat, my eyes finding Priest out of instinct. He doesn't give me anything, one brow raised slightly and a snide smirk on his face.

I love my brother, but he's a hard man to love. He always has been. You love him, but you'll always question if he loves you. It didn't matter to me. Mine was unconditional through and through, and when I was old enough to figure out this was what he was like, I had already decided that I would love him enough for the both of us. But for this reason, I knew that the second I agreed to step completely into the family order, I'd lose any softness that he ever had for me.

And it wasn't a lot to begin with.

Nodding, I straighten my shoulders and turn, surprised to see just how close War is. "Because I already know how they're played."

War's eyes search mine, azure blue framed by feathery sable lashes. His cheekbones are brutally sharp, his lips cherub soft, and his jaw…

That.

Fucking.

Jaw.

Some days I want to break it, other days I'm not sure if I just want to sit on it. We'd never so much as kissed. I hate that every time I find myself looking at him, I'm kind of envisioning what that would feel like.

The corner of his mouth twitches. "Or maybe you only know one game..."

I bring my hand up to his chest, shoving him away. "Where are we going?"

"You mean who are we going with?" War smirks. I almost forgot what it was like to be completely under his spell.

"Why don't you go trek out to the cabin and see what's happening?" Vaden's tone is level, smooth, and unbothered.

I slide my feet into my Louis slippers, making my way to the door that leads out to the bar, and then farther to where the business lounge and first-class areas would be on a normal double-decker 747. On ours, it's just cubicle bedrooms and a lounging area.

I bypass the stewardess and steward, padding down the steps that lead to the spa area and then farther down the twin stairs to the main cabin.

I pause at the entrance, blood draining from my face just as we hit turbulence and I reach out to the side to stop myself from falling.

"Halen, ma'am, you really should be back in your seat." A hand touches my shoulder and I scan over the people in the cabin area, coming up to look through the eyes of wolf white contacts and the skull paint that we're so famously known for.

This is the start of a game.

War was right. I hadn't known much. They kept it simple during high school, or for the most part away from me. I didn't know much about what they would do during the races and the games they would play then. But this? I knew this was different.

I move away as she sashays her hips through the aisle, clipping the empty glasses from the tables where people are sitting. The booths are lined more like business class. To leave it as coach wasn't happening on my mother's watch.

My eyes bounce over every head. I count eight heads. Every single one of them has one thing in common, and that is the skull blindfold over their eyes.

Fingers wrap around my hips, pulling me into a hard body as he shoves me back against a wall.

"Do I even want to ask?" I peer up at War with a curved brow. The area his hand is on burns as every second passes, but I don't care. *I'm starting to not care.*

He searches my eyes carefully, the tip of his tongue swiping his upper lip as he presses me closer against his body.

My eyes close out of instinct as I take a deep breath. "What are you doing?"

He lowers his hand from my back, down to my ass. "Kind of tired of the push and pull." He tilts his head, bringing me in closer. "Kind of just wanna pull…"

"I get it," I say through a whisper, searching his eyes. "Girls drop to their knees for you."

"Like you won't?" he challenges, and I hate that smug smile on his face.

"Me? Bow?" My mouth mirrors his as I lean up on my tippy-toes, bringing my hand to the back of his neck and forcing his down until it's a hair's breadth away from mine. "Now, you and I both know that's not going to happen."

He chuckles, lowering his mouth farther, but not close enough to be the first one who breaks.

I have thought about this happening so many times over the past few years, but I never knew what would happen once it came true, because I kind of always assumed it never would. He isn't just my brother's best friend, but he made a promise that he wouldn't. We always knew War could, at times, be impulsive, but this… the repercussions of us going down this path are ones we both want to avoid.

My shoulders deflate as I release him, attempting to put a smidge of distance between us. "What are you doing?"

He grabs the nape of my neck and forces me back against him.

He brushes my hair away from my cheek. "Whatever the fuck I want."

My eyes cross from his close proximity and my neck aches from being bent at this angle. I know I should push him away. Run away. Hell, anything.

"Don't even try, Halo. You won't get far on here."

I try to sidestep and head back to the cabin to figure out whatever the fuck is going on, but his hand is on my wrist and he's forcing me back, twisting my body around so my ass is against his thighs. He sprawls his fingers out over my belly possessively, and I hold my breath.

"You know what happens when you run, Halen?"

I don't answer, because the blood rushing behind the back of my ears is too much. Too loud. *Too heavy.*

I feel the softness of his lips graze the curve of my ear. "I *chase you.*"

My knees weaken and I hate that in mere seconds, he has me practically doing exactly what he wanted me to do.

Fall to my knees.

But Daddy raised a stubborn bitch.

A snide smirk touches the corner of my mouth as I turn myself in his grip. I'm about to laugh when his hand flies to my chin and he squeezes my cheeks together, backing me up against the darkest area where the exit doors are. Lights flicker on and off as the plane hits turbulence once again and I stumble slightly.

He runs the tip of his nose over the bridge of mine. "If you tell me to stop, I'm gonna fuck you anyway."

My heart hammers against my rib cage as his hand grabs my outer thigh.

My legs part a little, despite my words saying otherwise. "You know I'm not going to do that."

He leans farther into me until his lips touch the crease of my ear, and his hand finally travels all the way up before curving around to my inner thigh.

My breath catches when his palm eases over me, just as his teeth catch my ear. My clit praises his touch and my hips buck forward to beg for more.

"You're fucking wet." His whisper is rapacious. "Mine."

I grab the back of his head, fisting his hair to force him down to my lips.

Okay. So we both just dove headfirst toward each other instead of moving slowly.

Cool. Glad that's out of the way—but…

He chuckles playfully against my mouth, igniting a surge of heat, before his teeth sink into my bottom lip and he sweeps his tongue over the clefts left behind.

Tension snaps around us when he finally kisses me. *Oh my fucking God.*

I whimper beneath his touch as his tongue languidly circles mine, the ghosting of his fingers moving my underwear to the side. White heat surges around me as carnality sinks its claws deep into my nerves when he teases my entrance with a twirl of his finger.

My eyes burn with ardency as his mouth eases to a teasing pace, and my brain short-circuits as the world falls around us.

My breath catches as he slips a finger inside of me, and then another, before collapsing forward in a heavy surrender.

"Fuck."

I cry softly into his mouth when I feel my muscles tense and my back arching into his torment. I'm desperate and hungry, only his kisses are patient and his movements calculated.

Right now, I don't care that there are people blindfolded behind this wall.

I don't care that the flight attendant could come back at any second—and I kind of hope she does.

I don't care that there are people upstairs who could throw us both off this jet if they caught us.

My toes curl and I tighten around his fingers as he continues to stroke me like his pet. His tongue sweeps over mine and I suck it into my mouth, his piercing catching my teeth.

Kicking my leg wide, his cock grinds against my stomach as I reach between us to take him out. My mouth waters, my chest caving in at the thought of tasting him.

He withdraws from our kiss and rests his forehead against mine. "The shit I wanna do to you will need longer than the time we've got."

Fine.

I find his mouth again, and just like the first time, my skin sizzles as my brain whistles to a hypnotic tune. His tongue explores my mouth in a way that leaves flames blistering over my heart. The kiss turns frantic as he buries his hand in my hair, groaning when I tilt my head to the side to give him more access.

I'd give him anything at this point.

With my lips bruised and swollen, he detaches and dips down, catching my exposed nipple between his teeth as his tongue laps my piercing.

"Who else has seen these?"

Many people, my dear.

"Shut up," I whisper, sweat beading between my breasts when he works his fingers inside of me, his teeth puncturing my swollen flesh.

He curls his fingers and caresses me roughly, my mouth popping open as the familiar flames ripple through my veins once more like a vine of poison ivy dipped in gasoline. I don't even have a moment to realize I'm tipping over the edge before he catches my strangled moan as I dissolve around his fingers.

The shadows do nothing to hide the hunger in his eyes as his lips part and the corner lifts. Dragging his tongue over my breast and to the center of my chest, he trails the sweat all the way up to my jaw and bites greedily.

He stumbles backward, his eyes heavy on mine. I hate how much I ache to have his damn hands back on me. How obvious his presence is now that I don't have it rubbing up against me.

I wish I never knew now.

A pang of regret bounces through me, but not for the reasons I want it to. Because I know, this was a taste, and like the gluttonous bitch that I am, it won't be enough.

The dim lighting casts perfect lines over his features when he slowly lifts his fingers to his mouth, his tongue lapping over my cum.

I knew he would.

Asshole.

I straighten my shirt and put the girls away. "Fuck, I can't believe we just did that."

And I don't regret it at all. Aside from… the part where now I know what he feels like and I never want to go a day without feeling him again. Shit.

He hasn't said a word, and when I finally make a lame attempt at forcing my hair down from the nest at the back of my head, his lips roll behind his teeth to stop his smirk.

"What!" I snap at him, unable to hide my own. "Stop fucking staring at me like that."

I'm looking to the side of where the aisle is when his next words catch my attention.

"Little Halen Hayes…" He stumbles backward slightly. "Who knew you tasted *so good.*"

Fuck. I'm in so much trouble.

WAR

I'M NOT THE KIND OF MAN TO LIVE WITH REGRETS. Everything I do in life, I do because I fucking want to. Halen Hayes included. I could still smell her on my fingers when we landed in Perdita. She is a King, which means she's fair game.

I'll keep telling myself that.

I follow Vaden and Priest down the stairs that lead out onto the tarmac and awaiting cars. Four SUVs and a blacked-out Mercedes minibus.

Kinder meets us at the bottom, his ice-like eyes void of emotion as he looks over my shoulder, finding Halen. "The princess is finally in, I see."

I step in the way of his sight. "Yeah, but if you look too much—" I lean to the side to catch his attention, since he's so fixated on her. "—you might lose those pretty eyes, Lost Boy."

Priest turns over his shoulder again, looking between Halen and I with indifference. Priest isn't stupid. In fact, he's entirely too fucking smart for his own good. It's not a matter of when he's going to figure it out. It's a matter of when he's going to approach it.

Kinder's head dips somberly, stepping back as he gestures to the minivan. "How many are in this load?"

"Eight." Priest points at the SUV nearest to us. "And they can go straight to the gully. Have them waiting for us."

Kinder bows and I respond

with a wink, heading to the SUV. I slide into the back as everyone follows, with Halen directly in front of me and her brother
beside her.

I run one of the fingers I used to fuck her with over my upper
lip, grinning around the movement.

She clears her throat. "Uh, so who is going to fill me in?"

Vaden snickers, glaring out the window. "How much do you
know about Perdita and what it's used for?"

She shrugs, and it's amusing. As much as she thinks she can
handle what happens, I'm one hundred percent sure she can't.
Which is fine. It just means that she's easy to mold into whatever
the fuck we want.

I.

Whatever the fuck *I* want.

"Only what is told in the Hayeses' grimoire." Those fucking old
tales told by equally as old ancestors who couldn't shut the fuck up.
Some things would have been better left a mystery, and everything
inside of each family's grimoire included.

"And by told, you mean secondhand?" Vaden comes back to her.

Her cheeks turn pink, and I know it's getting to her that she
doesn't know what we're talking about.

"When our parents got pregnant, they decided to move us all
back to Riverside. They spent their young years in the Hamptons,
but they knew that when the time came, they would bring us back
here. While they were gone, Riverside was a fucking mess. Filled
with crime and drugs, it took our families coming back for it to
leave. But it did just that. It disappeared. For them, it was fine because they didn't have to do anything extreme. The trash took itself
out. Until a couple weeks ago."

She blinks at me and I fight the urge to laugh.

"Hmmm…" She crosses her leg over the other, her matte black
fingernail beating against her thigh.

A thigh I not long ago had in the palm of my hand.

I grab onto the crotch of my jeans to readjust myself.

"And what has that got to do with the van load of people?"

Priest turns to her. "It's why they're here. This is part of what we do."

She seems to muse over his answer before her hands come together with a clap. "Okay. Since we're switching stories, which, by the way, I didn't know, so thanks for that—" She leans over and her fingers wrap around mine when she reaches for the bottle.

My jaw tenses when her touch ripples through me like thunder.

I release it and she falls against her chair, covering her lips around the rim. Lips that need to meet my cock ASAP.

"What is it…" My brows lift.

"Yeah, what is it that you need to tell us?" Priest baits her, and I know—I just know—she's about to slap us all in the face. The tension in the air shifts as the car stops, but none of us move from our seats.

She takes a swig of the amber liquid, swiping her mouth with the back of her hand. There's a knock on the window at the same moment her mouth widens.

She gestures outside. "Oh well. Isn't this a turn of events."

I look out the window to see River and Stella standing against the two pillars on the porch.

"What the fuck—" I shove the door open, ignoring the prying eyes of the two Lost Boys who have both jumped out of idling cars.

I point to Stella and my sister. "What the fuck are you both doing here?"

Stella rolls her fucking eyes to the back of her head, brushing her hair over her leather-clad shoulder. "What? You think that you're the only ones who are Kings? Or that it rests solely on Halen?"

River shakes her head. "Let's go inside. We can't do this out here, we don't know who is watching."

"Wait a damn—"

River cuts me off. "War, I swear to God."

My lip curls up as I force myself back down into the car, grabbing Halen from around her wrist and hauling her out.

"Ouch! War!" she howls but ambles out.

I shove her against the side of the car and when I catch movement in the back, I glare at Priest. "Don't fucking even…"

His eyes narrow for a moment, before his big shoulders lift when he climbs out of the car.

I know he isn't good with this, but he and I will talk about it later, and besides, he understands the way I feel about River and how much I have tried to keep shit from her all her life. She's even more sheltered than Halen and Stella. Stella has always done whatever the fuck she wants, but River was the good one. She did what she was told, never put her nose into shit she knew not to, and always kept to the girls.

"What the fuck have you done?" I force out from gritted teeth.

Halen has always been the diva. She got what she wanted, whenever she wanted, and no one ever asked questions.

Until now.

She tries to whack my hand away, but I tighten my grip. "Halo…"

"It's not me, you ass!" Her eyes flash with defiance. "We—" She gestures between her and the girls. "—have been doing more than you know. The Fathers approved a long time ago, War, so if you have beef, go take it up with them."

I shove her back and as soon as she's not in my grip, I fucking hate it.

Priest finally rounds the car, his eyes meeting the girls. "I thought he was joking."

Vaden flicks Stella against her head with a chuckle.

"What do you mean *you thought he was joking?*" I flex my fingers in the palm of my hand to stop myself from punching him straight in the jaw.

Priest turns over his shoulder an inch, to make sure no one is watching before coming back to me. "Years ago, he said the girls would join when the time was right, but I thought he only meant Halen."

"War!" River snaps her fingers. "I'm not a fucking kid anymore, and when we *go inside* we can talk about it all. Together. As a family. As it was supposed to be."

My jaw turns to steel. I need to put some distance between me and everyone standing here at this moment. Did I think this would happen? No. I didn't. I made the mistake of assuming that it would only ever be Halen who would be partaking in the ritual. I did the unthinkable so that she didn't have to.

All along, it didn't matter.

Shoving the front door open, I don't stop when Katsia halts halfway down the round staircase, her satin robe split enough to see a slither of her sun-bronzed skin.

A glass of brandy dangles between her fingers. "Lover boy, what's wrong?" Her crimson hair flows down the angle of her back.

I stop. "Did you know about the girls? That they've been training for almost as long as we have?"

She lifts the glass to her lips, her lovat-tinted eyes on mine. She doesn't have to answer because I already know what it is.

I ignore her, heading for the hallway that leads to the open space where we have our conversations while we're here.

"War! I was only doing what I was—" I kick the door closed once I'm inside and suck in a breath. I find what I want on top of the square coffee table nestled between two wingback leather sofas. I slump down into the cushions and reach for the platinum box that's on the table, flicking away the eight-ball of coke and nabbing the rolled blunt. My skin dampens from all the adrenaline pulsing through my system. Anger. Rage that I need to work off.

I grip the bottom of my shirt and shove it over my head, tossing it onto the floor.

I place the joint between my lips, blaze the end, and drag my fingers through my hair. I lean back against my chair and gaze up to the ceiling as I shove my jeans down enough to reveal the band of my briefs.

Fuck.

I should have fucked Halen instead of giving her all that fucking pleasure. Now I want to take it back and make the bitch weep.

I hold in the smoke and let the toffee-laced weed fill my lungs.

When the door opens again, I breathe out a cloud of smoke, letting it float up to the gold-plated ceiling. My muscles relax, but the rage still burns the back of my mind. It'll stay there. Until I make her hurt.

It's a shit place for her to be when I'm feeling this way.

As soon as she walks through the door, I feel her. Her emerald eyes sweep over my body before settling on my face. I give her nothing.

If I can't give her anger, I'll give her *nothing*.

Everyone files in around her and when the door closes, I've smoked enough herb to not see red.

Priest saunters to the computer desk and leans against the edge. His finger taps against the structure and I count how many times it connects with the wood. *One. Two. Three. Four—five.* He's bored, combating the hunger to sink his fingers into fresh meat.

"Start talking."

"Well…" Stella trudges her thigh-high boots to the sofa beside mine. She folds her leg over the other and spreads her arms over the edge of the couch. "Like Halen said. We have been training for the better part of ten years for this. We, just like you all—" She points her black coffin-shaped nail to all of us. "—made ourselves busy with little hobbies on the side."

"Where did you train?" Vaden isn't pissed because the way he sees it, and the way he's always seen it, is if she's close to us, she's safe. He wants his little vampire sister in the fold. This is a win for him and their Addams family.

I wonder just how much they have in common…

"Everywhere. Mainly in the art of manipulation—" She holds her brother's stare. "—false complacency, strategizing, that sort of thing." Her mouth splinters wide, flaunting her bleached teeth. Stella is a fucking kick in the nuts to people around the world, because the girl is famed for her beauty. But she's a little witch, and I don't mean her appearance.

I lean forward, resting my forearms on my thighs. "I wonder…" I tilt my head and seconds pass before Priest clucks from behind me. He no doubt knows what I'm about to ask. "Just how alike are you to your brother…" My tongue swoops over my teeth. "Wanna help me find out?"

If Halen thinks because my mom and Stella's mom found out that they have the same mom would stop me from being a piece of shit, she's wrong. Do I want Halen? More than I've wanted anything in my life, but do I love pain? More than anything in my life…

Stella's leg stops jiggling and she shifts her body toward mine. "Are you into incest now?"

My lip twitches. "I'm betting you're fucking worth it."

"Back the fuck up. Play your games with anyone else…" Vaden rolls his eyes.

Priest passes the sofa that's opposite her, reaching into the drug box and pulling out the bag of white powder. He tosses it onto the table. "He's just keeping it in the family."

And there it is.

I chuckle, resting my hand on my abs and the joint back between my lips. "Fine." My eyes move to River. It all makes sense. Why we were told that one day, we would have to switch off our emotions to allow logic in.

It was for this. Because this was the plan all along.

The Elite Kings are no longer three. There are six of us, and fuck me.

Consider my shit switched.

I blow out a smoke ring. "Well, you've all come at the best time."

Priest's eyes turn heavy. "Truly…"

Chapter Fifteen

HALEN

THE TRIP INTO THE FOREST IS QUICK. FADED STREET signs from the old suburb that used to exist here are wilted, some with vines overgrowing as nature claws itself back from death.

I didn't know much about Perdita when our parents were young, but the stories Mom told me were nothing like this. I'm guessing Katsia is nothing like her mentor expected her to be. It's obvious that she's operating it as she wants.

A single door stands beneath an ivory tree with branches that encase the metal. It looks like a portal to some fantasy land.

If only.

River clears her throat. "Is that not weird?"

I tuck my hair behind my ear as the boys' heads turn toward it. They stop for whatever reason.

"We've seen worse," I say through a tight throat. River stills beside me. It's the first time since we were there that I have mentioned it.

"Do you think it has changed?" River asks. She's not a princess by any means, but she does require more softness at times.

Stella's arm brushes mine. "Evie is wondering where you are, by the way…" We're good at this. Ignoring red flags, even the ones that signify a memory.

"I figured. I haven't texted her back."

"Why not?" Stella turns to me. She's not wasting time with jumping into the family business. She needs to model instead. "Evie aside, we also need to keep our own hobbies too…"

"I know!" I widen my eyes at her as River snorts on her laugh beside me. "Let's just… see what the fuck the boys have been doing."

"Blood, sex, pain, I bet."

We all stop when Priest stares back at us after opening the door. "Well, come on then…"

I take the first step, my Valentino boot crunching against the gravel. As soon as we're inside, someone closes the door behind us, and it's lights out.

"Okay, well, I guess we don't need our face skulled if we can't fucking see," River teases from somewhere in the dark.

I take a step back while trying not to lose my balance and by using my other senses, when I collide into a wall of muscle. He doesn't move, and I know it isn't my brother or Vaden. Both of whom would waste no time in moving because, unlike War, they're not into flirting with incest.

My heart jumps in my throat.

"You won't need them going forward," Priest says from somewhere in the dark.

My legs begin to quiver. I don't want War to be this close to me.

His hand settles on my hip and my breath catches. Blanketed by darkness, there's a part of me that wonders if anyone can see. His fingers pinch my skin, forcing me against the bulge of his cock. My breath hitches as I rest against him.

"You won't be needing your face painted anymore," Vaden adds from deep in the abyss.

My pulse drums against my skin when I feel the sting of War's teeth glide over the nape of my neck. What the fuck is he doing? At any moment, a light could turn on and we'd get caught.

He pushes past the band of my short skirt, his fingers grazing the lace of my underwear before they dip beneath. I gasp as my clit blisters for his touch.

His other hand settles on the front of my belly before he applies pressure, my ass rubbing against him, and *oh my God*. I need it. My body burns from the fire pooling in my lower belly.

He slides his index finger through my slit, thrusting against my clit before using the soft tip of his finger to circle my entrance. My muscles seize when he's inside of me.

"War, explain why we're not getting skulled?" Vaden's tone is low. If he didn't sound like he was on the other side of us, I'd think he could see what the fuck War is doing.

"Hmmm?" War breathes against my neck and the vibration of his voice sends shivers down my spine. *I need to fuck this man right now.* Get him out of my system. Do it for the little girl with a crush…

He clears his throat as if his finger isn't orbiting inside of me. "You all have your own diamond masks." His tone doesn't shift, and it bothers me that he's unaffected. My knees turn to jelly but he catches me by a thrust of his hips. "If you haven't noticed, they're replicated by your family skull, only now exposing parts of your face. Thousands of diamonds have been welded together by thin webs of molted metal—in the girls' case, it's gold. They're called Calvarias."

My hand dips beneath the waist of his jeans and my teeth catch my bottom lip when the weight of him rests in my palm. Beneath his smooth skin, I feel the violence of his veins brush the pads of my fingers.

His fingers curl and the bottom of his palm crushes my clit in warning.

He continues. "And they're down the hall. We don't have light until we get into that room."

"Walk straight," Priest instructs, and War spins me back around with his grip on my pussy, as if I have no center of gravity, before withdrawing his hand.

As soon as I'm far enough away, it bothers me that I can feel the distance.

I also hate that he's going to live rent-free inside my head until I can fuck him out of my system.

Goddammit.

There's silence except for heavy footsteps as we head down the corridor. Someone opens the door at the end, and a vermilion hue illuminates through the crack. I follow both Priest and Vaden through until we're all inside a small room with clear walls. On the other side of the glass is a bar. That same color light flickering from inside.

"Here." Priest points to a glass table in the middle of the room. Not even demure lighting could melt the ice coming off that table. It's flaunting a radiance so bright that it burns my retinas.

I catch his eyes when he slides one over to me. "Aw, brother… don't tell me you already knew we'd be here."

"I did." His pupils dilate, and I know he's gone again. "And you would need these eventually anyway."

I bounce over all the masks that are on display in front of me.

"What did I say, Halo?" War interrupts my admiring from the other side of the room. "What if the game is you?"

I watch as he slowly lifts his mask to his face. Flourishing in an abundance of black diamonds that shade all the areas his skull would, they leave a brilliant shadow over his cheekbones and eyes, lining the cracks of his original art in strings of diamonds. Where the white paint would otherwise be used, colorless diamonds fill. With only three quarters of his face covered, it leaves the soft curve of his lips exposed. His shirt does nothing to hide the tight cords of muscle, and I find myself enraptured by his fingers when his arms fall to his sides after securing his diamond mask.

A morbid shadow spreads over his face as the room tilts, and my breathing becomes tremulous as if it's just him and I in the room together and no one else.

His pupils dilate when they rest on me, and that mask is not helping…

Why the fuck did the Fathers sign off on these? I guess getting your face painted was time-consuming.

"Halen!" Priest clicks his fingers in front of my face. I hadn't realized I was the only one left not wearing her Calvaria.

I stare down at it and my throat dries. My finger glides over the abundance of white diamonds that would cover my forehead, cutting above the sharp boarders of my cheekbones and covering my upper lip. Where the shading of my eyes and nose usually is, the same black diamonds catch the lighting.

I blink up at Priest and reach out to touch his. Covering the same areas of his face as mine, there's not a speck of light, with the radiance of midnight diamonds. Where they glisten over his upper lip, six sharp icicles elongate downward as teeth. Over his right eye are three bars that are made up of finer black diamonds, imitating a cage, and other slate-gray colors add dimension to the harsher lines around the mask. It's different... yet perfect for him.

I look back down at mine. "Why so many diamonds? How much did they cost?"

Priest shrugs his shoulders. "Mom said at least a mill, which means it was three."

I stifle a laugh. "Ain't that the truth." Before I can fasten it, hands cloak mine and my skin prickles.

Priest bares his teeth at him and for a moment, everyone stops.

This is bad. If Priest knows about us, it could ignite a family feud.

War ignores everyone and lifts it to my face. In a second, I'm looking through peepholes while he tugs on the ties at the back of my head.

"Chill..." War dismisses. "It's not that deep."

Priest holds his stare for a moment and I'm silently praying that nothing comes of this. The only time I'd get to my knees, is to pray that these boys don't rip each other's hearts out.

"We can do this later!" Stella snaps her fingers between us, and around all the drama, River has managed to twist her blonde hair in two pigtail buns.

River's Calvaria is similar to War's, only where his has white diamonds, hers has a scattering of pink rarity.

"Word!" Vaden pipes in, and I take the moment to admire both his and Stella's. Vaden's is the only full face Calvaria. Black and gray diamonds forge together and cover every inch of exposed skin, only leaving his eyes. If that wasn't enough, two points of Devil horns climb up each side of his head in a trail of black diamonds. Stella's is a similar style, instead her horns are hellfire rubies. The black diamonds that panel the design of the skull is on a sideways angle, leaving a quarter of her face uncovered.

"So, this game…" I step away from War. He's clearly on some shit if he's being callous with his dominance.

Vaden pulls the last door open, leaning his back against it. He stretches his arm out to the room.

I step through to see eight people with their hands bound and tied, naked and blindfolded, kneeling to the ground.

I turn over my shoulder to find Priest and grab his hand. I direct him around the corner until we're away from everyone else.

"What is going on?"

The mask doesn't cover his mouth or jaw, so when his lip curls up a half grin, I know I'm going to wish I never asked.

Jesus fuck.

"They're pledges, Halen."

I lean around the corner. Their skin is bare of any marks. I take this time to notice the rest of the space, since I was too focused on them when we walked in.

Stella leans toward a girl with long blonde hair and twirls it between her fingers as if playing with a toy.

"What's the matter, Hales?" His head tilts to the side. "No longer wanna play?"

"Pledges from where, Priest? We don't *do* pledges. We do family. Family lineage and *that's all*. So where did you get them?"

Priest's specialty is making people feel inferior. He'll antagonize you with his glacial disposition until you second-guess everything that comes out of your mouth. "That man who cut you? These eight are who we caught when he tried to get away."

I grimace. "There were nine, with him?"

His face is stone. "There were twelve. We gave them an option. They could come here and be a traitor, or they could die."

The Elite Kings Club has never opened their doors to outsiders. Not ever. "Priest, they can't be here. They can't just join Perdita or link up with one of the ten Founding Families. That's not how this works!"

The muscles on each side of his jaw twitch, and realization hits me when his eyes glimmer for the hunger of debasement. "*We know.*"

I stand there a moment as he brushes past me. So they kill who doesn't want to come with them, and then bring the others to Perdita to torment before eventually killing them anyway? Or before what? Sending them somewhere?

I shuffle back to the line of eight *pledges,* as the red light that tracks around the bar radiates from behind them. Bottles of alcohol are splayed out in the glass cabinet behind the tender, who is an obvious Lost Boy. His gold mask covering the side of his face proof of that.

I can think up all the reasons why the boys do what they do, but I'd never understand. They like to torment people, humiliate. They get off on it—but they also bring them here to Perdita? The island that is sacred to our ancestors. Fuck me. If Dad knew…

I make my way to the bar, desperate to dull the throbbing in my head. Music strums in the background as Tupac raps about thug love.

As soon as I've slumped onto the barstool, the Lost Boy's eyes settle on mine. They're a warm mix of hazel and green. His jaw is cleanly shaven, but the hair on his head is slicked back. He's attractive. All the Lost Boys are. They always have been.

A Stuprum, who is what Katsia is, are who keep the feminine balance of our world. I don't know if that's why she is here, but it's who has always operated Perdita. For generations, a Stuprum woman has controlled the island, and how they do that is by breeding, raising, and grooming the Lost Boys. They may not present themselves as soldiers, but the morbidity of their violence is held inside their minds. You don't want to *ever* be on the receiving end of their wrath.

The civilians of Perdita are a little different. They're the retirees of Founding Families, secrets of the Fathers and their affairs, or families and people who take refuge here for various reasons. Some can be because they don't want to conform to the way of the world, and for others it's because they're on the run from someone or something. Whoever resides in Perdita must abide by their one rule.

You don't hurt your own.

There are no jail cells here and you don't get second chances. You abide or die. For a lot of people, that's easier than living amongst society. There are no taxes, no currencies, no questions asked when you see shit go down on the streets. You will be taken care of here—until you harm one of our own.

The Lost Boy doesn't say a word as he pours a shot of Don Julio into a glass.

I swirl the russet liquid, before allowing it to slide down my throat like silk.

"You don't want to play with the rest of them?" he asks with detachment. I'd never been *with* a Lost Boy, but I'd heard whispers about what they do.

"Maybe later." I lean back in my chair as he refills my glass. His pillowy lips curve up a little when he slides my drink over to me. My fingers flex around the glass but when they touch his, I gasp and my eyes fly to his. Maybe I'm acting out because of War's little back and forth with Stella, or maybe I'm agitated because of War's little game in the dark.

I spin my barstool around to see what they're all doing, when I find everyone already watching me. Except Stella, who's examining the pledges.

River's head shakes from side to side with an eye roll. I know what she's thinking. *Great. How fucking long is this going to take?*

"What?" I ask broadly, swinging myself off the stool while swiping the bottle of Don Julio from the Lost Boy. "I'll play. Just—" I drag out the S while turning to Stella, who lowers me back down beside her.

I bring the bottle to her lips while peering up at the three of them from the corner of my eye, purposely ignoring War. "Give us a second."

"What are you playing at, Halen?" War asks from behind Priest and Vaden.

This time I let myself find him and my stomach coils like hot wire.

His tongue sweeps his bottom lip.

Stella clears her throat, breaking the tension between us. "Are you going to pet a Lost Boy?" I throw a wall up inside my mind before her words can penetrate. "Halen… fire. You're playing with fire."

I need to move. To get up and *move*.

Pushing back up to my feet, I ignore Stella's warnings. "I can do what I want."

When I turn to my brother, his eyes are hard on mine. I'd never seen him look at me this way and I know where it's come from. For so long, he thought I had to be protected because that was what he thought I needed.

Until now.

Now he's questioning if I'm as insane as he is.

I raise a single brow at him, patting his shoulder. "Not quite, but enough to be a Hayes."

His thumb skims his bottom lip to hide his pride. "Well, shit." He buries his face into the side of my head and tugs me under his arm. "Then let's fucking go."

I turn back to look at the eight people kneeling in front of us, while taking yet another swig of the tequila. "Stand."

They obey, unfolding to their full height.

My eyes bounce over them as I amble down the line. I stop in front of one of the girls. She's pretty. Resting my finger against her cheek, I notice their hands are no longer tied to their backs. "Remove your blindfold."

She trembles as her fingers flex over the mask. She peels it back, squinting before her arms fall to either side.

"Pretty." I smile, angling my head. "Such a shame."

Her blue eyes rest on mine, her mascara having long since left a trail of ink down her cheek.

Vaden comes close enough for his hand to wrap around her chin, forcing her face in his direction. When her eyes brighten, he shoves her away.

"Your first task…" War steps closer to her while placing a cigarette between his lips. He pulls a Zippo out of his pocket and blazes the tip, inhaling tightly. He doesn't shut the Zippo and I watch when the flame draws closer to the blonde. Her pert nipples harden as her chest rises and falls, her desperation reeking over the nicotine.

My jaw clenches. Shit. *I can't show a single weakness.*

War continues, "Everyone, remove your blindfolds."

They drop the silk covering their faces. I don't care enough to examine them closer. They're merely pawns in a game where there is no ending.

"Game one." War puffs on his cigarette, turning over his shoulder and squinting around the smoke before facing the blonde. "Fuck for three hours. Show me something I haven't seen."

My eyes roll to the back of my head as I raise the bottle back to my mouth and turn to face Stella. She's entranced with what the boys are doing, so I grab at River's hand and direct her to a booth that's nestled far enough away from everyone to be able to talk.

The entrance door opens and people start filing in. It's probably a good thing that this place is in the middle of the forest and camouflaged by rocks.

River taps the joint she's rolled against the table, moving blonde hair over her shoulder as her mocha eyes rest on mine. "Why don't we just kill them?" She lifts the trunk to her lips and lights the end. Blowing out a cloud, she leans back in her chair. "I mean, why do they have to enjoy the chase?"

"Because they're Kings," I answer, plucking the joint from her fingers and squinting around the smoke. "And because we're all a little fucked up."

I inhale, just as a camera flash snaps and we both stare up at Stella who has her phone in her hand. I pass the J and pointedly ignore whatever War and the boys are doing.

"Question." Stella leans against the chair. She flashes me a reckless smirk as she passes it back to River without looking at her. "Do you think they'll let me choose the second game? I mean, clearly War is starting soft." She turns to the four-person orgy in the center of the room. The music has changed to Bone Thugs and my muscles finally ease.

I feel my mind drift away, my eyes heavy but mood lifted.

"They will." River coughs on the last smoke before squashing it out in the metal tray between us. "You get what you want. I, on the other hand, have War as a brother."

A bubble of laughter leaves me as my head tilts back to the ceiling. I can't help it. It flew out before I could stop. I bring my face back down to River, to find her staring at me with slanted eyes.

"I don't know why you're laughing! He's as bad with you as he is with me."

"Maybe," I tease, holding her in place. "But at least I can fuck his frustrations out of him if he annoys me too much."

Her mouth slams closed. It could go one of two ways. It's the first time I've ever said something like this out loud.

She relaxes in her chair again. "Honestly, just hurry up already."

We all fall silent.

I need a mood shift.

Pushing up from my chair, I shuffle out of my leather jacket. As soon as I'm standing in front of the bar, back where the Lost Boy is, I place the bottle on top and watch as he serves the civilians down the way. It's not too busy, but there are a dozen or so people in here. Some nestled away in corners, drinking and enjoying the show. Others unbothered, sitting near the bar. In any other place, what's happening would make people run in the opposite direction, but to the people of Perdita, this is tame.

They're immune to it.

"I'm bored."

The Lost Boy pauses as he reaches up to the top shelf to grab a bottle of whatever it is.

"Care to entertain me?"

His eyes glaze over. "I don't know." He leans in close, his palms on the bar. "Are you as crazy as your uncle?"

Chapter Sixteen

WAR

MY HALF-FULL GLASS HANGS JUST BELOW MY MOUTH. I keep my eyes peeled on her, watching every movement. The Lost Boys have been here since the beginning of the Elite Kings Club. From when it was formed all those years ago when the ten Fathers founded Riverside. Perdita is off the coast of Riverside. Technically, you could sail over here in a big fuck off ship. I've considered it. Just to mix it up a bit, but we don't like to. Everyone here needs to *stay here*. Just like the fucking Lost Boys. They're detached from civilization. They would be wild wolves set free on a full moon if they ever made their way to US soil. Perdita is an island that's right on the edge of international waters.

We can *do* whatever the fuck we like.

"You think she'll take it that far?" Vaden nudges his head to where Halen is sliding up onto the bar, her legs dangling over the edge. All he has to do is part them.

Then he'll die, but that's all he'd have to do.

"What's funny is how clouded you all are." Stella turns her focus around the group. "How very sheltered you *think* we have been all these years." She leans forward, plucking a fresh cherry from the fruit platter that's between the coke and weed.

Her lips wrap around it as she tilts her head at me.

"We're related, War. Stop looking at me like you want to eat me."

The corner of my mouth twitches. "Barely. Tillie and Saint didn't even know each other."

She throws the stem at me and I laugh, winking at Vaden.

His foot connects with my shin. "Gonna stop trying to sleep with EKC girls or what?"

I shrug into my drink. "Or what."

Priest's knee starts jiggling and I catch his eye. The music had long since moved to a slow Lithe song and I know that as every second passes, it's only edging Priest more, and the more he waits, the more messy it's going to be.

The group is still rubbing against one another, and I watch two girls in the corner. Her face is between the other's ass cheeks and her tongue slides down the crack. The other girl has two boys on their knees, her fingers buried in their hair.

"It was nice of you to start with something light," Vaden adds. "You know, for the girls."

Stella laughs again. "Hmmm… let me see." She swings her legs over her chair and skips toward the sexfest like a little maniac of destruction.

"You guys do know that we all had a life outside of you, right? And that we, too, had our own games we liked to play."

That catches my attention and I glare down to my sister. "What's that supposed to mean?"

River stands to her full height, her blonde hair braided into some weird twist shit that goes over her shoulder. "It means, my dear big brother." She places her hand on my shoulder. I'm a whole foot taller than River. We don't know how the fuck that happened. "That we've all been fucked more times than you could know." She spins around and follows Stella to the live show in the middle of the room. The ambience of the lighting weakens further, and I flop down onto my chair again, snarling at my sister.

"Let up, War…" Vaden kicks me again, and I hold his stare.

He looks so much like Brantley. It's like staring back at a doppelgänger, only the eyes are different.

The muscles on each side of his jaw jump when he raises his brows in challenge. "The more they know they get a rise out of you, the more they'll annoy you."

My tongue slides over my top teeth as Linkin Park starts playing through the speakers. "Hmmm. Then let's just see how far they'll go."

Priest glares at me. "For tonight only. Then, we do it all *with* them, War. They're part of this whether you fight it or not." I hate when he's right.

Pushing up from my chair, I keep my eyes on Halen as she wraps her legs around the Lost Boy, leaning into the side of his neck. She laughs into him and when her tongue touches his skin, I'm already across the room, my hand on the back of her neck and the other around his. I throw Halen into the large wingback chair nestled to the side, while keeping my eyes on the Lost Boy.

Lifting him from the floor, I tilt my head and tighten the grip around his neck until I feel the tiny bones in his throat splinter beneath my palm.

I flash a wide smirk. "Well, shit. I guess since we're already halfway there…"

"War!" Halen's voice breaks through my rage and I hate her for it. I hate everything about her and how much control she has over me. Something I'll *never* admit to her. Admitting your weakness to a woman like Halen only allows her to weaponize it.

My fingers sink deep into his skin, and I know that all I'd have to do… is apply a little more pressure…

Blood trickles down the crease of my hands.

"War!" Halen snaps.

I shove him back and he crashes against the glass shelves.

"Tsk, tsk…" Priest shakes his finger at the Lost Boy, as Vaden leans against the counter, shoving his hands in his pockets and disregarding him. "You should know better than to fuck with a King, Lost Boy."

He bows his head, blood dripping from the marks around his throat.

Priest turns to me after glancing sideways with a shake of his head. "They're harmless, and they're *ours*." He moves closer. "Pull your shit together."

He turns back to the orgy that's happening in the middle of the room, leaning against a table and keeping his eyes on the girls.

I swipe a bottle off the counter while glaring at Halen, who's staring up at me like I've kicked her fucking puppy.

Technically did.

The Weeknd's "Often" starts playing and I let the alcohol sit in my mouth before gulping another load. Halen fucking Hayes. Forever the trigger to every emotion I've kept condensed all these years.

Even more so recently.

My Zippo stays between my fingers, and I flip it open and closed a few times, bringing the bottle to my lips while observing the show, still not witnessing anything I'd never seen.

I spark the flame, watching a girl who's currently face to pussy with another.

Rolling my tongue, I blow out a whistle, and her back straightens like an obedient dog.

"What are you doing…" Priest leans forward, flashing his teeth.

"I'm bored."

The girl turns to face me, her long blonde hair falling down her back. Her tits jiggle as she pads toward me with a hollow stare. I flick the Zippo again and when she's directly in front of me, I hold her eyes with mine.

"Do you like pain?"

Her thin lips part. "I like whatever you like."

My tongue dampens my bottom lip as my other hand meddles with my belt.

"Damn. With your sister here." Priest pretends to be shocked, but his tone is flat.

"She can look away."

Halen's leg is folded over the other as she leans on the wingback chair, her hair curling around her face. A bottle of tequila dangles between her fingers as her eyes lower down to my belt.

The cords in my neck turn rigid as I allow the girl to fall to her knees in front of me.

I whack her hand away, glowering down at her with bared teeth, and catch her by her chin. "Don't fucking touch me anywhere except with this mouth on my dick."

She blinks up at me with unshed tears and I shove her backward onto her ass before she's back to fumbling with my zipper.

I take the rolled joint from behind my ear and bite it into my mouth.

Priest taps against the table I'm leaning on. He'll be watching Halen to see how she reacts.

Brittle fingers reach for my cock, but I whack them away just before warmth blankets me.

Lighting the joint, I inhale and slant my head to the side, holding a few seconds before blowing smoke rings out and handing it to Priest.

I don't touch the girl. Her hand stays at the base as saliva dribbles down her mouth.

I bury my hand in her disarray of hair and force myself down her throat until she sputters and closes around my shaft.

Wrapping her hair around my fist, I buck my hips forward until my cock slides down the tunnel of her throat.

I keep it there.

Her eyes widen in horror as tears roll down the side of her face and her hands fly to my arms, her fingernails plunging into my skin. Her cheeks turn a ravishing shade of purple as her body palpitates from the lack of oxygen.

As much as I don't want to, my eyes find Halen's. I thought she for sure would have looked away. Maybe been rubbing up against another Lost Boy out of spite, but she isn't. She's sitting in the same position I threw her into, only this time with the bottle slightly emptier than it was before.

She challenges me with an arched brow.

I mouth the words silently. "Let's play a game."

Her eyes come back up to mine after reading my lips.

It's not obvious, but she captures me with a simple shift forward. Nothing Halen ever does is obvious. She's resistive and unattainable. She has everyone yearning for her attention, only to feed them crumbs. I'm beginning to see the other side to her the more she's around. I allowed myself to shut off from her a lot growing up because we lived in separate areas of each other's lives.

It's easy to convince yourself not to obsess over someone who isn't there.

I want nothing more than to finish all over this girl's face to punish Halen since I can't fuck hers.

Even if this girl becomes a corpse.

I shove her off my dick and she stumbles back, struggling and gasping for air.

I'm no Priest Hayes.

Gripping my cock in my hand, the veins in my arm ripple as I roll my thumb beneath the head. Swiping at the bead of cum, I dampen the edge around the crown as I find Halen's eyes again.

The smirk is gone.

She lifts the bottle to her lips, breaking eye contact.

I won.

I shove my dick back in my jeans, leaving them unbuttoned to hang from my hips.

"You know, as much as I want to punch your fucking face right now," Priest declares, stepping over the naked girl who's still trying to catch her breath, "I'm pretty sure she'll do it for me one day."

A pensive observation passes between us that I'm sure no one else noticed. It's almost an admission that he's known all along.

He probably has.

I snicker around the joint. "Don't I know it."

"War." His tone turns hard.

I slowly turn to face him, his passive eyes on mine. Not as vivid as Halen's, more of a forest green in moonlight. Almost black. I don't know if that was nature's way of reminding everyone why there's not a smidge of morality to Priest Hayes. You can't call him the Devil, because he's worse.

The Devil is patient, Priest Hayes is barbaric. "This is bigger than my opinion. She can do what the fuck she wants, she's a King now. But this is bigger than that and you know it."

I flick the spliff out onto the ground, using my boot to put it out. "I know. I've been knowing." I turn my back to him. "It's just us fucking around. It'll be nothing more than that. Once we hit, I'm sure we'll both move on. Just been this fucked-up fantasy since she rubbed her shit over my dick all those years ago."

"She what—" Priest levels.

I smirk over my shoulder. "What?"

"Fucker…" He shakes his head, turning back to watch the on-going boring fuckfest. "You were gonna hurt her."

My blood turns hot, rushing to my cheeks. My stare on him darkens. "Which one?"

Priest pushes off the table and heads to the group. He kicks the guy that's fucking one of the girls doggy style, and the fuckwit stumbles to the ground while holding his dick. "I don't think any of you showed us anything we've never seen before."

The music isn't loud, but just enough that you can chat without worrying anyone can hear you. People have thinned out as time has gone on, leaving those who make a habit of drinking themselves into a coma before going home. They're all too busy drinking to pay attention to us, and besides, everyone knows to keep their distance.

"Game two." He rounds the group as River finally turns her chair back around to face us, flipping me off.

I use the bottle of whiskey to hide my laugh, allowing the liquid to sit over my tongue. I need something to take the edge off. I know what Halen feels like now, and fuck if I don't want to bury myself inside of her and fuck her until her body gives out.

Kind of want to rip her skull in half just to see what she really thinks of me.

The wall to the side of the bar splits in half as the sound of heavy metal screeches when it opens.

Priest gestures to the rectangular metal space. "Enter."

They scramble into the box, desperate for rest.

We follow not long after, and I can feel Halen's slow steps echoing from behind. As much as I want to address the fucking elephant in the room, I can't have a distraction. That's what she is—a fucking distraction.

Once we're all inside, the doors slowly close and silence settles around us.

Stella clears her throat. Always the first one. "What's the second game?"

I circle my finger and gesture to the other wall when it parts, opening out into darkness. Twigs snap beneath my boots when I step forward, following the radiance of the full moon that beacons through the forest.

Flames from a nearby bonfire caresses my skin, where Katsia waits by a stray tree trunk with a Lost Boy on each side. Her long dress splits on either side, the material tight around her waist before relaxing around her feet.

"You took long enough." She pretends to observe her nails.

I circle the confined blaze as everyone filters around behind me.

Katsia's heavy-lined eyes roam my body, stopping at my unbuckled jeans. She's always been a woman of habit. Too bad not even she would be able to satiate the hunger tonight.

"Game two," Priest addresses everyone in a flat tone. The wind swoops around us as the embers from the fire glitter the air. "It's simple, really." He lowers himself down onto a log.

Vaden closes in behind them. "Run."

They all jerk forward, their nude bodies disappearing through the condensed trees.

Stella and Halen remove their masks and make their distaste for Katsia obvious by staying as far away from her as possible.

My phone vibrates against my thigh, and I reach inside, seeing Bishop's name flash over the screen.

I force my mask off and answer. "B…"

It's silent for a moment. "Why do I get the feeling that you're all having too much fun tonight?"

I don't bother fighting the grin on my face. "Yeah, we may have got a little carried away."

"Son…" I know that whatever he's about to say isn't gonna be good. "We've got a problem. The girls there?"

I make my way to Priest and Vaden. "Yeah." I side-eye them both. "Why?"

Silence.

"Good. Don't let them out of your sight. I didn't want this shit happening so close to the ritual, but the same people you chased down could be connected to a group that we've been chasing."

I shuffle on my feet. "Bakers? Yeah, they are."

Bishop grunts through the phone. "Kill them."

Priest and Vaden both glower.

"We planned to. Is there a special reason why you want us to?"

The parents haven't had anything to do with this group since they have only just resurfaced.

"I don't know yet. I'll let you know once I do. And tell my son to turn his fucking phone on."

I hang up when the line goes dead.

"Dad?" Halen creeps up from behind us and I almost forgot that she was here.

"Mmhmm…" Priest eyes her suspiciously. It's a habit, keeping shit from the three of them as much as we can. A habit I'm aware we all need to break. "You ready for the ritual?"

Halen doesn't waver. "Yes, Priest. I'm ready, as are Stella and

River." Her mouth snaps closed, as she tilts her head to the side. She studies us for a moment, before leaning forward onto her tippy-toes. "Are you all ready?"

I lower myself down onto the stray tree trunk farther away, but annoyingly closer to Katsia. I can't be bothered with the sibling fight.

She uncrosses her leg, her bare feet coming into view. "Hmmm… can I guess that the little Queens are misbehaving?"

"Shut up, Katsia."

I should have known better than to expect her to listen.

My eyes drift up to Halen when Katsia trails her finger up my outer thigh. No doubt her cherry red lips will be turned upward. "Did your dad ever tell you about his and the last Katsia's history? He had a thing for her too."

I blink lazily, watching as Halen's eyes turn to slits before they fall to where Katsia's hand rests on my inner thigh. I could kick the bitch off. I don't want her rubbing up on me, and furthermore, her doing this doesn't benefit the bigger picture shit, but I keep it there, spreading my leg wide to give her more access.

The vein on the side of Halen's neck flutters, her lips parting slightly. Tension cracks through the air as her knee bounces. *Drop the fucking façade, Halen.* I won't let my mind wander back to what happened thirty minutes ago and how goddamn unaffected she was. I'm betting it got to her. *You're not as fucking slick as you think you are.*

This has nothing to do with how intimidated she is of Katsia either. I know that's a fucking lie. Yeah, Katsia is hot. There's no denying that. She knows how to do what she does, and she does it well, but she's easy prey. Merely something to pass the boredom while you wait for the chase.

Halen isn't hot. She's fucking lethal. The kind of woman to pluck someone like Katsia out and feed them to stray dogs so that she can be owned by the wolf.

"Katsia?" Her name leaves my mouth through a smirk, but I keep my eyes on Halen. "I'm gonna go ahead and do you a solid by—"

She moves her hand up, brushing my cock through my jeans as the tip of her tongue slides over the side of my neck. The damn bitch is calculated, and she's about to equal exactly eighty-six. "I miss your tongue in more ways than—" Halen throws herself at Katsia in a flurry of rage and silver.

"Oh, shit." I jump up from the trunk, my arms spread wide with a laugh. Leaning to the side, I bite down on my lower lip to stop myself from losing my shit as Halen has her straddled by the chest.

She presses the sharp tip of the Hayes family blade against the bottom of her chin, leaning in close until she's hovering above Katsia's face. She's at least smart enough to shut the fuck up now. "I don't like you much."

Katsia's brow arches. "I didn't notice."

Halen must dig the blade in further because Katsia's face pales. "You don't touch him."

My eyes roll and I bite down on the groan that ripples through me, heading straight for my cock. Before I can open my eyes, I feel the point of her knife against the zipper of my jeans.

My smirk turns into a flash of white teeth and dimples when I open onto her, tilting my head down to her height. She's a little fucking thing but, fuck me, she can hold her own.

Check. Fucking. Mate. My girl is pissed.

Good.

She leans in close with a wide smile, patting my chest with one hand while keeping the blade against my cock with the other. "I know what you're doing." Her eyes lower to my lips. "And I'd suggest you not do it again before I do something crazy, like... oh, I don't know..."

My hips buck forward in challenge, pushing against the knife. I bend to catch her jaw with my teeth while holding in a deep chuckle. "Kill me? Cut my dick off? Give me your worst. It's all foreplay to me, Halo."

I reach for the back of her neck but she dips out from beneath me, holding my eyes. "Who do you think you're playing with?" She lifts her chin in challenge but those fuckable lips twitch. "I wouldn't give you my worst, War. I'd make you watch while I gave it to some-one else."

My face falls and my blood turns cold. Well, shit.

"Yeah?" I call out to her as she steps backward, her eyes dark-ening like the fucking Devil she is. I mouth the next words to her so that only she can see. "Fucking try it." She turns her back to me and disappears through the shadow of the trees.

"She is ridiculous!" Katsia's arm brushes against mine, and I instinctively move away from her. "Now tell me, Malum…" Her eyes flare as she continues to glare at where Halen disappeared to. "Is it just me, or is she hiding something?"

Chapter Seventeen

HALEN

EVEN BEFORE THEY ALL DISAPPEARED INTO THE FOREST, I felt agitated. I couldn't pinpoint the reason why, but I'm sure it had something to do with the fact that everything felt… off. Maybe I should have just got lost myself in there instead of coming back.

I don't know much about what they do here, or in Riverside and the game they play in the guise of Devil's Cockpit, or even how the Fathers have spent their time training them. All we know is what we've been training to do. Mom once told me that she hated it when she was young. The constant secrets and never knowing what was happening. Tonight was the first time that I felt like I knew how she felt.

Things changed a lot. They changed *drastically*.

I'm flicking through my Instagram when Evie's selfie pops up on my phone. The photo taken after one of our weekend antics. One I desperately need to repeat. Evie has her whiskey-colored hair pulled up in a high pony, the natural swell of her lips the kind girls throw money to have.

My constant woman. The lucidity in my delirious life and family.

I swipe it to answer.

"Hellion…"

At the sound of her voice and the nickname she hardly uses unless she's pissed at me, my muscles relax, and I forget where I am for a moment.

"I have been trying to get ahold of you!"

I can imagine her standing with a hand on her hourglass hip, a plucked brow raised and the deep vertical frown lines between her eyes.

"I know, I'm sorry!" I stand from the log I'm sitting on. I need to get away from Katsia anyway, before I end up in another cat-fight. "I'm in—"

"Don't tell me." She sighs. After explaining to Evie more in depth about my family, I ended up giving her the option to know everything, or nothing. She chose everything. Which is ironic since she never wants to know what we're doing while we're doing it. "When are you coming home?"

I turn back to where I was just sitting to find River lying on her back, gazing up at the stars. Her ash blonde hair is sprawled out over the grass. "Uh…" I move to Stella, where she's eye fucking one of the Lost Boys. The hairs on the back of my neck rise when I find Katsia's eyes pinned on me.

"Tomorrow. We will be back tomorrow. Hey… I was going to ask about this weekend."

"I'll be there, Hales. I promised you I'd be there for your family's thing because it's important to you. I'll be drunk enough to not think about all the ghosts, but…"

I stifle my laugh. "I miss you. See you tomorrow."

"Love you."

After hanging up with her, I continue scrolling over my texts and stop at a number. My heart slows in my chest as I fight the urge to spin around and check over my shoulder out of fear that someone is watching what I'm doing.

I open a new text and add the number he's saved under.

You asked me what it felt like.

I wait a moment after hitting send, my thumb hovering over the screen. Goosebumps prick my skin as more seconds pass. When my phone vibrates in my hand, my stomach tenses but I open his new text.

And?

Shit. Before I can stop myself, I hit send.

Betrayal. It feels like betrayal.

I delete the message thread before anyone sees it and shove my phone back into my pocket, finding my way back beside Stella. I don't even want to ask Katsia how long the boys are usually out hunting for, because I hate that she knows something I don't. She knows a lot that I don't, because of her connection.

Had War slept with her?

Of course, he had.

I sweep up the half-empty bottle of bourbon that's tilted on the grass, blowing out a heavy breath as I fall back onto the make-shift chair.

I lift the bottle to my lips and let the poison sit on the tip of my tongue. "I thought we could at least play with them."

My phone vibrates at the same time as Stella's and River's.

We all pause, before I lower the bottle back to the ground.

War Malum started a new group chat.

I hate the way my body leaps to life. War and I have never really texted, unless it had something important to do with Priest, or some random shit like Christmas or vacation, and he couldn't get ahold of Priest. It never occurred to me that we didn't have much of a relationship outside of the Kings, and I don't know if that bothered or worried me.

War: Riddle me this…

There's a pause after the dots and Stella and River both push up to a sitting position.

"I thought they only played this game to figure out if someone's an enemy."

"They do," I answer through clenched teeth. The chat bubble lights up and I hold my breath.

War: What's both dead and alive, but has veins that rot?

"Hales," River breathes.

"I know." I sigh, blinking down at my screen. "They don't trust us."

"That's bullshit," Stella hisses under her breath.

"We knew they would do this. Especially off the bat."

"What do we do?" River flexes her fingers around her phone. The fire crackles and embers fly into the dark sky.

"We do what we're supposed to do."

My fingers fly over the keypad.

Halen: Trees. Next riddle...

"Damn, you're good." Stella grins, and then it disappears. "I'm still annoyed with them."

"Me too." River closes the group chat and shoves her phone into her pocket. "They know us better than anyone. Better than our parents. We're a fucking family, and they pull this?"

I swoop up the bottle, my mouth burning before I swallow the long gulp. I hiss through the trail of flames left behind as it travels to my gut.

"They have to," I whisper, careful not to let the witch on the other side of the fire hear us. For whatever reason, she's here. Fucking why? "Yes, they're our family and they would die and kill for each of us, but that doesn't deter from who they are to their core." I lose my thoughts when I bore into the scorching flames. "Elite fucking Kings, and they don't bend, or weaken, for no one. Not even us."

My phone goes off again and a new text comes over the screen.

Vaden: ... my death is laced with the rope that's tied around your mouth.

I tuck my lips behind my teeth.

River flips off my phone. "Fucking hangman."

She's right. I type out the answer.

Halen: Hangman.

Priest: Cheat... River got that one.

My back straightens as I allow my eyes to wander. The trees

are parted enough to allow for easy running, while being flat enough to camp out.

Katsia catches my movement before she starts following my eyes. Before I can answer Priest, my phone vibrates again.

Stella: My turn. Riddle me this…

"Stella…" I hold in my laugh. She's a menace. Put on this earth to push everyone. Once she's tossed your ass well over your limit and you want revenge, you'll find out that she has none. No limit.

Stella: A king is only a King, but a witch can be whatever she wants…

I bump Stella with my arm.
She shrugs. "What? I'm both."

War: Why aren't you running?

Fear brushes the nape of my neck as if he does it himself and I slowly rise to my feet.

"We're really going to do this?" River glares up at me.

"Yeah, why not?" I shrug.

"I can think of one reason," Stella grumbles, but still follows. "Like how about you need to get some sleep?"

I push my phone into my pocket and ignore her jibe once again.

"Going somewhere?" Katsia asks from her spot, both Lost Boys still protecting her on either side. Katsia is around our age, and has the wildness that Stella embraces. Her reputation is one to run from, not to chill with around a fire.

"Yes." My eyes narrow. "Why? Got a problem with that?"

She slowly lifts herself from her seat, her bare feet closing the distance between us. Pretty sure the small flowers growing in the grass wither around her. She's an arm's length away when she stops.

Her cleavage spills out of her dress when she crosses her arms in front of herself. "Do you know about the history between the last Katsia and Malum?"

"Are you asking if I, the daughter of Bishop Vincent Hayes, knows about the history of *my own family?*" She doesn't shrink, but the corner of her eye twitches. Not even the blanket of the night could hide that. I take this moment to draw closer, until my chest brushes hers.

We're hovering around the same height, but because I'm wearing Jordans and she's in bare feet, I'm an inch taller, and I use it to my advantage by staring down my nose at her. "Bitch, you are *nothing* to me." I lean in even further, bringing my mouth to the side of her cheek so only she can hear. "And *less than nothing* to him." I move back, the smirk on my face unmoving.

A hand squeezes my arm as River chokes on her laugh, pulling me back slightly. "Let's go." She studies Katsia, her head tilting to the side as she sweeps her whole body.

When she's back on Katsia's face, River looks her dead in the eyes. "You'd have a better chance of me fucking you than my brother touching you."

"He already has." Katsia's eyes glisten with pride, and it's the first time since really meeting her that I've seen her say, or do, something her age. "Multiple times. Four? Five?" She starts counting with her fingers. "And you can't forget the Prince Albert…"

My mouth snaps shut, and I hate that she knows something so personal about War. Again, ridiculous since he and I haven't had any relationship above flirting, hatred, and more recently, touching. As much as he was my world growing up, he did just that.

Grew up. Grew out of me. I couldn't even get him to fuck me once, and this bitch has fucked him multiple times. What does she have that I don't?

I keep my face straight. "See if he fucks you again, now that he knows what it feels like being inside of me." I meant his finger, but she doesn't need to know that.

River stiffens, but Stella ignores it.

Katsia snorts, but falls back on the stump, her hand coming up to one of the Lost Boys. I find his eyes as they stay locked on me. I never know what to think of the Lost Boys. I'd heard different kinds of stories. There were what we were told, and then there were the stories my mom told. More of which about my uncle Daemon, who was my mom's twin brother. A conversation I don't touch often, especially since it's one of the limited topics that can make my mom cry.

I turn for the clearing I saw the boys bolt through, River and Stella not far behind.

We hadn't even hit it when River speaks first. "Are we going to talk about the fact that you and my brother are fucking?"

"We're not fucking." I brush her off in hopes that she'll drop it.

"But you just—"

"We're messing around, Riv. Don't stress."

She sighs. "I can't say I'm surprised."

Stella's laugh is laced with mania. "I'm just surprised it lasted this long with you guys not going near each other."

"The promise he gave to Priest."

I stop walking, my hands coming out to stop them. "Shh." They both pause. "It's too quiet." There's not a single sound. Not a cricket, not a bird, no rustling, no—nothing. The wind clips my ankles as I try to adjust my eyes to the sable night. Every time I blink, I see the outline of a shadow, but when I adjust again, it's gone. Riverside is what's comfortable. It's familiar. I know what to expect there, but Perdita is free game.

The smell of copper travels through the wind and clings to the back of my throat. It's warm. A pungent scent of iron. "We're close."

"This is game two, right? There's still a third. Do you smell that?" River rasps.

I take another step, heading straight between two thick red-wood trees nestled between shrubs. We must continue for a couple of minutes before we break through.

I stop walking and someone crashes into my back from behind. "What—"

Flames crackle behind eight wooden stakes that stick out of the ground, as the pledges kneel in front of each one.

War sits on a stray tree trunk toward the front, his legs spread wide and his elbows resting on his thighs. He finds me instantly. Movement catches my eye behind him when Priest and Vaden shift.

"What is this?" I ask, gesturing to the scene in front of us. "It's all very original, what with the forest setting." I circle War. "Daddies would be proud."

Silence. Just when I think none of them are going to answer, the corner of War's mouth curves upward.

"What do you think we do here, Halen?" When I don't answer, he looks behind me. "Riv? Stella?"

None of us answer. I think I start holding my breath because as much as I play a big game that us three have been training and that we hold secrets, I know that they're the main characters here. Sure, the Fathers wanted to be more inclusive with us after my mother pulled the plug on the murderous misogyny from our history. But I'll never get it twisted. These three are the beginning and the end.

"I don't know. That's why we're here, War." Even as scenarios filter through my mind, none of them would scratch the surface of what they do.

War holds my stare. "Come."

One of the girls stands to her full height, her head bowed as tears streak down her puffy cheeks. She's slim and has a tiny tattoo on her hip. She turns to face War, displaying her entire back. A clean new cut starts from the nape of her neck, tracing her spine.

I swallow but my saliva almost recoils. This is not new to me. I'm aware of this life and what we do. *Do I? Or is there something I'm missing?*

"Kneel," War commands and she quickly falls to her knees, her hands behind her back. His fingers curl around her chin, tilting her face up to the sky, but his words are for us. "You're all in this world now, not just on the outskirts of it, so here's the first thing you're going to learn."

He stands from his spot, disregarding the girl. "Our enemies try to infiltrate every week. Some more than others. We never know when it's going to happen. We deal with the threat, and then bring whoever is with them back here to do with as we please. It feeds, fuels, and satiates each of us." He grinds his teeth. "After we've killed the ones we do, we fuck up the ones we don't and send them back to where they came from, broken enough that they will have to put them down themselves."

I cross my arms in front of myself. "Seems a little vile."

Vaden holds my stare. "Maybe. But this is how we handle our enemies now."

"Dad knows about this?" I ask, gesturing around the torture garden. "I find it hard to believe that they'd sign off on it since it's so messy."

"They know." Priest shifts around War. "They know because this is how they've *helped* me. Our enemies are our enemies, Halen. This lot?" He jerks his head to the eight. "Are part of a crew called the Bakers. They weren't too happy about us coming back to Riverside."

White noise pierces my ears. I step backward but trip over my foot, landing against Stella.

Her hands are on my cheeks, eyes pinned to mine. "You're okay."

I nod, swallowing and turning back to War.

War jerks his hand over the stake that the girl came from. "Go." She crawls back, cutting her hands on the sharp stones. Her head hangs low enough for her long hair to sprawl over her shoulders. She's beautiful. It's a shame that kind of beauty isn't the kind the world needs more of.

My drink of choice was betrayal.
And I stayed drunk on it for fourteen days…

Silent tears rolled down the contours of my face. I was tired of crying. The room smelled of burnt citrus, and every time I tried to move my legs, they'd ache. He'd left kisses in the form of bruises up and down my inner thigh. The kind that I knew was a brutal form of punishment.

The kind of punishment that digs its claws into your bones and rots like a piece of meat.

The mattress above me creaked as she moved. Her sobs became more frantic as the days passed. I couldn't. I couldn't allow myself to feel or I'd feel too much. I waited for—I didn't know how long. Hours didn't exist here. Locked in a time warp that seems to loop.

Morning, we wake. Night, we sleep. That was all.

I rolled onto my side, tucking my hand beneath my pillow. My body vibrated with unease. I needed to get out. To run. Holding my breath, I pulled back the covers and tiptoed across the floor, leaning down to shake him awake.

"Get up!"

He jolted, spinning around to face me. "Now? Again? We tried. They caught us, Halen. Go to sleep. I don't much feel like getting punished tonight." He dragged his blanket back over his body but I grabbed his shoulder, forcing him onto his back and glaring down at him.

"Get. Up. Now."

His eyes turned to slits from below. "No! My back is still sore from the last time. Fuck. I won't survive it again."

I wanted to tell him that was the point. To not survive. Maybe it was the selfish part of me, not wanting to leave him behind.

"What's going on?" a sleepy voice mused from behind me. "Halen! Again?"

I turned over my shoulder slightly, not enough to see her. "I'll—I don't know!"

He breathed out a sigh, pushing the blanket off his body. "Fuck."

Leaving him to get out of bed, I'd crossed to the other side of the room like a thief in the night. "Are you coming?"

Two lines formed between her brows as she searched my eyes. "I don't know, Halen, I think they'll really kill us this time."

"And if we stay here—" I made sure to pointedly glare at both of them. One on the top bunk of my bed, the other on the top of his. "—we will for sure die."

"I thought you didn't care about that," he snapped from behind me, and God I wanted to fucking kill him myself.

My jaw clenched. "I will not leave you behind because you are so fucking stubborn. Get up."

"And the others?" a soft voice drifted from above my bed.

I closed the distance, my hands resting on her cheeks. "Not right now."

Not right now was the kind thing to say. It just wasn't the truth.

Chapter Eighteen

WAR

"HALEN, YOU CAN'T FUCKING DO THAT..." I REACH FOR her hand as she zaps forward and disappears into the forest behind the cathedral of town square.

She spins around, her eyes meeting mine. She doesn't bother to stop walking back as she makes her way between the clearing of two overgrown onyx maple trees. "But I want to..."

Halen is a fucking tornado that rips through your life. We used to joke and say that the reason why Priest had no emotions is because she sucked it all out of him in the womb. It wasn't so funny when we realized we were right.

Rain begins to fall from the sky, a pebble hitting the tip of my nose.

"Hale—" The spot she was just standing in is empty. My stomach rolls as I look side to side, unease pricking over my skin. "Halen, this isn't funny!"

I turn to find Priest, but he's still chatting behind me with the girl he was with, his eyes meeting mine mid-sentence.

He nods his head for me to find her.

My feet couldn't move fast enough and before I know it, I am shoving through rogue branches. Where the fuck could she just disappear to so quickly?

I push through two larger trees that open onto a leveled meadow.

She's directly in the middle, her arms to her side and her face on me.

Void. Expressionless.

"Halen..." I step closer, fighting

with myself to not rush forward and slap the shit out of her for dipping, only the closer I get, the clearer I see. Her face pales and her pupils bloat until the entirety of her eye looks black.

She collapses as her eyes roll to the back of her head.

I dive forward to catch her before she hits the ground, my arm tensing around her small waist as I lower her down slowly, gripping her chin to force her focus back onto mine.

"What the fuck have you taken today?" I shake her face gently, even though I kind of want to fuck her up to wake her. "Hey! You're fucking fifteen. Get off the Molly."

Her eyes split, and when she gazes up at me, my panic subsides.

"You're a bitch."

Her mouth curves upward in a smirk. "Maybe. But you caught me anyway."

My brows tense together, and I look between her eyes and the swell of her lips. The perfect bow dips in the middle, surrounded by skin so polished my fingers itched to touch it. She's the kind of perfection you want to terrorize because it simply should not exist.

She smiles. She fucking smiles, revealing the two dimples on either side of her cheeks.

"I'll always fucking catch you, Halen." I move away from her as we both stand. "That's the fucking problem."

They've been gone for three hours. I hate them anywhere near this shit, but I respect that they need to be.

"Thoughts on Katsia and her suspicions of the girls?" Priest lowers onto the bed I use while we're in Perdita. The Hutt is tucked adjacent to the Perdita mansion. When we decided this was how we were going to handle enemies going forward, we knew we'd spend more time here, so we had a shack built on the same property as Katsia's, without being too close to her.

"You and I both know there's truth in it—" I push up from the sofa and make my way to the bar cart that's near the floor-to-ceiling window which overlooks the edge of the cliff and sparse ocean. Right now, it's showing nothing but darkness, blanketed by the caliginous night. "It's only a matter of time until everything comes out." I pop the cork off the bottle of scotch, pouring just enough.

The silence is tumultuous as liquid pirouettes in my glass. Not much bothers me, but the perpetual stench of death that continues to rot at the base of my throat isn't helping my drinking habits.

Priest leans over the bedside table and swipes his phone. "Let them do it at their pace. I enjoy watching them squirm."

I raise a brow at him from behind my glass. Alcoholism starts at an early age in our families. Probably has to do with trying to drown out that infamous stench. "You wanna talk about me and Halen?"

His eyes turn cold. "You both knew what you were getting yourself into. I won't pick sides when shit goes down, because you know shit will go down. You're both too messy. Too volatile. But there's a distinct difference between the two of you that I'm not sure either of you have realized." He plays on his phone, brows knitted in concentration, before tossing it onto the bed. His broad shoulders lift in a shrug. "And the difference is that she needs it more than you do."

Whiskey rages down my throat and I hiss through the aftermath, placing my glass on the counter as my door swings open.

Vaden lazes through with bloodstains littering his white shirt.

I angle my head. "Been having fun without us?"

Vaden removes his shirt from over his head and flings it into the corner of my room. He wipes his hand over his stomach, which only leaves streaks of cruor on his abs. Plucking one of the bottles from the bar, he drops to the wingback chair in the corner of the room.

"She ran." Vaden raises the bottle to his lips. He swipes the residue with the back of his hand. "So I chased her."

Priest and I share a look, before going back to Vaden.

He shrugs. "And then killed her."

I roll my eyes. "I think we've topped our yearly record."

"Eight isn't bad." Priest blows out a cloud of smoke.

"It's March."

His teeth glisten through the veil of smoke. "I guess there is that."

Priest's phone ringing interrupts our conversation and he reaches into his pocket to grab it. "Dad," he answers and puts it on speaker. "Yeah?"

"How was it?"

"It was fine."

"And Halen?"

Priest searches me up and down from behind sleepy eyes. "She was fine."

"Good. For whatever reason, they're tough as shit."

Priest's fingers work around his Zippo. "They're bred from it. Not sure what you expected. Nature always overpowers nurture."

Bishop falls silent. "Let's hope fucking not." He sighs. "I'm not sure if it was a good idea keeping them separate. They probably should have been with you all from the start. You need to pull them in closer. I don't care how you do it, just do it."

"Hold up!" I round the bar to get closer to the phone. "You want us to pull them in closer? How close?"

Brantley speaks next and Vaden freezes. "Do what *you need to do.*"

"What's changed?" Priest asks, leaning back on his elbow. "Why has it gone from show them the ropes, to expose them to it all?" His knee starts bouncing and I can feel his agitation overshadow the room as his fingers flex around his glass.

This doesn't bother me as such. They saw a lot of ugly last night.

"I don't want to have this conversation over the phone, especially when you're all in Perdita."

When our parents were young, the way the Elite Kings were run was a lot different. Priest and Halen's pop, Hector, had a lot to do with that. Once they all settled down with our mothers, they wanted to change shit. Mainly once Madison came about. Then my mom and her history with this fucking island, as well as my dad and his wandering dick with the women here. It's no surprise why I find comfort in the confinement of this island.

"We'll be back in a few days. Got some shit to ship out." My fists clench.

"The ritual is this Sunday. You all need to be preparing." He pauses again. "Eli's trying to call. I'll see you all when you land."

"Shit." I smirk. "Don't they have a daughter? She still around?"

Bishop falls quiet. "Talk soon."

He hangs up and Priest kicks my leg with his foot. "What the fuck are you talking about?"

I look between him and Vaden. "What? None of you remember their daughter? Eli, Kyrin, and Lilith's?"

Priest's eyes dilate. "Yeah, I do, but didn't she die?"

I shrug. "I don't know, that's why I asked. She disappeared when she was young."

Shit. Maybe I imagined it.

The next day arrives quickly.

Eat, kill, fuck, sleep. Repeat.

It's the following night when we're finally back in Katsia's house. It sure does have its advantages, I have to admit.

The wind is bitter when it nuzzles against my skin from the open French doors that lead to the small terrace, and I move to the side of the room and watch as one of the girls tug at the cuffs around her wrists.

My Calvaria is bound to my face as I cross my arms in front of myself and lean against the post of the bed. She wasn't cute. I mean, she was attractive, if you were into her kind. You know. The innocent, girl next door,' I bat my fucking lashes and shake my pom-poms and get whatever the fuck I want' kind. Never been into that. They're too easy. They say yes to everything and never challenge you because they're so thirsty for your attention.

She is one of them.

Her blonde hair sprawls over her slender shoulders, stopping just above her waist. The bland shade of brown that withers in her eyes is cloudy, and her skin has clearly sweltered beneath UV a few too many times.

She tugs on the chains again and they clatter against the wooden headboard.

The red bandana that's tied around her mouth does its job of keeping her quiet.

Angry. Blood. *Mine.*

Leaving my belt buckle undone, I push off the pillar and place my whiskey onto the small desk opposite the bed. I don't speak, but she follows me with unease. They always do. No doubt they have questions… none of which is *why are we here?*

She pulls at her restraints again. This is one we saved for a reason. She has a purpose.

"Stop."

The motion is instant. So obedient.

"Spit out the bandana."

Her lips pucker as they push the material out.

I lean over her body, unlatching the cuffs from around her wrists. Her hands fall free, as she swipes the drool of saliva that drips down her chin.

"Stand."

She wobbles to her feet, naked and bruised as the moonlight contours her every curve.

Nothing.

I feel nothing. Not that I ever did when it came to fucking women, but this feels different and I don't know why.

My jaw tightens as blood rushes through my veins the more I think about it. Not even a fucking twitch from my cock.

I rest my head against the post. Gesturing to the slightly open window, the corner of my lip curls. "Go to the patio."

She trips over her own feet a few times before finally reaching for the handle. It clinks against the metal before it widens.

"Sit on the ledge." I don't move, simply watching as she shuffles herself over the railing.

The wind catches her hair as she turns over her shoulder. "Can I come back in now?"

I tap at my nose and watch as her eyes fall to the ground. Her mouth turns downward as her shoulders sag with defeat. It's the exact moment she realizes that she isn't coming back in.

My head shakes from side to side. "Fall."

She swallows but without hesitating, disappears from the ledge. A moment later, the heavy thump of her body hits the concrete below.

And there it is. My cock turns hard. Looks like she didn't live long enough for her purpose.

HALEN

"**Y**OU GOOD?" EVIE ASKS FROM THE PASSENGER SEAT. WHEN I don't answer, she rests her hand on top of mine. "You're spacing out." My body jerks and I search the familiar angles of her face, desperate for anything to anchor me back down to reality. After everything that happened on Perdita, I can't seem to catch my feelings on it all. The boys are unhinged. I never would have thought it'd have been that extreme. It's not enough that they kill our enemies, they also have to use them as pawns for their morbid obsessions.

I think over everything we were trained in, searching for the clause, *how to dismantle the human body and get off on it*, but come up short.

Perfecting the art of removing your emotions for decision-making.

How to manipulate people and their own narcissism to get what you want.

Cues when someone is being duplicitous and misleading them into telling the truth. "*People don't tell you their lies. They show them.*" There was always a mixture of finance, combat, being around crews that operate beneath us, but when it came to our enemies, nothing. They gave us nothing on them, and that's when it hits me.

It's because the boys handled that. Probably on top of all the above and then some.

My smile widens on Evie. It's the kind that never fools her because she can see right through it.

"I'm fine. Let's go." I push the

button to start my car and breathe out a sigh when the RB engine growls.

Evie reaches for her seat belt. "You know, I kind of didn't think you'd be driving this tonight."

I pump the clutch and move the gear stick into reverse. "I know. But I want to *drive* tonight."

"Oh?" Evie raises a brow. "Maybe rebelling since the boys are away?"

I push it into drive. "Aren't we always."

Only this time Evie doesn't know why. The true reason. Before, it was harmless pushing against the fold for shits and giggles. Now it's not that. I know for a fact that whatever they've been doing all this time, it's one hundred percent more than what we've been doing. Almost like the Fathers put us on this path to distract us so we'd stay out of their way. I shouldn't be mad. *I'm not mad.* But so much for equal ground.

I should have known better.

I drive us forward and Evie plays with the radio until she stops on a song by Meek Mill and Nicki Minaj. She winds down her window and plays with her phone, snapping a few photos of us and a video, before turning the camera onto me. "Tell the people where to meet tonight, your majesty…"

A smirk touches the corner of my mouth. "Meet at the chapel." I turn to face the camera, dropping it down a gear and flooring it. "Then follow me." The force of power throws Evie back in her chair with a round of giggles.

She flips the camera to the back and keeps it recording as we drive through the opulent streets of Riverside. There were old tales that Dad told me as a child. I think all the dads told us the same story, and I think if I remember correctly, it came from one of our family grimoires.

Vitiosis, no doubt.

The tale spoke of a witch who put a hex on the men of Riverside because of all the trauma they inflicted on Swans. They had to restore the balance somehow. None of them told us what that hex included, but now that I'm older, I'm assuming it was making them all assholes.

I keep driving as Evie skips songs, dances in her chair while drinking from the bottle of Don Julio, and lip-syncs alone to the lyrics. I don't bother telling her to stop the streaming, because now that we're are all on the same page with the boys, I don't have anything to hide.

Almost.

I pull down Main Street, bypassing the shops and town center, before turning down the back entrance of the chapel and park in an empty spot. I leave my headlights on as the car growls beneath the music.

Turning to Evie, I mouth *mute it* to her before she taps her screen.

The silence will be short-lived because within minutes, this car park will be thick with cars. On cue, cars roll through the entrance of the parking lot in a roll of color, pulsing engines, and boisterous music. Once everyone is here, I press the accelerator and double clutch until the blow-off valve whistles.

"Everything my dad told me growing up, wasn't all of the truth." I direct us back out the way we came.

Evie pauses, the long-neck bottle almost to her lips. "What do you mean?"

"I mean, the dark shit I was prepared for when it came to the EKC, Evie, doesn't even touch the surface of the barbarous bullshit they've been toying with this whole time. It's almost like they used us as a smoke screen." I continue to drive us forward, through the streets of Riverside, and head north. Opposite of the way to New York and the Hamptons.

Streetlights whip past the deeper we are on the highway, until eventually it bleeds obsidian, with nothing but clusters of lights that line the center of the road.

"Bayonet Falls?" Evie pipes up, gawking out the window.

Goosebumps break out over my arms as I feel myself nearing the enemy's territory. It's like my body can feel Chevalier Hill looming closer and every instinct I have is saying to rip up the brakes and turn my ass around. But Bayonet Falls isn't Gentlemen territory. It isn't ours either, but if anyone knew that we were going there, it would have both sides prickling with tension.

The Gentlemen and the Elite Kings Club don't have a superficial beef like our other rivals. No. This generational hatred is deep-rooted and dates back to our great-great-great—whatever—grandparents. It's so volatile that even centuries later, there needs to be a damn treaty in place.

For years now, I've never heard anyone so much as whisper their existence. I don't think we'd have an issue in Bayonet Falls. If anything, the ghoulish, abandoned township and ghosts who occupy it will love the company.

In the rearview mirror, the lines of headlights follow from behind as my phone starts blaring from the holster it's connected to on the vent.

I swipe it unlocked when I see Stella's face.

"Where are you?"

Stella hides her smile behind her hair. "A few cars behind you. Riv wanted to do a detour on the way."

I don't bother to look at my phone, but Evie does, moving into full view. "Where?"

Stella must flash something at the screen.

"Good girl…" Evie blows them both a kiss.

"You know you're on stream, right?" Stella declares loudly.

I look down at my phone. "Yes. I don't care."

Her eyes burn with devilry. "Oh, are we finally breaking free of the constraints from the animals we have in our lives?" She pauses a moment. "Fathers included."

I wince. I don't want to touch Dad right now. I'd always been a daddy's girl. My mother drove me crazy for the better part of my life, so Dad's lap was my favorite spot. I would have done as he told.

I was his loyal weapon. Now I feel like I'd been loaded with blanks.

"Yes." Another call comes through, but I hit ignore when the photo of War invades my peace.

"Tsk, tsk…" Evie wiggles her finger in front of my face. I couldn't care less. They wanted this.

They did this.

I continue to drive us down Highway 88, the notorious stretch of power, and think over all of the possible scenarios to justify my annoyance with my dad and brother. The only thing I find is my hindered pride.

I sigh, leaning against the driver's door and attempt to distract myself with the lyrics of Big Sean.

"The group on Snapchat has expanded, which means there are a lot of people following us," Evie ponders, scrolling through her phone. It had been fifteen minutes since hanging up with Stella and Riv, and we're about ten minutes from arriving in Bayonet Falls.

I don't care.

The open road goes on for what feels like an eternity before the fabled hill of Bayonet swells so high that it looks like the end of the world.

I drop it into second and press my foot down until it redlines, before double shifting into fourth, then fifth. Headlights glow in my side mirror as River's S13 slides out into the other lane, launching up, and ducking right behind me.

I bite on my laugh as Evie turns up the music.

"Are you only doing this because the boys aren't here?" Evie turns to face me.

"Nope. I'd do it if they were too."

I fly over the hill as the rubble of what's left of Bayonet Falls appears. It's all shadows and malevolent structures, but if I squint my eyes, I can make out the old Ferris wheel that's snapped in half.

We continue through the main street with a loud purr of import engines, passing the Bayonet Falls sign that hangs from rusted nails, before continuing through the township. Buildings with boarded-up windows and burned-out cars roll by as I release my foot from the accelerator to slow. Graffiti litters the walls with a kaleidoscopic palette, and abandonment aside, it's surprisingly tidy.

My headlights beacon on a tortured structure that crests up to the sky in an arch, with the words *Cirque de Diavolo* written below a bilious clown with blood dripping from its mouth.

"Dang." Evie is still staring up at the sign as we drive through the archway. "What kind of shit went on here? How'd they all get booted?"

I park my car in the middle of the parking lot, shifting into neutral and leaving it to idle as Riv pulls up beside me. It doesn't take long for everyone to pile out of their cars and park in their little cliques. I hadn't even hit my window down to talk with Stel when a KE30 starts ripping up its tires.

I slip out of the driver's seat and slam my door closed. In a flurry of raven hair, she unfolds from the passenger side. "Damn. This place is actually creepy, but I love it."

Music is playing from one of the vans in the corner, the smoke and screeching of tires sending a thrill through my body.

"I know!" For a couple weeks now, I wanted to come by and check it out. I didn't know it would splinter my spine with its creep factor until I got here.

Now I kind of want to know the history of the town.

Around fifty cars are parked up here tonight. It's just what I needed after Perdita, but is also why when three luxury cars roll through and park directly opposite us, I notice them.

Rolls Royces aside. Nice. The kind of rides our daddy's drive.

Thankfully, no one outside of us notices the newcomers since they're all too busy enjoying a lawless space.

The door of the middle Rolls swings open but no one appears. "Halen, show you're not carrying…"

A smirk touches the side of my mouth as I stretch my arms

wide. I'd recognize that voice if it was blended with ten others. "Would you like me to strip for you, Bas?"

"Well now, that wouldn't be very *I promise not to tell people we fucked in the back of War Malum's car after he denied you* of me, would it?" Bas boasts as he closes his door.

I fluff up my cropped racing jacket, doing a three-sixty. I'm in a crop top, black cargo pants, and Jordans. "You can see my belly, Bas, I'm not wearing a holster."

"What are you doing here, Hayes?" He leans against the hood of his car, crossing his legs at his ankles.

Finally, I step to the side of my own, matching his stance.

He reaches into the pocket of his slacks and takes out a packet of cigarettes, biting one into his mouth. His hair is as dark as Vaden's, but his eyes are so brown that they're almost hematic. His cheekbones are shaved sharp, but his lips are thin. His nose is slightly bent from being hit in the face one too many times, but all it does is fail at trying to hide his classically handsome features.

He's hot.

Actually, that's probably being modest. When you've been surrounded by beauty all your life, it bores you.

Show me someone with scars. The kind that makes people quiver with fear, and I'll show you my kind of beauty.

"Maybe I'm just here for innocent fun?" I bat my lashes at him to add to my pseudo.

He snickers. "Doubtful. Do your daddy and sociopathic brother know you're here?"

My smile falls an inch before I collect myself. "What, forty minutes up the road?" I'm bluffing, and if Bas remembers correctly, he'll know it.

He puffs on his cigarette, the end crackling amber. For a moment, I forget where we are until a car backfires and laughter and music filter through once more. "What I want to know is, what you're doing here." I lean forward. "Are you following me?"

He pauses the cigarette before it reaches his mouth. "And if I told you that I was?"

I kick off the car. "Now, why would I expose all my signals? I wonder what I would do?" Bas Blackwell was the stray I dragged off the street the night War so ruthlessly put my ass in place.

Literally.

I didn't know who he was, and I didn't care. I broke into War's garage, pushed his RX4 down the driveway before starting her up down the street, and picked up the first guy I saw. It just so happened that Bas was in our estate. I didn't ask why at the time, or even now. I probably should have. In hindsight, I know that if I wanted to be the brat I always get called, I could shoot up this entire spot and be the fucking problem.

But I won't.

Not yet anyway.

Bas swipes the curve of his lip in an attempt to hide his chuckle. "Okay, Halen. I'll be seeing you." Then he's back in his car as fast as he came.

"Shit, you slept with that?" Stella taps her foot, her head bent to the side. "He's cute."

"He's regret," I correct, watching his taillights disappear. But why was he here, that's the question. I haven't seen Bas Blackwell in a long time. The last time wasn't something I wanted to relive.

"Okay, well!" Riv claps her hands, breaking the silence. "I don't know about you guys, but I kind of want to race. What do you say..." She bounces around me, her high heels clapping against the asphalt.

When I don't answer, River's hands come to my cheek as she forces my focus. "Since coming back from Perdita, I can see it in your eyes, Halen. So, I think we should *race*."

"You see what?" I widen them at her.

"The look of your brother."

Twenty minutes later, everyone has split into their collective groups. Stella sprays a line below the entrance sign to Cirque de

Diavolo as River fixes her makeup with one hand while looking into a small compact mirror, and clutching her Desert Eagle in the other.

"You want to set the track?" Stella leans into my window after I've positioned my bumper parallel to the starting line. Not everyone is focusing on the race, since a lot of groups are scattered around, dancing, smoking, and burning rubber, but I want to be the first one to put tread down on this particular track.

For one, I didn't know where I was going, so I just hoped that whoever I was racing knew that. It should have been Stella. She acts like she isn't as big of a car girl like the rest of us, but you put that girl behind any wheel and she'll smoke you off the line.

My muscles relax when I inhale the smell of hot exhaust pipes and rubber. "Of course! Who am I up against?"

There's always someone who needs to be humbled in the car scene. I liked to be the one doing the humbling.

Dad's name flashes over the front screen of my phone and my smile falls. "Hold that thought."

My finger hovers over the screen. He's never had to discipline me. In fact, he refused to. Probably explains a lot now that I look back to my past—and current—choices, but it's why I've always felt soft around him. He's never had to raise his voice at me.

Bishop Vincent Hayes doesn't have to raise his voice at anyone, because his name alone is enough to scare everyone. Except me, apparently, since I have decided to play on his nerves since suspecting he's been playing favorites.

I swipe, blocking one ear before I have a chance to wind up my window. It's impossible to get silence at these things, but at least I can hear his words.

"Halen."

I swallow but my throat is dry. "Dad, I'm just out."

"Doing? You were supposed to be home. Preparing for the ritual this weekend. You can't be out doing whatever you're doing with your car friends."

My eyes rest on the endless pit of darkness up ahead. It looks like the street materializes into nothing.

I ignore his words and focus on his tone, putting some of my training to work. It won't work. Dad is a master at everything that I was merely just learning, but there's a coat of honey over the harsh edge of his tone, as if he is wondering what exactly we are doing here and why we aren't with the boys.

"I'll be home later, Dad."

I hang up my phone, breathing in a shaky breath.

Lowering the window once more, the wind picks up and curls its fingers in my hair as I brush it back behind my ear. Fear prickles down the crux of my spine when I feel it.

Shaking off the skepticism, I turn to Stella, who has reappeared at my window. "At least you can't run anyone off a cliff here…"

She laughs, shoving me in the arm with a side-eye. "I didn't! He drove off himself!" Her eyes widen on me with mock insult. Yeah. Sure. We all know that's a lie.

Stella steals the microphone off Kevin, who's leaning against his Mazda 323. He presses his hand to his heart, as if offended. He isn't. He knows the rules.

She lifts it to her mouth, widening her smile so far that her straight, white teeth almost blind us. "If you haven't dropped your phones in the basket, do so now before you're checked. You know the rules. If you're found to have it on you, you're out." She bats her long lashes at the spotlight on her. "This is our new spot. As expected, Nismo Hayes will be the first to burn the way. We ride how we do back at Devil's Cockpit—but let's…"

My eyes narrow on Stella when I see her brain ticking over. I know that look. We've all seen it one or two times growing up.

Her shoulders straighten as she lifts her chin. "The loser has to do whatever I say for the rest of the night."

I roll my eyes as people whistle and hoot. How is she going to threaten everyone with a good time? Now they're going to want to lose just to have her attention.

"And trust me—" She turns to me, her eyes darkening. "—no one wants to be my pet."

Once a few of the boys who chill with Kevin have checked everyone's phones, except mine, Stella continues, "Twenty races. One final. One winner. Since Halen wins all hers, like always, she doesn't go into the pool of winners. We have to make it fair..." She pauses a moment. "I have a little something special for the losing team tonight."

She lowers the mic and throws it back to Kevin, who pushes off his car and waltzes toward me.

"You make me question my sexuality, little Nismo. You know where you're going tonight?"

I chuckle, revving my engine. "Who am I racing, Kev?" I had barely turned my head to him when a Honda pulls up beside me with its windows down.

When the driver shifts his arm out of the way of his face, my smile hits the ground hard. Words fail me because my chest tightens as I try to suck in deep breaths.

Fear.

This is what fear feels like.

WAR

ITAP MY PHONE AGAINST MY THIGH AS PEOPLE FILE THROUGH my parents' front door. Thank fuck they're never home, and even if they were, you've got a one hundred percent chance of my mom smoking a joint with you instead of her throwing you out.

It didn't matter. They were here through all the parties we threw growing up. And we threw a lot of them. Kind of still do since we all find ourselves with a lot of time on our hands.

This time was different, because this time I was fucking *pissed*.

Halen thought we were still on Perdita, but between her ignoring our calls and Evie going live on TikTok long enough for us to figure out that they were all up to some shit, it warranted a flight straight home. They left Perdita in a hurry, with no text or call. We hadn't spoken to any of them since showing them our extracurricular activities. Was she turned off? Hardly. She could pretend that she wasn't as fucked up as the rest of us all she wanted, but the truth is, she's just a better liar.

Just when she thought she wasn't like her daddy...

And don't get me wrong. I ain't mad at it, but the girl is pissing me off.

D12 raps in the background as people scream from the pool behind us. The lounge isn't as busy as the backyard, but it's enough for us to all talk, hear the music, and do whatever the fuck else.

"How do we know they'll come back here?" Vaden asks, leaning against the chair opposite me. My knee doesn't stop moving. I'm on edge. We didn't get to finish what we were doing tonight because of this, and now, I'm fucking agitated. And that's not at all where I want to be when I'm anywhere near civilians on land.

Fuck.

"Because I've made sure they do…" Priest murmurs, dodging a girl who has her hand on his shoulder from behind.

He flicks it off like one would a piece of trash, before glaring at her coldly. Her lips roll behind her teeth, her cheeks pink. He rests back on me. He knows every single thing that's going through my head right now and all of them don't put his sister in a very good position.

Literally.

"You know that at the ritual, by oath, we shouldn't hide shit from them."

Another girl screams from the pool and my teeth clench. "I know."

Vaden kicks my shin with his foot, and I tear my eyes away from the front door. I can be patient with my wrath. I don't have to tear her apart out of rage, because I'll fucking dismember her with a smirk. "So what is it with you and Halen?"

Priest laughs coldly. "Like you didn't know?"

"It's nothing like that." I bare my teeth, agitation wavering too close to my final straw.

"She's going to be a King after this weekend, War." Priest holds my stare, and I watch as the cloud from ganja pillows around his face. "Which means she's an equal. You can do whatever the fuck you want, you know."

The corner of his mouth twitches, just as the front door cracks open and I watch as River pauses at the threshold, her eyes finding mine instantly.

Her face drains of color. Good. She's fucking lucky that's all that is being drained from her tonight.

But then I notice the bloodstains on her clothes, splattered all over her white dress.

She backs up, almost tripping on her feet as she makes her way back the way she came.

I fly up from my spot on the couch, without so much as telling Priest and Vaden, though by the sounds of their heavy footsteps they're not far behind me.

I catch the door before River can shut it, just as Halen climbs out of the GTR with Stella.

River clears her throat, most likely thinking of some bullshit explanation. "Um, what are you guys doing back?" She quickly steps into me and closes the door, her eyes bouncing over the three of us with disbelief. The door opens from behind her and she closes her eyes in defeat, cussing beneath her breath.

"Why the fuck are you all covered in blood?" I point to all three of them.

Halen blinks down at River's dress. "I told you not to wear white—"

Fuck my sister, I go straight for Halen and grab her by the chin to force her eyes up to mine. "I'm fucking done dancing around the teen angst, Halen. Now, why the *fuck* are you covered in blood?"

The makeup under her eyes is smudged, her cherry red lipstick smeared down her chin. "Someone died."

"Oh?" I raise my brows. "I gathered that. And?"

Her mouth closes, so I slip my thumb between her lips. "Keep going, Halo."

"And I killed him."

My jaw tightens to stop myself from doing something stupid like fucking yell at her. "I didn't sign up to be your peace, Halen. You want peace, go to your daddy. What the *fuck* do you mean you killed someone?"

She reaches up to touch my arm, forcing my hand away from her mouth. If I want, I could ignore it, but I don't. I need the distance from her before I lose it completely and we have two murders to clean up tonight.

I point to the car. "Get the fuck in."

"War!" She spins to follow me as I round her GTR. "We can't go back there!" Her eyes widen with panic, but it does nothing to simmer my rage. If anything, it fuels it.

"We'll follow you both out." Priest snatches the keys from River as we ignore the protesting of the tantrum-throwing, bloodstained brat.

"Wait!" Halen yelps, and I find myself stopping with the car door slightly open. She starts pacing up and down the length of the car, combing her fingers through her hair. You could snap the anxiety coming off her like a rubber band.

"Halen..." River whispers. "This time, we need them."

I glare at her from over the car. I'll touch on the 'this time' another time. "What did you do?"

Halen comes to a halt and the silence rings through my ears. We've always thought the girls lived somewhat of a normal life. They were sheltered from the majority of the shit that goes on.

Well... we thought so, until recently. So this could mean anything.

Halen blinks between Priest and me. I know she's battling internally with whom to address. On one hand, she's always had an unorthodox bond with her brother. Not the conventional kind because you can't with someone like Priest, but Halen showered him with love. Affection. Everything. Priest took it, even though he hated it. If it came from anyone else, he'd have killed them.

She settles on me and my stomach coils around itself in a blaze of ember. "We need to take one car. An SUV. And this one needs to go to the cleaners."

I slam the door closed so hard she jumps. "How the fuck do you know about the cleaners?"

She rolls her eyes, her hands flying out to her sides. "I'm a fucking Hayes, War! Shut the fuck up. Yes, you all may have protected us from the creepy high school boys, but I was born in this, and you need to not forget that!"

My mouth closes because…

Well. She's right.

It's really as simple as that.

She closes the passenger door. "We need to take the Range."

I scan her from head to toe, before looking to Priest. He holds my stare, his finger tapping his bottom lip. Can't get shit from him on the best of days, let alone when he's trying to figure out how they managed to off someone on a night they were out racing.

Priest finds River. "Go grab the keys."

She disappears into the house before returning to silence. She hands Priest the keys and we all make our way to the outer garage that sits directly beside the house. He taps his phone and the garage rolls open.

I hang back, counting down from ten.

Vaden shoulders me in passing as Priest unlocks the blacked-out Range Rover. "You better fuck something that doesn't break tonight."

My jaw clenches, fingers flexing in my fist.

Priest eyes me as he slips into the driver's seat.

"Vaden in the front!" I fling the back door open and slide in.

River glares at me from the other side of the car, hesitating whether she wants to sit near me. Don't blame her. I'm not the greatest person to be around when I'm pissed. "Get in the back, River."

She nods, jumping through the side to get to the *very* back. Stella doesn't argue, following her.

Halen finally saddles in beside me, shutting the door and blanketing us all in darkness, except for the lights on the LED dash.

"Where the fuck are we going?" I turn to her, ignoring the impulse to wrap my fingers around her delicate neck.

Vaden turns in his chair to get her attention.

My knee continues to bounce as I rest my head back against the chair, squeezing my eyes closed.

"Where?" A simple word from someone like Vaden and she spills her guts.

"Highway 88."

My head snaps to her. "What the fuck! Why the fuck were you on Highway 88?" For whatever reason, we thought they were in the back streets of Riverside. Fuck. I gotta GPS this bitch ASAP.

She ignores me.

Priest turns the music on.

"Hale, you need to say *something*." I don't miss the perplexity in Stella's tone when she says *something*.

"Well, shit, someone better say fucking something!"

Vaden's taps on his phone, finding the cleaner.

Leaning over, I unbuckle Halen's belt and drag her over to the middle seat. It'd be my lap, but hand… throat… rage.

"War…" She quivers and just like that, all the wrath I'd felt build up over the past week diminishes. *A little.*

She blinks up at me from below and a tear slips from the corner of her eye. "I can't—"

"Something," Stella urges quietly.

"You're not so slick with the undertones, Stella." I catch Halen's chin with my thumb. "What is it?" When a tear falls on the top of my thumb, I slide my arm around her waist and pull her in closer.

She takes a deep breath. "You're going to be mad. All of you. This is bad—it's so much."

"Yeah, well, I'm pretty fucking mad at you right now, so I doubt it can get worse."

She huffs.

Stella clears her throat.

River moans a little.

My fucking stomach drops because, what the fuck could she have possibly done?

She swipes her tears and shakes off her sadness. "I did something."

Silence.

I catch Priest's eyes in the rearview mirror, and he holds my stare for a second before going back to the road.

"Do you remember that one winter when everyone got snowed in, in Perdita so the jet couldn't run? The mothers were in Milan."

"Yeah, you were fourteen." I trace the curve of her jaw with my eyes. "You girls had the nanny here, though. Why?"

HALEN

I run through the long hall, sliding to a stop with my fluffy socks. Stella and River have long since crashed, and I am bored. Of all the times for us to be snowed in, it had to be when the parents are away. We could have had a movie night. Dad would have failed at making Mom's favorite pancakes, and then Unc Nate would have to come fix them. Then we'd have to listen to the banter between him and Mom as Aunty Tillie threw fruit at them both and Dad threatened their lives for the millionth time that year.

Now I am snowed in inside the Castle with no one to annoy. Not even War. He is my favorite to work up because he pretends to have patience for me, but really, he has anger issues with a capital I. I use the line that separates the two as a jump rope.

I saddle up on the railing of the stairs and slide down before landing at the bottom. My feet ache when I land on the hard floor. I kind of like that. The feeling of something other than the hollow abundance of luxury and privilege.

"In a hurry?" Linda, our nanny, rests against the wall opposite me clutching a mug. My attachment to her is displayed in the wide smile on my face. My cheeks sting from it, but she makes me happy. Linda has been in our lives since before my brother and I were even born! That's how long. I am the only one who has a nanny. The other aunties and uncles like to rile Mom up about having one, but Linda helped raise them too. She is everyone's second mom. Even Mom's second mom.

"What are you drinking?" I singsong, dancing up to her and sniffing her mug.

She whacks my arm playfully with an eye roll. "Listen, I'm off the clock!" She waltzes past me.

I turn just as she hits the middle of the stairs. "Lies! You're never off the clock!"

She flicks her wrists over her shoulder. "Probably. Since I'm having to sleep in the main house instead of in the comfort of my granny flat!"

I bite back my laugh because that granny flat is still on our property, just tucked deep away in the nestle of trees. Dad said he didn't want us to scare her when we got to our teen years. We've just arrived and I've gotta say—my tits are not growing as fast as I would have liked.

Sighing, I stop near the window that looks out to the pool and parterre. The cover is pulled over, waiting for summer, and the trees are blanketed with pillows of snow.

A shadow moves past the patio and I fly to the glass door that opens onto it. As soon as I swing the doors open, a glacial gust of wind curls around my body.

Rubbing my hands up and down my arms, I try to narrow in on one of Mom's fancy shrubs that lines the end.

"Halen." His voice is somber through chattering teeth.

"Who is it?" I slide my socks off my feet and reach for one of the knit couch throws.

Slipping into Priest's Jordans that are a few sizes too big, I shuffle the blanket over my shoulder and step outside. You have to bypass security to even get into the estate. Whoever this person is, was legit enough to not raise alarms.

The shadow steps out from behind the shrub and I blink. He is tall with narrow shoulders. Or maybe this is the normal size of the average boy and I'd just been surrounded by monsters all my life.

"Can I help you?" I ask with a raised brow. "Are you cold?" He's in nothing but a plain black shirt, black pants, and black shoes.

"You can." The snow crunches beneath his boot when he takes another step. "I need a favor from you. You think you can do that?"

I cross my arms in front of myself. "I don't know you."

"I'm a friend of your father's."

I pause. He probably is, even though Dad's friends don't come to our house. They go to his office in New York because they're not even allowed in Riverside. "I've met my dad's friends."

He steps into the line of light coming from the lounge. He's around the same age as Pop. We were working on human interactions and cues this week. We are required to know these skills for this reason.

Blasted. I'm on my own.

"Hmmm. What is the favor?" My eyes narrow. His shoulders are slumped over, his eyes droopy and weak. His beard is unkempt, his brows as thick as hell. He really needs to pluck those.

He reaches into his pocket slowly and I straighten with unease.

My eyes flick to the outdoor table, where a Glock is strapped.

"No!" He raises his other hand up. "I'm just going to give you something." He pulls out a small envelope, keeping his eyes on mine as he lowers it on top of the puffy snow, a distance between us.

He straightens and steps back, slightly behind the shrub. "Watch that. You will not say a word to anyone. If you skip to the end, it'll show you why." I open my mouth to argue but he shakes his head. His eyes are no longer droopy, they're hard on mine. "When the time is right, it will happen."

I stand straighter. "What the hell do you want from me?"

He leaves before I can say another word and I dash for the envelope, running back inside and closing the door. I drop the blanket on the couch and make my way to Dad's office.

I type in his password—riddlemethis—and shove the SD card into the laptop. I click on the mouse and a video pops up on the screen. A bright yellow light comes into view, and the camera shifts downward...

WAR

"Who? What?" The rage is back, only more aggressive and not aimed at her.

She ignores me, before answering, "Go to Bayonet Falls."

I blink at her when she leans back in her chair. Motherfucking Bayonet Falls?

Priest cracks his neck, leaning into the glove compartment and taking out two Desert Eagles and a large sheath. "Any reason why you would all want to be fucking around in that ghost town?"

Vaden checks the chambers. "And why you thought it would be a good idea to not tell us?" He clicks it back into place.

I steady my anger. "GPS. Every single motherfucking one of you."

Priest places the sheath on his lap, before his eyes meet mine in the mirror. "What'd the video show, Halen?"

She breathes out a shaky breath and the chair jerks from someone in the back.

"Stella. I'm gonna fuck you up," I deadpan. "Keep whatever secret you all think you need to. The ritual is this weekend, so either way and by oath, we're gonna know the full story before Monday. Play as you will and we'll entertain it for now, children."

I flash Priest a dark smirk.

He settles back on the road, driving us forward. I rest back in the chair, closing my eyes as my heart slows to a harmonic pace.

It doesn't matter. Whoever it is or was, they are dead. There's comfort in knowing that you can skin a human alive with your bare hands, and whoever is left of the ones who crossed paths with any of the girls are about to get a package gruesome enough to turn them vegan.

I reach between Priest and Vaden. "Tell me what happened tonight."

"I may have started a war..."

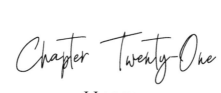

HALEN

Three hours earlier

M Y HEART RACES AT A MERCILESS PACE. I HADN'T realized I was holding my breath until my head spins fast enough to make my palms prickle.

"Do I look familiar to you, young one?" He flashes a gold-toothed grin.

My mouth dries and white noise rings through my ears as panic rises in my throat.

"Why are you here?" The weight of my anxiety holds me in place as I glance up to the rearview mirror to find River and Stella. I need to make sure they're safe.

"Oh, now where would the fun in that be if I told you?" I keep my eyes locked on the road ahead. I hate that I can't seem to find the words I want to say to him, as if choked by fear.

I clear my throat, fighting the tears that prick the corners of my eyes. As a Hayes, I don't have the luxury to expose an emotion as fragile as fear.

"You look like him." It's a hoarse whisper, a telltale sign of the pain it caused to say it.

He chuckles and acid burns the back of my throat. "I guess that's because he's my father."

His engine opens up and I blink once more to help my blurring vision. I've never lost a race, but I am willing to throw in this one.

The world slows around me as

a shirtless guy wearing a Ghost Face mask walks between our two cars, grabbing at his crotch. He pulls out a gat from each pocket and raises them both in the air. When they pop off, I bite down on the inside of my cheek. The emotional barrier I'd been trained to feed materializes in front of me as I slam the gear into first and floor it forward.

Pain.

Regret.

Anger.

Pain.

My car shoots forward as I short shift into gears. The buildings cave around me, but driving is a natural skill for me, so I drop down into second and tear up the brakes, drifting around the first corner I see. The map on my dash displays a perfect loop that continues through a few town streets, before rounding to the back of the park. I have no idea what kind of state the park itself is in, but I'm thinking we dodge and dip, before swerving around people and their cars, and skidding back to the starting line.

I correct the drift before flooring it forward again. The Honda wouldn't have a chance, even with a DOHC VTEC, but I can hear that whatever is under the hood, isn't that. Sounds more like an SR engine or 2JZ.

My jaw tenses as I slide around the final bend before we hit a straight. The speedometer strokes two hundred, and my eyes fly between the dash and to my left. Where the fuck is the back entrance? There has to be one here.

My engine cackles when the rear tires lock and I slide through the chain that hangs across the back entrance.

I zip past withered old rides, a haunted fun house, and a carousel with headless horses and unicorns. Hooking the steering to dodge an old food truck, I reach into the side of my door, turning the steering until I've swung front on with his car.

I slide the mag release over my thigh before hitting my window down.

His eyes widen and his smirk falls when he realizes he misread me. I'm a product of the Elite Kings, and we don't cower to our fear, we shoot it between the eyes and call it a win.

I lift my hand out the window with my index finger on the trigger, before emptying the clip into his skull. Blood explodes from his forehead as his car skids sideways before flipping four times and landing at the base of the Ferris wheel.

I slam on the brakes, my heart galloping in my chest. I've never taken a life before. Not ever. I've seen dead bodies and people die, but never at my own hands. *I fucked up.* In the haze of my rage, I was blinded by the hunger for vengeance. *It was his son.* I just dipped the igniter to a war in gasoline. One that will not only leave a trail of death in its path, but unearth old skeletons that had been buried for years.

Skeletons I buried.

I reach for my phone on the passenger seat, swiping my tears angrily from my cheek and dialing the *for the girls* group chat. One of them will answer.

"Crash?" Stella's face pops up first with a curled smirk.

I shake my head, my face paling.

She stiffens and her smile falls. "We'll be there in a second."

"Don't bring Evie…"

Stella pauses a moment. "Shit."

I have to protect Evie from as much as I can. For her own safety. For her little brother. For her parents who are about as close to a second family outside of our lives as I'll get. I'd never want any of this to touch them, and neither would Dad.

No.

Me and the girls need to clean this up, bury him where he needs to be, and then call it a night.

I end the call and send her the map, telling her to follow the track I did so people don't get suspicious.

Silence claws at the memories I'd locked away.

I squeeze my eyes closed and start counting in my head when headlights beam through my lids. They roll to a stop beside me.

River's eyes bounce between me and the wreck. "You really just can't let anyone else win, huh?" she jokes, sighing and turning off the car.

I watch as Stella makes her way to the mess, and once enough time has passed, I slide off my belt and open my door.

"I see…" Stella teases, casting a quick glance over her shoulder before leaning down to get a better look inside.

"This is bad." Panic grips me around the throat, forcing me still. "I shouldn't have reacted like this, it's just—"

River reaches into my car and takes my gun. "Who is he, Hale?" Her tone is gentle. "Do you know him?"

I shudder. "He's—he—was." I stop, my tongue stuck to the bridge of my mouth.

"Hey!" Stella brings her hand to mine. "We will figure this out. The boys don't need to know. We can call in the cleaner after we do our thing, and then there's no evidence left, okay?"

My muscles relax a little when I see her logic. That would work. "Okay. I'll pick up Evie and drop her home. We can meet at my house."

River tosses my gun into her car. "Do mine. No one is there right now."

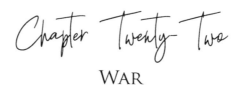

WAR

"**P**ULL BACK…" I HIT THE HEADREST WITH MY PALM.

"Why?" Priest hesitates, Bayonet Falls dead in front of us. Even from here, the town is so dark and lifeless that any kind of light is easy to spot. A train of imports flies past us as they leave Bayonet one by one. They're a mess over the road, as if being chased out by something.

Or someone.

I don't look at any of them as I say my next words. "Because we don't have the armor to take on what is waiting for us over that hill." My eyes land on Halen. "Right?"

Halen swallows, her lashes fanning out over her cheeks. "Right."

I kick Priest's chair. "Back up. We need a plan."

He reverses, just missing a 200SX before sliding into the convoy. I send out a text to shut down the party at my house and we all drive back in silence.

The Castle comes into view as soon as we hit the estate.

No one spoke a word. Not when we were driving up the long cobblestone driveway that's lined with perfect, manicured trees, and not now when we pull into the horseshoe driveway of the Castle.

Priest parks and we all sit for a moment. After this weekend, everyone in this car will not be able to so much as shit without one of us knowing about it.

Yet right now, I can't help but feel the separation between us and the girls. Has it always been like this, but we have never all been forced to be around each other?

Probably.

"Everyone out. Meet in Halen's room," Priest bites out tonelessly.

I watch as the girls pile out of the car and shuffle their way up the marble steps to the front door.

"What do you think happened?" I'm the first to ask because it could be a number of things.

Priest is silent for a moment. "Twin-tuition... this is something that has been going on for years. I can feel it with her. How she's responding to it. Almost conditioned. She's acted out of haste, and now she's freaking out about the repercussions, which means this has something to do with people we already have tension with."

Vaden removes his belt. "Yeah... but what? And who? It can't be the Gentlemen because Riverside would be on fire by now."

"Well, I'm about to find out." I reach for the door handle when Priest's words stop me.

"I get that the two of you have got all of that going on... but I wouldn't in this house. If Dad catches you, I ain't helping."

I shove the door open, ignoring Priest. Please. I'm the favorite fucking child.

I jog my way up to the front doors before climbing the imperial staircase until I hit the second floor. Taking a hard left, I stop outside her door.

A fucking door.

A basic-ass beige door with patterns carved into the wood.

She's hiding something. And I'm about to squeeze it out of her.

I don't bother knocking, but the natural scent hits me in the face and almost catches me off guard. I haven't been in here for a long time. There's always an aura of flowers and cedar, but tonight, that's fused with a pungent hint of iron.

Her bed is in the center, with its feet facing the door, and the

California king is decorated with feminine plush blankets and one hundred and fifty-two pillows. Her bathtub sits openly to the side, with a floating wall that separates the *actual* bathroom. For whatever reason, she wanted her bath in the open. On the other side is her closet. If you can even call it that. The thing is basically a fucking two-story jewelry store surrounded by other shit.

A satin black bar is nestled in the corner, with a bright pink neon sign hanging over the face that reads *Cocaine is bad for you*, and beanbags spread around it. A big fuck off TV hangs on the opposite wall, surrounded by random cutout photos of everyone over the years. Even fucking baby photos of us.

Halen and her sentimental bullshit.

"Okay well, don't worry, you don't need to knock." Halen rolls her eyes, making her way into the bathroom and leaving River and Stella on the beanbags. Even though both hers and Priest's rooms are the same size, somehow, she manages to fit more shit into hers. Borderline hoarder.

I ditch them and follow behind Halen like a fucking puppy.

When we're out of earshot, I grab her elbow. "Talk. Now."

Her eyes come to mine in the wall-sized mirror. "No."

My head jerks back. "The fuck do you mean 'no'?"

She reaches for the bottom of her crop top and tosses it into the corner of the room. "I can't do this with you. You're just going to have to trust me."

"Trust you?" I follow her to the stream of water that's falling from the raindrop shower. "Halen, I barely fucking like you right now."

She spins to face me. I'm so entrapped by her eyes that I don't notice her hand go to the back of her bra until it falls to the ground.

My eyes drop to her perfect tits.

"Are you sure about that?" She steps closer, her bloodstained hand coming to the tattoo on the side of my neck. "Or are we going to keep pretending?"

"Why not?" My brows rise in challenge, looking from her lips to her eyes. "It's not like we haven't been for years now."

She falls back, stepping beneath the water while shimmying out of her cargo pants and kicking them away.

I draw closer, leaning against the wall as beads of water roll over her body.

"You're looking too hard."

"Am I?" My head tilts. I don't realize I'm doing it until I've reached for the back of my shirt, throwing it onto her pile. I step into the shower just as she turns to face me, swiping water from her face.

"War... everyone is in my bedroom right now."

"So?" I whisper over her lips and my cock swells against the zipper of my jeans. "Then you're gonna have to be quiet." Before she can protest, my mouth crashes against hers as I bury my hand into the back of her hair. She fucked up when she let me taste her, because now I'm gonna ruin her. Slowly. Bit by bit until she doesn't realize she has nothing left until she realizes *she has nothing left.*

Releasing her hair, my hand wraps around her throat and I force her backward. Her head bounces off the wall before her long brown hair fans out over her shoulders. My fingers bruise her thighs when I lift her from the ground, as she wraps her legs around my waist and my tongue traces the hard lines of her jaw, all the way down to the soft curves of her tits. Sucking her nipple into my mouth, my teeth catch the piercing as blood seasons the tip of my tongue.

She cries out through weakened whimpers, but I catch them by covering her mouth with my other hand.

My tongue swipes over my bottom lip as my eyes darken on hers. "Can you shut up?"

Her eyes turn to slits.

"Awww..." I tease, flashing a smirk and moving in closer, until the tip of my nose grazes over the bridge of hers. "Halen doesn't like being told what to do. Fuck. Can't say that I'm surprised."

I let my hand slip but before she can start popping off, my

mouth is on hers once more. There's a faint echo of a door closing in the background, but neither of us stop.

Her movements are frantic as she slides her hand between our bodies, tugging at the belt around my waist. After forcing my jeans and briefs down and tossing them out of the shower, her lips are back on mine and her kisses become more desperate.

Needy.

Wet.

My hand rests on the wall beside her head as a chuckle vibrates between our lips. "Grab it. Go on…" I stay fixed on her, and fuck if she didn't look goddamn perfect right now. With her cheeks licked pink, her kiss-stained lips, and her hair brushed by the carnal obsession of madness, she is exactly where she belongs.

At my damn mercy.

When warmth curls around my cock, I bite down a groan as I thrust my hips into her touch.

"Halen," I warn, my body shaking to contain the primitive hunger of every damn thing I'd ever wanted from her.

My eyes dilate on her and I watch as she bristles away a little. "I simply tasted you and hours later, I have you here. With your brother outside the door and your tits in my mouth. But if I fuck you, Halo?" My hand slides down the wall, bringing us closer. "If I feel your tight little cunt mold around my cock like a fucking ownership title, well…" My lips skim the velvet pillow of hers. "Then I'm gonna fucking surrender."

She slides the cushion of her thumb over the curve of my helmet. "So fuck me."

Jesus.

I palm her pussy with one hand, pressing it against her clit while putting some distance between us. Just enough to watch her. Her chest rises and falls as her lips part, allowing the shower to rain into her mouth.

Her brows crease when my thumb finds her clit and I slow my strokes. I want her to come apart in front of me so I can put her back together inside of me. Swallow her whole so she can never fucking leave.

Fuck. She's turning me into a damn madman.

She reaches for me, but I duck away from her.

I need to feel it. That hallowing rage before I give in.

She tries to push into me again, but I counter it while keeping my hand on her.

"War…" she rasps. "If you don't fuck me right now, I'm going to get loud in front of everyone."

"You think that's a threat?" My lip curls as I circle my finger inside her wet entrance and fight my eyes from rolling to the back of my head when she tightens around me. "I want it, Halen. I want my name to leave your lips as I fuck you so everyone knows that you're… *whose?*" I bait her, my eyes glistening with mischief. She won't give it to me, but I'm gonna get it whether I have to reach inside of her cold heart and tear the word out myself.

My fingers find her mouth as I drag them over the base of her tongue, arching them down her throat until my fingertips touch her tonsils.

She doesn't even gag as saliva slips over the palm of my hand and I gloss my cock with her spit.

She crawls up the wall a little further and I position myself over the mouth of her cunt.

Fuck.

Her body hardens as my cock splits her open.

My teeth catch her cheek. "Yeah, you're fucked." My tongue tastes the dimples I left behind before I stand straight.

She collapses against my shoulder as I drive my hips further into her and her back arches off the wall.

Shit. I ain't gonna survive her.

She bites at my shoulder as my fingers flex around her hips and I force her all the way down my length, until the tip of my cock collides with her cervix.

I hiss as my hand travels up her chest, landing on her throat.

Her tongue cleans up the blood on my shoulder, before she blinks up at me with the kind of innocence only a demon could suit.

Shit.

Fuck.

Drawing back, I can't fucking control myself when I thrust inside of her with enough force that the fat on her ass claps against the soapy wall.

"Shh…" she whispers over my lips with a grin. "They—"

My grip on her throat tenses. I'm done whispering. I keep to a deliberate pace, sucking down her kisses as she tightens around my cock. Her hand knots in my hair as her chest rises and falls against me. She tries to calm her breathing but fails, so I catch her mouth with mine again as my balls pull together and her hips tremble.

She whimpers into my chest to mask her orgasm as tremors twitch from the slick walls of her pussy, her cum sliding over my balls like velvet.

Every muscle locks up and my eyes roll back to the back of my head as I switch speeds. Harder, not faster.

I beat into her wet cunt without releasing her throat as my blood turns to lava, pumping roguishly through my body. Goosebumps litter my flesh when I detonate, and hot cum fires out of my dick as I empty inside of her.

Silence for a moment, with nothing but the starving panting of our lies stripped bare between us.

We peel away from each other as I stumble backward, releasing her delicate body as she slips to the ground.

The sooner I get away from her the better, before I carry her into the room and tell everyone to get the fuck out. "I'm not nearly done with you, so hurry up in here."

I exit the shower and tug my jeans back on, swiping the panties she was wearing all day and shoving them into my back pocket. I make my way back around the floating wall, ignoring the stares.

Heading straight for the bar, I swipe a bottle of bourbon and the packet of smokes beneath the dresser, before dropping my weight on top of her bed.

Stella and River are both glaring at me from the beanbags, but Priest and Vaden remain silent across the two sofas in the corner of the room.

I lift the bottle to my mouth, catching Priest's eyes. Nothing. Nil. Void. Because he is who he is, and now… well, now, she's mine. Even if she didn't fucking say it. She didn't have to.

Priest's knee starts bouncing, and it's probably the first bit of *anything* I've seen from him since that time…

The time we don't speak about.

"What happened today?" I ask no one in particular, hoping the girls just spill.

I open the packet of cigarettes and bite one into my mouth as the shower cuts off and both Stella and River look over my shoulder to Halen.

"Hmmm?" I pipe. "Well, come on. Or we can wait until the ritual tomorrow where you're obliged to after we're all linked together as one. In front of five hundred members of the EKC."

River sucks in a deep breath and my eyes sway to Halen as she saunters past us and buries herself in her closet. Annoyingly so, I drag my eyes back to my little sister.

"We decided to create a new race spot in Bayonet Falls as a way to get out from the suffocation of literally this—" River waves her hand around the room.

Stella touches River's arm. "What she means is that we were sick of going far and wide just to be able to fuck."

"Stella," Vaden barks and she at least has the common sense to jump a little.

I pause my drag. "Continue."

Stella rests her head back on the beanbag. "We would do what we do at Devil's Cockpit, only the losers are my bitch."

"Blah, sounds basic. Keep going…" I edge her, my left eye twitching. I said to Priest that I wouldn't lose my shit over this whole *they had another life outside of us* thing, but this is testing me. We'd give Halen whatever space she needed, sure, but the vanilla shit can be eaten now.

River stares at Stella, as if waiting for her to continue. She sighs. "The winner who made it, had to race Halen at the end of the night. If they lost, they would give us two things."

The room falls silent.

River's eyes widen on Stella, a tickle of a smirk on her lips. "And *if* you made it through the actual race after losing to Halen," she shrugs and picks at her nails, "you play Russian roulette." She pauses again. "While live." Her mouth twitches as she pins me with a stare. "Naked and in front of everyone."

More silence.

Halen scoffs from where she's leaning against the wall.

"What?" I snap at her, no longer bothered to hide my agitation.

Priest's demon-like eyes fly up to his sister. "Care to enlighten us on why that's so funny?"

"It's not…" She shrugs. "That's exactly as it is. Like River said…"

"Halen?" I don't hide the cynical tone in my voice. "Now, the truth."

"That was all a lie, but whoever lost would be with Stella and whatever she wanted to do with them. That's all."

"And what happened tonight?" I'll try the trauma anyway, because we all know vanilla isn't my thing.

Her face pales. "Oh. I was breaking in the track when my opponent pulled up beside me. Honda Civic—"

I scoff.

She glares at me. "—with a *not*-Honda engine. Anyway. He looked familiar. I knew him, but it wasn't *him.*"

"The man from when you were younger?"

She nods. "Yeah." When her voice cracks, she clears her throat. "He said he was his son. We raced, I panicked, and I shot him. His car flipped and landed near the Ferris wheel." She glances at the girls. "That's all we know."

"Who is this man, Halen?" I lean forward, wrath clawing its way up my spine. "What did the video that he gave you show?"

She smiles but it doesn't reach her eyes. "The man who gave me the video? I don't know. I've never seen him again since."

Priest turns over his shoulder. "Where's the video?"

She shakes her head. "I don't have it. I destroyed it straight away."

"You—" Priest stands slowly, turning his full attention to his sister. "—fucking why?"

I slow my exhale and watch them with careful eyes. Priest would never hurt his sister, but then Priest puts the Kings first and above all, so if he thinks she's betrayed us in any way, there's no telling what he would do.

"You protecting them?" His eyes flash a brilliant shade of murder.

Halen doesn't back down, crossing her arms. She'll never bitch from a challenge, even if her biggest one has always been her brother. "I hate you."

Shit, she's mad.

And making it obvious that she's avoiding me.

"Who is he?" I ask, apathetic to her obvious hostility, even though I'm having massive regrets about not dragging her ass back into that shower.

Her shoulders lift again, as her eyes move to the girls. "I guessed a long time ago that he was with a rival group. Not sure who."

I trace the lines of her features in an attempt to domesticate my wild thoughts.

With her arms at her sides and her mouth turned to a frown, I know she isn't lying.

"So, why the bloodbath tonight?" I ask, tilting my head. "The passion? I mean, you gotta be filled with some pretty volatile hatred if your first instinct when you see someone is to pump a whole chamber into their skull."

She falters. "I told you. He looked like the man. I panicked and killed him."

My jaw twitches a few times. "I'm fucking tired. We can finish this shit tomorrow." I know Halen, and the harder you push, the more she pulls away. Whatever happened, there has to be more to it than what she's letting on.

I fall back as my hand rests on my abs and the circle light dims from above her bed. My eyes follow her when she saddles up with the girls in the corner. With how big the space is, we can't hear each other talk if it's hushed, and something about that just doesn't sit right with me.

The mattress dips as a rolled joint comes into view by tatted hands. I reach for the trunk, glancing briefly up at Vaden.

Bringing it to my lips, I ignore the faint chatter from the girls and the evident silence from Priest. I inhale and hold, until I feel my muscles relax around the THC.

Vaden takes the spot at the top of the bed. "Gentlemen?"

I bend my head back to look at him. "Naw. Don't stress that. This is too messy for them, and they'd never go for one of us. It's why the treaty is in place." I blow on the ember when it dies out. "Danny Dale is a crazy sucker, but he loves his kids. He'd never do anything to fuck with that. Because we would," I clarify, even though Vaden doesn't need to be reminded. "Fuck with them. I've heard his daughter is hot. She'd make a good little target."

His mouth falls into a straight line. "Damn. We turned into the bad guys, huh? Killing and shit for fun, not purpose."

I choke on my laugh until my eyes water. "I wouldn't say it doesn't have a purpose if they're fucking with one of ours first."

"Hmmm." I hate when Vaden gives noncommittal answers.

I should tell him that we should take the Gentlemen anyway, and that Moses and his brothers wouldn't be able to do shit about it. Danny Dale is sick with cancer. It is only a matter of time before he goes down and his oldest son rises up. Then what? Then it is fucking on because I am certain that Moses Dale wants our heads just as much as we want his. Or maybe not. We don't know. The Gentlemen are wild cards, but we are the dealers.

Chapter Twenty-Three

HALEN

I STARE BACK AT MYSELF IN THE MIRROR, MY FINGERS GRAZING the white paint that's smudged down my jaw. I've been waiting for this moment for as long as I can remember—we all have. The process of becoming a King is sacred amongst our kind, but a practice that historically took place during a different time for our parents. Many will be born into one of the ten Founding Families, but not everyone will become a King. *Officially.* We wear our marking with pride, but it signifies a lot of things to many different people. The rest of our lives start after tonight.

Quod Ritualia. The Ritual.

Stella peers at me over her shoulder, as Saint—who is far too sweet to be her mother—works on her face skull. "You're thinking too much into it. Mama, tell her she's thinking too much into it." I love the girls, but one of the many reasons is that there's a toxic recklessness to Stella, who could put a man three times her size in the ground without blinking, and then River, who'd write poetry with your blood as she declares her underlying love.

"Thank fuck!" My mom rushes through the door in a flurry of panic, before her shoulders sag. "Why are you so hard to fucking find lately?" She places a hand on her hip.

I love when she does this. Pretends she's my mother and not my sister. She's more than I could ever ask for in a mom, but damn. The woman's spunk just won't die.

"Probably because she's beneath War."

River's tone is drunk with sass.

Tillie pauses on River's makeup, my mom's eyes are lazy on mine, and Saint clears her throat.

"Thank God!" Tillie exhales, clutching her belly when she curls over. So dramatic for no reason. Also, love Tillie, but damn… "Oh *thank fucking God!* I was almost afraid that he'd bring home a stray, or worse…"

I know she's implying Katsia.

She uses her hand to fan her face. "I want all the tea!"

I shoot River an icy glare before softening back on Tillie. "What your daughter meant to say, was that we are nothing. There's still a very real possibility that he could bring home a stray. Or, like, ten…"

Tillie blinks at me as if I spoke a foreign language. Maybe I had, but it's more Stella's habit to randomly break out in Latin, not mine. "Nope. I know him. He's exactly like his father."

She turns back to River, swiping up a makeup brush. "So, on that note." Her cheek crinkles when she tries to hold in her laugh. "How's the trauma?"

Mom's hand comes to mine. "I need to show you something."

I don't know why we decided my room to get ready for the event of the century would be best.

I squeeze her hand with mine and smile, placing my glass of gin down on the vanity while tightening my satin robe. "Okay, Mother."

Her smile widens, and I don't think I've ever seen her so beautiful. Actually, that's a lie. She was forged by an angel on the day of the joint wedding in Italy. All to marry the Devil.

She directs us down the long hallway. Arce Hayes has twenty-three bedrooms, twelve bathrooms, two theatres, a shooting range, an indoor basketball court, an underground fifty-car garage, and a pool that would make Elon Musk cream his panties. The kind of wealth our families have is disgusting. Thankfully, every six months, our mothers hold prestigious charity events, and then match every dollar that they raise. The next one will be in a month, and we'll officially all be Kings. Without our parents' involvement.

They've phased out slowly over the years, but once that gavel is in Priest's hands, they're officially done.

Not that my brother hasn't been holding the gavel since he was in his senior year of high school, because he has… metaphorically. He and Dad share an outlandish bond. One that kind of feels like a secret society in itself. My brother would burn the whole world down if anyone hurt Dad, probably killing him along with it just to prove a point.

After following Mom to the end of the hallway, we walk up a level and she stops outside a door that's smaller than the others in our house. She squeezes the handle and cracks it open.

I peek inside to see a swivel staircase that grows to the ceiling. The walls are barely wide enough for the stairs, let alone me—a claustrophobic.

She leans against the wall, the worry lines around her eyes deepening. Well. The lines that are there, since she religiously gets them frozen. As much as she would *love* to say it's genetics, we all know it's not.

"Your father and I have been waiting for this day for a long time, Halen. I have to admit…" She rolls her eyes. "If anyone had asked me when I was at high school if this was the life I would like for my children, I would have shot them on sight." Her lip twitches into a smirk. "But it occurred to me that that in itself is why I would never be satisfied with a prosaic life."

She pauses, her hand settling on my arm. "I need you to know that from now on, all of you are going to find yourselves in situations where you might think you've got no way out." The corners of her eyes soften, but her mouth flattens. "But you always do, Halen. You're more like your father than you are me, that's for sure."

She blinks back the tears I can see forming in her eyes.

"Mom…" My heart sinks. I hate seeing her upset, because she never is. She's the toughest woman I know, and I know this because she married my dad.

She winces. "Go up. I'll be right behind you." She stops for a moment, holding my eyes. My stomach twists like she's the one holding it. "I need you to take what I'm about to show you with a softness you only share within the family. And by family—" She reaches out to touch my cheek and my eyes close. "—I mean the *entire* family. Incest aside…"

"Mom!" My eyes widen, choking on my laugh.

She wiggles her brows at me. "Go. I'm right behind you." I don't know what kind of secrets I'm about to walk myself into, and in the back of my mind, I wonder why she had to do it right now. Before the ritual.

But I take the first step anyway.

The door closes as Mom follows behind, and we get blanketed in darkness, tiny specks of LED lights creeping over the rail to guide the way. It doesn't take long to reach the top, and after a few moments, my feet hit the final step.

I turn to her. "You know, you're going to have to repaint my face because I didn't sign up for a workout today."

Her laughter echoes as she passes me, and my eyes fly to where she grips the handle to the door. "You'll be wearing your Calvaria anyway."

We're both around the same height now, and she makes it her mission to tease me about getting her height when Priest clearly inherited Dad's. "If you're worried that I'm going to run, I'm not, Mom. I'm going to stand here and fight for our family until my very last breath. I love you, but nothing you can show me will scare me away from this life."

Her mouth parts, her face frozen. *Literally.* Without another word, she pushes the door open.

Air leaves my lungs as static prickles down my spine, leaving a plethora of fear in its wake.

The concrete walls match the ceiling in starless radiance, but it's the fluorescence of scribbles that steal my breath. A single wing-back chair sits lonely at the center, sewn with satin black suede and gold curvatures. Paired with a neat ebony table where a bottle of

Louis XIII Black Pearl, it's spine-tingling how morbidly elegant the room is.

As soon as I see the label, I know who occupies the space. I'd know even if it didn't, since every breath you take in here leaves the venom of Priest D'mon Hayes behind.

"At least he didn't steal Dad's Henri IV Dudognon Heritage this time."

No—just an easy sixty-five-thousand-dollar limited edition bottle of cognac. When I say limited, I mean Priest bought all of them. He doesn't share with *anyone*. It's his whole personality at this point.

Mom steps inside farther, tracing the writing on the walls. She drags her finger over one of the names.

Dylan.

I blink back to my mother. "Did you bring me in here to ask me to save him, Mom? Because I can't. No one can." I wrap my arms around myself when the temperature drops. I don't know if it's from the inverter or just because he who occupies it is the Devil, but it's cold. Soulless. It's what I'd imagine death to feel like right before it takes you.

"No. I know." Her body shifts to mine, her head shaking gently. "I brought you here so that you'd understand that your brother may lead this generation, but you will be the one to keep it in line. We love you all equally, but we also know that out of the six, it's you who has the most humanity. You may be like your father, but you have a heart of your own." She smiles, but it's not a happy one. "You hold yourself to a caliber where you try to do good."

I wince, my gut laden with guilt. "I killed someone the other night."

Oh God. I can't believe I'm telling her this, but I need her to know that I'm not the angel she thinks I am.

She brushes off my confession nonchalantly. "And how did that make you feel?"

I reach inside of myself to comb through the sensations of that night. "It felt like he deserved it."

She smiles once more, this time wide enough to reach her eyes. "And that is exactly what I mean. Your decisions are powered by logic. The rest of them, with the exception of War, can be callous."

She wanders over to the chair, lowering herself down and swiping the bottle of brandy. "When I met your father, it was during a different time. Swans were forbidden, and your pop was still carrying on the traditions of the Old Kings. The original Founding Fathers." She twists the cap off. "They kept a lot of secrets from us during this time. Kept us in the dark. I rest knowing that this won't happen to you."

"So why did you show me this?"

She swallows a shot of Priest's forbidden love, swiping her mouth with the cushion of her thumb to hide her smugness.

She places the bottle back to where it was. "Because I need you to know that none of you are perfect. That if you've made a mistake, made a wrong choice, or feel as though you're alone, you're not. You're the logical one. The one who will keep them on track when they go rogue." I can't tell her how wrong she is because... no the fuck I won't. "You'll always be your daddy's *amica mea...*" My heart tightens in my chest at her words.

Forcing the tears away because I don't want to smudge my skull makeup, I soften. "I know, Mama."

She watches me carefully, and I hate how it feels like she's reading every thought in my head.

She probably is. Maybe Aunty Saint taught her how to be a witch.

"Okay!" She claps the necromancy out of the room, pushing up from the chair and hooking her arm through mine. "Let's go and get you anointed, or whatever it is called."

We both laugh as we make our way back down the stairs and away from Priest's—whatever it is. Once we are back in the hallway and Mom has locked the door once again, I follow her back down to my room.

River and Stella turn when they hear the door open, with Tillie and Saint right beside them.

Mom squeezes my hand, but her words are for everyone. Probably even for themselves. "Ready?"

Embraced by the shadows of a crescent moon night, we all stand in a line outside the entrance to the tomb. It was my great-great-great-grandfather's bunker for the Elite Kings Club when he created it one thousand and fifty million whatever years ago. The stories that have come out of this very place are too hellacious to think about. It's why I stopped reading the Hayes grimoire and left it for Priest. I don't need more reasons to hate my ancestors.

The graveyard itself in Riverside was assembled around this tomb. It started as the place they'd bury the bodies of every single Swan that they killed. There are so many unmarked graves throughout the forest that every time someone else needs to be buried, they find human remains.

The quiescence of the forest gives me a moment alone with my thoughts, as the skeleton of trees loom over us. Six linked from the blood of our ancestors, and after tonight joined as one. Our morals and what we believe are about to change.

As much as Mom tried to reach inside of me at some final attempt at saving our generation, after tonight, my loyalty will no longer be to her or Dad. It's to the five of them first before anyone else.

I think that's why she showed me Priest's little box of terrors tonight, to prove that it didn't matter if us girls haven't been with them for long, that if I felt that way, I needed to pull it in and be the person I need to be for the order.

Stella shifts. "I haven't been here since I was little."

"I come here often, obviously," River replies softly, and none of us question why. Her obsession with death and high heels aside,

River visits her sister often. Sometimes we come with her, other times she just wants to be alone.

The exhale of old ghosts curls around my ankles as I tug the black hooded cloak down so it further pools around my feet. We all lift the hood to our head, and I play with the clasp that clicks near my collarbone.

Built from fossilized concrete, moss flowers through the veins of the archaic structure, leaving ropes of ivy to climb freely. A tilleul hue glows from beyond, and I take in the hostile archway and twin columns on either side of the entrance.

Stella plays with her phone. "Of course, we were all born into the creepiest families known to mankind." She shuts it off when Priest hushes her, before taking the first step forward.

Priest leads, followed by War, Vaden, me, River, and Stella. Not in order of importance.

Priest shifts over his shoulder a little, his eyes bouncing down the line. "In sin, and until the last drop, long live the EKC until our hearts stop." His skull mirrors mine, if only his ash-colored contacts could hide the emptiness that resides inside of him.

We all repeat the chant, excitement finally zapping through my body. *Holy shit. It's happening.* Before I can absorb the thrilling buzz, a morbid overtone of a trumpet horn howls all the way down my spine.

I swipe my damp hands down my thighs in a poor attempt to unknot the anxiety that's coiled through my body.

I'm ready for this. *I've been ready since I was fourteen years old.*

The swarm of emotions aren't ideal. I can't lie.

As soon as we descend into the tomb, I shudder around the earthy perfume of nightmares and death. The recited hum of the EKC mantra echoes up the stairs that lead down to the underground bunker, and fog drowns our ankles the deeper we go. I swear, even the candles that line the walls surge as we pass.

The chants become raucous when we hit the bottom, and I keep my head down to follow Vaden's steps. Ancient relics carve the way to the shallow platform, along with riddles in our native tongue.

None of us have ever been down here, since it's considered the holy ground for the Founding Kings. If I listen closely, I'm certain I can hear the screams and cries of every soul that's trapped here. The sacrificial home to slaughter, cannibalism, necrophilia, and rape. The list could go on, but I'd have to ask Priest.

Thank fuck for my mother, or us three girls would be cooked meat.

I take a single step up as Vaden stops walking and the recitation ends. When he's no longer in view, I stride forward and lower to my knees.

We know the routine. We've been taught it since we could walk.

Vaden's presses his arm against mine gently, as Stella does the same on the other side. A silent *you good?* The concrete floor gnaws at my knees as I blow out a steady breath.

"Tonight we witness the inauguration of the six progenies of Kings. Hayes, Vitiosis, Malum. I want to start by acknowledging the last surviving Founding Families. Hayes, Malum, Vitiosis, Venari, Ditio, Divitae, Rebellis, and Stuprum. Hunters of the night, the Elite Kings Club was formed by the power of three who desired to live lawlessly outside the scope of mankind."

He pauses, looking out behind us. "They then found seven other members who would share their philosophy, before building a legion so strong that not a single sector of power amongst civilians could touch them. But in doing that, and because they existed during a time of anarchism and destruction, the ritualistic events that took place over the years, though barbaric, were worshipped amongst those who both idolized and feared them. Humphrey Hector Hayes was both monster and man, who continued his legacy the way he saw fit. The extirpation of Swan's born into the Founding Families continued until I met my wife—" I gaze up from below my lashes just in time to catch Dad smirk at someone. It'll be Mom.

He continues. "—who broke through generational curses so

that our children wouldn't know the pain and suffering that so many did before us. The Elite Kings started as a conspiratorial disassemble by becoming just like them. Every Founding Father had a purpose, placed in the ten highest points of power across the globe. Hayes, the Devil; Malum, evil; Vitiosis, vicious; Venari, to hunt; Ditio, power; Divitae, wealth; Rebellis, rebellion; and finally Stuprum, debauchery."

A smirk touches my lips at the mention of Tillie's last name. I don't have favorites, but it's no secret how close she and I are.

"Over the years of training, Kings would slowly part into their titled positions, leaving Hayes, Vitiosis, and Malum to run the Kingdom from the inside. So tonight, we welcome all who have traveled from around the world to bear witness to the first of what I'm sure will be many more generations to come."

I pale. Hell no. I'll leave that to Priest.

We all stand to our height, lifting my head to face the line of Fathers. All eight that are still alive. Right in the middle, dressed in a dashing Armani suit, with the strokes of our family skull painted over his face, is Dad. He broadens his smile when his eyes lock with mine, before he dips his head at my brother.

A thrill of euphoria blooms in my chest, and my chin lifts a little higher. I won't let him down—ever.

The Fathers part, exposing a copper barrel that's wide enough to fit us all inside. Latin is engraved at the front.

Carpe Noctem.

I shudder. That is clearly the place of—everything. Sometimes I wonder if we all should have just stayed at the Hamptons instead of coming back to the mother ground.

But no.

No, because there's no need for us to be there anymore, because they captured their swan and she turned into a crow.

"*Quod Ritualia* will begin with three steps. The first, the soul knot that will bind all six of you together." I hear a ruffle of approval from behind us and excitement ripples through my veins as the minutes pass on. I don't know if it's the tomb, or the five hundred or so people at our back, dressed in similar robes without the patterns down their sleeves, but all painted with the skull of their ancestry, or if it's that right beside Dad, is Aunty Saint, holding a brass bowl in her tiny hands.

Her silvery hair flows out from her robe, her Vitiosis skull a little distant to Brantley's. With a palette of white and gray, the corners of her eyes sparkle with two diamonds. I remember overhearing the talk of the Calvarias a few years ago before they were made, and it was her who helped inspire the idea. She suggested that they be forged by tracing only half of our traditional skull, and the other left uncovered, or as she put it, to display our humanity. Ironic since the lot of them have exactly none. I don't think that reference stuck.

I love our Calvaria, they only add depth to a century-long tradition. It kind of helps that we don't have to go through the painting process every time too.

When she steps directly in front of Priest, the air becomes dense.

"Recite after me. As I give you my blood, I submit my soul to tie with another, until the sixth is completed until forever."

Priest quotes the words back to her, taking the Hayes dagger as his fingers wrap around the bone of Humphrey Hayes. It's seen more death than the Reaper.

He squeezes blood into the bowl, finishing the final line.

Saint moves down, repeating the process until she's finally standing in front of me.

Plucking the dagger laid over the rim, I hold her stare, careful with my expressions. It doesn't matter what I try to hide, because if there's anyone who can see through me, it's her. Created from witchcraft and sunshine, Saint Vitiosis is from a line of light empyrean witches. It's a little terrifying. They started learning more about her linage after she had Vaden because they wanted to know if the gene could be passed down.

Spoiler alert. It can. Twice. With different crafts.

Needing to get this done as fast as possible, I press the sharp side of the blade against my palm and recite the old line. My skin splits as the wound opens, and I lift my hand to hover above the bowl as blood trickles into the broth.

After Stella, she circles back to where she started. I can't lie. This part doesn't necessarily excite me. Freaky fucking ancestors and their traditions.

"Drink." She hands the brass vessel to Priest, his head tilting back when he swallows.

A beat later, War repeats the process. Blood stains his lips when he turns to pass it to Vaden. My chest tightens when War's ocean eyes suck me into the undercurrents of their maelstrom. The room spins around me, but before I can completely lose myself in the abyss of his particular destruction, he breaks eye contact.

Vaden takes a long—and questionable drink—before it's my turn.

I hold it in my hands and stare down at the contents. I take a moment.

Please forgive me.

Moving the bowl to my lips, iron lubricates the base of my tongue, flowing down my throat like a glass of claret, only, unlike Vaden, there's flinching on my part.

My nose wrinkles as I pass the bowl down. Stella swallows without hesitation, the corner of her mouth turning up in a merciless smirk. *Menace.*

Dad steps forward once we're finished. "The first stage is complete. The second…" He pauses, resting on each of us before moving to the next. "You are to bring us the body of your first kill. Place their remains inside the grail of birth and death, where a bed of Carva will be scattered." Carva is a sacred herb which is only grown in Perdita, but for the most part it's a mystery. "Go."

Shifting around to follow orders, it's the first time we're able to take in the magnitude of our audience. It's no wonder the EKC have the name they do if this is how many people are connected to the ten Founding Families. It's surprising that we've not already taken over the world.

Following the line ahead toward the exit, I ignore the descriptive graphic sacrifices illustrated over the ground. When we near the end of a steep incline to the exit, I hit a wall. Vaden's wide frame blocks my view, so I bend to the side to find Priest motionless, looking directly ahead.

The hairs on the back of my neck rise when Priest deliberately angles his head to our left.

Painted with the Rebellis skull, each eye is drawn with four pointed ends to epitomize the other side to their family—the Kiznitch side from Midnight Mayhem.

Kyrin and Lilith, the two who make up the throuple with Uncle Eli. With Lilith's silver hair and Kyrin's brooding energy, they're hard to miss. But that's not why Priest stopped.

It's the girl standing closest to the aisle beside them. His head cocks to the side, as if studying a foreign animal.

"Priest!" The soles of my feet are aching already. The sooner we get this done the better. "Kind of want to get this shit done ASAP." He draws his attention from her, continuing to lead the way as if it didn't happen.

Before passing their row completely, my curiosity is insatiable. "It's been a while, Nala." The nickname we all called her growing up before Priest decided he found a better one to torment her with that includes her name and ends with 'tic'. It had been years since she disappeared, but once you'd met her, it was easy enough to spot her in any room.

Luna doesn't move but the corner of her skull-covered lip widens in a smile. "A lot to catch up on."

"See you soon?" The question comes out hastily as my feet patter to catch up to Vaden's long strides, leaving her answer behind.

"What was that about?" Stella asks from behind after finally catching up with Vaden. "Wait, was that Luna?"

Stella must stop walking because River growls, "Move."

"Yes!" Luna was a friend to all of us, even to Priest at one point. The term isn't what he would call her today.

We hit the top of the stairs and tread back through the entrance. Cool wind billows through the rustling trees before I inhale it into my lungs. "I just buried mine. He's going to be ripe. Gross."

"Gross. Even for me." Stella smiles wide, showcasing sharp fangs.

The boys are quiet as we pass the headstones of residents who have passed over the years, stopping when we hit the boundary made up of historic stonework.

All the blood leaves my face.

Shit.

They're going to see who I shot that night. What if they know the man he resembles? They'd connect the dots the same way I did. They'd surely know, since nothing passes the Kings. Which means they cannot see his face.

"This place is in serious need of an upgrade." River leaps over the edge first.

Landing with shock waves over the soles of my feet, I dust off my hands. Grass and overgrown weeds blanket the unmarked gravesites, except mine.

He's not going to be decomposed enough. Dammit.

Cursing my ancestors, I shuffle out of my robe and grab one of the shovels that are leaning against the boundary. Brushing my hair to the top of my head in a high pony, I unclip the robe and let it fall to the ground, exposing my clothes underneath.

"What the fuck are you doing?" War's tone has more bite than the cool breeze.

"I'm being practical, War. You should try it sometime." Forcing the spade into the bed of loose soil, I start shoveling fresh dirt.

"Oh, so practical, wearing ten-thousand-dollar shoes to dig up the corpse of your first victim."

"Shut up, War." He's clearly going for a new record of how many times he can piss me off in a twenty-four-hour period. Moments later, the boys have stripped their own robes and shirts, leaving them in nothing but their jeans.

Music and laughter reverberate in the distance. "Well, at least they're all having a rad time." River wipes the sweat from her forehead, her long blonde hair curling around her neck. She gives up and ties it to the top of her head.

"I wonder what the third step is." Vaden shovels into the next layer of dirt. Knowing that there are only three steps isn't exactly comforting when you consider this is the first.

"Honestly, could be a six-person orgy, for all we know," Stella teases.

"That would require a lot of incest!" I need to get this body out of this shitty little hole and pray to Lilith that he's decayed enough. Multiple holes in the head has to account for something in the anatomy of decomposition, right?

"So?" War's unrelenting mention of incest has my agitation multiplying. "You do know that incest wasn't a taboo thing between our families way back then. Wouldn't be surprised if we're all related somehow down the line, especially with all the secret baby drama from our grandparents."

"You mean, my grandparents." My spade hits something hard. "Yes!"

"How the fuck did you get to yours quickly?" Vaden glares up at me from the cavity of his grave.

"Because I panic-buried!"

Everyone pauses.

Priest is the first to break the silence. Of course. "Hold up. Let me see him."

My mouth falls open. "Ah… sure!" Terror wells in my stomach but I keep myself composed. "I need a break anyway." The barrier hits my back when I stumble backward, my skin sticky with sweat. How long does it take for a body to decompose? It's cold, but not winter. *Shit.*

I rush forward when he stops shoveling, blood cursing through my ears.

No! This is—

"I'm all for innovative slaughter, but this is… damn." Vaden's head tilts to the side, examining what's left of the body.

My eyes burn as relief washes through me. His forehead is a montage of brutal lacerations, not an inch of skin recognizable. The wounds are still flamed crimson, but instead of resembling the very reason why I killed him, he looks more like Freddy's brother.

"Now I'm mad." Priest's eyes fly up to mine, catching the final tremors leave my body.

"Ditto…" War swipes his hand over his abs. To fight my wandering eye, I jump back into my shallow grave.

"My turn." War tugs on Priest's collar and he shuffles out, leaving me to deal with the one person I don't want to right now.

Suddenly I'd prefer my brother in the small space.

He leans down and continues to tear open the bag the body is wrapped in. "Get out, Halen."

"What the fuck are you doing?" Dirt crumbles from the edges when I do just that. Get out.

Moments later, he stands to his full height after searching his body. "Why?"

My mouth opens, but nothing comes out because if I said I did it, they wouldn't believe me. I don't have the mindless rage that it takes to be able to carve someone up like you would a ham on Christmas Day.

"I have never seen face muscles before, okay!" Stella's hands are flying in the air. "I'm sorry, but I am who I am." They all hesitate, before War climbs out of the hole and shoulder barges past me.

Once everyone is back to their own corpses and the attention is off me, I mouth a silent thank-you to Stella.

She winks, casually going back to digging. I kind of want to know who she has down there.

An hour later, everyone has their bags filled with rotted corpses out of the graves. The girls go first and we prop ours against the concrete hedge, climbing to the top, before dragging it over as we jump to the other side. The boys make it look easy by throwing theirs over their shoulders as if they are a sack of potatoes. Theirs are considerably lighter than mine.

After our robes are secured back on, my sweaty palms slip on the handle of the bag as I start dragging it back to the tomb. Static prickles the nape of my neck when the penetrating gaze of the star-less night whistles over my spine.

With a rush of unease, I twist around, expecting the harsh glares of War, but I'm met with the watchful shadows of this god-forsaken cemetery instead. To be fair, a lot of the ghosts that haunt this place would hate me by association.

"Halen!" River calls out loudly from up ahead.

"I'm coming." I drag my eyes away from the dark forest, heading back inside the tomb. The air grows thick once again, but the music vaporizes rather quickly. Waiters duck around the crowds of people, balancing rock glasses filled with whiskey. With nothing but the sound of plastic chafing across concrete, we're back in formation on the platform.

Dad's eyes bounce over each of us. What could he possibly want with dead corpses?

"Phase two, which is important for the finale. Unzip your bags and place the remains in Noctem."

My knees hit the ground as I unzip the bag. Death has long since passed their bodies, but it does nothing to stop the smell of decayed liquid flesh and dusted bone marrow. I think I prefer theirs to the perfume of rotten eggs and rust.

With my bag now half open, the ambience of one thousand candles showcases Stella's expertise. Jesus. She really did a number on him. I need to stay focused. If I allow distractions to slip into my head, it allows a window of opportunity for one of them to ride in with it.

Dad's shoes come into view before he kneels to my eye level. "Mea…"

Everyone had already tossed theirs in Noctem and I was still staring back at the nightmare below.

My tongue sticks to the bridge of my mouth as I tremble on fragile legs. Dragging the bag up the bowl of metal while stepping around the side to use my foot as an anchor to haul him up, I pull back until it unfolds in. Unzipping the other half, his body rolls out of the plastic.

After tossing the bloody bag to the side, I stumble back to my place in line.

"Kneel." Dad's demand is as powerful as his energy, and we're all once again at his mercy.

He flicks a match against the metal before tossing it inside. "Recite the tale that's in front of you." I shuffle backward until the Latin passage is as clear as day. Sable and gray smoke clot the already swollen air, as death settles around the charcoal fragrance of rose and oud wood. The herbs. I've never—seen them—

The room becomes cloudy, and my eyes burn as the riddle leaves my tongue. "*Here I kneel, for you to take, accept my sins as payments, until my final date.*" Weighed down by the dense congestion of air, my chest caves in as everything tilts in threes.

What the fuck.

Delirium too thick to swallow, I'm suddenly weightless, before everything turns black.

Something heavy and long slaps my cheek with cadence. Cotton replaces my tongue as my eyes open to opaque movements and a throbbing head.

"Wake up, sleepyhead." Stella wiggles her finger above my face, her midnight hair tied to the top of her head.

Stella has the aesthetic of a demonic goddess. Even during

times when we should all look like shit. Like after fainting. "You were out even longer than I was."

Rolling to the side, I push up from the ground with my palms. I'm still trying to brush away the fog from whatever the hell *that* was, when the lingering smell of ash and lavender lulls me awake.

War sits on a slab of concrete, with Mom directly beside him. The buzz of a tattoo gun draws my attention when she dips it into the same copper bowl we all drank from and brings it to his chest.

Stella squeezes my hand. "Look!" She turns her head to the side, exposing the EKC insignia on the side of her neck. Stella has no tattoos, but as per usual, she goes to the extreme. Things like slicing up a man's face like she's Scissorhands and getting her first tattoo on her neck. The familiar shading of a city built on top of a skull. It's up to every generation what tattoos they decide on, but they all have to match. I don't remember what Dad's is since all three of them have so many tattoos they look like a walking sketchbook.

"Where are you putting yours?" We both head to where Mom is. I once heard that she worked in a tattoo shop in her younger days, after running away from Dad for the billionth time and trying to start a new life in New Zealand. Her art is a sugary glaze of destruction. It's still only her pieces that hang on the walls of the Castle.

"I don't know." I turn over my shoulder to find the concrete seats that were once filled with people, now empty. Our parents are chatting amongst each other with Pop and Nanna, and it's not until my eyes swoop back ahead of me when I notice Priest motionless on the ground.

A merciless web of protectiveness fractures my heart as my feet instinctively move toward him, but hands catch my arm.

"Leave him, *Amica*. He will come out when it's time." Dad's tone is gentle, the kind he only uses for me and Mom.

"What happened?" What if I said something I wasn't supposed to?

His weak smile isn't enough to bathe my fears. "I'm sorry, *Amica.*"

"Sorry for what?" I ask, but his back is already turned to me as he saunters back to Mom. "Sorry for what, Dad?" Everyone falls silent.

His arm laces around my mom's waist as he finally turns back to me. "For what may come."

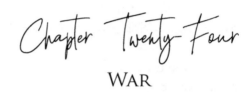

Chapter Twenty-Four

WAR

IT'S BEEN THREE HOURS SINCE WE'VE COME HOME FROM THE ritual, baring tattoos inked with the ash of our first kill. How fucking convenient for the boy Halen killed to be marked up so badly that none of us could recognize him in the off chance that we did.

The tumbler resting against my mouth swirls with whiskey as the endless glass walls circle the rotunda-style tower. Offering a full three-sixty view of Riverside, it's a watch tower, but no one is actually here to watch. It's more of a space away from everyone and everything except for the people in this room.

"You gonna move the tower over to your property?" I ask Priest as he lights the tip of his cigarette.

"Yeah, in a couple months." He blows out a billow of smoke. "Completion should be in a few weeks." Lucky bastard. Bishop and Madison have been building Priest's palace of nightmares since we were in high school. Vaden and I only just approved our plans last year.

It's not surprising that the tower will be moved to his property, considering it's burrowed in the mountains of the highest point in Riverside, behind the Castle.

Fitted out with opulence, a neoclassical-style bar centers the room and sets the overall vibe, beside a rustic industrially designed table that's paired with eight modernized velvet chairs. No rooms, but two king-sized beds on either side, and if that won't do it, there's a monster U-shaped sofa. You're up shit creek with the chesterfield if you miss out on the beds and sofa.

My mind keeps drifting back to the ritual. Bishop was older than Priest when he took the gavel, yet somehow, I know Priest is ready. Even if he isn't, he's going to have to be.

"Sit." Priest gestures to the chairs around the table after rounding the kitchen that's built into the back of the bar.

After Priest lowers to the head of the table, Halen sits to my right and Vaden falls opposite. River hooks her arm around Vaden as she lowers beside him and opposite Halen, as Stella connects to Halen's right.

"We can start with what you have been doing for the past five years. Any hidden skeletons that we need to bury?" Priest's gaze filters through the three of them.

The heat of Halen's tension burns as the tongue of flames lick the side of my face. Nah. We ain't doing that.

My chair scrapes against the marble floor when I push back a smidge, just enough to notice the cues when she's trying to hide some shit.

The muscle in her jaw bounces when I snicker around the hollow curve of my glass. The only woman walking this earth who is close enough to flip my detonate switch.

"We'll go first." Air hisses through my teeth when the liquor burns down my throat. "What you saw on Perdita wasn't the only time we were playing around. Pledges are for our enemies, but we also have recruits. They're who are offered from families who owe us favors, money, whatever, and can't pay up in time so they give us a kid—"

Vaden shuffles in his chair.

"Dark." Stella gazes off into the distance.

River glares at me. "A bit much, don't you think? Even I have damn boundaries."

I flip her off. River's said boundaries are why she and Vaden get on so damn well. I wonder what will happen if—*I mean, when*—that changes.

"What I was about to say before being interrupted, is that we eventually let them go. We set them up and fuck them off to another connected organization or order."

Priest's finger works his upper lip. "Sometimes. We *sometimes* set them free. This is a new thing after reaching a compromise. I don't give a shit about their lives, but War does, so we agreed that we'd eighty-six the parent who sent them in instead. How it unfolds, really just depends on, I don't know," his eyes darken, "my mood."

It's painfully obvious how quiet Halen is.

"What organization or orders?" Stella's head jerks back. "We don't fuck with anyone else."

"Midnight Mayhem." I cut her off without addressing her. "You're right, we don't fuck with any other societies or orders, but these young people are not one of us. They can go wherever, and since Midnight Mayhem have now split into four different countries to run four styles of… acts," I pause when the last word leaves my mouth because we all know they're anything but, "it's made it easier for us to distribute out the human payments. Again, we've only done this a few times now. It could change."

With the risk of triggering him, I push through Priest's earlier confession. "Or there are times when the recruits come from people who are connected to the world through a lesser family line, but want a closer title. They come to us as they are—" The bounce of my knee intensifies as I tap my Zippo against my thigh. "—and they leave us in a box, because none of us want a fucking groupie as a wife. Except maybe Aire. Pretty sure he'd hit."

Halen's eyes slant on mine as the Zippo snaps closed.

"You mean you groom them?" Her tone is as flat as the expression on her face.

I shrug, leaning back in my chair and kicking out my leg. My gaze flickers down to her wrist, before traveling back to her face. "Sure, if that's how you want to put it."

"Then what?" Stella pipes up, and if I know Stella, which I do, I'd say she is way too happy with this. "This is kind of... hot."

Vaden runs his hand through his hair. Stella stresses him right the fuck out. Unlike Priest, he has emotions. He shields them from most, but he has them. Not to be confused with soft, because he'd still take your head off.

He blows out a breath, his raven hair a mess and his cheeks pinched pink. "Stella. We don't bring home strays. They're for play, not to stay."

River leans back, resting her head against the top of her chair. "This is fucked up. Even for us."

Vaden continues. "As you may have noticed, Perdita isn't exactly as it was when our parents were around. The new Katsia has run the island for a few years now, and other than the odd rogue Lost Boy, there have been no other issues." I know what he's doing. Implying that we can step in and tear the crown from her head.

We shouldn't.

"Vaden's right. We could kick the bitch if we ever wanted to, but leaving Perdita to draw out its own infections has always been the best way to go. The island has a way of choosing its residents. We have to respect that."

Halen ignores me. "We all know Perdita is purgatory for everyone who passes through, and it has nothing to do with the island choosing. It's us who does."

"Maybe so," Priest murmurs. "But we ain't changing that right now. Whether you like it or not, this is how it's going to stay. She will stay." Priest's subtlety has never been his strong suit, and the smack he just landed on Halen to remind her to pull her head in where Katsia is concerned is proof of that.

Halen shrugs, not bothering to hide her cavalier. "You can have your toys. That's not what this is about." When Halen is annoyed, her tongue turns into a fucking weapon. I know her. Katsia isn't what bothers her.

My thumb grazes the curve of my bottom lip. "I can share them if you want."

"No thanks." She reaches for the glass in front of her, swirling liquid around the edge. "And you already know everything about what we've been doing. Parties, jumping city to city to get laid, racing, you know—" No one says a word as she pauses.

Her hand rests on her bracelet to adjust the chain. "—the usual. I'm tired. I'm going to head to bed." Without hesitation, she stands and makes her way to Priest, kissing him on the top of his head.

His jaw tenses but he lets it happen. He always does. In small doses, because she doesn't do it often.

She throws up deuces before the elevator closes on her.

There's no point censoring around the girls, so my eyes find Priest. "She's hiding something."

His finger beats a tune against the table, his metal ring clattering on contact. "Obvious. Knowing her, she's not going to come clean. Not until she wants to. And as we all know, if you pull, Halen doesn't pull back." His pupils dilate. "She cuts the fucking line."

He's right. I just don't know if he's reminding himself, or warning me.

"How's that gavel feel?" I change the subject. We're all fatigued, and right now if I think too much, I'll snap.

Shadows form beneath the hollow contours of his cheeks. "Like I've always had it."

"Okay, well, I'd love to chill all night, but I'm fucking tired." River claps her hands and scoops up the stray keys on the table.

The silence from them both was discernible tonight, until the elevator doors close around Stella's burst of laughter at something River says. The bond between the three of them would be terrifying, if we didn't know that it only meant they were always safe so long as they were together.

Before my wayward thoughts go rogue, my legs carry me to the floor-to-ceiling glass walls that flaunt the freckled lights of Riverside.

A single light flickers on from the Castle, stealing my attention. All it takes is one, when that one means so much.

With one hand on the glass, and the other holding the tumbler to my mouth, I follow the shadow of her silhouette. "Whatever she's hiding aside, there's something we didn't tell them either."

"The Hunt," Vaden agrees from somewhere behind me.

"We keeping it that way?" I ask them both, unable to move.

Priest's silence is the calm before the storm. "Halen is smart, logical. She's a lot like Dad, but she also hides a side that she refuses to allow people to see. She's been my sister all her life, so she has always felt as if she has to make up for what I lack. It's a guise. One I've always let her have."

My body turns rigid. Everything is spot on. I'd felt the thunder of her dark side over the years, but I was yet to taste its rain.

What makes people like her and Bishop incalculable, is that it's not their humanity that's a guise, it's the reason why they're lethal. A monster is still a monster, no matter how sharp its teeth are.

"Is that a yes, or no?" My finger taps against the glass wall. Moments later, her bedroom light is out.

Vaden's eyes burn the back of my head. "That's a no. I'm sure they'll find out sooner or later, so it can be later rather than sooner. And anyway, they'll be too busy with college."

"Yes, they will be, especially since I planted the idea in Mom's head about the old EKC frat house that hasn't been used for fifty or so years." I swallow the remainder of whiskey. "I'm sure that'll keep them all nice and busy."

My mouth curves, but I don't bother turning to face him. I can't take my eyes off her, even if she's not in the room. "Luna was there tonight."

"Hmmm. And that's been a while, hasn't it?" Vaden teases Priest from the same spot on the table. "What happened between the two of you all those years ago? You never talk about it."

I catch Priest's reflection in the window, but it's obvious he's going to ignore my question.

His body lowers down onto the same chair. "Halen?"

One of these days, that scale is going to tip inside of him. "Let me handle it."

The front door swings open before my feet have touched the marble steps. In a haze of beige and black, Halen rushes out in a designer hoodie and yoga pants.

"Where are you going?" The suspicion in my tone travels down the tight curves of her body, and before I can say another word, she moves to the side.

Her shoulder brushes mine, and instinct has my hand flying out to stop her. "You gonna tell me where you're going?"

Every time her eyes meet mine, she strips away the shadows of who I am. The parts of myself that I have hidden, because she's not ready to see the carnality of the creature that's been craving her since it felt the weight of her body in its lap.

"No. I'm not." She yanks her arm out of my grip. It's not until she's at the door of her GTR that her head curves over her shoulder. "Maybe I'm going to see a boy."

Jealousy coils in my gut but I bite it down with a snarl. "Yeah? What's his name? I just wanna talk…"

She clucks her tongue tauntingly before disappearing through the driver's side door, the loud RB engine purring into the darkness like a cat in heat. Circle backlights fade as she drives farther away, and my hand digs into my pocket to fish out my phone.

The photo staring back at me weaves memories like a connoisseur. Aspen. Would have been our junior year of high school and the first time back there since we were young. Boys in the back, girls sitting in the snow at the front, all holding our boards.

I tap on the locator app and the little green dot dances its way through the map of Riverside. The torching embers of the sunrise couldn't hide my grin as my tongue dampens my bottom lip and I lower down onto one of the steps.

"You going to bed soon?" The familiar tone of Bishop Vincent

Hayes slides over my shoulder as I lean back on an elbow and stretch my leg out.

His body fills the wide space when he settles on the step beside me. Not too close, but enough to be able to clip my jaw if I say some smart shit.

"May as well stay up now, since the day is almost here," I rasp through tense muscles. Fatigue weighs down my eyelids, but like fuck sleep is an option until she gets home.

Bishop chuckles, running his hand over his beard. I swear the motherfucker got better looking with age. "The weight of love can be trained to strengthen you, or it will be the anchor that drowns you."

"I'd prefer it be the hammer that kills it." Plucking the rolled joint from behind my ear, I bite on it and spark the tip. "Love is like cocaine. Easy to snort, hits fast, but then you realize it isn't worth it."

Bishop pauses, his narrowed gaze on the joint. "Jesus, you fuckers can at least pretend that we're your parents."

The smoke curls around my laughter. Neither of us want to touch on what the fuck he just said. "You and I both know you all lost that privilege the second we heard all the crazy shit you used to do."

"Fair." He stares off into the distance as I hand him the spliff.

His eyes narrow between it and me, before he finally takes it. Embers crackle when he inhales and the blister at the end burns. "Did you just compare my daughter to cocaine?"

And there it is. "Who said anything about your daughter?"

Smoke streams out of his nostrils when he turns to me. "You did. The second you were born. That aside, because clearly neither of you are ready for that conversation, you've been there for her more than her brother ever has. Not that it's Priest's fault, but what she needed from her brother as a young girl, she got from you. Don't get me wrong, he protected her when needed and where it counted, but that's not what we're talking about here." He passes it back and I blow on the dwindling end.

Dried herb crunches beneath the base of my thumb and forefinger. "I don't know. It got complicated."

Sorbet orange sweetens the bitter dusting of purple over the sky when he pauses a moment.

"It's not complicated, you're overcomplicating it. Just like your old man."

His words leave a trail of footprints in my mind, but instead of seeing where they lead, I stomp the fuckers out and ignore them.

The lull of hot exhaust fumes mixed with the spice of burning rubber on asphalt is more intoxicating than any liquor I've ever tasted.

Except her.

No one bothers to ask why Halen's throwing her fourteenth birthday out here. Apparently owning your own track isn't enough when your kink is destruction on the streets.

Cars line the parking lot of the cathedral in town square. The night is young, but people are already rowdy. I fucking hate being around people from school. The stress of constantly having to stop Priest from murdering students aside, I can't fucking stand any of them either.

Vaden pushes his body up the hood of my car, his lithe legs rippling over the edge as we watch the scene unfold in front of us.

"Why she gotta be this way?" Priest fixes on his twin. Candles on the GTR lettering cake that Evie is sashaying over to her illuminates the wide smile on her face. So carefree. Happy. Content. I could never ask for more than for her to be exactly the girl she is now. I fucking hope that never changes.

"Because she can." Vaden lifts his heavy-set shoulders, but he doesn't shift his gaze from her as Evie starts singing Happy Birthday. "Good thing we own this town. Imagine not being able to drive since you were ten because the law says so."

Fifty or so other drunken voices join Evie in the famous tune.

Halen glares at her best friend, and whiskey catches my throat when I choke on my laugh, with Vaden's hysterics following closely behind.

Priest shakes his head. "She'd fucking hate that."

"Torment." The word leaves behind a bitter aftertaste of images of me doing what I'd prefer to torment her with. None of it includes singing.

My phone lights up in my pocket, and Bishop's face flares over the screen. Tapping Vaden's shoulder with mine, Priest turns just in time as I take the call.

"What's up?"

"Halen's birthday?"

"Yep! You wanna talk to her?"

Silence. Anytime Bishop Vincent Hayes is silent, it's a bad sign. For one, his genius is working overtime and I already know that whatever he's about to say, I ain't gonna like it. "It's about the ritual. Are you all there?"

Priest and Vaden both move in closer, and I tap on the speaker button. We're far enough away that no one can hear, yet close enough to watch the girls.

The tone in his voice is tight, as if he struggled to say the words. "We've found some old translations of the possible events that could unfold during the ritual. It never happened with us, or with Hector's generation, so we're trying to figure out what it means and how a certain herb could be of importance."

A certain herb? Well, fuck. It better be ganja.

"You think it was true?" I stub the spliff out.

His hand brushes his beard once more, as if battling with the very thoughts that triggered the delay of the ritual to begin with. "What'd you see?"

"I wasn't out long enough to see shit. Or if I did, I don't remember."

Early morning sunrays capture the stress lines around Bishop's eyes. "You'd remember. That much Hector did know. I know you can't tell each other, but if you have suspicions, you should voice them." He shifts his gaze down to my phone. "You tracking her?"

My brow arches. "You surprised?"

"Not a single bit." He stands, patting my shoulder before disappearing behind me.

⟡

The heady bass of Tech N9ne stirs me from my sleep.

Fuck.

My legs swing off the bed as I roll to the side, pinching the corners of my eyes. Once I'm sure my body has caught up, I push off one of the beds in the playroom. It was another area for us to throw parties growing up, but when we were toddlers, it was an actual playroom. Six bunk beds constructed into the walls, all handcrafted into castles. The space was kitted out with all the best toys. I'm pretty sure we all slept here more times than we did at our own houses growing up, since we've always been one family.

We kept the name playroom, only now there's a pool table tucked in the darkest corner, and a wide industrial bar that's lined with electric blue LEDs. The main parterre garden is on the other side of the room, behind a glass wall. The room uses a lot of the space from the floor plan in the top levels, which is why it's so large.

Vaden makes it snow over the coffee table he's in front of, as Priest's shirtless frame saunters by, his hair in disarray and a bottle of bourbon clutched between his fingers.

It's fucking Monday and I slept away most of the day, including seeing what time she got home.

Tapping on the GPS app to see where she's at, my body relaxes when her location picks her up here.

A hundred-dollar bill lands on my lap. "You've slept long enough, Sleeping Beauty." Vaden leans back against his chair, the muscles in his arms rippling when he rests them on the top.

"You know, you're starting to lose your beloved title of the nice boy of the group, Vade." My hand finds my hair. That joint this morning knocked my ass right out since it's now six p.m. "I might need to check you all into rehab."

Priest eyes me closely as he drops onto one of the single sofas near the pool table. "You find her?"

"I know where she is." I tap the locator app on my phone.

The door closes behind me and the hairs on the back of my neck rise.

"*She* snuck out for a dick appointment—" Halen strolls past, snatching the rolled bill and glaring at me over her shoulder. "Stalker much?"

I flip her off. "Do I look like the kind to give a fuck?"

Her hair flows over her shoulder when she turns her back to me with an eye roll, and my eyes land on the curve of her ass.

My finger twitches, mirrored by the corner of my upper lip.

A sheer black bodysuit cradles every bend of her body, except the black g-string. Murder nonnegotiable if a motherfucker looked too close.

The note disappears up her nostril as the dust of snow vanishes.

Clearing one side, she swings around and lands on Vaden's lap.

Priest has always had a way of being able to hold an entire room without saying a single word.

The silent echo of his stare locks mine in place as Halen pops off on whatever bullshit she's going on about.

"So, I've discovered something seriously concerning." She pretends to play with her long, coffin-shaped nails. You have a sister like River, and you get a brother knowing what the fuck *coffin*-style nails are.

"What?" Priest's lip twitches.

"Well…" Her head angles to the side, regarding each of us evenly. "You see, it's very unfortunate that we're all kind of related. Except for War and I."

"And?" Vaden stares up at her through dark lashes. He curls a lock around his finger, regarding her with the kind of patience only Vaden has.

"And I don't find that very fun. Do you?" She shifts her body into Vaden, linking her arm behind his neck. "You may be our holy child, oh dear saved one, but even you have to want sex."

"Why would it matter?" My brows rise, saving Vaden from Halen's persistence. That's not hers to pry into, much less assume. It's easy enough to because he's a King.

"Well, since we have to consummate our coming into the Kingdom—officially—and it's Friday the thirteenth this Friday..." I look back down at my phone. Fuck. It is. "I've planned a little party."

My body turns to stone.

The corner of her mouth twitches when she notices my subtle reaction. "Not just for us girls... I got you all someone too."

Yeah. She's really going all out with the whole *I'm an official King now, suck my dick.*

"Halen, I don't want or need anyone on my dick," Priest snarls at her.

"First of all, ew!" Leaving Vaden's lap, she swipes the *Scream* mask beside him before stopping in front of her brother.

She slides it over his head. "What if I told you, dear brother, that I want to help you? That we could all do what we wanted, without one, our parents finding out, and two—" She pauses. "—without it implicating the EKC—" She leans in close, but because Priest is opposite me, I get a direct view of her from behind. And by the theatrical arch in her back, she knows it.

"—and without needing to go to Perdita."

For the second time since she's walked her ass into this room, she's done the impossible.

Left me fucking speechless.

"Elaborate." Nice ass aside, she's beginning to show the temperament of her brother.

Just how much does she know about Priest?

Halen dances around the three of us, humming a tune.

Grabbing at the collar of my shirt, I head for the bathroom that's nestled at the far end of the room.

"War, what do you say?" Her voice stops me. She knows what the fuck she's doing.

I'm the one who makes sure the train doesn't derail.

I'm the one without bloodlust, or the prickly halo of a fallen angel. My damage is different from theirs.

Mine makes sure that if I get my fill, I don't have to self-destruct.

The muscles on either side of my jaw bounce. "I think, that if you wanna make that mouth useful for something other than talking shit, you could just come slide it over my dick." I throw open the door and loosen my belt.

The spray of water hits my face a moment later, my palm finding the wall as I angle my head beneath the scolding temperature. Tension tightens its knots in the deepest crevices of my body as my hand finds my cock. Gliding my thumb over the head, frustration oozes from me with a growl.

I'm a lost cause.

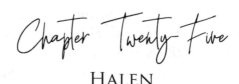

Chapter Twenty-Five

HALEN

MUSIC IS THE BINDING AGENT TO A DECAYING SOUL, and right now, there are many. All entrapped within sweaty bodies laden with alcohol and drugs. Some I don't know, others I'd seen, but most of them are who we're about to meet when we start college.

New paint glazes the halls of Riverside Elite University, suffocating the souls that cry for help. Beneath the glistening gold, it's the decay of hidden secrets that fossilized over the years. We'd been waiting on Stella for a couple years before enrolling, and in a few months, it was happening.

The glass rests against the swell of my lips as a girl I don't know grinds her ass into a shirtless guy wearing a Billy the Puppet mask.

When a shrill scream bathes through the music, I'm back on Billy the Puppet. She continues to dance around him, her nurse outfit glowing in the moonlight. Friday the thirteenth to us is just like Halloween, and we celebrate it every time. That means that every few months, we get our favorite holiday.

A date with the Devil.

"You should go rub up on that..." Stella's head jerks to where I'm looking. My eyebrow perches at the boy on the floor at her feet, along with the two at her back. Always busying herself with toys.

Stella isn't humble with her confidence. As soon as her feet touch the ground of whatever room she's in, people fall to their knees. As shallow as it sounds, her beauty is the first thing you notice about her.

The second being her eyes.

We would joke about what kind of man she would settle down with. He would need to have the hostility of her dad to put her in place, but enough swagger to terrorize her with.

"Hmmm…" The couple don't part, but the way the girl paws at Billy the Puppet makes it obvious who is thirstier for who. "I feel like I'd be doing her a favor. She wouldn't know what—"

"Halen…" Evie warns from between my legs. She peers up at me behind a flutter of lashes. "Be nice."

I raise my brows at my best friend. "Since when?"

Her head shakes side to side with a snort. "Keeping you in place in college is going to be fun." Evie's parents agreed to her starting with us. It allowed her to figure out her major, and decide what it is she wants to do going forward.

"I'm still annoyed that we have to attend at all." River's red bottoms flare against the tinted lights. I don't have to know her to know why she's hesitant to go. She's not as obvious as her brother, but the wildness of Nate is strong. She just doesn't show it. River's the girl who steals every moment. With her long, beachy-blonde hair and flair for anything remotely artistic, she's a force that takes whatever she wants, when she wants. The problem is, she never knows what she wants.

Or who.

"It'll be fun. Think of it as a new playground," Stella teases from the chair beside mine.

The two I'd been examining finally part. Her hand slips into his as she leads him toward the pool. Inflatable crows and sunbeds float around the mass of rowdy drunks, and achromic lights twinkle in the thick of Mom's garden and trees.

The alcohol raging through my blood has me wobbling my way through people, as my untamed hair brushes my tailbone with every step. With "Toxic" by RealestK playing through the speakers, it's obvious whose playlist we're listening to.

My feet stop at the edge of the pool, where Billy the Puppet and his friend are chatting. He's a foot taller than me, but that's not hard to be when you're five-foot-whatever.

He doesn't cower away in fear of who might be watching.

He doesn't show any hesitance because of who I am.

Instant turn-on.

My hands slide down his chest, bumping over the hard edges of his abs and stopping above his belt. Nurse aside, whoever the fuck she is, can wait. Because I need this more than her.

The mask is mediocre, not at all at my caliber, but whatever. I won't be able to see it when he's taking me from behind.

Then it hits me. Billy the fucking Puppet. A bubble of laughter lodges in my throat when I try to fight the irony of that, since my dad and uncles spent the better half of their high school life tormenting my mother and her friends with riddles.

The leather string around his neck connects to a sable-colored emblem, as my fingers trace the lines of it. "Want to play a game?"

Silence.

My hands trail back up his chest until they reach the bottom of his mask. My finger hooks beneath the plastic but he catches me by the wrist.

"Fine." The *F* falls from my tongue. "Keep it on. It's my thing anyway."

Snaking his other arm around the curve of my waist, heat waves pull me against him like a riptide, until my back hits his front and the cool touch of his mask grazes the nape of my neck.

But then it all stops.

The violent brush of a familiar flag sends a sizzle of *red* heat through my veins. Around a dance of recited flames, War's eyes are fixed solely on me. My breath catches when they move over my body the same way his hands do.

Death perfumes the air like any other party we have, only this time a girl is slumped over Priest's lap. A varnish of pale skin, she glows against the tongue of flames like a mannequin to admire. With two metal buckets on either side and slits that travel from her wrist to her elbow, it's clear that she's dead.

He's unhinged, no doubt, but Mom will appreciate the effort he took to keep any evidence off her grass.

Priest keeps her limp body on his lap, her head tucked into the crook of his neck and her legs slightly parted over his. Jesus. The only step above his already demented soul is exactly where I draw the line.

Necrophilia is a hard no.

Resting my hand over the stranger's, my eyes close as his knuckles skim my belly. Wrath blasts my skin as if I wore a bullseye on my chest, as my eyes peel open and land on a snarl so wicked it could make the Devil run.

He wanted to play games but forgot who he was playing with. He simply led with a pawn, where I always started with a queen. I didn't need the detachment of my brother, or the wicked finesse of War. I don't even need the virtuous charm of Vaden.

The thrill of every game pumped through my veins like DNA. I'd tear out my own heart and use its strings as teeth floss before I'd ever let him defeat me.

Checkmate.

The party dissolves around us as the seconds feel like minutes, neither of us breaking eye contact.

With a bubble of thrill, I lower the guy's hand and he finally dips beneath the band. My lips part, forming a perfect 'O' when fingers finally skim over the smoothness of skin.

Arching back into him, my eyes roll a little when his finger splits me open and wisp over my clit. With the hand that's on the barrel of his neck, I force his face to my shoulder. The pant expelling from beneath the mask would be desperate in other circumstances.

But queens and pawns…

His finger thrusts inside before lining the crease and anchoring on my clit. The length of his cock billows against my back when he shifts his hips forward. With both of us refusing to break, my knees weaken and the hand on my pussy tightens as the guy catches me when I almost fall, only aggravating the fire that continues to burn between War and I.

I break.

Curved in a pillow of rage, War's lips are the gates of hell, his tongue the Devil's shrine. Even with the vicious warning of his scowl, my teeth silence my pants by catching my lower lip.

The familiar sway of elation tightens around me—

War is off his chair in a flash, swallowing the distance between us like the beautiful monster that he is.

The music is suddenly too loud, the people too close, and a yelp bolts out of me as I shove the guy's hand out and duck behind a group of people. I needed to get out of here or at the very least put some safe distance between us. I may have moved my queen into the wrong row.

My hands fly out to move people when Vaden shifts from beneath the light, turning a girl who's in his arms. His tongue cleans the blood on the corner of his mouth.

Shock holds me in place. Vaden? No. There's no damn *way* I'm seeing what I'm seeing.

Maybe I'm drunk.

These parties had always been nightmarish. It's our version of Halloween, and everyone is too high on drugs and alcohol. Until we stopped coming.

Now, they'd hopefully have to be so fucked up that they don't question anything. Shit. I should probably call cleanup now before I forget. Whoever dies simply never existed. The Hayes Castle was their path to death.

"Unsainted" by Slipknot counteracts the adrenaline and alcohol as my shoe catches the wrong angle and I'm falling—until my back lands on something hard.

My smile widens when I spin back to my puppet, only to find rage glaring down at me from the most beautiful face to ever touch mankind.

His hand lands on my throat before I can say *fuck*, squeezing out what's left of the air in my lungs. He can push around all he wants, but fear doesn't exist here.

The cushion of his fingers bite into my flesh when he lifts me from the ground, forcing us closer. Even through the chaos of what's going on around us and the alcohol that's masking feelings I don't want to touch right now, it's the way the bruise of his attention feels days after I have it that leaves me hungry for me.

"We're gonna lay down some ground rules." His other hand moves with greed when it slips down the front of my skirt. "This is, and always has been, *mine*, and I don't share my fucking toys, much less the damaged ones."

He glides his thick, long fingers over the swell of my clit, rousing the sharp talons hidden in my heart to claw against my rib cage. My body shudders, and the whimper that leaves my mouth tastes a little too close to surrender.

His shoulder catches my forehead when I collapse against his weight. Sweat rolls off his hard, coiled muscles, drowning me with his scent.

I can claw out my heart later. Right now, I need him.

The sadistic cadence of his chuckle has my skin prickling. "You think I'm gonna get you off?" My feet hit the ground and his hand is out of my skirt in a flash. "Fuck no, Halen. You can sit on my lap for the rest of the night without a release, and if you're fucking lucky…" His movements threaten my space again, only this time I don't want it.

War is nothing like my brother or Vade. He's different in that he's intentionally vicious with what he wants. The other two will deprive themselves just to bathe in the suffering. War, I've begun to learn, is the one who likes *inflicting* the suffering. Not necessarily a fan of being on the receiving end of it.

A thickset band snaps around my throat before I can protest. Blood drains my face when my fingers skim leather and metal.

"You collared me!"

The party is in full swing, but without his body against mine, it suddenly feels too empty.

He answers me by tugging on the leash that's connected to the collar. I bury the heels of my shoes into the grass in a poor attempt to stop him, but with a facile pull, I tumble forward, reaching for the lead out of haste and dropping my glass in the process.

Nature billows her bitter fog at our feet as silent prayers leave my lips, begging that no one sees me in such a vulnerable state.

Moments later we're brushing past herds of basic Halloween costumes and coke dusted naked bodies until we're directly in front of the fire I admired him through not too long ago.

Chairs litter the wide space, curving around the copper pit in a horseshoe. The presence of my twin lingers, but before I can seek him out, War drops his weight back down to his chair… and me to my knees in front of him.

Before he can tug me further between his wide-spread legs, I push off the ground and stand to my height. Ignoring the amber shadows that accentuate his hard features, my fingers find his chin and I force him to look up at me. "I'm no lapdog."

Amusement clings to him like mortality, as if toying with his prey.

Fine.

Let's play.

A rogue blast of wind sweeps my long hair over the nape of my neck, and movement shifts in the corner of my eye. Right now, I don't care who it is. I see nothing but victory.

My hands land on his shoulders and he shuffles down an inch, tilting his face up at me. I lower my body down until I'm straddling his lap, knuckles skimming my outer thighs when his arms fall to the sides of his body.

"Well, fuck. If you're gonna stake your claim…"

There's a conceited type of security that comes from being a King, and a lot of it is that no one approaches you unless instructed to.

Times like tonight are one of those moments. And they have every reason to be, since Priest is parading his lifeless doll like a fucking trophy he won.

"You think I need to stake my claim on you?" The grin that kisses my mouth tastes like poison.

His gaze catches the movement. I hate that it looks fucking hot.

Warmth from the open flames caresses my back as he considers me a moment. "Are you saying that they all know I'm yours?" His tone is deep enough to bury every single emotion I'd ever felt when it came to him.

"Was there ever a time that you weren't?" The challenge is clear when our faces are an inch apart. Crippling heat singes the back of my throat when our lips brush, a daunting reminder of everything I've denied myself all these years.

With a sluggish tilt of his hips, the curl of his devilry touches the corner of my mouth. "Not even when I hated you."

His tongue swipes at my lips and that's all I need to swap out my queen to a damn pawn.

For now.

Our lips collide in a punishing pace of pent-up vengeance, and for this very moment, I'll take what's rightfully mine.

The Kingdom, and the boy. *Both mine.* Because I'm a greedy bitch, even if he's going to hate me when it's all said and done.

Chasing the surge of electricity that cackles between us, my hips flex forward as the material of his jeans rasp against my inner thighs.

His fingers knead into me as his tongue battles with mine. It's the first time we've outwardly claimed each other in front of everyone.

With a gentle stroke up the pillar of my spine, deceit takes over when he grips the back of my neck, forcing me deeper into the kiss.

Our teeth collide before he finally pulls back, his face one bad decision away from mine. "If you don't want me to fuck you in front of your brother and his dead toy, I'd run. Now."

"I don't run." We both know that neither of us are backing down.

A violent rush of dominance gnaws at my chest when he rests his hands my outer thighs, using them to draw me in closer before he lifts his hips into me.

Shit.

Hunger scathes over my body every second that there's clothes between us and in this moment, I don't care about the people behind me. Priest has had more than enough warning to find another place to pet his toy, and as far as the girls go, they're probably already occupied with their own. Rhythmic waves of Tupac's lyrical genius rasps through the air as my fingers find the side of his corded neck.

"If you think this is gonna go down as some cute little secretive sex show that no one knows is happening, you're wrong."

My hand finds the button of his jeans as I catch his bottom lip between my teeth. "You mistake me for one of your minions, oh wicked one." After I've worked his button, my hand slips beneath the waistband of his jeans, the greed in my movements obvious as my fingers close around his weight.

Wrapping the leash around his wrist, he gives it a tug and I fall forward, tightening my grip around his cock. A thread of rippling veins pillow the surface of his cock as the cushion of my thumb swipes the metal piercing.

Lost in the maze of his face, my hands itch to touch the hollow shadow of his cheek, until the corner of his lip arcs to a smirk. "You've got two seconds to climb on it before I bend you over Priest's toy."

Falling forward, I nestle my face into the crook of his neck. "But then you'd have to share me?" Warmth feathers my clit, igniting a firestorm of desire that burns roguishly through my veins.

My teeth catch the familiar scent of his flesh when I bury my cries into the crook of his neck.

"Do you want murder or dick?" His fingers bruise my hips

when he forces my weight down and I bite into his jaw to stop the scream from escaping. "Gonna be both in a second."

With an emptiness only he can exude, his pupils swell and the muscles on either side of his jaw bounce. He's mad. Good. He can stay mad. This isn't about him—it's about me. I need this.

With the purpose of not touching me clear as day, he spreads his palm over my lower back without messing with my pace while keeping the other to his side.

He leans back lazily, holding my eyes hostage.

This. Is. For. Me. Because if I start doing things for him, then I've already lost.

My hips mark their space with intention and a subtle growl vibrates from his chest as his cock disappears inside my body with slow yet hungry thrusts.

The battle of control between what he wants and what he needs continues by the torture of his restraint. That's where he and I are different. I can take what I want without needing anything.

He wants everything.

Burying my fingers into the side of his neck, I taste the edge of his lips.

His body tenses. So close to pushing him over the edge.

With the weight of vengeance between us, my grip around his cock tightens and my body convulses when he pulses inside of me.

My own restraint wavers when I drive my hips up, allowing the metal of his piercing to carve his name into the walls of my pussy.

A whimper claws its way up my throat as my body convulses around him and suddenly, I don't want us to be in public.

His mouth catches my cries, sucking my bottom lip into his by the curve of his tongue. "Yeah, fuck, I'm done." Using the weight of his arms to hold me in place, his body swallows mine as his hips drive into me with lazy thrusts.

Finally.

Flames spread over my skin as if sweating gasoline, and the back of my eyes prickle when the varnish of his body slaps against mine.

The steel square of his Zippo catches my attention as he slips a familiar ring over his finger.

His eyes land on mine and I pause mid-ride. All the boys have one, gifted down from the Fathers.

"Still wanna play a game, Halo?" A flame burns between us. "What about now?" The WM etched into the metal glows a brilliant shade of orange. With time lost around us and the ache in my body persistent for no one but him, I'm pretty sure I'd do anything right now.

His tongue dampens his lip. "Come here."

The simplicity of his command ravages through my body and lures me to his mouth. Our kisses spin a web of dominance and power, and the more I allow his pierced tongue to lick mine, the faster my heart pounds.

Refusing to release each other, he presses his palm against my lower back with a growl that sounds more animal and less human.

Grabbing at the corded muscles in his neck, the angry tip of his cock teases me to the edge of insanity. "I can't—I can't. Can we go?"

With the release of our lips, his attention is back on his ring, burning the initials once more. The hunger for my release is relentless, even when the hand that's holding the ring slowly disappears between us.

Knotting my fingers together at the back of his neck, I peer up at him from damp lashes as his intention becomes clear the closer he gets.

The flesh of my pussy sizzles with blinding pain as his other hand slams against my mouth to muffle my cries. His fingers mark my hips as the weeping swelter of my fresh wound lingers.

His pace picks up as he drives his cock into me with a rare kind of carnality that I never knew existed. Even with tears pricking my eyes, it does nothing to calm the crazed obsession to have him fuck me until it hurts.

And it hurts already.

"Give it. To me." His hand lands on the back of my neck, forcing my attention.

"I—" My lips brush his. "—want it to hurt."

He groans.

A trigger only he can reach is flipped when the weight of my surrender slides over his cock. Watching him come undone shouldn't make me feel the way it does. Like his fist buried in my chest and not knowing if he's there to mend, or tear me apart.

It's the way sin stains cheekbones that are clearly carved by gods.

It's that single moment of vulnerability when he pants through lips so supple, they melt against mine.

Or more obvious, the way his eyes darken in an attempt to hide the very monster I just brought to its knees.

Violent tremors of my orgasm rip through me as the evidence of every dirty secret between us drips down my thighs.

His thumb circles my clit as the remnants of my rapture forge my body forward and I collapse against his chest.

When my whimpers fall into his mouth around the teasing of my tongue, his teeth snap at my bottom lip.

"Fuck," he gasps into the kiss he doesn't finish as his cock throbs against me.

Music lulls us back to the party, and if the thought of anyone so much as seeing him didn't make my hand reach for my nine, my knees would hit grass to clean him up.

His chest catches my sudden fatigue as I collapse into him.

"I still win." The bubble of laughter floating up my throat bursts his answer.

"Who said we're done?"

Maybe it's through the delirium of my comedown, but I don't care who saw. Not even Priest. The only thought that orbits my brain right now is that I kind of want to do it again.

Does he like inflicting pain? Is that it? Has he always been this way? And why did the thought of me giving him what he wants fuel me enough to go another round?

Our bodies peel away from each other's, and not even the wave of heat that throbs over the branding is enough to replace the torment weighing in my gut from the mere distance between us. After tonight, it didn't matter. None of this mattered.

We would play.

We'd fuck.

Then we'd hurt.

I'm beginning to read the poems sewn into the literature of his carefully crafted lies.

Shuffling my skirt over my ass, my pelvic floor tightens so he doesn't drip down my thighs.

I fail.

Leaving his belt buckle undone, he plucks a rolled blunt from the table beside him and leans to the side.

"Should we worry where everyone is?" Brushing my fingers through the front of my hair, it flows down one side when I tap on River's name in my contacts.

"Nope."

The smoke that was once in his lungs now clouds my vision, as my fingers find the joint he's holding.

With ganja in one hand and my phone that's calling River in the other, he's dragging me back down onto his lap with the curl of his arm around my waist.

I hit the end button. "They've probably all run away."

Heavy smoke fills my lungs as War catches my chin with his hand, forcing my lips down to his. As soon as our lips touch and I release billows of smoke into what's beginning to feel like a familiar place, the flash of a camera snaps.

Fucking Stella.

The anchor of my arm that curls around his neck holds me in place, since my feet dangle so far off the ground. Monster.

His thumb taps at my chin with passive strokes as he holds my stare. The unspoken pull between us nothing but an invisible barrier.

It might be a good thing that I have tunnel vision when we're like this, because I can't imagine the scowl on Priest's face right now. I'm praying he does whatever he does with his conquests and leaves me be.

Shadows draw around his face and it's the first time since I stupidly allowed him to collar me that unease crawls up my spine.

My movements stop, eyes narrowed on his. "What are you doing?"

Call me paranoid, but I know who this man is to the very core of his being.

A dark brow lifts, but even beneath the ambience of dim lighting, the pleasure he's attempting to hide leaves a dusting of color over his cheeks. "You fucked me for assertion. Last I checked, I didn't it. So tell me. What do you think I fuck for?" The conceit that laces his tone when the final word falls from his mouth has my leg swinging over his lap.

Both his hands land on my hips, forcing me still. "Where the fuck do you think you're going?" This time the hardness of his body has nothing to do with the iron he lifts.

"To finally fuck someone who *wants* to fuck me." My hand hadn't even hit his chest to push him away when he catches me by the chin and forces my face down until it's just him and I and the tension that seems to constantly bathe between us.

"Don't do that," he hisses, his tone above a whisper.

"Do what?" Our lips skim.

Both lost in a marinade of confusion, neither of us can take our eyes off the other, even in this close a distance. "You think I forgot that just moments before you were bouncing on my dick, you had another's hand down your skirt?"

His mouth twitches when his eyes land on someone behind me.

Asshole. Fucking asshole.

I bounce off his lap as fast as I got on it, ignoring the leash that dangles between my breasts.

With a blunt nudge of his head, War whistles at whoever it is that has been watching for however long. "Don't act like you're scared now."

Following War's line of sight, Billy the Puppet stands in the direct path of it when he lands beside me.

Vaden chokes on his laugh as he kicks out his chair. "You two about fucking done?" I'm guessing everyone is back. You don't see one without the others.

War's eyes bounce between Billy the Puppet and I, ignoring our best friend.

What the fuck is he doing?

"Touch her inner thigh." He pauses, pinning Billy the Puppet with a glare that's borderline deranged. "And *only* her inner thigh."

"Jesus, War!" River's annoyance with her brother isn't needed, but relief floods through me when I notice they're all back. Pointedly ignoring Priest.

Billy the Puppet shadows behind me when he moves, clearly following instructions.

War palms the leash that hangs between us, resting his forearms on his thighs. "Touch her."

"What are you doing?" It leaves my mouth as a whisper when I try to swallow around the coarseness of my throat. His scent still clings to me. The poison of his hungry kisses and the demand of his possessive touch running rampant through my blood.

The boy lowers himself to his knees. When a palm feathers my ankle, my heart fractures in my chest and leaves splinters of betrayal stuck in my throat. *You motherfucking cunt.*

With Seether's "Fake It" playing, I know what I have to do.

His palm moves farther up the inside of my leg. I hate it. Where War's hands are calloused, scarred from murder and pain, his are soft and sheltered.

Standing to his full height and positioned slightly behind my body, he stops at the top of my thigh, probably pushing it a little high, to be honest, but he stops.

The tip of his finger leaves a subtle warning, grazing the crease to where my pussy meets my thigh.

"You get it?" War antagonizes with cold possessiveness. "If you come near her again…" The glimmer in his eyes shouldn't look as menacing as it does right now. His mouth widens, exposing the full set of his white teeth. "I'll cut your fucking head off and feed it to my pet pig."

A finger slips between the fold and my breath catches. If I make one movement or inclination that this guy just did the one thing that would guarantee him sitting on my brother's other lap, it'll be messy. They won't even bother to hide their rage. They'll kill him on the spot and then we'll have a party of witnesses. Too many to pay off, kill, or intimidate.

Just as fast as his fingers arrived, they're gone.

War leans back in his chair. "Put that same finger in your mouth."

I glare at War. "You're a piece of shit."

"What?" He doesn't move his focus from Billy, but then his eyes land on mine and the rage that tightens between us tugs at my chest. "You were gonna anyway. Did you not just threaten to fuck him again? On my lap? After coming all over *my* dick?"

Ah. So this is what this is about.

"Steady…" The subtle warning from Priest would usually raise my hackles, but all I see is War.

Now I want blood.

Billy moves, lifting his hand to where the hole in the mouth of his mask is. My jaw seizes when his finger disappears, along with my emotionally charged turmoil.

I will not cry from anger or cause a scene. I will just kill him. Yes, I will. Murder. Murder is the answer. Aunty Tillie always says that.

The reverberation of War's snicker almost matches the baseline of the current song playing.

"Tsk, tsk, Malum. You lit a fire I'm not sure you'll be able to put out..." Stella teases from somewhere near Priest.

War ignores her, his attention solely back on his target. "You taste that?"

The guy doesn't answer.

Fingernails bite the palm of my hands, leaving clefts of crescent moons.

He drives his intention home. "That's the taste of who the fuck she belongs to."

The resistance against War is obvious when he disappears from my view. It's admirable but stupid. It's not what should bother me that does. It's that he's implied to everyone that I'm yet another girl he plays with.

"I'm glad I'll never date a King." River's eyes roll, shifting her legs that are slung over the side of her chair.

"I hate you." Humiliation strangles the words as my eyes prick with unshed tears.

Asshole. It wasn't enough. *It will never be enough for him.*

"We know." His stare holds me in place. "And if you keep it up, Priest's trophy will have a mate."

"Why do you care?" I've never been a yeller, but my arms fly out to my sides and the anger surging through me has no other outlet. I can't let him have the last say.

A gentle tug on the leash that's connected to my collar. "I don't."

"Liar!" The whisper leaves behind a residue of ash from my charred voice box.

With one hand tight on the leash, he reaches over to the side with his other, swiping the bottle of liquor. He draws my body close before our fingers weave together. I want to pull away.

I want to fucking punch him. Still might.

But for now, I follow his lead through the sea of people. War and I haven't had much of a friendship in recent years, but there was one thing that has been constant, and that was how safe I felt around him. It didn't matter that he was a bad person, or that he had even done anything bad to me.

I loved him. That may have changed after the public humiliation tonight.

Beneath the turmoil of tonight, I can't hide the way my skin continues to burn and how fast my heart beats. *Why the fuck do I like it?*

If love is freshly plucked flowers on a Sunday morning and being told how lovely I am, then I don't want it. I wasn't made to be handled with care. To me, love is the wilted flowers from last month when most would call them less desirable. It's being craved to the point of insanity, and the only way to feed the primitive nature of his hunger, is by giving him one simple thing.

You.

His six-foot-four frame towers over almost every guy here, his wide shoulders stretching under his hoodie.

The longer our fingers are laced, the heavier the weight I feel over my chest. Shit. This feels a lot like *I fucked up.*

I follow his lead, through the playroom and to the elevator in the corner. It's giving Little Red Riding Hood if she was in love with the Wolf.

His palm lands on the elevator button and obsidian doors open.

"Where are we going?" I bend to look up at him but the mirrored walls surrounding us sway beneath my feet. My hand flies out to keep me steady. "I'm not joking, War. I hate you. That part was too far."

His chuckle rolls down my spine. "What was? The part where I'm—" The weight of his body forces me against the mirrored wall, as the warmth of his lips trace the line of my cheekbone, stopping at the corner of my mouth. "—not gonna worship the ground you walk on, because I know that the legs doing the walking, would much rather be spread open and fucked?" All the air leaves my lungs. He did not just say that. "Hmm? That part?"

He nips at where his lips rested against mine, using his palm to push off the wall. In the absence of his vehemence, I draw in a deep breath. The doors split open, allowing music to replace the vicious energy of his words.

Frozen in place, panic replaces all else when I realize he's taken me down to the basement that was reconstructed to a showroom-style garage. Using the entire space from the foundation of the Castle, this is where every car is kept until our houses are built.

Using the first ever EKC private jet as the center piece of the setting, ivory lighting outlines the collection of cars that surround the satin black Learjet 23. People dance around them, almost swiping the paneling of Priest's McLaren. Anxiety knocks me off my feet when I think of any of these idiots damaging War's LaFerrari, Vaden's Hennessey, or any of Priest's collection of JDM cars, since they're here until his monster of a garage is built.

Whose damn idea was it to allow this party to expand to down here? I can feel my anger wavering as the alcohol leaves my body. The fist of sobriety pounds against my head, hammering me back down to earth.

I hate him for real this time. I don't care how horny he makes me. Regardless of how I'm following his steps as he leads me through the open space, or that my fingers are back to being intertwined with his.

"War. We need to talk." My chest collides with his back when he stops walking. Clearly, one of War's past conquests have found him out and about.

He releases my fingers, and that crippling anger is back because, *excuse* the fuck out of me.

Stepping around his mountain of a body, my mouth opens to cuss out whoever the fuck is on the other side, when I pause. Forget cussing, I'll just straight swing.

"Katsia?" My arms cross in front of myself. For her own safety. "A little far away from Perdita, isn't it?"

Her brows hit her hairline in surprise, her stare bouncing between us. She settles back on him. "Anyway, I need you."

"Busy—" He moves her out of the way with his arm, and we hadn't taken two steps before her next words stop him.

"I *need* you, War…"

My chest hits his once more and I raise my arms around a loud huff, my annoyance obvious. What the fuck is he doing?

His head turns over his shoulder lazily, whacking a stray skull balloon that floats up between us and glaring at her over my head. Both muscles on each side of his jaw tense. "Fuck."

He pushes me out of the way with that same arm he did to her, knocking my balance.

I follow his movements as he grabs her by her arm. "If you walk away from me right now, I'm fucking done with you and these games!" With blatant neglect, he ignores my words. They step into the elevator and right before the doors close, Katsia angles her head over her shoulder with a swift smile, shifting her copper hair over her skinny shoulder.

The humiliation of tonight weighs heavy, keeping my feet cemented in the spot. I can't fucking believe he just did that.

My hand finds the latch of the collar around my neck. I force it off, before stumbling to where his blacked-out RX4 is parked. Guards flare over the cambered wheels, as I plant my ass on the hood, swiping up a stray bottle that's sitting on the ground.

My fingers tangle through my hair, moving the mass of waves over to the side. My eyes wander before my mind does. Groups recording videos, dancing, and yelling. A big part of me hates that they extended the area to somewhere so sacred like the garage, but another part of me—the bigger part right now—wants one thing.

Revenge.

War so publicly used me like I'm one of his lapdogs that fawn over him. No. I've clearly misread the situation for too long. My mistake. I won't waver off track again.

"Penny for your thoughts?" A deep voice startles me from my heat of rage.

I jerk up to see Billy the Puppet watching me with eager eyes.

My head tilts. "No pennies here. Just hundred-dollar bills."

He chuckles, closing the distance between us while burying his hands in his pockets. Tailored slacks hang off his hips, leaving his chest bare. He saddles up against the wall directly opposite, flashing a rolled bill.

"Like this?"

My eyes bounce between his. "Maybe."

He kicks off the wall and draws closer, until his boots hit mine. My eyes slant.

His finger strokes the barrel as the silence between us stretches wide. I find myself tracing the lines of his lips through the hole.

The curve of my smirk is wicked when I reach out to stop a passing girl. If he's going to touch me again, it's going to be on my terms. Since War snatched all the power by using this guy, it's only fair I take it back the same way.

She spins, a scowl on her face until she sees it's me. Her eyes flare to life. "Oh, hey, Halen."

"Hey!" *Whatever your name is.* "Can you do me a favor?"

Her brown eyes brighten as she lowers her red Solo cup to the floor. "Of course! Anything!"

I hand her my phone after swiping to video. "Record until I say stop."

She looks between my hand and my face, slowly plucking it from my fingers. "O—okay."

My elbows catch my weight on the hood of War's RX4, keeping my focus on the boy in front of me. "Take your next line off any part of my body." Angling my head to the side, I bat my lashes up at where he stands while curling my tongue over the base of my thumb and sucking it into my mouth. I dip the same one into the bag of coke that hangs from between his fingers before sliding it between his lips.

I clean the residue off with my mouth. "Please?"

He pauses a moment. "You sure your bodyguard isn't gonna tear my head off? Apparently, he has a pig."

My finger finds the waist of his jeans. "By pig, he means himself. And anyway—" I trace the familiar colors of his eyes. "Are you sure *you* care?"

His laughter is about as sarcastic as expected. "Um… yeah, kind of. Not to stunt on my own game, but getting on the bad side of one of the Kings isn't really on my list of things to do before I die."

"You touched me…" A gentle whisper that's loud enough to be heard on the video as the girl draws close. "Now you can get as much of it as you want without hiding behind my skirt."

My lip twitches as my eyes flick toward the camera for a second before returning.

My legs part. "Your finger doesn't have to be the only thing that knows what my pussy feels like."

Hands move up my thighs until my skirt is pooled at my waist.

The metal of the hood cools my back as I spread for him. Powder scatters over the fresh branding of my skin as I find the camera lens. The sound of him snorting the line has my hips tilting up to his face as his tongue replaces the drug when he laps up the residue.

I lift a single brow in challenge, glaring through the lens as if it wore the skin of evil himself.

Billy moves the mask enough to do what he needs without exposing his entire face, but it doesn't matter. I won't need him long enough.

One lick.

Two.

"Okay, get off." The heel of my foot lands on his shoulder and he stumbles back.

I reach for my phone with a smile, harnessing my inner Evie. Evie's lack of appearance to these things is always obvious, but she's never far. "Thanks."

The girl shuffles nervously. "Aren't you worried I'm going to tell everyone, or that people around us saw?"

I cut the video slightly so that it doesn't show me kicking him off, before hitting *post*. "Nope. I'm counting on it."

After covering myself for the last time tonight, I pause on the rubble of man on the floor. "Bas. I'd be careful where you step going forward."

With one knee drawing up to his chest, he rests an arm over the top.

I draw home the seriousness of my words by pinning him with a pointed glare. "Not even my grandfather would be able to save you if they found out it was you."

Tonight can go fuck itself. All I want is my best friend, my bed, and food.

With a pounding head of dread and a crippling weight of fatigue, I drag myself back through the party with the direction of my bedroom in mind.

My feet hit the main foyer and I find myself fixed on the family photos and portraits that scatter the walls leading up the staircase.

My blood turns cold when I land on one of Tillie, Nate, War, and River.

I rest against the rail, kicking off my shoes while lifting the bottle to my lips. If I'm going to bed, I'll go shit-faced. Before I can stop myself, my finger traces the glass. I remember this trip like it was yesterday. I would have been nine or ten. It was around the time I *thought* I had a simple crush on my brother's best friend. Turns out it wasn't a crush. It was a fucking stampede of bad choices, and there was no stopping it once it started.

"*Amica*, go to bed." Dad's voice travels down from the top of the stairs.

I point to him with the hand holding the bottle. "He's worse than Uncle Nate, isn't he?"

His palm rests over his abs as his eyes shift to the photo. "He's who he is, *Amica*. You can accept it or leave it. Come on."

I stagger my way up the steps. *Leave it*. The lie hovers in my head for a nanosecond.

Dad catches my body when I skip a step, a gentle growl vibrating off him. "Baby girl. Bed."

I pat him gently over the tattoo on his chest in passing. "I don't think I can."

As soon as my bedroom door swings open, my muscles ease. She's here. Of course she is.

"Girl…" Evie's working moisturizer over her face, already buttoned up in satin pajamas with two burgers in the space that separates us. I don't have to look at my bedside table to know that she would have already put Advil and water there. "Your drunk posting tonight may just go down in history."

"It was to my close friends list." I roll my eyes, pulling back the fluffy cotton sheets.

Evie glares at me, pausing her skincare. She's left her hair out in soft waves that flow down the curve of her back. "You are not getting into bed without washing away your sins." She lifts a single curved brow. "Shower. Now. And no, I'm not helping you."

The bottle slips from my fingers when I belly flop onto the mattress. "I hate him."

"Yeah, well, maybe give your vagina the memo because it seemed to miss it."

I push to roll onto my back, but the room spins around me. "Turn off the lights."

"Go to sleep."

"It hurts…"

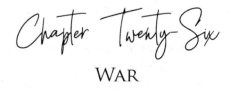

WAR

THE DOOR TO THE ROLLS ROYCE SLAMMING CLOSED echoes through the eerily silent street. Perdita isn't exactly bright lights and laughter, but it's never like this. The destruction of whatever has happened tonight is visible in the details.

Katsia's door closes on the other side of the car as I trace the road of Main Street. "What the fuck is going on?" Splintered shop glass windows, nests of fires, and the outline of half a dozen bodies scattered around the town, facedown in their own blood.

"They came in quick." She turns her whole body to me. "But you know us. We're quicker."

"The bodies?" Perdita was supposed to be a safe place for our people. If they're here, they were and always have been under our protection. The fact that someone has fucked with that is big. If we lose people here, it makes us look weak. They'll want retribution. I'll make sure they get it.

"Not ours. We lost a couple, but the Lost Boys fought them off and killed many." She gestures out to the road. "Clearly. Sorry about dragging you here. I didn't mean to… interrupt whatever was happening."

My jaw tenses. "It's literally your responsibility to do what you did. Don't fucking apologize. Forget all that."

I hate that she and I have history, and I especially hate that it's not the kind I'd usually have…

"Do you think our mothers will

ever get on?" *Katsia asks as we both make our way down to the docks. No one knows where the fuck the old Katsia found this one. She was island born. That was all that mattered. That was their business and we stayed out of it—until we didn't.*

"We're thirteen. I think if they were going to, they would have by now. I think it's safe to say that their hateful friendship isn't going anywhere." *I don't bother to tell her that it most definitely has to do with my mom. I'm also pretty sure my fucking dad had double dipped.*

Katsia's leather boots hit the wooden dock, her red sundress dancing through the wind.

She turns over her shoulder, her green eyes resting on mine. "Wanna go burn some time?"

Katsia and I had grown up around each other over the years, as did the other boys, but she and I were… well… a little different. She sprawls her hand out to me, her eyes flashing with rebellion. "Come on… I can almost guarantee you'll like it."

"Because you forget that easily?" It's not that I fuck around with a lot of people, but the ones I do, all know that I give nothing but my dick. If they start showing signs of wanting even a smidge more from me, I'm out.

Katsia and I were each other's firsts. We were thirteen. *Doesn't matter that we continued for years after.* She never asked shit, never expected shit, and more importantly, I thought she didn't feel shit. The first time I noticed her flinch was when a Lost Boy's sister was on my lap.

Well, shit. That was over a year ago. Had I made an exception without even realizing?

I ignore her. "They only took out two of ours?"

She sighs, folding her arms around her waist. She never gave up those damn sundresses. A complete contrast to the girls we hang with. Halen would shoot you before she'd allow you to put a dress like this one on her. It's long and flows down to mid-calf. The material around her chest is tight, making her tits spill over the seams.

Priest has had his share of toxicity, and shit, I've had mine.

Unfortunately, mine are always holding a pair of tits and a bad attitude, where his are always leaving a trail of bodies behind. Vaden's golden boy status should be classified as one on its own.

"Young soldiers. Good kids. Kind of reminded me of us at one point. But they did that before they were gunned down." Her finger points to four statues that tower over the gardens of Perdita, each of them carved to represent the Founding Kings. That's not what catches me off guard, it's the four bodies strung up and hanging by their feet from each sculpture.

Poetic. Typical.

"I hate to say it, but we did create them…"

I ignore her rambling and pop the trunk, lifting the hidden compartment to reveal the array of weapons. Semis, knives, grenades, whatever the fuck we might need offhand.

I pluck out the military knife and Desert Eagle.

Katsia glances down at the equipment with unease.

The wall she keeps up to hide all the emotions she condenses slips. She must feel my gaze on her because just as quickly as it fell, it's back up.

"Time to change your taste in men?"

She bristles. "God no. I have my ways of doing things and you have yours, Malum."

The trunk slams closed. "Just like the old days."

She smiles but it doesn't reach her eyes. Since Halen and I have been fucking around, I've ignored Katsia. It wasn't purposeful, but I can't be fucked with the girl drama. Not that I owed Katsia an explanation to my ghosting, but even bad habits die hard. It just so happens that she's been one of mine for a fucking long time.

"You stay here. Get in the car."

Her brow lifts. "Um, just because I don't want to use guns to pull this island back together, doesn't mean I'm a child, War." Her shoulder taps mine when she passes me.

We pass store after store, where bodies lay sprawled over the pavement. I pause a moment at a chocolatier shop with cursive writing on a sign that reads *sugar and blood*. The lights flicker inside, illuminating red stains over the glass display. A Lost Boy lays lifeless on the floor with a gaping hole in his forehead. Gary and his wife own this place. There's no doubt in my mind that they would have shot anyone who they deemed a threat, but I'm glad there was a Lost Boy here to help anyway. Even with the cost of his life.

Perdita has a particular scent that I haven't smelled anywhere else. I could never put my finger on it. It was the perfume of pine and something sweet like floral. I now know that the unfamiliar note is the herb we drank at the ritual.

Flames from the small pockets of fire release embers through the silence. There's not a single sound except for the crunching of my boots over the loose gravel.

The deeper we walk down Main, the worse it gets. It's like a damn bomb site.

"Tell me everything." The sensitivity of my vigilance doesn't waver, as my head swivels from left to right. The rest of the Kings would have no doubt heard by now, as much as I tried to ignore it.

Ignore *her* coming here. I don't even want to allow my mind to wander to Halen. I may have pushed her away a little too hard tonight. Let's just hope I don't end up with a matching bullet in my head like that Lost Boy.

The soles of her shoes clap against the cobblestone the farther we move through the street. We're only a couple hundred meters from the end, where her mansion is.

Moments later, we reach the high-wire fence that's slightly ajar and unprotected. I've never seen this place left unprotected before.

"I was down at the docks. A shipment was due to go out, but I got a notification from an unknown number that I had to be there to retrieve it. When I got down there, men piled out of a black jet boat and started shooting."

"They all missed you?" I gesture to the front of us. "And why is the house unprotected?"

"Because the Lost Boys wanted them to think it was. Easier

to clip them off one by one." I follow her line of sight to one of the corners of the roof, where a barrel looks down at us.

She shoves the gate open. "And thankfully, yes. You know me, War. I run."

I do know her. And she does run... too well.

I don't bother raising my gun. If anyone's gonna shoot me, it better be a fucking kill shot because mine sure as fuck will be.

Three bodies lay sprawled out on the driveway, but music plays in the distance. "You leave a radio on?"

She shakes her head. "No. But there was a party happening when it started."

"Do I even need to ask what kind?" My boots slosh through the puddles of blood and brain matter when I climb the steps that lead to the front door. "Have you checked them?"

The empty foyer displays nothing but the diamond chandelier that hangs above.

"Yep. Nothing on them that we could see. No ink, no ID. Nothing."

Glass stairs lead up to the second and third floors, but I turn a sharp right to follow the music. Columns line the path down the wide hallway, before we reach the twin doors directly at the end that lead into her office.

My palm lands on the wood as I push it open, the music now even louder than it was before.

The step is careful, but I haven't even lowered my heel when something flies out from the side. I turn just in time, catching his gun that's coming for my temple and whacking it out of his hand.

I grip him around the throat and force him back against the bookshelf, squeezing so hard I feel his organs splinter beneath my palm.

"Yeah? So much for your fucking security, Katsia!" The venom in my words are for her and she knows it.

"I don't know how he got in!" The panic in her tone releases some of my annoyance with her. For now.

"Maybe you're not as hot as you think you are, and your seductress ways are a little rusty?" I tease, keeping the intruder close. It's a lie. Katsia emanates erotic, feminine energy. Even when she's naked, there's a softness about her. She doesn't like to kill, which is not only why she has the Lost Boys, but is how she chooses to use them. She could seduce her way into any motherfucker. We'd even caught Priest eyeing her once. He'd never, but you could see he admired it. It isn't just about her appearance, nah. It is more than that. It is her to her core. It usually only comes from a blood Stuprum. Old Katsia clearly trained her well.

"Actually, he was captured and left for you."

The color in his face drains, his eyes widening. "You're—" He stops abruptly. Probably smart.

He doesn't look like a Baker. Not a Gentleman, not that it would be them, but we still have to consider our biggest threat. Fuck.

Shuffling rustles in the background and I don't bother to turn and see what Katsia is doing. She's not weak. She can handle her own; it's just that she loves when people do it for her.

"Who the fuck sent you here?" He's young. Has to be younger than us, which would otherwise make me think he's a Lost Boy, had we not known all thirty-five of them.

When he doesn't answer, the barrel of my gun slides between his lips as I force it to the back of his throat. "Who the fuck are you here for? If you don't talk, I'll be happy to make you…"

His green eyes harden on mine.

"Okay then." Using the strands of his hair, I drag him back to the office desk in the middle of the room and toss him into the chair.

The brief moment that I glance up at Katsia, I catch her naked body disappearing into the steam of her Luxor bath. I don't question her need to bathe right now or why she has to do it *right now*, because I already know.

It's already started.

"I think they've all left, War. Or are dead. He's the last one here. Their mission failed," she singsongs smoothly.

"Good."

The doors of her room open and two Lost Boys stammer inside, bloodstained suits and gashes on their faces. The boy sees this as a way to leave, but I grab him by the back of the collar to force him down onto the chair without taking my eyes away from the Lost Boys.

Their bodies bend when they bow to Katsia, as she releases the clip that's keeping her long, copper hair tied. With a trail down her slender back, the ends skim the water, following the waves her body creates as she moves to the other side.

She lifts her attention up to the boys.

"*What is our current body count?*" Her tongue's flawless when it wraps around the dead language.

They both nod, but nervously so.

The first one is the bravest. "*Four. We found one other floating near the docks, and a second one not far from him.*"

She ponders for a moment, before curling her finger at the boys. "Come here." I take that as my cue to continue.

I squeeze his cheek by the grip around his chin. "Talk. Now."

His lips tighten closed.

"Or not." I aim my gun and squeeze the trigger. *Pop!* The ripple of his screams tear through the sound of the bullet, as his hand squeezes the wound on his thigh.

I kneel to his eye level. "Just between us girls, I could do this all night. I know one hundred fifty-seven ways to kill a man without *actually killing* a man. So…" Standing to my full height, I grab the poker stick near the fireplace and go back to Mr. Chatty.

Ignoring the rage of memories that come with it, I flip open my Zippo and let the flame heat the end. "We're going to play a game. It's called, how many times can you be shot, healed, and then re-shot, before your limbs sever off?" A wide smirk stretches over my face when he looks between me and the stick.

As soon as the point glows hot, I slowly place it over his wound with a resounding crackle of skin melting together. His screams are loud enough to draw blood, only agitating my annoyance. I didn't want to be here. I was supposed to be fucking the stupid out of a certain pet.

"FYI, if this part here isn't hot enough…" I flick it with my finger. "It makes it worse."

My fingers unclip the holster, finding the handle of the knife. "I need a name. An organization…" Silver catches the bright light that hangs from the center of the room.

He spits to the ground, glaring up at me with a snarl. It's obvious he's not going to help.

The sharp point of my knife finds the top of his shirt, as I cut a perfect line down the middle until his chest is bare.

Inkless. That's different. I don't think I know one person who doesn't have a single tattoo, but then in our world, sometimes they're a bad thing. If he had a black tie displayed as a knife, it would be the Gentlemen. Then there are things like their clothing. If it were any pastel colors of blue and pink, they'd be Bakers. The fuckers who have been antagonizing us since we came back to Riverside and drove them out. But Bakers are brainless. A rogue operation run by young twits who are too drugged out to make good choices. They come, we take, and repeat. They never learn their lesson. If they have *any* style of thorns tattooed on them, whether it be a single vine, or one that covers your whole back, well… it's probably too late for you.

I rest the knife against his manubrium, right where it dips between his collarbones. "Number four on my list of how to kill someone without killing them…" My head tilts. "Ever heard of jacketing?" The more he doesn't answer, the faster my heart beats.

Blood pools around the end of my knife as I apply just enough pressure. How that must feel, to be cut right there…

His groan is throaty and desperate, so I press the blade in. "I can take it as slow as I want. Name. Now." Baring straight teeth, saliva sprays from his mouth as the veins in his neck swell.

"You've got balls, I'll give you that." I direct the blade down even farther until his skin splits open, exposing the chalk of flesh beneath. This is child's play. Painful, sure. Kill you? Naw.

Of course, unless you get a nasty infection, then well…

The more time that passes, the more impatient I get. Usually Vaden handles this, since he's the more patient one out of us, but not tonight. I need to get as much as I can out of him, and then kill him before Halen is anywhere near breathing Perdita's air.

Don't know why the fuck I give a fuck, but I do. I always will. It's not about the why. It's about the since *when*.

Truthfully, that extends to all the girls.

My hand pauses as I stop. He knows I'm going to kill him anyway, so he'd rather go down without talking.

Two hours pass.

Three hours.

Four.

Sunlight splits through the windows behind us when I finally toss the knife toward Katsia. He ain't gonna talk, and now he's unconscious with blood dribbling from his mouth.

My fingertip slips beneath the outer layer of skin, pulling it away like you would pork skin.

He doesn't move.

"Did you kill him?" Katsia calls from the bath.

"No. He'll stay alive for a while like this, while simultaneously wishing he would just die. This is drying him out. Make him think about who the fuck he's working with and whether or not it's worth dying for."

I stammer backward, turning just in time to catch Katsia sliding up to the edge of the tub while massaging one of the Lost Boy's heads.

Her legs part as she swoops up a glass of champagne. She must have popped one open sometime between my focusing on the piece of shit in front of me and fighting fatigue.

Blood streaks through my hair after running my hand through it for the hundredth time tonight. Fuck I'm tired. The throbbing of my muscles is one thing, but the burn of my eyes is another. I can barely keep them open, and the more I sit here with nothing to do, the more I replay the party from last night. She fucked me in more ways than one, and now I don't know what the fuck that's going to mean going forward. I'd always known she was too important to start anything with. Shit, I wouldn't be surprised if there was something between us before either of us even knew the other existed. Which was exactly when we were in our mothers' wombs.

Or maybe it's just an obsession.

Katsia's sipping from her flute as the Lost Boy moves closer, until his face is between her legs. "I need it, War. I hate that I need it, but I need—" Her breath catches when he takes her, and the ache in my muscles eases as my head rests against the wall.

Unshed tears glisten over her eyes but she keeps them on mine. It'd usually be me there. She and I had an interchangeable situation. We both gave as much as we got—and we knew what the other needed.

She'd yield, allowing me to do as I please.

And I'd fuck the nightmares out of her.

I know what she's doing now. The way her chest rises and falls and her eyes remain on mine.

She wants it to be me. It never will be again.

The Lost Boy's tongue slips over the opening of her pussy. "War... keep hurting him. Please."

I know what she needs, and I'm well experienced to be the person to give her the release she craves, but I can't be the one doing it anymore. It's not even about Halen, or whatever bullshit we've unconsciously started, but the thought of touching, or so much as putting my dick inside anyone's tight gap that isn't hers, just seems—pointless.

Boring.

Games and torment aside, I only have interest in her. I don't need to tell her that. She knows. She's seen how I am with her and how I am with others.

Except last night happened and she probably thinks I put her in the same category. Which are thoughts that I would have fucked out of her, right after reminding her that not a single fucking girl walking this earth has ever been publicly claimed by me in the way she was last night. But I didn't need to claim her more than she thought she needed to claim me, because there's never been a moment in her life where she wasn't mine. And fuck. There's never been a time in my life where I wasn't hers.

But none of that mattered because she and I would never work.

Katsia's fat tits rise and fall as she sucks in deep breaths. There's no denying Katsia is a sex beast. Not only that, but she's as fucked up as I am in bed. No one wants to cross her, and it has nothing to do with murder.

I grip the back collar of my shirt, tossing it into the corner of the room after wiping the blood from my hands. It's humid as fuck in this room from the steam of the bath. Now it smells like a murder spa with the heady scent of metal fusing with soap.

"I need to go make a call." My hand is in my pocket to fish out my phone, and I haven't even taken two steps toward the doors when they swing open.

Halen's body fills the space, with the rest of the Kings behind her.

"Well... why am I not surprised by this?" Her green eyes slither to Katsia. Fuck the guy bleeding out behind the desk, nah, Halen only cares who I've had my cock inside while she hasn't been here.

This. This is why we could never work because we'd tear each other apart—and possibly our families too. We put the EKC first. Above all. There has never been a King with a King—that we know of. Halen and I would be the first.

Beginning to think there's a reason for that.

My hands are on Priest and Vaden, dragging them back out the door by their arms. "I don't have time for drama, Halen."

"It's not drama, War!" she yells at my back, but I ignore her. The doors close her into the office, but River and Stella stay behind.

"For a minute, and I mean just a fucking *minute*, War..." River glares, her high-heeled foot tapping against the floor. "Can you not be a complete fucking asshole to her? And I get that you have this whole twisted history with that crazed bitch in there, but Halen is—"

"Um, no? I won't—" River steps up to me, her chest to my stomach.

My head shifts to the side as laughter bubbles out from between my lips. Before she gets comfortable, I pin her with the kind of coldness that I've never used on her before. "—baby sis. This is cute, but back the fuck up. Think about it, Riv." I take a menacing step into her space, but she holds her own. "If you think that girl doesn't need to be loved by toxicity and poison, then you may not know her at all. She may not be a coldhearted killer like the rest of us, but she has her own demons, and they all have to do with the way she needs to be loved *and* fucked. So back. The fuck. Up."

River's anger dissipates the more she blinks, her eyes finally widening with understanding. She knows I'm right. They all do. Regardless of how I love Halen, the fact is that I do. The only way I know how to love, just so happens to be the only way she craves it.

The girl is fucking mine. Period.

My attention is back on Priest as if that didn't just happen. We don't have time for the theatrics of who's on whose dick. Someone just shot up our island. "I don't know anything right now. Katsia came to find me—"

Priest clears his throat.

I pause.

When he doesn't say anything further, my shoulder rests against the wall and I arch a brow. "Got something to add?" I should have known he would. Considering we haven't exactly had the time to talk about the party.

His pupils swallow the color of his eyes. "You're my family, War. The only people I ever gave a fuck about are in this room, our families included. At any other time, sure—" The glow of his teeth is blinding against his tanned skin. "—I'd threaten that if you continue to fuck with my sister, I'd break your face. But we both know that what you said was true. And anyway, I know she can handle herself, but I will say this. Don't be using that bitch to get to her. Katsia and all the fucking ones before her have a long line of fucking with the Malum men. Now, continue with what the fuck you were saying."

I don't bother to address any of his shit. He knows about Katsia already. I don't need to repeat myself.

I continue. "There were bodies everywhere. As I'm sure you saw. Katsia had one held captive in her office, waiting for me to interrogate."

His eyes don't move from mine. "I don't suppose you raged out and killed him, did you?"

My mouth opens a little. "Not exactly."

"Gentlemen?" Vaden's question comes out from gritted teeth. The beef between the two families tracks back further than him, but he's a loyal fucker.

The need to put him out of his misery outweighs the tension emanating from Priest. "Nah, as resourceful as they are, this wasn't them. Why would they, it makes no sense to hit Perdita. They'd just rip Riverside apart."

Vaden's eyes darken. "They could try."

"They'd start a war..." I look between both him and Priest. "It lacks the finesse of their style to be them."

Stella sighs.

We all turn, my arms crossing in front of myself. "Spit it out, Stells."

"Well, I don't know... why would Katsia have one held

captive and he didn't run? Was the door unlocked? Was he locked in? Was he bound? How have you not asked these questions?"

We all fall silent.

Priest's heavy strides eat the space between us and the office. He shoves the doors open and my stomach hits the floor. Empty. Everyone is gone.

My heart thrashes against my ribs. *What the fuck?*

I trip on my feet as I stumble backward.

"Well, fuck!" Stella waves out to the setting in front of her. "What did I say?"

Chapter Twenty-Seven

HALEN

THE WORST PART ABOUT HAVING AN EMPIRE LIKE THE Elite Kings, is the enemies that come from it. You can't have a kingdom without villains.

I tap on the three numbers on my phone and press it to my ear. It rings three times before someone picks up.

"Did you find him?"

The tears that roll down my cheeks shouldn't be there. They should be dried up by now. "We're driving to the helipad. Someone needs to meet me there." The groans from the back seat become louder, but I ignore them.

"They tried to take Perdita!" My mouth slams closed before I allow my emotions to control me. "It doesn't matter. I have this idiot in the back."

Silence. "That wasn't supposed to happen. What do you mean they tried to take it?"

I drop it down into second. "You think? And I mean as in they shot up the entire fucking place. Of course, we came out on top, but they *tried to take it down*." The leather of the steering wheel complains when my grip tightens.

"The chopper will be there in a few minutes." I hang up the call and direct the car down the first right turn that leads up Mount Esther, the highest point on Perdita.

"Should I thank you for saving me?" How Deacon can ask anything through his panting is beyond me. He coughs loudly, swiping his mouth with the back of his hand.

Trees zip past as the road swirls up higher in elevation. When the wired gate appears, I press on the accelerator to crash through it, skidding to a stop outside the helipad.

The driver's door swings open, and I reach inside the clove for my Glock, checking the chamber. Helicopter blades cut through the air above, and I slam the door closed before moving to the back.

He blinks between me and the gun in my hand, while clutching his stomach. "Do it. I know you've wanted to for a long time, Halen. It'll fix everything, wouldn't it?"

I grind my teeth. "Everything but *that*. And if I kill you now and leave you here, they'll examine you and realize who you are. If I kill you and put you on the chopper, I'll have too much explaining to do."

His chuckle turns into a fit of coughs as blood spills down his chest. "I guess that could be a problem. For you."

I take his hand with mine, shoving my gun into the back of my jeans. "Get up."

"Aw. Come on. You gotta love me just a little."

Hitching his arm over my shoulders, I kick the door closed and ignore him. The loud rotors of the chopper paddles through the air as the wind knocks us both around. The helicopter hadn't quite landed when a voice calls out from behind me.

"I'll cover you. Make something up so they don't panic," Katsia calls and the hatred I have for her wavers. I haven't always hated her.

No. Just since I found out that she became important to War and vice versa.

I keep my back to her, dragging Deacon up the ramp as someone on the other side catches him. Headlights bounce off the trees below and anxiety prickles around my heart.

I quickly slide inside the lavish leather, with one last glance at Katsia before the door slams closed behind me. We lift off the ground with a sideways sweep, and I move Deacon over a smidge to sit beside him, peeking out the side window at Perdita down below. My throat swells when I swallow. All the emotions I had prepared myself to feel for years suddenly overwhelm me. It doesn't matter how much I try to fight it.

Darkness fills the space around a flashing blue light in the middle of the cockpit.

The girl moves forward, tapping the light between us. When it clears, I come face-to-face with teal hair. "Are you new?"

I rest my head against the window, ignoring her.

The heavy breathing.

His hot body.

The sweat.

Pain.

My eyes close as white noise buzzes behind my ears. I refuse to allow any weakness to leak down my cheek, but then I feel the familiar images scratch from inside my brain.

"Do you know who I am?" the girl asks, but I turn to the bleeding idiot beside me.

Shuffling out of my coat, I rest it to the side of his chin where a droplet of blood has dried. "I don't care who you are. I know why we're here and there's no point with small talk."

She snorts. "She's funny..."

I ignore her. She's not very anything. But it's not her fault.

"Hey!" My palm rests on Deacon's cheek, but it's met with the cool nearness of death. Frustration has me grinding my teeth. "Hey!" I slap him gently and he mumbles back to life.

His green eyes stir, blinking past the clunks of dried blood on his long lashes. The lump in my throat swells the more I stare at him.

"Little Hayes. The perfect one. *The chosen one.*"

I sigh, my chest falling as I expel the leftover oxygen in my lungs. "The wrong one."

Past
Halen 14 years old

I jiggled my leg as I kept my eyes on the entrance of the chapel. War was taking ages. *Bet he was doing his pretty hair.* Or maybe asking God to forgive him for all the sins he had already committed.

Maybe asking for an STD cure.

I rolled my eyes and threw myself off the bench, my Doc Martens hitting the dust with a thud. I swiped my hand down my ripped jeans as my eyes locked on the statues outside the chapel. They looked bigger today. All of them towered over, shading me from the sunlight. Dad had said they were moving them to the chapel on Perdita, that they didn't want people to ask questions, or worse, google the names carved into the stone.

I stopped in front of my great-great-whatever's one. Humphrey Hector Hayes. I'd heard a lot about him. More so recently than before. How he killed all the girl babies to build an army against a system that was fitted out for civilians to fail. Apparently, it was what inspired our generations-long secret society. It was a society where only the blood of one of the ten founding members could exist in, and one you only ever left in a box. There were no initiations. If you were in the Elite Kings Club, you were in by blood and birth. No options. If you tried to walk, well...

Sometimes it felt more like a cult. Without all the... I don't know... cult-ish things that people do. Like worship gods and—

Wait.

I swallowed around the lump in my throat. We were not a cult. *I knew for sure.*

"You know, he wasn't all that bad." I heard Pop's voice from behind me and a wide-toothed smile spread over my mouth. It was the first time in a long time that I'd felt my fingers prickle with glee.

I quickly dashed forward, my arms locking around the back

of his neck when he dropped to catch me. Pop always smelled of aftershave and cigars. I loved it. He was my safe space.

He swirled me up in the air, catching me before gently placing me back to the ground. I loved Pop so much. I knew he was a bad man and he'd done really, really bad things, but recently, I'd realized that, well, he could be worse.

He could be *very* worse.

Even when he was busy running the country for two success-ful presidencies, he made time for me. He wasn't a bad man. I—

I blinked back the sting in my eyes.

"How's my favorite girl?" He twirled my hair around his finger and traced my cheek. "Staying out of trouble, I hope?"

"Never..." I smiled so wide I was sure my cheeks cracked. I didn't have to force it around Pop. He made me warm and fuzzy. Same as Dad.

He chuckled. "I expect no less, my little hell-raiser."

He stood to his full height. "Who are you here with?"

"The boys, of course. War's new R32 comes off the boat today from Japan. The asshole wants to rub it in that he got one before me."

He kissed the top of my head. "Well, now. We can't have that, can we?"

His eyes flew over my head, stopping himself before he could say anything else, and I turned to see Lisa, our nanny.

My mouth closed. What was she doing here?

"Can I have a word, Hector?"

His head tilted as his hands dove into his suit pockets. It was weird. I'd never seen Lisa need to speak with Pop. Oh my fucking God. I hoped he wasn't cheating on Nan again.

Ew. I'd snitch for sure.

Pop nodded, ruffling my hair playfully before making his way to her. I watched as her mouth turned to a frown and her brows knitted to the middle. Something was wrong—and just like that—

My blood turned cold.

She was telling him.

Now

"You're thinking back, aren't you?" the girl asks. If we didn't land soon, I was about to jump. Deacon has long since fallen asleep, or died, and the moments that pass now are numbered. Numbered because I have a choice to make. Would I continue as if I don't know everything that there is to know about what the fuck is happening here, or do I kick this bitch back into her place and remind her exactly who I am? But then, who is she… How is she of importance? She has to be someone, because you can't be a no one and be here.

"Actually, no. I'm thinking about my grandfather and someo—" I study her closely. Her long, sea-green hair and brilliant blue eyes. The only time I get a glimpse of her features is when the light above us flickers on.

I leave it there. I shouldn't talk. I know better.

Deacon groans again. Good. He's not dead. If he does ever die, I'd prefer it to be me who's holding the opposite side of the knife. Since he is the idiot who almost ruined everything.

"None of us remember our grandfathers. You're not one of us," she whispers sadly.

My back rests against the chair. I need to focus. It isn't supposed to go down this way. There is a method to the madness that we need to follow, but somewhere down the line, something happened, and now we're here. With Deacon almost dead, Katsia putting on the show of her life, and the most important people in the world to me none the wiser. I know Katsia will feed them some bullshit line about how I'll be back and that I'm not in danger. She is good at that. Lying. Almost as good as I am.

The chopper landing jerks me from my nap. I must have only been out no more than half an hour, but it was all I needed. The whirling of the engines dies as I rub the sleep from my eyes.

When I turn to Deacon, I notice his wounds first. Thread has now closed the long cut down the middle of his chest. I don't look up at the girl as she packs her kit away, afraid that if I do, I'll get too close.

Maybe she's also a nurse.

My fist lands on Deacon's arm with force I know will bruise. "Get up."

"Ouch!" he whines, his palm resting where I hit. "Everything fucking hurts. Could you not?"

The doors fly open, and my eyes sting from the sun. A couple of shadows stand in front of us, and I shade my head to block the rays.

"You made it."

The grumpy mumbles of every cuss word known to mankind don't go unnoticed as my arm hooks Deacon's. "Just. And by the way, he almost didn't. Since you thought it would be a great idea to drop him in the middle of a shoot-out."

One of the shadows steps forward. "We didn't know what was happening on Perdita when we did that, my little hellhound."

Breathing out a sigh, I help Deacon to his feet while ignoring the girl who is opposite. "Well, it's fine. Katsia is handling the boys, so I'm sure they'll be too busy trying to figure out who this idiot is, and hopefully think he's with, well, them." I don't want to touch on the way I felt when I saw Deacon slumped in that chair in Katsia's office. Even if she was working on trying to wake him in a panic as soon as I had entered. I hate that I felt it. I felt his pain as if it were my own. The crippling fear that he was dead tore my spine out of my back and had me almost losing consciousness.

Stupid fuck.

I direct Deacon down the steps, the metal ramp complaining beneath our weight. "I hate you. I hope you know that. I should kill you for almost getting killed, Deacon."

"I love you too." With his eyes closed, the hint of a grin on the corner of his mouth shows more life in him than I've seen since finding him that way.

As soon as my feet touch the grass, I inhale the scent of burning herbs and freshly cut grass. The building that's almost complete sits near the cliff. Inspired by neoclassical architecture, it demands to be seen as soon as you set foot on the tarmac. There's a rotunda beehive that peaks up to the sky in the middle, with stained glass windows and garden beds growing from the ceilings. It's not finished yet, but it's close. It has been years since it was started.

"Who's all here?" Deacon collapses all his weight in my arms. This time I let him fall to the ground with a thud. I glare down at him. "You truly are so unimpressive. Seriously. Pull your shit together."

He clutches his stomach, his brilliant green eyes blinking up to the sky. "Well shit, I'm sorry if your psycho little boyfriend got off on torturing me."

"War got him?" Pop breezes up from behind, the corner of his mouth curving up in a smile as he shakes his head. "You're lucky you're alive. And she's right. Pull your shit together. You're making us all look bad."

The girl from the chopper stumbles behind, trying to catch up. "Wait… who are you?"

I don't bother addressing her. She may be important, which she clearly is or she wouldn't be here, but she's not worth the shit on my shoe right now. Especially since Deacon is fucking bleeding on my Jimmys. It's refreshing when people don't know your name after being raised in a world where everyone knows exactly who you are before you've even laid eyes on them.

"Halen Hayes." Deacon chokes on his laugh when he notices how much I'm trying to stay away from her. One of the men dressed in a military-style uniform lowers himself down to help him.

I clean my shoe with the back of his jeans, my eyes lifting to the girl beside me as Pop follows Deacon.

"What's your name?" My shoulders straighten when I stand at my full height.

Nervous tics aren't something I am familiar with, unless you count Priest's hobby, War's obsession, and Vaden's purity.

"Salem." With two fishtail braids over her slender shoulders, her makeup is flawless, but that aside, she carries herself with the kind of confidence that is made from mishandling.

We make our way down the path that leads to the building. I don't bother filling the silence with empty words or chatter. That's not my style, but I get the feeling it isn't hers either.

I pause at the entrance, scanning the lines of maple trees with thick, black leaves and trunks. The wind breezes through my hair and leaves a dusting of shivers down my spine.

This should be something I'm happy about.

But betrayal tastes bitter no matter how it's swallowed.

I clear my throat. "Furniture?"

One of the men helping Deacon takes the space beside me, cleaning the blood from his arm with a bandana. I peer up at him through tired eyes.

"All there. The harbor is through the forest to the back. It gives you direct control from *there* to here." I don't have to ask what he means by there.

"Kinder…" His name falls from my lips the same way it did all those weeks ago, when we were on Perdita. The sun sneaks through the clouds above, displaying the brilliant gold flecks in his mossy green eyes. "You've done well. You should be proud."

He remains stoic, offering nothing at all. "As you know, we are not familiar with the feeling." The pause he takes is long. "It is my honor. Your uncle Daemon meant a great deal to me."

"I'm sorry for your loss all those years ago. He was before my time, so I didn't know him." Priest inherited his middle name from him. If the stories about my mom's twin brother are true, which I know they are, I'm thinking the uncle-nephew apple may not have fallen far.

I touch the side of his arm, squeezing the tight muscle. "And you'll get used to the feeling."

We all will.

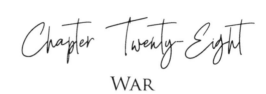

Chapter Twenty-Eight

WAR

SKIN SPLITS FROM BENEATH MY PALM AND BLOOD STAINS my hands the tighter I squeeze. I've killed many times. All the fucking time. It's as easy as breathing for all of us, and to some, like breathing down the neck of a Victoria's Secret model. I can count how many times I've killed in a blaze of rage.

None. None at fucking all.

The lifeless body slips from my hand and onto the ground. The scene in front of me is pure chaos. Not just a blaze of rage, but the whole fucking fire. White noise screams through my ears as my feet catch and I almost fall.

The scream of people running for their lives finally replaces the toneless tune, as my foot lands on a faceless corpse. Bodily fluids swell around the sole of my combat boot as I fish out the packet of cigarettes from my back pocket.

My teeth catch the trunk with a hiss, as I light the end with my Zippo. The glimmering metal of my ring reflects off the orange flames, igniting that same hunger for her that I've craved even more since that night.

I need to shut it all out. This. Her. Me.

The spillage of mountains hides in the distance, as more gunfire resounds around the valley. I expected more. Somehow. All this time, these motherfuckers have been here? With a bunch of rugged-up weirdos doing—whatever the fuck they're doing. A large house is built in the center, encased by a pebble of smaller shacks.

The screaming dies into the darkness as people dressed in white robes run for their lives, scattering like feral cats. It doesn't occur to me why they all seem to be running in one direction, until a Jeep speeds up beside me with a flick of grass.

Priest stands with his machete in one hand and the torn flesh of a severed head in his other. The sound of skin splitting open against a sharp blade bellows through the air as intestines slip through Vaden's fingers.

The holy one still bends for the Devil sometimes. Not usually. *What the fuck?*

The Jeep stops, and the back door swings open. "We need to leave. Over that mountain is around fifty or so men! Get in!" Baylee yells, gesturing over Samson who's in the back. Luckily, we managed to wrangle them both for the last-minute mission... since just twelve hours earlier, it was a much different tone.

Twelve Hours Earlier

Suspicion has my eyes flying between Katsia and the car.

"She's okay! She said she will meet you all back at home. I promise." Her words don't mean shit.

She takes a large step back when she notices I'm drawing closer, her head shaking. "I promise you, War! Please! She's fine. She will meet you back at the house."

"And where's the boy?" Priest asks from behind.

"He got away. Sorry. I couldn't stop him."

Agitation has my fingers craving her throat, but I throw open the passenger door and find Halen's phone on the seat.

I tap at the screen and her screensaver lights up.

Try and find me with your GPS now. Asshole. Be home later. – EWBOMH

My breath is heavy when it leaves my lungs, as if I'd held it for too long. *Even with blood on my hands.* She put the acronym there because she knew I'd ask questions.

I kick the door closed, passing her phone to Priest.

"You!" I point to Katsia. "If there's even so much as a fucking strand of hair missing on that girl's head, I'll fuck you up."

The realization of how important Halen is to me weighs her mouth down in a frown. "I know. And don't worry. She'll be okay."

We hadn't even made it back onto the jet when Priest answers his phone.

"Fuck… now what?" Vaden rests his foot on the table opposite us. We need to find out who the fuck it was that tried to take Perdita, and who that little fuck was that was in Katsia's office.

They're both dumb as fuck if they think we don't know that something is happening between her and Halen. We don't ask questions. We find answers.

"Who?" Priest's body turns stiff. The width of his shoulders spread as the muscles in his jaw turn taut. For the first time since he took the gavel, I see it. I see his father in him. It's a simple change of gears, not the whole man.

His eyes hold mine before shifting to Vaden's. When they come back to me, I know it's not the Gentlemen. "How can I help you?"

Lowering his phone and taping the speaker button, he places it on the table between us. "We can all hear you."

My brows knot as lead fills my gut when his voice comes through the phone.

"I'll make this quick. The people who shot up your island were part of the Factory." My body turns to ice. Archer Thorn isn't a man you want a phone call with. We had never spoken with him before. In fact, we didn't know shit about him until his father came up out of nowhere when we were young. His father and Bishop knew of each other. Our families pointedly made an effort to stay the fuck away from one another. Not that Archer was an enemy, because he wasn't. He was just… Thornhill's monster, and no one—and I mean *no one*—wants to die on that hill.

"Why are you telling us this?" Vaden asks, his eyes bouncing around the two of us, with the two girls watching carefully from the back. They'd been surprisingly complacent throughout the whole Halen leaving debacle.

"I won't be the one blamed. They ran up in there with ski masks, dressed in black and wearing a black rose. They knew what the fuck they were doing trying to pin that shit on me."

My knee bounces. "The Factory? Never heard of them."

He falls silent. Seconds pass until Priest jumps back in. "Who are they?"

Finally, Archer snickers, and the motherfucker, I swear. If half of the stories are true about him and his crew, then I'm not sure we want his help. I mean, yeah, we could take them out, but we'd both lose. Their savagery matches ours. We've always known we could fuck up the Gentlemen. They'd be tough, and they're the biggest threat as far as enemies go, but that's only because Thornhill isn't an enemy.

We'll need to keep it that way.

"It seems you need to pull your resources in line. Look…" He closes a door in the background. "The Factory is where the Bakers run out from." The air drops to an icy level. "They're not the crew you assumed they were, and that's where you've made your first mistake. I'll send you coordinates. Go in, take out who you can, and get out. You do not want to be there for longer than two minutes. You hear?"

"I owe you." Priest's jaw tenses as if it physically pained him to say the words, but I know that's not all that he's pissed about. It's that we didn't know whoever the fuck these people are.

"Actually, yeah, you do, but not for this."

I lean forward, ready to ask him what the fuck he means, when the phone goes dead. "Well, fuck. How's that gavel feeling now?"

"This is how it's going to be from now on, right?" River surveys us all, clipping a bottle of water when Amber strolls past with the cart. "I guess we won't have to throw parties when we're bored anymore."

"We threw too many when we should have been doing this."

Priest is cold when he answers her, and I know that from this moment onward, everything is about to change.

Now

As soon as we're all in the Jeep, Baylee floors it forward and we zip over the valleys of greenery, back the way we came.

Just as we're passing a line of trees near one of the huts nestled away, a flurry of white glows from between the bushes.

Priest taps at the back of the driver's seat. "Stop!" The Jeep skids to a halt as Baylee turns over his shoulder just in time for Priest's door to swing open.

He reaches for the girl and I half expect her to run.

"Hurry up, bruh! We gonna be cooked damn meat if we get caught!" Baylee complains, his eyes flying all over the place.

The girl doesn't move. She peers up at us all through wide eyes and dark eyelashes. I don't give a fuck much about her right now, but Priest forces her into the back seat with us, even though she almost got in willingly. Baylee resumes as the tires rip up the grass. We fly back through the dense forest and onto the track we created to get here.

Shit.

As unsatisfying as that was, our point was made. Don't fuck with ours or we'll fuck with yours. Only now, we need to review just who these Bakers are and how the fuck they've been hiding the whole time. They're not just bored young idiots dealing drugs on the street.

There's so much more to who they are. For the first time ever, another organization has surprised us. This isn't fucking good.

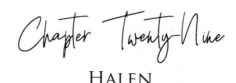

Chapter Twenty-Nine

HALEN

I STARE DOWN AT MY PHONE THAT WAS PLUGGED INTO MY charger when I got home last night. I woke up feeling like I had slept for days, but it has only been hours.

Shutting the screen off, the glass of rum on the counter finds its way into my hand as I swirl the liquid around the rim. My head should be clear, especially after yesterday and the close call with Deacon, but the more I'm around them, the more I need to drink.

Storm clouds roll in from behind the woods of the backyard, as a cackle of thunder growls through the sky. Tonight will go smooth. I will make sure of it. Pop will too.

"I'm not drunk enough for tonight." Stella steps down the platform that leads into the main family room, where large glass doors are opened out onto the back patio. The gardens are so well manicured that I sometimes wonder what my mother would do if I ruffled them. Fucked with them. Messed them up a little.

My bare feet touch the marble patio and I hold the glass to my chest. "Well, you better hurry then."

"There's something I need to tell you before the boys get here." Stella brushes up quietly behind me. It's the first time she's used her gentle voice.

I turn slightly over my shoulder, the silk of my gown parting when the hint of winter teases my skin. "They're suspicious?"

Movement behind her steals my attention and the smile falls from my lips when my eyes land on them. I scan their bodies quickly, noting the bloodstained clothes, but it's War that stops me.

With dried blood smeared over his face and a small cut on his chin, the room spins around me.

The glass is back on the table and my feet are moving forward without thought.

He stumbles drunkenly, his eyelids heavy. We hadn't spoken at all since the party two nights ago, and somehow, all that delayed time did was piss me off even more.

My fingers are on his chin, forcing his lazy eyes down onto me. "What the fuck happened?"

His teeth chase my hand, but he misses.

I shove him back slightly when he laughs. "Priest!" I summon my brother while keeping a close distance to War. If he falls… I'll catch him.

His shoulder brushes mine when he passes, removing his shirt by the back of his collar and heading to the alcohol cabinet in the corner of the room. The open flames burning from the large open fireplace do nothing to soften my twin's hard features when he looks down at me.

"Nothing."

I hold his eyes. The opposite to mine, yet so similar. "I hate you all. Something *clearly* fucking happened!"

They continue to ignore me.

"We're not talking about me right now, Halo…" Glass clatters together as he fumbles around the bar. I still haven't turned to face him, mainly because I don't think I have the restraint not to kill him. Finish the job of whoever *clearly* failed. Betrayal is a wound that most girls cannot forget, it cuts deeper than love itself. That's why it lingers in our blood as a reminder to us that men like War exist, and why at the end of the day, they'll only ever be some guy you thought you loved.

"Mmm, good point…" Priest's dark brow lifts to a perfect arch.

I rest my body against one of the columns, folding my arms

in front of myself. "Spit it out." It could be anything. It could be the video, or the fact that I disappeared in the middle of a war on Perdita, leaving them with nothing but Katsia, and my phone. I think it worries me most that they're not questioning that more.

My heart burns in my chest.

My fingers play with my earlobe, running circles around the soft skin.

I catch War watching my movements behind his glass as his head bends slightly to swallow. The longer we stay locked in this silent conversation, the deeper my stomach sinks. I want them to ask. But the fact that they're not is a red flag.

Heat travels down my neck as my tongue sticks to the roof of my mouth. The fireplace rages against the wall, rolling off gentle reminders of what happens to me every time he and I are in the same room. Being around him is like finally completing a five-thousand-piece puzzle, only to find out a piece is missing because he didn't give it to you.

"Sorry I'm late!" Her voice is starting to feel a lot like being waterboarded by acid.

I don't bother to break eye contact, since I know who it is. Did he think her covering for me was an invitation to family dinner? Or was this part of them not asking me where I went. Did they believe whatever story Katsia gave them about Deacon?

I doubt it.

The glass slowly lowers, revealing his smirk. He doesn't bother hiding the cynicism in his response of Katsia entering. If I'm hostile, he'll love it too much. It'll show my hand. Not that it's been much of a secret how I feel about her recently.

My eyes almost roll off him as I push myself off the pillar and make my way down the steps. I don't stop walking until I'm in the kitchen. It isn't the kitchen that the chef works in. This is the one Mom shows to pretend she cooks. The chef has his own commercial-size kitchen in the west wing. Closer to the dining cube.

Sucking in a deep breath, my fingers flex in my palm to try

to calm my raging emotions. They're doing this on purpose. He's doing this on purpose. He brought her here to agitate me. They know I'm hiding something and they're trying to pull it out of me by their torment.

"Are we fighting someone?"

And just like that, my anxiety releases.

The smile that spreads over my face is wide enough to split my skin open when I turn to find Aunty Tillie leaning against the long marble counter. Over the years, she's kept her pink hair. I love it. "Yes. Please."

She laughs, rounding the counter and going straight for the cabinet. "I know your mom keeps all her good shit up here." She's up on her tippy-toes, before finally lowering back down while holding a metal tin.

"I don't know why I thought you meant alcohol."

She slides up onto the counter opposite me, popping open the lid. "You know, when I was your age, we were snorting cocaine off each other's titties. Thank *God* you guys know better."

"Mmhmm…" My lips roll beneath my teeth to stop myself from laughing. "No, yeah, sure…" Some of us just snort them off corpses now.

The corner of her mouth twitches. I know what she's thinking. "Talk to me."

Her fingers work the bud of flower as she pulls it apart, crumbling it onto the blunt paper. "If we're fighting someone, make sure she has a momma."

"Oh, she does." My feet dangle over the edge. We've been told stories of our parents' days, but not too much detail. I think they'd probably leave shit out even if they did try to tell us what they'd been through, but I know. I *know* Nate was a menace in his young days. Dad used to say that War is kind of like him, but more like Dad. More controlled. Whatever the hell that means.

She places it between her lips. "Yup. Still got it."

Leaning back against the window, I kick off my Louis Vuitton slippers and cross my legs. The kitchen is far enough away from the family room that we can see if anyone is coming. I know it's just her and I in this moment.

"I don't really want to go there, because if I do…" I drift off over her shoulder, losing my thoughts on the photo hanging on the wall beside the fridge. It was a winter holiday in Aspen. We would have been ten, and everyone was there. I think it was the last time we saw Luna.

"Halie!" Tillie's fingers snap in my face to get my attention, and I'm back in the kitchen with her, the candy smoke of marijuana blowing into my face.

"What?"

"I said we don't have to go there if she's already in this house…" She hands me the blunt and I take it.

"How did you know?"

Tillie leans back on her hands, her head tilting to the side. "Let's just say that the apple doesn't fall far from the tree."

I choke on my inhale, fist banging on my chest. Squinting around the smoke, I hand it back to her. "You too?"

She slips it from my fingers. "Oh, sister. You have *no* idea."

"Perdita was rightfully yours, was it not?" I ask, searching her eyes. I hadn't heard much, but what I did hear was that Tillie could have taken Perdita all those years ago because of her bloodline. Everyone thought she was just an average hang-a-long to Mom, but she wasn't. She was a queen. "Why didn't you take it?"

"Because she wanted my King too." She leans forward, squashing out the blunt. "Are you going to allow her prodigy the same?"

I think over her words. If she had said this to me a couple weeks ago, I probably would have blushed. Nothing was going on between him and I but what was on the surface. Now I know that I have to say something. I can't brush it off. "There's nothing between War and I."

She ponders a moment. "Honey…"

I swallow roughly, but the splinters from my rib cage fracturing are stuck in my throat. "It's hopeless, is what I mean." I've never out-wardly expressed my interest in War. The sex? Whatever. Sex to us is a game. A tool. We don't dive too deep into it, but this is something else. I've never shown my vulnerability toward him. Has he been gentle with me growing up, during the times I needed? Yes. One hundred times over *yes*. But more so recently, I've seen the shadow side to him, and the more I stepped in, the further he stepped out. It is a classic game of cat and mouse.

The breath I take feels like a knife in the heart. "I guess in sim-ple terms, the boy I fell in love with doesn't exist."

The corners of her eyes fall. She's the only one out of the moth-ers who has never touched Botox or plastic surgery. Aunty Saint only dabbled with Botox, but my mother... well. Vanity. There's nothing wrong with it. I know for *sure* I'd be freezing my face as soon as I see a wrinkle. Mom would always add that she'd go out exactly as she'd been played like.

Like a toy. Plastic.

Their inside jokes never made a lot of sense to any of us and I kind of don't want to know what they mean, since I'm almost certain they had all kind of slept together. Happy families and all.

"Halen." My eyes drift to hers. "You don't have to be that per-son around me. I know there's a lot of pressure with being Bishop's daughter and a Hayes in general, but with me, you can just be a twenty-year-old young woman who is confused about who she loves."

"It was an accident." The words burn my throat like I swallowed cyanide. "I shouldn't have fallen in love with him, Tillie. Somehow, somewhere along the journey, I did. I gave him my whole-ass heart without realizing, and now, the only person in this entire world who can break it doesn't actually have one himself."

She pauses a moment, her brows lifting just enough to show her surprise. Her shoulders relax as she places her hand on my knee. "He does. I know he does. I'm by no means making excuses for him, because you know you're my girl, but in this world, you know how it is. We go by a different set of rules than other people. He may not show it the conventional way—"Ya think?"—but it only makes the love that we all share that much more special. It's the kind of love that survives shit. To love a beast, you must be a beast. Unless you're Saint, then you better fuck like one."

We both burst out laughing and it doesn't die out until my chest burns and tears have dampened my cheeks. I probably shouldn't have said all that. *Fuck.*

I sigh. "Doesn't matter, because I'll deny myself the feeling for as long as I need."

Movement catches my eye in the corner of the room. "Now, this is a scary scene…"

I push myself off the counter and land on my feet. I don't have it in me to go another round with him. Not right now.

Tillie's words stop me before I reach the other side. "Dinner party at twelve!" We already know. And I'm definitely not prepared for it.

Before this family dinner party, I need to mentally prepare. Too many Kings in one room can either be a very good thing, or a very bad thing.

Kicking my bedroom door closed, I lean my head against the wood. The week after the ritual has been testing so far, but the weight of my secret is becoming heavy. I always knew it would sink me over time.

Blood strums through my ears rhythmically, releasing the tension in my nerves as the minutes pass. The claws of my consciousness gnaw at the cavity in my chest as I move to my bedside dresser.

I lean over to plug my phone in to charge when the cord falls between the crack of my bed.

"Of course."

My knees hit the floor as I aimlessly reaching for the cord, when my fingertips graze a hard surface. I slide it out from beneath my bed with a waft of ancient leather.

My finger traces the lines that are engraved over the top. I think back to the night I found it, in the back of the boy's car from Bayonet Falls. For whatever reason, I wanted to take it.

The backs of my thighs hit my bed as I lower to the edge, tugging at the leather strings that keep it closed. It falls open and the papers give way...

Today was like every other day. I stared back at myself in the mirror for minutes. Or maybe it was hours. It wasn't a good day, but I'd decided to finally journal. Try to make sense of the days that seem to lose me. Maybe one day, I'd be able to come back here, to pages so familiar that they could almost whisper my deepest memories back to me. Well, I'd hope so anyway.

The scar on my face looked worse today. A brutal reminder of everything I'd been through. Ironic how it started from my temple and curled around the contours of my eye.

My fingertips brushed the swell of it gently, but when the memories crawled over my skin, anger slammed the mirror closed.

I've never written before. Watching the ink spread over the page is somewhat therapeutic. The trust implicit. I wasn't sure if I liked it. This might only end up being one entry.

I hated this place. I wanted the buildings to turn to rubble and to run.

But I could never.

Every day was exactly as the last. The same routine. Tediously repetitive. The sun would set, and the sun would rise. In between that, we would cook, feed, and then clean. None of those were the worst of what we'd do that day. My hands ache so terribly by the end of the day that I'm barely able to continue writing this paragraph.

Today, I sat and watched as the clock in the common room ticked by as we all sat around the common table during lunch. We were always dressed in white, hence washing them seemingly tedious. There were twelve right now. Not including the soldiers, and others that I would see walking around every now and then, but for us cloth wearers, there were twelve.

I knew exactly how many people were here because I counted. I was never sure if there were more, and I never asked. We weren't to speak unless spoken to.

Heavy footsteps pounded against the wooden floor and my body froze.

"Holy day to thou." His voice was hard. Rougher than usual, and I was sure this was a warning. He was never in a good mood, but no one wanted him in a bad one either. "Sit. Eat."

We all lowered ourselves to the wooden bench, awaiting his next command. The material of my robe was extra itchy today, and my skin burned, as if it knew I did not belong here. No one damn well belongs here, yet even when my oldest memories were hazy, others would tell me that I needed to obey.

He was evil.

Pure evil.

At first, they thought I was naturally rebellious. I always felt as though I didn't belong. Like my legs wanted to run to a place that didn't exist. A world that didn't exist. Maybe even a time that didn't exist yet.

We drew pictures as kids of what the world looked like. The sound of strange flying objects in the air.

The pictures stopped long after that.

Long after, we were told who we were and why we were here. At that time, there were only three of us... there were now twelve.

But there has always been me. And him.

And I hated him.

"Eat." His words were soft around the sound of meat being torn from bone. Dried white meat and withered green leaves. I pushed my food around and my stomach grumbled. I found it hard to believe that this was the only thing humans could eat. Surely there were other things you could do with a potato.

We all ate in silence.

We drank in silence.

The lights flickered up ahead and I stared up at the concrete ceiling. Acid burned my throat the longer I stared.

Sweat dripped down my palms and I released my fork.

I didn't want to be here anymore. I wanted to live in a world that I knew didn't exist.

At least maybe not yet.

I felt his eyes crawl over my body the longer I sat here. Exposed to whatever pain he wished to inflict on me. He wasn't the man I thought he was... and he wasn't always like this.

I reread over the words, then fly back to the start with my own stomach rolling. I don't even realize I've stopped breathing until my lungs burn. What was this doing in the guy's car? Did he know this girl?

I pause a moment, retracking that night. I knew who he was. And I knew what had changed and why they had come to Perdita— it was because of me. Everything was because of me.

The time flashed over my phone screen. 1:32 p.m. I have a while to go before the dinner party, so I peddle through the page. There doesn't seem to be too much writing.

My fingers graze the torn pieces near the spine. Or at least there isn't any more.

I continue, tucking my legs beneath my ass and shuffling up my bed.

I felt like an outsider around people I knew most of my life. I guess the first lesson in life is betrayal. Everything else comes after.

The bedding was cold to the touch and littered all over the place. The sins of my ancestors maybe, or the punishments I'll be passing on to my future self.

"You may go back to your chamber."

The brutal routine day in and day out, a silent punishment from God.

I braved myself to count how many of us were here today.

Nine.

We did have a lot more than what we do now. They'd slowly been plucked away or taken. No one knew how. I could feel him get more agitated as time went on. As if he couldn't figure out where they'd gone or how they had.

I wanted to find my own way out. I would find my answer.

I could no longer wait for him to save me. I didn't want to be saved.

My legs shook as I swung them over the bench. I had to hitch the ends of my robe up to be able to move, but I moved fast. I followed behind the girls who sat beside me as we walked out of the room in a single file. The sun beamed down against my forehead and my chest cracked a little. We moved like cattle. The single file split off into separate and smaller lines as I continued forward with no one else in mine.

The chamber huts curved around the building where a yellow door glared back at me. I used to think it was a pretty color. It reminded me of sunshine.

I wasn't sure if sunshine was the right word for what went on in there. If I could never reenter that place again, it would be too soon—only I'd be back there tonight.

Bile rose in my throat as I took the steps that led to the front entrance of my chamber.

A single bedding area and a single mirror that hung on the wall. I made a small desk from old wood I found in the forest during a hunt, but other than that, it was simple. All I knew.

I at least got my own room during the day. Whether it was his punishment or his apology, I didn't know yet.

I should stop writing. I'm afraid that I can hear people outside. Maybe I did… or maybe I was finally going crazy. I was told I would. I just thought that I would have more time than I do.

Time. What we measure everything to, simply doesn't exist.

Tonight was different. I spent an hour beneath the stream of water, desperate for anything to make sense. Nothing did.

Then I ran. I was running so fast through the forest that my lungs burned with every breath I took. The ground bruised my feet the longer I went on, but I knew that I needed to continue. I'd never get another chance.

But I slammed into someone hard, my hands flying out to stop my own fall, but it was too late, and my head hit the ground.

A shadow came down over me as my eyes tried to adjust to the dark night.

He gripped my throat and my muscles seized. No. No. Please. No.

I dug my fingernails into his hands, desperate for release, but it was no good. I knew it wasn't. I was going to die.

He took me for all I had. All of it. He and his brother made sure to keep me close. Just enough for them both to play with as they pleased. To have sex with for as long as they wanted.

I couldn't walk for days after their last antics, and they never gave me a break. I still felt the prickle of stitches against my insides from when they split me open.

I never had enough time to heal. I was a walking infection that the healer despised. I was an annoyance. She had asked multiple times to get rid of me.

She was an awful woman.

She'd no doubt leave me there to bleed out this time. Unlucky for her and me both, her husband was too damn obsessed. And because I started as his mistress, she had even more reason to hate me.

I didn't have long left. They say you could feel the shadow of death before it took you. And tonight, that shadow was here.

The book leaves my hands as if laced with poison. Anger streams down my face and no matter how many times I try to swipe the tears away, they return.

Oh no. No, not right now.

The quake of my shoulders turn violent as my lungs ache for air, but this particular panic is malignant. It holds no prisoners.

It can't be. Surely not.

What the fuck is happening?

I hold my breath until I feel the slowing thud of my heart, balling my fists so tight I'm sure there are new marks on my palm.

There's a knock on my door and my eyes pop open as I slide the book beneath my ass.

"What?" Tension leaves my body when Stella enters, a bottle of tequila dangling from between her fingers.

She beams a wide-toothed smile. "I thought we could warm up to the evening?"

"You mean you want to also talk." I slide the book further as she kicks the door closed with her foot. She never knocks, but she must have known I was upset.

"Well, yes."

Great. Of course, Stella chooses now to come and interrupt me. I can feel the book burning my cheeks the longer it sits there. "So, you and War have finally given in, huh?" She slides over my computer desk, shuffling the papers and photos around.

I don't answer. The girls are good in the way that they've never pushed me.

She changes the subject like I knew she would. "You know that our glorious mothers have restarted that ancient-ass prestigious sorority house, right?" Her lips cover the top of the bottle as she takes a shot, leaving the stain of obsidian lipstick behind. "It has been one hundred sixty million years since it was running, so we kind of have a lot of work to do, but I have this whole idea, and River is on board too. But first, we have to sit down and think of a new name. And by we, I mean all of us. We need to find a gender-neutral name, and— Oh my God, we should—"

She loses me. The fraternity will be crazy. I'm not ready to touch on that. Stella is the girl we go to when we need to be told something straight. Somewhere in the DNA of Brantley and Saint, they managed to conjure this spitfire of a weapon who is terrifyingly smart and constantly minimized by the potency of her beauty.

She exhales, obviously picking up my drifting. "Halen, we need to talk about you and War."

"We really don't." I wince.

"Or what about the fact that you released a sex tape out of

spite. How about that?" The corner of her death-stained lips curves up a little.

My smile cracks, swinging my legs over the bed and quickly shoving the book farther beneath my pillow. I swipe up my phone. "No regrets."

My door swings open again as River turns, slamming it closed with a huff. "Assholes."

"Can we go back to the time where we had our own lives, away from them?" Stella ponders, the bottle of tequila hovering over three tumbler glasses. She pours equal amounts of 42 into each glass, and I take one, resting it against the skin of my chest where my gown splits.

"I think if I had known just how different it would be, I would have fucked more people," I whisper through the sweet burn, and they both burst out laughing. There's a reason why I love being around them. They're my reminder to show up.

Even when I don't want to.

River kicks off her Valentino heels, falling onto the bed and crossing her long legs. "My brother's a cunt. There. I said it."

My thumb catches Don Julio residue below my lip. "He is. But... he has a nice dick so I'm a little conflicted."

"First, ew! Second, I don't want to go to this dinner party tonight."

I release a steady breath. "Neither do I." The monthly dinner parties are traditional. It was one of the new implications our parents started when they took over. They're not bad. It sometimes feels like a therapy session with family members. But then it's not always good. It's just that—a dinner party. Except for that one time Pop brought his mistress and Nanna stabbed her in the throat with her steak knife.

Because every new system that is brought in has to be carried through to every generation after, means these will continue with us too.

River's phone starts blaring, and her smile slips when she sees the name on the screen. She is a replica of her mother. It's creepy. They could almost pass as doppelgängers. Only River has ash blonde hair, and Tillie always keeps hers a shade of pink. We've been telling her to dye her hair for years.

"Ugh!" Her fingers fly over the screen, and Stella and I both share a look.

"Trouble?" Stella asks with a perched brow.

River doesn't answer, continuing to text whoever it is. She hands me her glass without looking up, and I pour more tequila.

"Why is it that the person you want to text, doesn't? And then the one who you don't want to, does."

My fingers flex around the glass. "Do we have to have that little intervention again about how you should not be fucking Katsia because she's a piece of shit?"

River's fingers pause, sheepishly lifting her eyes to mine. "No. I got it the first six times."

I glare at her.

"It's not my fault! She's crazy! Crazy makes for good sex. And anyway." She goes back to texting. "She was leaving War alone when she was with me."

"I don't think that girl has ever left War alone…" Stella muses. "Honestly, Hales, I would have slit her throat on sight."

I ignore my unhinged witch.

Four rounds later, River's lying back on my bed, her hands sprawled over her belly as she stares up at the ceiling. "Do you think Vaden is okay?"

Stella has her phone out, snapping selfies.

I lean into one just in time. "What do you mean?"

Stella flicks through the retro filter app and opens Instagram. "She's right. Something is going on with him."

The photos pinned on my wall display a story of family, trust, love. I couldn't imagine a life without everyone in it. I never want a life without them all in it. War included. Could we be jeopardizing that by being too involved?

I doubt it. God himself couldn't rip this family apart.

"I think it's just because we hold him to such a high standard, so if he does something considered remotely normal for us, we're all going to question him. It's no secret he has blood on his hands. Maybe he's just—" I don't even believe my own words. "Yeah, maybe you're both right."

Our phones light up at the same time.

Dinner party postponed to tomorrow.

I read over the words again. "What? That's never happened…"

"Everything is suspicious." Stella's staring down at her phone, the two lines between her brows deep.

The bedroom door swings open as I'm sliding off my desk.

Priest fills the space, holding the door open as if waiting for someone.

"Dashing, darling…" Stella eats up what he's wearing. Denim jeans, a black-and-gray Hermes shirt, and the latest Jordans. Stella and Priest should never be allowed together unattended.

Ever.

His head jerks out the door. "You all need to go downstairs."

"Why?" I leave out the fact that I don't want to and that every second Katsia is in my house the more I crave murder.

Ignoring my question, he crosses the room and shifts the curtains out of the way.

"Because you need to go downstairs and stop making it fucking obvious that you've gone soft for War." He releases the curtains, turning back to me. "And what happened with you on Perdita? Where'd you go?"

The urge to snap at him for his comment has me glaring. There's no point arguing with Priest. You could sit there and insult him all day, and all it'd do is make you exhausted and him bored.

"I left."

"You left." His catatonic voice parrots my tone. "Downstairs."

My mouth snaps closed.

"What happened to the dinner party?" River shuffles off the

bed. "Why has it been called off?" The air around me tightens. I'd never felt claustrophobic in my own bedroom until now.

Priest ignores her. "Now, Halen. Don't fuck around." As soon as he leaves, we all sit in silence for a moment.

"So..." The unmistakable sarcasm in River's laugh would otherwise work into the tension of my muscles. "You want me to go rub up on Katsia, or?"

"No." I cross the room to my closet and drop to my knees, sliding open one of the drawers beneath the center compartment. My fingers wrap around the handgun before standing back up and placing it on the top. I need to find something to wear.

"This—whatever that's happening tonight. You think it has to do with Perdita?" Stella asks the question that I'm sure everyone is wanting the answer for.

My hands pause on a tight gray suede skirt that buttons to the side, and a black leather automotive drag racing jacket that hangs to my waist.

I toss them into a pile in the middle of the island before searching for my knee-high, heeled leather boots. "If I have to sit down there and tolerate that bitch, I'm doing it on my terms."

River slides in from behind, her energy infectious. "So, what jewelry are you going to wear with this outfit?"

I face them. "Well, the severed limbs of an enemy, of course."

Stella chews on her laughter as she disappears back into my bedroom, but River draws in close, handing me my phone. "Who could possibly piss off War?"

I take my phone from her, opening a new text message. "Oh, don't worry. I know someone. I just need you to go and get him from the back entrance and bring him up."

River lifts her shoulders in a shrug. "I can do that."

HALEN

I TAKE MY THINGS INTO THE BATHROOM AND SCRUB UP IN the shower. I can't let my mind wander too far, because if I do, it's too hard to bring it back. Whatever is happening between us all, is bad. They haven't said who attacked Perdita, but do they already know?

I swipe the condensation off the mirror and dry myself off, throwing a bunch of skin products over my face. I keep my towel wrapped around my body as I pad back into the room. Stella's dancing recklessly to the music that's playing, and River is still fighting with someone on her phone.

My phone lights up as I place my glass of tequila onto the desk. I open the text. **Here.**

My fingers fly over the screen. **I hope you're wearing a bulletproof suit.**

Ha… ha… Your psycho ass plaything has anger issues. Actually, he doesn't. He knows exactly what he's doing and who he's doing it to.

Sending River down so no one shoots you on the spot.

I get started on my makeup. "He's here."

River's long legs carry her out my door. By the time it re-opens again, I already have my foundation, contour, and shadow done.

My eyes meet his in the vanity mirror. "If it isn't my favorite villain."

Bas flashes me a wide smile, sliding between River and the door. Dressed in dark slacks and a button-up shirt with the top left open, you can see the defined lines of his lean chest. His black hair is ruffled on the top of his head in effortless waves.

The warmth of his brown eyes heat. "If it isn't my favorite cherry…"

The small wand I'm holding stains a deep mauve over my lips. "Do you know why you're here?" I trace my bottom lip with my thumbnail to clean the edges.

"Because as always, I'm whatever you *need* me to be."

My eyes snap to his, before looking around the room.

I relax. "Exactly."

His long fingers wrap around the bottle of 42. "I'm going to need this more than you, though, especially if I'm dealing with EKC's finest psychos."

"Four. There are four down there." I grab my phone before we all follow Stella out.

Bas hisses through the alcohol as our heels click against the marble hall that leads to the staircase. "This is still classed as work, technically speaking."

"Keep telling yourself that." My hand moves aimlessly to the bracelet on my wrist, checking the clasp.

"You're evil." His arm falls to his side.

Stella and River stumble down the stairs in a fit of laughter, as we follow not far behind.

"Watch yourself here, Bas…" River jokes from over her shoulder.

Silence. "Thanks for the heads-up, little queen…"

Once we hit the foyer, the air grows tense the closer we get to the family room.

Petty? Maybe. Do I care? No. I probably get it from my mother.

The room falls silent when we enter, and to distract myself, I settle on where Priest is leaning against the doorframe on the other side. I pointedly ignore War, but I know he's on the sofa near the fireplace, and I *know* Katsia is right beside him.

Movement from War as Priest's shoulders harden when he sees Bas.

No movement from Vaden, but that's no surprise. He never announces his moves.

"You got a fucking death wish?" I don't' know if War is directing his question at me or Bas.

Priest holds my stare. *You just had to go lower.*

Yup. Yes, well, I did.

"How are you doing, Bas?" Priest's cool assessment remains stoic, as Bas sits on the curved sofa directly in front of him.

"You know, not too bad, considering…" His eyes widen on my brother, placing an ankle over his knee. Bas could say a lot of shit in this moment, but he won't because if there's one thing about Bas Blackwell, it's that he'll always protect my pop. "You know what, though, if I missed out on watching the show Halen put out on her Instagram story because I was too busy helping my dick warmer do her job—" His eyes settle on War. "—I'd be mad too." He grins from behind his glass.

I take that back.

"What's he talking about?" Vaden shifts his weight forward, turning over his shoulder to find War.

Shit. Fuck.

Katsia bristles, sinking deeper into her chair.

River whines beneath her breath, cussing while heading to the bar.

Stella waves her hand with a sparkle in her eyes that looks a lot like anticipation. "Actually, it was great. Here."

"Stella," I growl through the grit of my teeth.

"I ain't watching that shit." Priest turns his back to us, facing the glass wall.

War snatches the phone from Stella, dragging his eyes from mine but not without shooting daggers right through my heart.

"Okay, one! This happened in the moment. I was drunk, pissed off, and you had—" My mouth stops, that same humiliation reminding me why I did it in the first place. "Actually, you know what?" I ignore the hardness of his jaw and the way his knuckles turn white when he squeezes the phone. "Fuck you. You get nothing from me." I relax back in the chair beside Bas, his thick thigh pressing against mine.

War taps the screen before tossing the phone back at Stella. "Interesting choice of car to do it on. Can't say it's not obvious who your intended target was." There's no guessing who his words are for, but his eyes are distant and cold, refusing to meet mine. "Unfortunately, you're a shit shot."

My chest deflates. Other than the tightness of his shoulders and the swollen muscles on either side of his jaw, he's giving—nothing.

"Speaking of cars and sex—" My fingernails find Bas's thigh when he doesn't shut the fuck up, but instead of stopping, he chokes on his laugh, spreading his leg out carelessly. "I mean, what a lucky guy..."

War's cold eyes move up Bas's body, stopping on his face. The tension in the air crackles around us when he says his next words. "I wouldn't go that far. She's not that great."

My skin prickles but I collect myself quickly, swallowing a long gulp of alcohol to numb the pain of his words. Unlike me, he didn't miss his target.

"Why are we all here?" Stella lowers to the other side of me.

"He can't be here for this, Halen." Priest rolls his eyes, relaxing against the frame again. As much as I don't want them to know how much War has hurt me, I can't push the words out. I can't give them anything because I'm afraid of what emotion will be laced with my tone.

"Actually, he can." Dad comes in from behind us, and I hold my brother's stare. "Bas isn't an associate with the Gentlemen like you've all suspected." He moves to the bar in the corner and pours himself a drink. "He's with us."

"Nah," Priest snickers. "I've seen that motherfucker's Instagram. He's with them. Seen it with my own eyes, him and Moses together."

Dad lowers his glass to the bar, holding my brother captive. "He's working *for us*, Priest. He's the son of a good friend and has been working for Hector since he was fourteen." With Dad in the room, my pain evaporates into the air.

Priest blinks between Bas and Dad. "What? How?" He finds me. "And did you know?"

"Yes, I knew." My leg crosses over the other as my chin lifts an inch. "I've known since the party I crashed when we were all fourteen and War dropped me home. Of course, I didn't stay home." Was I doing this? "After stealing War's new RX4, out of sheer spite, I found Bas wandering down the estate." I pause, a wide smile spreading over my face. I guess I was. "Sorry, Papa, block your ears."

"Oh God," Dad groans behind his tumbler, turning to my brother.

I lean forward as if in a fighting stance. "He made sure *I knew* who he was in the back seat. Gotta say," I blink to my side, tracing the lines of Bas's jaw. Nothing like War's but I don't care enough, because Bas isn't hiding the smugness directed at War. "I think we preferred the hood. Right, B? After all, I did warn you, War." My eyes flick back to him, but his face is as hard as stone, never moving from Bas. "*Don't say I didn't come to you first.*"

"Wait!" Stella bites back her laugh. "That was you that night? Who she's with in this video? The one wearing the Billy the Puppet mask?"

The corner of Bas's mouth lifts. "Yeah. And, shit, Hales, am I very good at following instructions. I mean, he said to not go further than your thighs, but I just had to make sure my memory—"

All hell breaks out. Stella yelps, grabbing me by the arm and dragging me to the floor as War grabs Bas by the throat and throws him across the room.

Around the pounding of flesh and bones fracturing, vases

smash to the ground when War shoves him up against the wall so hard plaster explodes around them.

Priest stares up at the ceiling with vacant boredom, as Vaden watches with calm observation.

"Jesus Christ." Dad lowers his glass with an eye roll. "Separate them, Priest, before they break something important and your mother shoots us all."

Priest lowers his head back down, swallowing the last of his drink before taking long strides toward them.

He forces his body between them, but keeps his hand against Bas's throat, and now it's the Mad Prince in his face.

Bas's nose is busted red, his lips swollen, and his cheek split open. Blood oozes from every wound on his face, and a pang of guilt wiggles inside my gut.

I caused this.

"*Amica*," Dad says softly from the other side of the room, as if hearing my thoughts.

The apology hangs off my tongue as I look up at him from the floor.

His hands disappear into his suit pockets. "You know better."

My head dips docilely. I know I fucked up.

Stella and I both help each other back up off the ground.

"Go home and get cleaned up, Bas." Bas bows his head slightly, scattering up the steps that lead to the foyer. Before he can disappear, Dad clears his throat. "And stay the fuck away from my daughter, or next time, I won't stop him."

And there it is. The favorite child.

A soft growl leaves me bitterly, and Stella's hand tightens around mine.

My attention lands on my brother, only to see he's already watching me. He shakes his head a little, and he doesn't have to yell it out across the room to know what he's thinking.

I'm losing control.

"The dinner party has been moved to tomorrow because of

what's happened on Perdita. We suspect who it is, but until we know for sure, doing anything else other than trying to find them would be neglectful."

"We heard the call that came through on the flight back," River says when Dad finishes. "Are these people a real threat to us?"

Dad loosens his shirt around his collar. "Yes. We didn't think so until now. The Bakers is what they're called. We always assumed that they were young criminals who dabbled with street drugs and petty crimes. Every crime they've committed never raised flags with us. It was street shit. The shit we don't associate with. Recently, we've come to find out that that may be what they wanted us to think."

I block out the white noise ringing in my head until he's finished talking.

"The dinner party is happening tomorrow," Dad continues. "By then, we'll have heard back from Archer Thorn."

My fingers prickle when blood drains from my face.

"Am I interrupting?" The only voice that could ever replace the cool caress of death.

I shoot to my feet at the same time as Stella and River, turning to see my best friend, who is looking around the room nervously. I've never been more thankful for her timing in my life.

"Of course not, Evie," Dad says with a genuine smile. Dad kind of took her under his wing when she was a little girl. Her father is the only man outside of the Kings that my dad considers a friend. He doesn't have friends, he has family, but Evie's dad is considered that. I think he loves Evie more than I do.

"Good…" She dangles a set of keys. "Because I need to forget about the crazy family drama I just went through. And I'm driving."

"You're not going anywhere, Halen…" Priest ignores Evie.

"Actually, I am. I need it."

"Go." Dad waves his hand. Before we've hit the front door, he calls out, "And you better be carrying!"

The girls jump into the back of Evie's blacked-out Porsche and

I take the front passenger seat. The force from my door slamming blows my hair around my face. "Get me out of here."

No one says another word, but Evie searches my face. She's worried.

"What?"

"You're going to be fine with leaving all that in there?"

"By 'all that' do you mean Katsia? Because yes." I pull on my belt. "I don't care anymore."

Chapter Thirty-One

HALEN

THE ROOM IS DEATHLY QUIET, MY BREATHING THE ONLY sign of life as the galloping in my chest quickens.

My hand flies out in the darkness of the room, until they land on the lamp on my bedside table.

Dread continues to pour into me as my eyes adapt to the room.

I'm in my bedroom. In my bed. With no one beside me.

My hand flies to my throat as tears fill my eyes, and I feel the familiar sticky residue slip between the cracks of my fingers.

No. No. Please no.

Goosebumps spread over my skin when I draw my legs up to my chest. They're worse now. As if being this close is only opening the access it already had.

My door opening summons my panic, and the muscles in my body turn to stone.

The annoyance that's displayed over War's face instantly disappears when his eyes land on me. "What's wrong?"

He's in front of me in an instant, swooping my body with careful eyes. He doesn't say another word as he lifts me from my bed like one would a child, placing me on my feet. "Hey! Are you hurt?" His palms skim over my legs in his search, trailing up to my hips.

His head dips when my cheeks warm from his hands. "What's wrong?" Whiskey stains his words.

I shove away from him sleepily, the serpent of my heart rattling against my rib cage. Whatever weird shit I was dreaming up just then is suddenly irrelevant, because I remember.

I remember that he was probably in bed with her. *With her.* Like he used to be. I remember his words in front of everyone and how much he has hurt me over the past couple of weeks.

Lowering myself back onto my bed, I rub my eyes with the back of my hand. "Leave me alone."

"What are you doing, Halen?" His voice is a distant memory, locked in the haze of my own mind.

"Nothing. I'm doing… nothing." I push back my covers and turn off the lamp. I don't know if he's moved, or if he's going to just stand there all night, but I can't care right now. Because I need sleep.

If I wasn't so tired, all I'd be able to feel are the new wounds over my heart. I said I didn't care.

I clearly do.

The mattress dips beneath his weight but I curl deeper into my covers, my arms slipping beneath my feathery cold pillows.

"I don't know what bullshit you've filled your own head with, but whatever it is, stop fucking thinking it—" The covers move and cool air wraps around my thighs. "—or I'll tear it out of your mind with my bare hands."

The words I want to scream at him clog my throat.

A breeze whisks over my swollen lips when his massive body lays back. If I shift my leg even just a little, I'll feel him.

So I don't.

Fear keeps me frozen in place, only it's not from him.

What the fuck is with me? I should be kicking him out of this bed, only I don't. I don't because even through the hurt we both continue to inflict on one another, there's one thing I've never lied about, and that's the fact that I need him.

"There's so much you don't know." My lip trembles around the confession.

"What?" His body shifts, and I slowly flip back around to face him. I blink through the darkness, trying to imagine the expression he's giving me right now. Probably a scowl for being vague. "What happened?" Silence stretches between us, and the mattress moves again. This time I don't need to see him, because I can feel the heat of his body radiating from his chest.

"There have been times, where I don't—" I pause. "I don't know. I think the brain isn't the greatest place to hide your secrets."

I roll onto my back, resting my hands on my chest. "I should have washed my hands."

More silence.

Swinging my leg over my bed, I quickly shove the blankets off and turn the lamp back on, desperate to wash the blood from my hands.

Clean palms stare back at me. "What?"

"Halo…" I'd never heard such softness from War.

"What the fuck!" I spin around to face him.

He notices my panic and launches up from the bed, grabbing me by the wrist.

He forces my body against his. "What are you talking about?"

"It's gone!" Tears fill the corners of my eyes. "The blood on my hands. It's gone."

His eyes flick between my hands and my face, before his fingers run rampant through his unruly hair. "Shit, Halen. What?" He casts a quick glance to the side, confusion pulling his hard features in tight.

Before I can answer, his hand is on my chin and he's forcing me to look up at him. "Baby, there was never any blood."

I try to move out of his grip again, but all it does is make my lip quiver. Confusion sinks its ugly talons into the most hidden parts of my brain, and I'm once again reminded why I hate War.

I hate War because all I've wanted is peace. *But I'll never have it.*

"Hey." His voice softens to that same tone. The one I've never heard. Even as kids, all through our early teen years, he'd be gentle with me, but never soft. That turned to shit recently, obviously.

The cushion of his thumb skims over my bottom lip. "Talk to me, Halo. Fuck. It's *me*."

More tears roll down my face when I try to blink them away. "Right. *You.* Did you shower before you got into bed with me? Or if I take your dick out, would I still be able to smell her on you?"

Anger flares in his blue eyes. Gone is the gentle nature I just saw moments ago. "Keep going, Halen. I can do this dance all fucking night if you want to, or you can saddle your ass against me in bed and go to sleep. Your choice."

"Leave me alone." The words set fire to my throat.

He didn't say he didn't.

"No."

Simple answer. No effort. No need to prove anything to me.

My eyes harden on his. "Leave."

"I'm not fucking going anywhere, Halen. So shut the fuck up and get in bed."

I shove him away with my hands on his bare chest. "War! I said go the fuck—" He catches my hands with his and flips me around until my back hits the mattress with a heavy thud. The lamp on the bedside table rattles as the weight of his body presses into mine.

His thigh widens the distance between mine. "No."

The air thickens around us as I struggle to breathe, and the thin material of my camisole does nothing to hide the swell of my nipples against his chest. "I hate you." The words leave me as a sob, but his lips brush over mine anyway, as if he'd take whatever I say to him however he could.

His fingers above my head lace with mine, and everything inside of me detonates. Suddenly I'm aware of everything. The breath expelling from his lungs that leave a whisper of promises over my lips, and his skin that burns as a threatening reminder of his rage.

Not even the infinite muscles that ripple over his chest can hide the pounding of his heart over mine. His thigh shifts higher until it's a wall against me. The gasp that leaves me only has the hardness of his cock grinding against me.

This is a problem since we're so goddamn close. Everywhere. Except there.

His finger twitches against mine. "You don't hate me, Halen."

My mouth dries. I don't like him being close like this. I like our sex when it's careless. Angry. Emotionally sadistic when he's inflicting pain. That's familiar.

This is dangerous. This is forbidden waters for both of us.

"I do," I whisper, braving myself to search the speckles of gold in his cyan-tinted eyes. My gaze falls to his lips when I can't take looking into them any longer. It doesn't help, since his lips are carved for every girl's wet dream.

"You don't hate me."

A single tear rolls down the side of my cheek and he shifts his weight, as the warmth of his tongue follows the path it just fell from.

The anger is crippling as my head tilts. I'm angry with myself for showing too much, and angry at my traitorous heart for wanting the only thing that could destroy it.

With his cheek pressed to mine, his lips brush my ear. As if trying to remain in control of whatever he's been fighting recently. "Fuck, Halen."

A simple exhausted cuss, and my insides are gravy.

The cushion of his lips glides over the hard bone of my jaw. His teeth catch my skin, as he nibbles his way down to my chin.

He raises himself up by his elbow, until he's staring down at me with the same blue eyes that I've both loved and hated simultaneously throughout my life.

I shouldn't. I really shouldn't. But my legs fall open, allowing him full access.

The corner of his mouth twitches as he slips his other leg in between.

Brushing his nose over mine, he pauses, a whisper away from my lips. "I didn't mean anything I said." His words hit their intended target when the butterflies in my stomach burn to ash.

"Which part?" My eyes cross as I peer up at him. This is the first time since we've fucked around that it's just him and I in one room. Alone. Not being interrupted, watched, or to prove anything. It feels different.

My fingers trace the corded muscles in his arms, following the deep contours of his biceps. I want to ask him again, but I'm too afraid it'll start a fight. A fight that I don't have the energy for tonight.

He thrusts against me with such slow finesse, the pressure of the movement lifts my hips from the bed. A hand slips beneath my thigh to catch me from falling. "You fucked up by letting me hit, Halen. I'm a jealous man, even when it comes to your torment." He dampens my lips with his tongue. "Especially when it comes to your torment. So now I'm gonna fuck you until the only pain you ever feel going forward will be the bruises left over by my cock."

Words fail me, but it doesn't matter because his mouth covers mine and the silk of his tongue tastes every inch of my own. The room tilts to the side as my stomach strangles itself in an attempt to slow the fire that's spreading through my veins.

With lithe, methodical pacing, his lips mirror mine, sucking my lower one into his mouth and catching it between his teeth.

My fingers flex around the back of his neck to hold him in place, leaning up further to deepen the kiss. I wait for him to do something so *War*—like deny me of it just to be an asshole, but he doesn't.

My demand is met by the mania of his appetite when our teeth collide mid-kiss.

Fumbling between us, I shove his sweats down after he lifts for ease. My legs lock around his back, as my nails leave their signature down the smooth surface of his back.

He buries his face into the crook of my neck, sucking the skin near my jugular into his mouth. My hips rise to meet his when the tasting of his tongue quickly turns to pure predatorial greed that leaves teeth marks in its path. The desperation of my cries become tameless when the smooth end of his cock rests against my opening.

His thumb dips beneath the string of my underwear before the distinct tear of him ripping them off fuses with our heavy breathing.

I catch his lips with my teeth, every other emotion I was once feeling long since dissolved.

Now I just feel him. All of him.

The thin strap of my camisole meets the same violence, as the fat of my cleavage spills out of the thin material. His mouth is back on mine as my legs widen once again. I wonder if I should see how far I can take him. Does his sadism stop at emotional damage? Or will he smack me around too? *Kind of want to test that.* If only to give me a reason to swing on him.

I rest my hand on the back of his neck again, circling the swell of his veins with my thumb and forcing him deeper into my mouth.

"Fucking missionary?" He chuckles against my lips. "Really?"

I know he's joking... but he's probably not.

Lifting my hips as my answer, I trace the hardness of his cock with the slit of my pussy. My body shakes with uncontrollable violence as my clit suckles its way up. I hadn't even reached the end of his length when his eyes roll to the back of his head, baring his teeth with a cruel hiss.

He tastes of cinnamon rose and seawater as I lick a straight line up the center of his neck, exactly as one would mark their territory, before stopping at the corner of his mouth and whispering, "You haven't fucked *me* missionary." As soon as the final word leaves my mouth, his teeth sink into my neck. I need to make sure he doesn't do anything like hang me upside down to bleed me out while fucking me until I cry.

Using the slippery end of his cock, I circle my hips against his girth in hopes to prime myself for his size. Every second that passes feels like an eternity. It's never enough. Just as I'm about to roll my hips over his length to coat his size, he drives his hips forward with a single thrust. His balls hit my ass as his pelvis smacks against my throbbing clit.

A scream tears through my vocal cords as my nails bury

themselves deep into the muscles of his back. He catches my noises with his mouth and finally releases the hand that has been joined with his above my head, the residue of our joined sweet sliding down my arm. He seems to hesitate before completely letting go, his fingertips bruising every inch of my body on his way down to my upper thigh. My body vibrates against his in a tornado of unstable arousal, as the torture of his pace starts. With every forceful drive of his hips, my body jolts up the bed.

"What's that you were saying, hmmm?" His smirk teases my lips. "I haven't fucked *you* missionary?" He circles into me again, and my teeth catch the inside of my cheek when the metal of his piercing strokes over an area inside of me that has my body surging off the bed to chase the euphoric high.

With fingers on my chin, he holds me in place, his eyes searching mine when he draws out again. This time is different. Like the banging of your palm against the other with loud thuds. Harder, but not faster. A merciless pounding so deep, my head smacks the headboard of my bed when the violence of his force has my pussy latching around him with the kind of dependence you'd expect from an addict.

My insides coil like the braiding of exposed power lines, toasting everything that comes too close.

"If you move again, I'm going to make a mess..." I whimper into his slick flesh, losing the fight I'm pretty sure I started.

His pierced tongue ravishes every inch of my cheek, nibbling a line to my lip. "Then be my good little slut and show me." My grip around the back of his neck tightens, as beads of sweat pool between my brows.

He picks up to a brutal pace, every pump harder and more relentless than the last. It's not just fucking, this is owning. It's an unmerciful thirst for blood and finally letting it consume you.

The gore of my orgasm explodes through my body after the grip of my pussy turns homicidal. The brutality of the convulsions that charge through me are crippling, every muscle tensing up as the waves crash over me with no sign of receding. "Oh my fuuuck…" I'm barely able to say the words when the room around us tilts and I come apart beneath him once again in a rush of unrelenting orgasms that aren't letting up.

He doesn't slow or stop, seeing the torment of my own body and the restlessness of every orgasm as if it won't stop until I die. The primitive slapping of our bodies colliding has the monster inside of him clawing at me to release mine. My soul leaves my weightless body for a moment as a scream pulls from my chest with an arch of my back. I'm going to die.

This is it. He's going to kill me by fucking the actual life out of me.

My body wouldn't stop shaking as I suck in deep breaths around the wrathful pulses of my clit and the stream of my evidence dripping down my thighs.

His sweaty body slides over mine as his tongue licks its way to my nipple. He flicks the piercing with his tongue while peering up at me through eyes I wasn't sure I'd ever recover from. The chill of his own piercing massages my nipple before his white teeth snap around it again, tugging back so hard I feel the sting all the way down to my toes. My orgasm never leaves, tearing me apart from the inside as the monster weighing down on me toys with it like it's his pet. He draws himself all the way out, and I hate the stab of loneliness that leaves a wound where he once was. I instantly need him back.

He disappears down my body and I lean up on my elbows as his tongue sweeps over the ache near my entrance, leaving ecstasy prickling through my limbs. The tip of his nose glides over the pleat of my pussy before he gently nibbles at my clit. "Kind of wanna pierce this."

"It's not enough that you branded your initials on me?"

The vibration of his chuckle shudders over my sensitive flesh, his tongue curling in a way that has my heels stab into the feathery mattress and my fingers twist with the sheets.

"Nothing will ever be enough for me, Halen."

I ignore him as his tongue works the space by using the same pattern. He doesn't stop before I feel the metal from his piercing cools over me. My flesh pebbles and my nipples harden as my body once again prepares to come apart. I wasn't sure I'd survive it this time…

Heat spreads through my body as the sweat drenching our skin slides between us.

His heavy arm lands on the lower part of my abdomen when I try to grind my hips forward. It does nothing to calm me when the blistering spread of pleasure only pools around the weight of him.

He flattens his tongue against my clit.

"Yours." My breath catches in a hiccup as my skin cries sweat.

"Mine." His thumb circles its way inside, slipping his pinky between my ass cheeks before it hits the entrance of that too. His lips close around the well of my clit and everything goes black.

I don't know how many minutes pass when I wake to the brutal charge of my body, but I'm on my back once more, arching off the bed as my fingernails splinter from the grip I have on the sheets.

My body fights the merciless tremors of yet another orgasm, as my body lays powerless and vulnerable beneath him.

I swipe at the glistening of sweat over his chest as he moves back up my body and when he fills me once more with a single thrust, my body quivers through the rippling return of pleasure.

My finger traces over the familiar tattoos, and down to his pierced nipple.

"What did you wanna ask me tonight?" I feel the weight of his gaze on me but I'm too afraid to look up at him.

His hand settles on my cheek, squeezing hard enough that I wince, and the size of him expands against the tightness of my pussy. My teeth pierce my lower lip at the exposure of what he does to me.

"What did you want to ask me?" he repeats, trying to move himself into my line of sight.

I'm ready to force myself out of his grip, but he shoves me before I get the chance. Asshole.

"Did you fuck her?" The words leave before I can stop them.

"Well, shit…" I finally let myself look up at him, just in time to catch the smugness of his grin match his tone. "Guess you'll never be able to smell her now, huh?"

My last nerve snaps and my hand slides into the side of the bed, between the mattress and the frame, until the cool brush of metal touches my fingertips.

That same hand swings back, racking the slide over the muscles in his back and pointing it at his forehead. "Does it look like I'm joking?"

I knew I fucked up the moment his eyes flared like I'd handed him the greatest gift I ever could.

His lip curls up in a snarl as his forehead meets the barrel. "You look like you're *mine*." His hips circle against me once more and the familiar pull stirs me back. "Pull the trigger."

"What—"

His pelvis slaps the sensitive pulse of my clit as his cock hits a wall inside of me, working my back off the bed.

"Pull." He kisses me. "The." His tongue tastes my lips. "Trigger." He applies more pressure against the barrel.

"I—no!" I scream at him. I don't know why. This was my idea. I have never pointed a gun at someone that I didn't intend to shoot.

"Fine."

His fingers close around mine to take it away and I blow out a steady breath. Why the fuck did I do that?

With slow movements, he flips it around until it rests against my temple, before lowering his weight back down and kissing me hard enough to split the inside of my lip.

"Let's play a game." I would have missed his chuckle had it not vibrated against my chest. "Every time I lie, I'm going to pull the trigger."

His cock tests the limit of what I can take as it expands inside of me. The curve of his head drags over the ribbons of my walls as he finds a lazy yet potent rhythm. His body rides mine with mastery, as if he'd been doing it all his life.

My clit aches to be beaten as he sucks my lip into his mouth.

Thrust. "I really do hate you."

I squeeze my eyes closed as a loud *click* bellows through the air. My heart flatlines and he groans, pumping a little faster around the loud gushing of his cock stroking my pussy.

I don't get another second to prepare myself before the next one leaves his mouth.

"I've never fucked myself to thoughts of you wrapped around my cock..."

Click!

My lip trembles as fear poisons my blood. His pace becomes a torture of restraint and there's a primitive darkness inside of me that clings to him as tremors ripple over my flesh.

Close. So close.

His lips swallow mine as his tongue laps over my own in a way that has my chest squeezing. The cold metal of the barrel against my temple pulls me out of my lust, but not enough.

"You scared, baby?" It's a taunting whisper, the kind you'd imagine death to sound like.

I swallow past tears with a curt nod, but my pussy strokes his cock as if it were her pet.

That gun is always loaded. He knows that.

"Good." He bares his teeth as he hammers into me at a pace so animalistic, my body quivers and my vision blurs. Sweat drips from his forehead and beads over my lips as I come apart once again with a violent cry of whimpers.

The corner of his mouth curves into a frightening smirk. "I don't fucking love you."

Click.

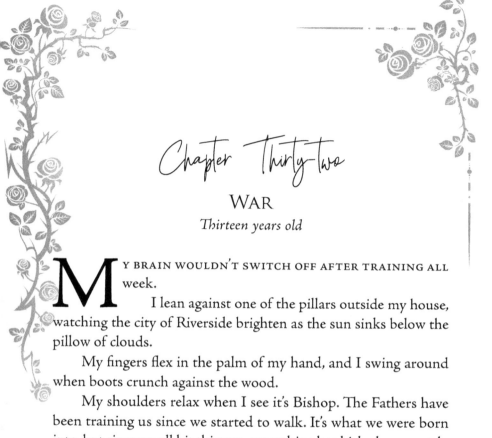

Chapter Thirty-Two

WAR

Thirteen years old

MY BRAIN WOULDN'T SWITCH OFF AFTER TRAINING ALL week.

I lean against one of the pillars outside my house, watching the city of Riverside brighten as the sun sinks below the pillow of clouds.

My fingers flex in the palm of my hand, and I swing around when boots crunch against the wood.

My shoulders relax when I see it's Bishop. The Fathers have been training us since we started to walk. It's what we were born into, but since we all hit thirteen, everything has kicked up a notch.

I took my first life today. I don't know how I feel about it. Am I sullen like Vaden, or am I void like Priest? Somehow, I don't see how either of them are better than the other.

"Son…"

My thumb brushes over my knuckle. "I thought we had to all be packed by tomorrow? I've seen Madison's bags when we go away, Bishop. You guys won't be ready in time."

He laughs, shoving his hands into his pockets. I've seen photos of our parents growing up. I wonder when they moved to the suits.

Silence stretches between us before he clears his throat. I already know what he's going to say.

"You thought much into what I asked you?"

I follow the hard lines between my knuck-les. "About Halen?" Bishop doesn't answer. "What makes you think that's going to work? With any of them?"

He doesn't bother to offer me any animation to his answer. "Because when you're around, she doesn't see anyone or anything else but you. It's temporary and the other two will follow her lead. We can only draw out the ritual until you're in your early twenties, so if we don't find an answer by then, it will just need to go ahead."

I straighten. "I can't do anything to distract her."

"You being around is enough, but we will do what we need to on our end as well. Madison is adamant on what she wants." His brows pull together.

"And you?" The question is an obvious one.

He doesn't hesitate, as if he'd recited his answer over and over again. "She may be my princess, but her crown is one of a King. She will deal with it. *We* will deal with it when the time comes."

I'm not sure I will if it's her.

Present

Satin sheets fall from my body as my legs swing over the bed. Fuck. I came in here last night with the full intention of fucking her to death, but I think it ended up being the other way around.

I drag my hand down the side of my cheek, turning over my shoulder to check on Halen. The spot where she was sprawled out on last night is empty.

I'm off the bed in an instant, adrenaline swallowing my fatigue. I check the bathroom.

Empty.

Closet, empty.

Shoving on my sweatpants and leaving everything but my phone behind, I make my way out the door and down the wing of their level, just as Priest is closing his bedroom.

"Where's Halen?" The pounding of my heart doesn't let up. I'd never felt panic to the full extent, and if it's anything like the insistent tempo thrashing against my rib cage, I'm out.

He scans me up and down. "It appears I should be asking you that?"

"She wasn't there when I woke." Her door clicks shut.

After a minute of what I'm sure is him counting down from ten to not kill me, we both make our way down the stairs in silence. There's an echoing void in my chest that makes me want to shove my fist inside and tear out.

"Nah, something's wrong." Even though the absence of her twists in my gut, I still search through every room she'd usually be in, settling on the family room where Stella's laying out across the sofa.

Her face pales when her eyes land on me. "What's wrong?" The spoon she's fisting drops to her bowl.

"Halen wasn't in bed when he woke up this morning and now he's freaking out." Priest's tone may as well had come from a fucking corpse.

Color pumps back into her face. "We chilled at Evie's last night. After you told River and I to leave you both alone, we crashed in the playroom." She rolls her eyes. "So long as you didn't say anything dumb like usual, she'll be fine."

"I didn't." I can't be bothered with an argument, so I start scrolling through my phone with my thumb. "She wasn't right in the head last night. Thinks she saw some blood on her hands or something. I fucked her back to sleep but I don't know. Haven't seen her do something weird like that since she was young."

"Wait—what?" Stella leans forward and places her bowl on the table in front of her. I have her attention. Good. I think.

Priest watches me carefully from the other side of the room. The fact that he's silent only means he's processing everything.

"I don't know!" I grind my teeth to stop myself from snapping at her. "There was this one time years ago where I once found her asleep in the middle of the field behind the church. She seemed fine but I still watched her for a little while after since this asshole didn't." I jerk my thumb at Priest.

"Careful…" Priest warns.

Stella's shoulders fall as she releases a breath. "Okay. We need to go."

"Hold up!" Priest lifts his hand. "What the fuck are both of you talking about? And where the fuck is my sister?" I take it the processing is done.

Stella tucks her long hair behind her ear. She's nervous, which in turn doesn't help my unease. Stella is hardly ever anything but confident.

She picks up her bowl and stands. "Call Vaden and River. We need to leave. Now." Her shoulders brush mine in passing, but my hand flies out to stop her. "Stells." I search the different colors of her eyes. The weakness of her smile tightens. "We don't ask for much within our family. We trust each other enough to respect when the other is ready to talk, but you need to tell me this right now. Is she in danger? Because if she is, they can fucking wait."

"I don't know where she is. I believe it's happened enough times for her to not be in any real danger, but—"

My grip releases from around her arm before I swing my eyes to Priest. "We're leaving, now."

Priest blinks back at me, the shadows around him darkening.

"If—" I step closer so no one else can hear but him and I. "—you can reach inside that dead little soul for your sister and help me figure out what the fuck is going on, you need to do so right now, before I shove my hand into that cold heart of yours and tear it out. The EKC is priority, I know, but Priest, *she is* the EKC."

His shoulders straighten. It's pointless. He's the product of every Hayes ancestor that ever walked the earth. Humphrey included.

Disappointment has my head shaking from side to side.

His words stop me from leaving. "If you're implying that I don't care about my sister, War, you're wrong. I shared a whole womb with the brat, you don't think that means anything to me?"

I want to say no. He continues. "If there's one person walking this earth that can force me to bend, it's her. Don't get it twisted. Put your fucking dick away. You have my support."

"Good."

I climb the steps that lead up to the main foyer, stopping when I'm at the base of the split staircase.

Bishop stares down at me from above. "Find her. Now."

The front door opens onto Vaden and River. I ignore them both, moving out to the patio. Anxiousness gnaws at my chest. Everything with Halen has always been too much. It's why I ignored it for so long, why I need to continue to ignore whatever it is that we've started.

I carry on through the garden that leads to the Lighthouse. It's not until the elevator closes behind me when my phone vibrates in my pocket. I pull it out and answer without looking. "What?"

"War…"

The world around me stops and my phone almost slips from my grip. "Where are you?"

I could kill the little shit for removing that damn GPS.

"I—" Her breath catches. I try to pay attention to the outside noises. Wind. So much wind. Water? Waves against sand? "I shouldn't have stopped. They're back."

"What?!" I'm already shoving my feet into a pair of socks and grabbing at the stray pair of Jordans near the kitchen.

"They won't go away." The choke of her words has my brain short-circuiting as the elevator opens behind me.

"Listen to my words, baby. Are you listening?" Rage burns through my veins. I need to calm the fuck down if I'm going to have any chance of finding her. I can fucking kill whoever *they* are later. All of them. "What do you see in front of you?"

Priest moves to the other side of the room, opening the floor-to-ceiling cupboard that's behind the conference table. Weapon after weapon lines every inch of space as Vaden and the girls follow closely behind him.

She pauses. "On the cliff of Devil's Cockpit."

Vaden throws me a semi and I catch it with one hand. "Step away from the cliff, baby."

The whimpers of her pain tug at something feral and wild that lives deep inside of me, that only exists for her. The grip I have on my phone tightens until I swear I hear the screen crack.

"It doesn't stop. It won't stop."

The phone line goes silent and the realization of every-fucking-thing we didn't want to happen floats to the surface like the fat of boiled meat.

Maybe we were wrong. Fuck.

My phone's back in my pocket and I'm across the room once more, my palm hitting the button to the elevator. "Devil's Cockpit." We all pile in together but I know Priest and Vaden are both asking the same question I am.

Did we have it wrong? Surely not possible.

"Talk. Right now!" I snap at the girls. They'd been hiding shit for Halen for a long time, if I'm going by the little hints that they've left over the past month. Priest's thumb flies over his phone as the elevator reopens onto Creed. He's the head of our security, and by security, I mean his hands are in everything.

His beady eyes bounce around us all. "Get in the caddy. I'll drive." We slide into the back and as soon as we're on the road, Stella opens her mouth.

"The first thing you need to know about what's happening right now, is that you can't kill them."

I squeeze the barrel of my gun to stop myself from choking her out. "Oh, that's real funny, Stells. Next joke. This time be sure it's funny, instead of making me want to kill you instead."

She glares at me. "Jesus Christ." I wouldn't. Or maybe I would. The control I've spent so many of my years honing is weak right now, and I know that at any given second, I could tear someone's head off if they so much as joke about her being in danger.

Her exhale is steady, but before she can continue, River interrupts her.

"*Maledictionem...*"

The word sucks warmth out of the space and my eyes land straight on Priest, and then move to Vaden.

"What?" My head tilts to the side. Priest's eyes narrow on mine for a second, before understanding settles around him. "What curse?"

River's head shifts to the side window. "We don't know a lot about it, but I'm sure Halen will tell you." Yeah, because she's been so forthcoming leading up to this moment. "There's a curse that runs through Riverside, and now, through her."

I find Priest again, his eyes falling to his phone before lifting back to mine.

"We don't have a curse," Vaden answers smoothly. "Pretty sure we'd all know."

"Faster, Creed!" I call out, but keep my focus fixed on River.

Her thumb plays with the strap of her semi.

I sit back in my chair. "Hurry the fuck up, River."

She clears her throat. "There'd been tales in the old days about it, but since it didn't get to our parents' generation, they didn't warn us." Outside ceases to exist as she talks. "It seems to skip a generation, which is why there's always one generation of Elite Kings who are sane and morally in line, and then there are others who are deranged. Filled with rage, hunger for power, and do *bad things*." Her words leave her mouth in a whisper.

For the first time since this morning, a steady breath leaves my lips.

"What the fuck has this got to do with Halen being in danger *right now*, and I swear to fucking God, River, if you don't hurry the fuck up and spit it out, I'm throwing your whole ass out of this car!"

"It has to do with her, because this is what it does to you, War!

Are you not listening?!" she yells back as tires hit gravel. "This!" She gestures around us all. "Doesn't leave!"

"I'll kill them." Priest shoves his gun back into the band of his jeans, and I place mine to the side, away from my thigh.

"You're not listening," Stella repeats. "The curse isn't there for you to touch. It exists inside your mind. Coming only when you're asleep, when your mind is at its weakest. They visit you. They come to you," she says with certainty.

I feel them both out. "Who?"

River's fingers rake her hair to the top of her head. "It's only affected her so far. We don't know why, but we know it's just on her. Halen has said that it will only affect her. We've helped her how we could over the years, but if she stops, they start back again."

I shake my head. "What the fuck are you talking about?"

Stella blinks at me from the side. "Why are all three of you so damn quiet?" Anger ripples over her face. "You think our parents could just change history? Change generational damage because they could? No."

They're not making a shit lot of sense right now.

"And… You all didn't think to tell us this from the fucking start?" The tires kick up dust when we stop and has barely settled before the door swings open. The soles of Priest's Jordans fly over loose stones until I'm at the edge. Tracing the man-made steps that lead down the cliff face and to the bottom that's only sandy at low tide, I find her.

"Halen!"

Her arms fan out, and she falls.

Chapter Thirty-Three

HALEN

Drowning pain wasn't enough.

You had to burn it first, and the easiest way to turn anything to ash, was to love it.

FLAMES FLICKER AROUND MY LUNGS WITH EVERY INHALE. The pain was unbearable. I knew I shouldn't have let it in, and now I was fucked. I had to bathe in it to exist.

This would be my final attempt.

My final attempt at scrubbing my own memories of every goddamn thing they had not only put me through, but everyone else around me. I couldn't fix this. I knew that now.

My lips parted as I counted the people on the field below. I was about to die on hell's doorstep, and I couldn't be happier.

I stopped counting after ten, my fingertips grazing the cuff of my bracelet. It was a gift. I still remember the day he gave it to me. Back then, it meant everything to get something from him.

Past

"Here." He tossed the box onto my lap when I wouldn't stop swirling around his computer chair. They hadn't been back long from their trip to Perdita, but he had come back… weird this time.

"What's this?" I asked, eyes

wide on him. Priest and Vaden weren't here yet and since River was once again late, I came to annoy War.

His shoulders lifted when he shrugged. "It's your thirteenth birthday in a couple days." He swallowed, his eyes glassing over as if remembering something he didn't want to. They'd been through a lot already. It was probably something to do with training—

My eyes fell to the bruise on his neck, and my stomach tightened as if he had reached inside of me and squeezed with his bare hands.

He may as well have.

I guessed he'd had sex now. You didn't get a hickey like that by just making out.

Whoever the fuck she was, I hoped her teeth fell out.

I collected myself, swiping the heartbreak from my face before he could notice, but when my eyes collided with his, I knew it was too late. His face had turned to stone, his jaw tight and eyes hard on mine.

"Open the gift, Halen, okay?" It was a plea. A desperate attempt at shutting me out so we didn't have to have the conversation that we both had ignored since we were old enough to realize.

I wanted to say something, but the words were stuck in my throat.

Envy bloomed beneath my skin like liquid heat.

I knew my cheeks were red, but I didn't care. Suddenly, I didn't care if he wanted to ignore it. He and I had never so much as flirted. Never stepped out of line. But I knew that this wasn't one-sided. That he felt what I did just as much as I did because it couldn't just be me.

"Halen…" he groaned. It was supposed to come out as a warning, but instead it hit every trigger I had kept hidden inside of me and triggered the sparks that flew across my skin. How could we not say a single word, but both of us knew exactly what the other was thinking?

Fate was a fucking bitch. No doubt he'd fuck her too.

I squeezed the box in my hand. "Do you love her?"

He held my eyes sternly. "I won't say this again. Ever. And if you repeat it, I'll fucking lie."

I held my breath.

"No." Honestly, I knew that. The day any of the Kings fell in love would be the day I did. Which would be never.

He leaned forward an inch and the hairs on the back of my neck rose. "If I ever fall in love, Halo, there'll be warning signs."

I tilted my head, eyes locked on his lips. They were perfect. Soft. I wondered what they tasted like.

Then I remembered he would have kissed her, and jealousy flared to life inside of me.

"Like what?" This was good. Distraction. Do not think of whoever the bitch was.

He spread his legs a little and my focus dropped to his lap before quickly diverting back to his face. Shit. I was screwed when it came to him.

The corner of his mouth twitched before it was gone. "Trust me." He held my eyes with cool assertion. "You'll know."

Before I could ask what he meant by I would know, the door opened and just like that, the conversation evaporated as if it never happened.

Back

I hated that even though the memory of him giving the bracelet to me wasn't exactly perfect, since he clearly lost his virginity that fucking weekend, I still kept it. Because after all these years, it reminded me of what I was capable of. I'd never felt jealousy like I had that day. Now it reminds me that if I can pet an emotion so aggressive as envy, I could fucking get over anything.

War was one half of my soul. I was sure of it, but we were too similar—too much. We'd destroy one another before we'd allow love in. Neither of us were going to open for what we knew was true, so we'd rip each other apart until we could damn well fucking take it.

I hated that he wasn't mine first. I'd never admit that. I never would need to, because I was sure I was going to die today. I'd make sure of it.

I wanted to be his last.

My brain was turning hazy as my heart slowed and my foot slipped from the edge of the cliff as I peeked over once more. There was a line of trees that hid in the back, and I squinted my eyes as I noticed a figure appear. Over six foot tall. Even at this age.

His arms fell to his sides as the gun he was holding dropped to the ground. He dashed forward but everything played in slow motion.

I remembered his face paling just as I turned my back to the edge, spreading my arms wide.

Then I let go.

Even with blood on my hands.

Present

I don't feel the land of his arms when he catches me. Shit... Did he drop me? *Am I dead?* Did I—no. I couldn't have. That's not how this goes, if only it did.

Wait...

Water spills from my lips as my lungs rattle with fluid, and my body rolls to the side in a plea to relieve pressure.

"Hey!"

Voices yell from afar, hands on my cheek—hands everywhere. So warm.

My lungs corrode as I gasp for air and my eyes fly open onto the shadow of War kneeling over me.

The real War.

This is real.

"Fuck. Halen!" Stella screams at me, falling to her ass and swiping the tears from her eyes. "Goddammit."

"I'm sorry, Stells." I rest my hand on her arm.

The misfire of her sob has her exhaling loudly. "It's not your fault." She collects herself. "It's okay."

Except it isn't.

War's arms slip beneath my thighs as he scoops me up from the sand and cradles me against his chest.

He carries me up the steps against the cliff that lead back to the top. "You need to explain everything, Halen. To all of us. I mean it." His eyes come to mine.

My hand catches the back of his neck. "I know. I'm sorry."

"And with everything else going on between us all, you couldn't find a better way to tell us?"

Saliva burns my throat when I swallow. "I know. The EKC comes first. I know."

"That's not what I mean," he growls, and I know he's fighting with himself. He wants to yell at me. "I mean, you've been dealing with this on top of that."

"Oh." I blink, as we finally get to the top.

I tap at his neck to let me down, but his eyes snap to mine with a harsh snarl.

My eyes roll.

His arm tenses around me. "Roll your eyes like that again, Halen, and I'll toss you off this cliff myself. This time leaving you there to fucking drown just to teach you a lesson."

We reach the car and he holds me with one arm while using the other to open the door. He slides me inside as Priest shuffles out of his hoodie and throws it to my lap. As soon as I'm nestled in warmth, I sigh.

"The girls filled us in on a little, but not all." Priest leans forward, just enough that I can feel him close. His eyes soften around the edges for a moment. That one percent that still exists inside of him is the only reason why he isn't locked up in a padded room. "We need to know everything, and you need to talk right now."

My throat crackles when I try to clear it as Stella hands me a bottle of water, her thigh pressing against mine. I relax knowing she and River are close.

A sip just enough to coat my voice, before holding the plastic in my hand. There are moments that happen in your life that you're met with one of two options. Kind of like a crossroads. If you take one side, the road is bumpy, and you'll get lost. You may even get a little scared when you can't see around the tight bends. There'll be times where you'll want to turn around and wish you took the other way, but when you look around, you have the most important people in your life beside you.

Then there's the other. A narrow, flat road with no bumps or hurdles. You'll reach your destination quicker because the surface is smooth and straight. There are no sharp corners to fear, wondering what you'll find on the other side, because everything is out in the open. But when you look beside yourself, not everyone will be there.

Because they'd be dead.

I'd decided what road I chose.

"It started when I was fourteen. I remember waking up in a place I don't remember going to." Arms snake around my belly. "I came to in a field. I don't remember how I got there, just that I was—"

"You were with me," War says gently. "We were at the chapel in the town center. We were all talking, and you were tired, so you went to the bench to chill. None of us thought it was weird since you had started pulling away a lot."

A smile touches my mouth, but I don't want it there. I want to carve it off my face and throw it away. "I remember turning around and War was standing on the other side, staring at me. He was mad. I don't know why. I didn't think anything of it."

"So you just black out?" Vaden asks with a curved brow. "This *curse* makes you black out?" He's staring back at me with an empty void, one I'd never seen on him before. Speaking of changing…

I shake my head. "Not so simply. I guess I get sleepy, and then I see figments in my mind."

"What are you trying to say?" Priest leans back in his chair. "That you're hallucinating?"

If only.

Forcing away my tears, the muscles in my body tense when everything closes in around me.

"I've been trying to work it out, and then I found—" I flex my fingers when the words don't find me. "—some help. It came in the way of a palm-sized notebook."

"This is sounding familiar," Priest muses, a jab at our mother.

I shake my head. "No. It wasn't *Tacet a Mortuis*, or a family grimoire."

Priest tilts his head. *Oh God.*

"This one is different. For one, it's tiny, and the words written inside are in a different language, not Latin. I'm not even sure I recognize it." I stare between them, and just before I'm about to continue, Priest's eyes flick to War before quickly resting back at me.

That was something. I don't bother to touch on it. "It's formatted like a recipe book, I think."

War's thigh tenses against mine.

"Where did you find this book?" Vaden asks, not stupid enough to look at anyone else but me. Probably honing in one of his many creepy skills.

I pause. Probably a moment too long for him. "It was a gift sent to me the same day War gave me this." I flash my Van Cleef bracelet.

War shuffles, leaning against the window. I don't miss the sudden tension that fills the space the more I talk. *Focus.*

"I've only picked away bits as the years went on, but I can't find anything on the language online either. At one point, I thought it was similar to Arabic, but has distinguished differences that I can't put my finger on."

"And why didn't you say something before?" War's tone is cold and distant. Not at all the man who carried me up the steps.

"Because part of what I did manage to translate, if I was even a smidge right, is that I *wasn't to speak amongst the crown of a King,* which I'm guessing, means you guys. I told the girls because when this book would have been written, Swans would never exist. I was hoping the technicality of it wasn't as sharp for our modern age."

Vaden's hand works over his jaw, turning to Priest. The angst that rolls between him and War is palpable.

"Ask me!" I yell, annoyed with their lack of engagement. This isn't at all what I expected. I thought there'd be more. "Ask me anything and I'll tell you. I couldn't tell the moms with the risk of them spilling to the Fathers, and I don't know about you, but our families have a history of creepy shit. I wasn't too keen on testing that."

Not even a fight. No questions. Maybe even a plan to fucking fix it all…

A distraction.

I sigh, releasing the tension that's knotted in my muscles. "I can give it to you when we get back. Maybe you guys can figure the translations out."

"What happens inside your head?" Vaden ignores my offer. Probably because it goes without saying. It didn't matter. They could have at it.

I hold his stare. "I die. Multiple times. From different points of view, in different ways. I *die.*" Plucking the material of the hoodie, I look down before bringing my eyes back up to Priest. "Sometimes it's strangers who kill me, and sometimes, it's, well…" I pause.

"It's what?" War snaps from beside me.

"It's someone I know."

War pulls at his hair before his hands fall to his thighs. He taps at the screen of his phone, his eyes moving over the words as he reads. He locks it and pushes it into his pocket with a clenched jaw.

We drive through the high gates and stop on the bend of the driveway outside of the Castle. "And since you asked—"Sarcasm drips from my tongue. "—I've used cold water immersion to keep them at bay over the years. Recently, the terrors came back because I hadn't been practicing. The cliff works because of the adrenaline too. It just… helps keep it all away."

Priest looks between me and War, before resting on Stella.

"No one asked, Halo." War disregards me with cruel indifference.

"Stay with her at all times!" Priest says to Stella.

"Hold up!" Stella's hand lands on Priest's chest. "We know. Have any of you ever noticed that none of us have *ever* slept alone?" She blinks at them all as if they're slow. "We are always together. Always here, or at one of our own houses. We live with each other. And none of you thought that weird? Not that she's ever did it to that extent, but the terrors—all of that, we've known about."

"Honestly," Vaden shrugs, "kind of just thought that was normal."

War's next words stop me. "You said you didn't know where she was, Stells. So which is it?" His head swivels toward the both of us and now that his eyes are on mine, I see it. The detachment. The betrayal, maybe? "Did you or didn't you know that she was there?"

Stella bangs her head against the top of the chair. "I did when you told me she saw the blood, but I thought she was with River. I was hoping one of you would say something when I told you to call her and Vaden, but you didn't. When River came home, I knew she was in danger but by then she had already called you. Besides that—" Stella's annoyance rests on me. "—she promised she wouldn't do it without any of us there."

"I'm sorry." My hand rests on Stella's thigh. "I wasn't sure I was going to until I heard the car pull in. It really was bad last night."

"All three of you are to not leave our fucking sight." War shoves his door open and storms up the steps to the front door as everyone slowly rolls out.

This isn't going well.

"He's mad." I stare off into the distance, shivers racking over my body.

"Yeah, well… We knew he would be." River shoos me out the door.

"Priest!" He stops, his back still turned to me. I wait until everyone disappears through the front door.

I want to tell him. I should tell him. "I'm sorry."

"You could have told us, Halen." He finally turns his body, giving me all his attention. "We could have figured it out together, but that doesn't matter anymore."

My arms fold in front of myself. "So you all haven't been keeping anything from us?"

"Honestly?" His brow kicks up and I hate when he gives me this look. It's too similar to Dad. "Yeah, two things. One of which you're about to find out *real* soon, and the other is what we do during Devil's Cockpit parties, which was a new tradition that we carved into our generation for *us only* and is only known by *us*. The fact that you've acted this way only proves you're not ready to learn what the fuck we do on those nights, but the only real reason why we haven't told you all about that, is because you haven't asked."

Before I can tell him to elaborate, his back is to me and the door slams closed. I have ruined everything. Maybe I made a mistake. Took the wrong turn.

I force my feet forward and run up the stairs, not stopping until I'm in my room. I can't be around anything right now.

I close my door with the force of my back, bending down to reach beneath my bed until the familiar two books touch my hand. One smaller, agile, and filled with words I don't understand, and the other all too familiar. The reason I suspect everything has come back.

"It's ironic." River rustles with a packet of chips as she lowers herself onto one of the lounge chairs near my window. "How all this time, the enemy was our past."

"It's not ironic," I say, leaving the booklet with the foreign tongue on my bedside table and flicking through the pages of the letters I found to pick up where I left off. "It's fucking creepy and inhuman. Like everything in our fucking world."

I woke tonight with an intense pounding in my head. Sweat bled over my face and down the back of my neck. I tried to rethink of what had happened the night before.

I had died.

Someone killed me.

Was I a ghost? Did I imagine the dagger slicing me?

My fingertips brush where the ink dries out over the paper, before I continue.

I pushed up from my bed and made my way to the mirror in my bedroom. Touching my throat, I focused my eyes on the faint finger marks around it, before stepping backward and hitting the counter behind me. I spun around, searching the room. What was that? Confusion ran inside me. It was like being trapped in your own body and not being able to find an out.

I needed an out.

I scooped up my robe and placed it over my shoulders before my hands came to the knob. I wasn't going to get any answers here. Indeed, I needed to get out. I was going crazy.

The door swung open and the wind whipped around my ankles as I took the first step. The camp was asleep. The night too ripe for anyone to be awake. I lived with one memory that always clung to the back of my mind on repeat. Kind of like a constant reminder of where I was. Who I was. It was like my blood was on fire the longer I stayed. The longer I fought for a love I didn't know.

I tiptoed down the steps until my feet hit the grass. That was when I saw it. A bright light blew up above my head like a star, before it exploded with a loud bang. I dropped to my knees, covering my ears with my hands. Crawling to the side, I stayed curled as fire rained down from above. People screaming, shouting, running around the camp like someone was chasing them. I stayed still. Quiet. Curled up in a ball of protection.

I rustled my way into a side bush and opened this page.

This is the final time I can do this, and I'm now in a hurry. I feel the panic reaching up my spine the more that time ticks on. Gunfire erupts around me, but I have to scribble this down, with the hopes that one day, you will find it.

Yes, you, whoever you are that reads this.

I can hear a machine. Or a—automobile? I think that's what they're called. There are young men climbing in it. They look like bad men. Maybe even worse than the ones here. Maybe even worse than the ones I come from.

This place, save them. Please. I will pray, leaving my Tie to the Crucifix tucked within the pages. I pray this finds its way back to my home. There's water down below, but there's a road not far off. I know because I've seen it. I've seen the sign that reads Riverside…

I flip through the pages, but they're all blank after this one. Not even a torn page.

"No!" I flip through, but nothing is there. "What the fuck!"

I slam the book closed and toss it over my shoulder. Swiping my phone, I type out a text to Pop.

> **She said she saw a Riverside sign, but there's nothing else after that. Did she die? She saw men right before it ended. She spoke weird.**

Stella leans back and grabs the book, opening it onto the first page. "Who is it?"

I pluck it off her. "It's—I don't know yet. I think it has to do with the curse. Maybe?"

"We can help figure out who she is." Stella holds my gaze, the corners of her eyes softening.

"Sure, Stells." I smile at her gently.

"We have to get ready for this dinner party tonight." River lowers herself down in front of me. "Don't worry about this curse. We will figure it out."

Guilt tears through me once more. "I know."

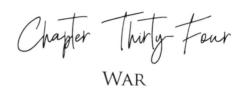

Chapter Thirty-Four

WAR

MY ZIPPO FLIPS BETWEEN MY FINGERS AS I IGNORE THE commotion in front of me.

Priest leans against the wall, and I watch as he studies the woman closely. Her legs hang off the mattress of the four-post bed. "We have to decide how we're going to go forward with this."

I snap my Zippo closed. "She's a fucking liar. How about we start with that?" I've thought about one hundred different ways to approach the Halen situation, and they all end with my hand on her throat.

Fucking professional bullshitter.

I shift my weight forward, resting my forearms on my thighs as the girl's chestnut brown hair falls over her shoulder.

I kneel in front of her. "You see that guy behind me? The one staring at you? He's the one who decided to pluck you from the bush. Not me. So I have no problem killing you." I smile widely at her. "How many people you got? What do you do in those little huts? Why the fuck is it set up in the bush, right between Riverside and Bayonet Falls?"

Her dark blue eyes shift to Priest, but her lip quivers. Shit. The palms of her hands find her thighs.

"So, you don't actually speak." I lean back in my chair. "Kind of hoped that was a temporary thing." Priest and his dumb ass picking up stray fucking cats off the road. Or worse. Off some fucked-up compound we know jack shit about.

She glances up at Vaden, her brown skin flawless as the lighting above hits her. She lingers on him a moment, before moving back to Priest, tucking her hair behind her ear until her robe shifts with the movement.

"Who are you?" Priest's eyes narrow on her.

She shuffles up the bed, pulling her knees up to her chest.

Priest stays in his spot. "How fucking old do you think she is?" Her body is small, but she may just be malnourished.

She doesn't lift her head.

My head cocks. "I don't know. Old enough."

The door behind us opens and then closes. Katsia brushes in and the hairs on the back of my neck rise.

My hand flies out to stop her before her hand touches me.

"So moody," she whines with sass, circling around my body. "Who do we have he—" Her smile falls when she sees the girl, but she recovers quickly. "Who do we have here?"

"What the fuck was that?" I glare at Katsia. We should have put her in our house, but we couldn't risk the girls rolling in unattended now that they all have full access to their trusts and to every resource ever collected for the EKC. So, we've kept her locked in this room.

"Nothing!" She purses her lips, as if I'm being ridiculous. "She's just beautiful is all."

No lie.

"Find her something to wear. Our little guest is coming to the founding members' dinner party," Priest announces casually.

I follow him as we head down the stairs to the kitchen, leaving Katsia and Vaden with the girl. Not sure if that's the best idea.

"Why would we bring her?" A muscle in my neck turns rigid and I reach up to massage it with my thumb.

Priest shrugs. "Because I want to see if anyone there recognizes her."

I cross my arms in front of myself, leaning against the wall. "As in what?"

"As in that shit has been not too far off our backyard for how long, and we didn't know?" He flicks off the lid to a bottle of bourbon. "This has Bishop Vincent Hayes all over it."

"Priest," I hiss. "This hasn't got shit to do with him. That may have been off our land, but it isn't Riverside, and you know that we don't fuck with shit outside these borders unless we have to. Besides," I snatch the bottle from his hands with a glare, "it was a fucking three-hour drive inland. It wasn't close to fucking anything."

Priest glowers at me. "How are you so sure?"

I bare my teeth when the alcohol hits the back of my throat. "Because he would have said something. Every single person has done everything in their power to ensure those girls aren't going to be harmed, even going as far as to drag out the ritual until we had figured a way to counter the herbs we had to drink. Then there's your dad asking me to watch out for her, for us to keep them busy while they searched. Now this—" My fingers flex around my head.

"It's sleepwalking, nightmares, and the occasional sleep paralysis. It ain't that uncommon," he counters flatly. "And it sure as fuck ain't the curse. My sister is her daddy's girl. She's a master manipulator and can whisper secrets into the ears of *anyone* who will believe them." Priest cracks his neck. "You've been thinking with your dick when it comes to her. She probably did it on purpose, have you thinking you're only looking after her for my old man when she's used that as a weapon to blind you this whole time."

"Damn. I was going to say who hurt you, but I already know who hurt you."

He ignores me. "She can continue to think we believe her about the curse, and in the meantime, that booklet she has needs to be given to Saint. She's the only one who can translate it."

My lip curls but I can't fight the smirk. "Are you still mad about Bishop asking me to be the one to look out for her after that time in town square? I was just being a big brother to her since she didn't have a present one."

"Last I checked," Priest holds up a single finger, "you don't fuck your little sister."

I flip him off.

Priest holds my eyes, before they move over my shoulder to where Vaden appears. "I'm serious. She's more like BVH than she is my mother. She doesn't answer with emotion. She's a brat, sure, but she understands this life more than anyone." His mouth lifts a smidge and I want to punch him. "Then again, she could still hate you from the other night, because although she handles herself like Dad, she can hold a fucking grudge like Mom." Priest throws back the rest of his drink. "She's coming tonight. Watch how everyone reacts. I wanna know who this bitch is and if there's any connection between her and us."

"Her name's Eloise," Vaden says from behind and I shift over my shoulder.

"Motherfucker, you got her to talk?" My brow lifts. We haven't been able to get a word out of her in days.

His hand rubs his chin, using the other to pluck the bottle from me. "That's all she gave. I'm guessing it's her name." Vaden stares between the two of us. "For the record, I don't think these people have anything to do with the shoot-out in Perdita. We need to call Thorn and see what the fuck he's onto. There's a chance he has used us as a weapon."

He isn't alone in those thoughts.

HALEN

MUSIC DRIFTS AROUND US AS I READJUST MY MASK. My fingertips graze the crusted diamonds before resting it back on my lap. Energy prickles over my skin. I can't sit still. *Do they know?* It's not that we were having a Founding Families' dinner party, because we had them often, but it's that we're wearing our Calvarias to said dinner. *Why the fuck are we wearing these to dinner?*

My blood turns cold.

The racing of my thoughts works through my fingers, as I tap against the silver handle of the knife. The heat of his stare is hotter than the candle that burns between us, but I'm thankful for my Calvaria. It gives me more confidence to do what I'm about to do.

My mouth accentuates the syllables as I whisper a snide *fuck you*. It's not like he didn't miss it, because unlike Vitiosis, mine isn't a full front.

The music offers the perfect background behind the chatter that pools around the table. Roast meat has been carved with the precision of a professional killer, and fresh salads have been tossed using Mom's favorite dressing. Even in the spacious dining room of Hayes Castle, we all know why we're here.

I just hope I'm wrong, because if I am… I reach up to touch the side of my mask again. *Then I know what these are for.*

Stella's hand rests on the knife in front of her, and River swipes up the tumbler filled with whiskey. The silence between us down this end isn't loud, since the pianist won't shut the fuck up, but the tension in the air is deafening.

"This is going to get interesting," River murmurs from behind her glass, her long blonde hair brushing my arm. It's a subtle reminder of the sins we have all drowned ourselves in and what possibly led us to this moment.

"Good," Stella exhales blandly. "I'm bored."

A foot collides with mine beneath the table and my eyes fly up to the half mask in front of me. The hard edges of the Malum Calvaria, slightly different to River's. I wish his did cover his face. Then I wouldn't have to stare at the pillowy swell of his lips, or the sharp lines of his jaw.

My foot flies forward, hitting his shin. *Asshole.*

"Let's begin," Pop Hector, a recovering villain from our parents' younger days, announces from his side of the table. I guess we can't really be mad at him for fucking shit up during their years. He didn't create this world; he merely drove it forward so it would never stop.

And it never stopped.

It will never stop.

A wave of electricity prickles over my skin. My smirk deepens as I tilt my head to the side while keeping my eyes locked on War.

My heart stops beating when he leans over, tattoos slithering up both of his arms, and my eyes fly back to his when he finally stops. His lips part, ready to say something, when Dad interrupts from the opposite side.

"Halen."

War's annoyance swings between my father and me.

The room falls silent. Cold. So cold. Like the final fucking ride.

I come from a line of powerful men, and only since my mother and nan, women. All of us here tonight yield the kind of mass influence and power that you can't replicate or marry into. This isn't a matter of *do you want to join the EKC?* It puts a new meaning to the term ride or die.

I can taste the blood in the air already, as if my suspicions are the centerpiece of our night. But we all have secrets. Mine just never wanted to be found.

Stella's hand squeezes my thigh and I rest mine over the top of hers. Spellbound with divine feminine energy, Stella is the Devil's goddess and she damn well knows it. Only this time, she can't prance her way out of what I've gotten myself into, because she doesn't even know the truth.

I clear my throat. "Yes, Papa?"

Seated around the ornate skull-carved marble, is my pop at the head, my father to his right, and Nan to his left. Beside Dad is Mom. Opposite Mom is Brantley and Saint, and then Nate and Tillie, River, Stella, and me on the other side. Beside me is Vaden, who has Priest next to him at the opposite end of the table facing Pop, and then it goes War, and five empty seats.

I don't much like empty seats.

The tension is crippling, and I can't believe I used to *actually* enjoy our monthly dinner parties.

"I'm proud of you, *Amica*. Of all of you." Dad lifts his whiskey glass to us all and a smile touches the side of my mouth. My attempt to not look at Pop fails when my eyes drift there of their own accord.

Pop nods his approval at me and lifts his own as we all chant the thousand-whatever-year-old riddle. "In sin, and until the last drop, long live the EKC, until our hearts stop." We lower our Calvarias from our faces and place them onto the table beside our plates.

But the truth is, we have a job to do. Our ancestors made sure to scratch it in thick enough to bleed into our bone marrows, so no matter what, I'll always do what I am born to do.

Whatever that looks like to anyone else. War included.

"We're just waiting—" Dad pauses, lifting his glass toward the entrance of the dining room. Like the rest of the Castle, it follows a Romanesque design, only with Mom's light-handed changes. "Here they are."

Everyone follows Dad's line of sight except for me. After

allowing the warmth of the tequila to rest on my tongue, I swallow and finally turn.

Holy shit.

I throw myself to my feet. "Oh my fucking God!" I'm around the table before anyone can stop me, only instead of hugging Eli, since I'd seen him already recently, my arms tighten around Lilith.

She buries her laughter in the mass of my hair. "When the fuck did you get so tall?" Her hands come to my arms as her eyes sweep over me. Her head cocks. "Such a shame. Bet you could work a crowd."

"I've missed you! Why has it been so long?"

Dad clears his throat, and we both turn to him with a silent apology. My hand squeezes hers before I hurry back to my chair. I had only just lowered back down when I notice a fourth person with them. Her ash blonde hair flows down her back in gentle curls, the sides held up by a casual claw clip with tresses falling around the sharp contours of her diamond-shaped face.

Her smile widens to two deep-set dimples on either cheek, and the eerie color of her eyes rest on mine. Her mom, Lilith, has unique lilac pigmented eyes, rimmed by dark edges. Luna's are similar, only she seems to have gray more than lilac, until you're up close, then you can see the wash of lavender surrounded by a web of obsidian.

I return her smile, eyeing her satin, beige, off-the-shoulder minidress. She turns her head to look down the table and I catch the black bow tied to the back of her head. I need to talk to her. Right now. See where she's been for the past seven or so years.

"Thank you for coming here tonight. I didn't mean to make it so theatrical, but it turns out that once you call a dinner party and cancel it, people talk."

The familiar wave of War's attention sends prickles up my spine as I play with my drink. He keeps me pinned in place and I fight with everything inside of me to not throw my drink at him. Why must he always be hostile? *Or see through my lies.*

Dad raises his glass. "Enjoy your food. No business talk tonight."

"Hold!" Priest pushes up from his chair and now everyone turns to the opposite side. I hum into my glass as the waiter moves around the table and refills everyone's drinks. Her hips sway past the boys and I roll my eyes.

The detachment of Priest's voice sounds a little less like death tonight. This can't be good. "We've got one more guest before we can start."

My forearms rest on the table when Luna's eyes bounce between River, Stella, and I.

I'm the first to ask, "Where have you been?"

Her nose wrinkles. "You don't want to know. What's your number?"

The numbers leave my mouth as Luna punches them in her phone. It's not until she finishes that I realize how deathly quiet the room is.

I'm met with the glare of my brother when my eyes shift up to him. "You done?"

"No, but carry on, I guess." I lean back on my chair. The only good thing to come of tonight is Luna.

I catch movement near the entrance once again. Great. Now what?

My blood turns cold at the sight of her. With the knife fisted in my hand, I use it as a distraction, counting back from ten. What the fuck is happening?

The silent echo of Pop's warning is as though he's sitting right beside me. *Don't flinch. They're watching for any movement.* Sweat coats my hand as my body thrums a tune I try to sing to.

Sliding the metal down to the table with slow movements, I try to calm my breathing. Maybe I'm thinking into this. It could be a complete coincidence.

My stomach hits the floor when my eyes swoop up from my plate and land on War, who's already watching me. His mouth is in a straight line, his eyes dark on mine. A moment passes when the side of his lips twitches. I can't make out if it's a smirk, but either way, this isn't good.

With my blood buzzed from tequila, dinner is served.

I pick at the food on my plate while losing my focus on the sparse windows that display the back of our property. Remain calm. That's all I need to do. Don't look at her, don't even—

A shadow zips between two maple trees outside and my hand instinctively lands on my thigh. My fingers pull at the silk of my dress to expose my holster, but I stay fixated on the outside with no sudden movements.

"Dad." The calm call of my tone fails to reach him, as a flush of adrenaline prickles my skin when my fingers unlatch my gun.

"War!" The scream that shreds my throat will leave abrasions long after tonight, as the hand that's holding my gun lifts not even an inch before the violent blast of the explosion erupts around us in a rain of shattered glass.

The end of my gun follows the movements outside the new hole in our wall where the window used to be, as I fire round after round. The ones I hit drop, but not fast enough, before a round of bullets spray through the room. Chunks of meat and salad fly around us, just as I catch the amber glow of his assault rifle. I swing my hand up and empty the rest of my chamber into his face.

The sound of bullets being fired are drowning out the ones coming from outside, so I take this moment to check on everyone.

"Stella!" I grab her by the arm, ignoring the shards of glass cutting into my hand as I force her beneath the table. "Where's your fucking gun!"

"I left it behind!" More bullets rain through the room, and I push back to my feet. Before I can shoot the next, a weighty arm forces me back down, and now a pissed-off War glares back at me.

"If they don't kill you, I sure as fuck will. What the fuck are you thinking!" The pits of his eyes balloon, swallowing all the color.

"Why are you yelling at me when people are dying?" I scream back, shoving him by the chest.

"Get the fuck out of here. All of you!" The anger in his glare falters for a moment when someone behind me catches his attention.

I turn to see who he's looking at, when my eyes land on Luna as she's lifting the end of her feminine dress, displaying a crown of throwing stars on the strap of the black garter around her thigh.

Holy shit. I would have never pegged it. Soft girl got a baddie side.

"No!" I bite back at him while he's out of focus, grabbing the next round from around my holster.

Stella's little body crawls across the ground, dodging the flying bullets, before ducking behind the slab of concrete that houses top-shelf alcohol.

River and I share a look of disappointment, as I point to our wildcat. "Stay with her."

War's fingers wrap around my chin, forcing me still. "Listen to me. Bullets spraying aside, I love you. I need you to know that. I need you to know that whatever it is that you've been hiding from us, from me—" His eyes harden. "—I can handle it."

They do know. Shit.

I swallow past the guilt knotting in my belly. "Not now."

With a gentle release, I move backward from the table, ignoring the stabbing of glass biting into my knees. More bullets pour from the sky, and I draw in a deep breath. Not a second passes before I swing back to my feet, my gun aimed to the first one I see, and I start firing. His head disintegrates into fragments of brain matter and blood, before I move on to the next.

I make sure to stay low every few seconds and change location, busying myself through the room. It's not long before I've bottomed out, and I toss the gun to the side, crawling beneath the table to check on everyone. Not a single person is down. That's a good thing.

A semi slides over the marble floor, connecting with my knee, and I look up to find Mom with one in each hand as she fires. Tillie's pink hair glows behind a white wall, an AK tight around her chest before Nate, Dad, Priest, War, and Vaden disappear through the smashed window, straight into the firing ground.

"Shit!"

A few more loud blows echo through the air before silence falls around us. I shuffle backward quickly, leaving a trail of blood from my hands.

I start to count. Dad. Mom. Vaden. War. Priest. Stella. River. Luna. Eli. Kyrin. Nate. Tillie. Brantley. Nan and Pop—though Pop looks hurt. Saint— *Pop looks hurt.*

I shove someone out of the way and as soon as I can reach him, my fist finds Pop's gray suit. I don't ask questions, simply tearing open the buttons to assess the damage, as my blood rushes through my veins the longer time goes on.

"My little hell-raiser. I'm okay. Flesh wound." I ignore his words and grab his wrist, counting his beats per minute. Low, but steady.

My shoulders sag in relief, as I take a moment to check no one is within earshot. "We need to tell them, don't we?"

Pop shuffles up against the wall, touching my cheek with the familiar coolness of his palm. "We do, princess."

Then it hits me. This could all be because of *her.*

The flurry of mania has me spinning around, my eyes moving over the destruction of the room. Broken glass, food sprayed up the walls, smashed half-a-million-dollar bottle of brandy, empty guns, knives.

None of it matters. Just her. I need to find her.

"Halen!"

Someone calls my name, but I don't care. The relentlessness to protect my family is crippling.

An arm catches my waist, forcing my attention. "Where is she?"

"Not. Here!" War's eyes bounce between mine.

I exhale the simmering anger, turning my attention to the bodies littering the grass. Dressed in all black, with ski masks.

Familiar to that of Perdita.

I shove myself out from War and swing my leg through the window frame. As soon as my feet hit grass, I start ripping off the ski masks.

"Do you know anything about this, *Amica?*" Dad asks gently from behind me. Tonight is one of the rare occasions where we don't have any wind, yet my eyes are bone dry, and a breeze rolls down my spine.

I force the tears off my face, clearing the emotion from my throat. I don't even know why I'm crying. I don't cry often, yet the thought of this being my fault, on top of what I'm already responsible for, is too much.

My hand flies to my mouth to conceal my sob but it's too late. I'm too slow.

A blur of people charge to comfort me, but I wobble back, holding my hand up to stop them.

I can't. I can't say the words that I need to, not here. Not like this.

Dad has always been weird when it came to Pop. He always has been, and maybe he had his reasons to hate him. Scratch that, I know he had his reasons to hate him. But Priest and I don't. I love him as much as any child can love their grandparent. Maybe I loved him even more because he was so messed up. But I knew. I knew that once everything came out, it would be catastrophic to the family, as much as it will be to the EKC.

A rule has been violated, and blood will be wanted.

War breaks the silence when he moves to the body closest to him, bending down and tearing off the ski mask. He flips him onto his back and lifts his shirt, as if searching for something. Probably ink, or anything that can identify who they are.

"Where's Eloise?" I whisper, and just like that, Wars stops.

Everyone. Stops.

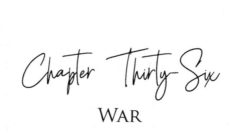

Chapter Thirty-Six

WAR

MY EYES BOUNCE BETWEEN HALEN AND ELOISE. NOT everyone is out here. Eli, Kyrin, Luna, and Lilith are inside with Scarlet. Hector is seated on a stray pot plant, staying close enough to Halen, and for whatever reason, that makes me queasy.

"This about the curse?" I leave a bitter sound around each syllable.

"Curse?" Saint's voice is careful, as her eyes take a moment to land on Vaden, Priest, and me. "Halen, are you talking about *Laena Daraetha Tayir?*"

Halen doesn't answer. We're not at all surprised. Bet she's fucking shitting herself.

Saint continues, her fingers tucking her colorless hair behind her ear. "*Laena Daraetha Tayir* translates to The Curse of the Darkest One. Spoken in the language Laheamayac, which originated from one of the first settlers of witches back in the days of the Messiah, it's said that during one of the many generations of Kings, a witch put a hex on Riverside for all the wrongdoings the Founding Fathers did. The curse itself is complicated, sure, but so is the way you obtain it." Saint pauses. I think she's giving Halen time to process, but it doesn't work.

Halen doesn't move, and every warning sign in my body starts going off. Why isn't she saying shit?

"The curse is true," Hector interferes from his spot. "The last generation it came for was the one before my father's. They were, at the time, the worst reign we have had." He swallows and the tattoos on his neck swell. "Until, I'm thinking, this one."

The wind bites at the loose strands of Halen's hair, and before anyone can say anything else, Hector whispers, "Princess?"

HALEN

My tongue clings to my upper mouth. No. I can't. I can't do it.

I rush toward the back patio, passing the pool house before anyone can stop me. After closing the glass door, I turn to find Katsia sitting on the single sofa in the family room, her leg crossed over the other. That's not what shocks me, though. I mean, having her in my house, yeah, but it isn't that.

"I know you want to run." The purr of her assumption grates on my nerves, as her arms visibly tighten around the baby she's cradling in her arms.

A baby? From where? The only person I know who has a small baby lives all the way on the other side of the world.

She moves the blanket away from its face as if moving the curtain from my eyes.

"Whose baby did you steal?"

"I know you want to run," she repeats, her tone harder this time.

"You don't know *shit*," I snap back, even though I know that it's not true. I don't know what I want.

"You and I both know that isn't true." She hums a melody against the covered head of the small child as it jerks awake. "Halen. You can't run."

"Whose baby is that, Katsia?"

Her eyes swing up to my face, and I swear the seconds feel like minutes as she holds my stare. Acid rolls up my throat and my whole world flips on its ass. She doesn't answer, but she doesn't have to. I hear her loud and fucking clear.

I fly up the stairs and up to my bedroom, with nothing but the footsteps of my heart palpitations trailing behind.

I settled into Dad's office chair and plugged in the USB. Shit. What the fuck could this be and why did he think I'd care? I'd met all of Dad's friends, and they were more like family, except Mr. Paige, Evie's dad. He and my dad were tight. They played golf together—weird! Dad never plays golf!

The file pops up on the screen and my finger hovers over the play button.

Shoving through the bathroom, I turn on the tap and collect cold water into my palms, splashing the puddle against my face to swipe away my tears.

Dabbing my wet face with a towel, I stare back at myself in the mirror, my fingers dancing across my cheeks.

Even if they knew. Even if Pop was right and it was time. Would I ever be enough? And I don't just mean to the EKC, or to even Dad.

She had a baby with him? They had a baby together? Is that why they are the way they are? Why the only person who has ever pissed me off when it came to War was her?

I'll never be enough. I'll never be trusted.

Fear grips me around the throat and before I can think twice, I swipe up my phone from the bench and rush to my closet. Three minutes, and a flurry of stray clothes flying over my shoulder later, my suitcase is packed.

I've been strong. I've done what I needed to do like a good little princess. I've stood by every single person when they needed it. I've swallowed pain so that the people I love didn't have to taste it.

I need to get out. If only for a little while.

I drag the zip up on my small suitcase and grab my charger and a hoodie, shoving it over my head. With fresh blood on the soles of my shoes, I kick them off quickly before reaching for a pair of thigh-high black boots.

Swiping the keys to my Hakosuka, I rush down the hall to

the other side of Priest's bedroom and all the way to the fire exit on this level.

It closes quietly with a click as I remain still. A black van pulls down the side of the Castle and toward the side entrance of the yard.

Maybe I should kill Katsia and leave them one more body to clean up on their way out.

Dashing down the stairs, I'm thankful I parked out the front as I throw my suitcase into the back seat and stare back up at my home with a swarm of mixed emotions stuck in my throat.

Just for a few days. I need a minute.

Even with the door handle in my grip, my chest tugs me back to the people inside. I don't want to do this.

I shouldn't do this.

I slam the door closed and fire the car to life. Shoving into first, I hit dial on Evie, and she picks up on the second ring. "Hey, girl. How was the dinner party? Anyone die?"

I almost laugh. "Well..." I direct the car out the gates and onto Elite Boulevard, before hitting the main road that leads to downtown Riverside.

"You okay?" she pipes up, and the noise in her background dies down. She must be watching reruns of *The Vampire Diaries* again.

My eyes fly to the rearview mirror. "Yes. No. Not really. Look, I'm going to be away for a while, and I need you to know that I'm okay."

"Is this one of those things that you told me about? Because if it is, I thought we both agreed—Daddy Bishop too—that I get my own passport as well!" I can see her lip dropping from the other side of the phone.

"It's not that."

Silence. "Shit, Hales. Are you running from your family?"

My heart skips in my chest as the realization of what I've just done hits me. I should pull this brake up and spin around. "Shit. I am not my mother."

Evie doesn't attempt to hide how funny she thinks that is. "Uh, no. I don't believe you are. Why? What's Mama Mad got to do with this?" I hear a fridge open and close in the background.

"Nothing. Old joke. Keep talking to me, please." I pull to the side of the road, just before the withering *Leaving Riverside* sign.

My car idles beneath my ass.

"Okay. So. Get this, I was waiting for your text back tonight when that guy I was telling you about sent me a Snapchat." She bites into food and it's probably something her mom cooked the night before. Lucky bitch. Miranda is a professional cook and has a famous TV series for it on Netflix. She's kind of a big deal.

"What was the Snapchat and what are you eating?" I can feel my muscles relax and my heart rate mellow.

"His dick! He sent me a photo of his dick!" That does it. I burst out laughing and I can't stop. My stomach aches and tears roll down my cheeks, only this time it's for something other than shame and disgrace. "And I'm eating coconut shrimp!"

My nose wrinkles. "Okay, you lost me."

I rest my head against my window. "I love you, Ev. Thank you for always being my rock." I don't even have the heart to tell her about the real reason I ran tonight. The thing that triggered it.

"Aw. Come over and stay with me. We can perve on Damon all night."

"You mean Ripper Stefan."

"No. I'm pretty sure I mean Damon."

"Kai?" My brow curves with hope.

"Halen V'cent Hayes…" She pronounces V'cent correct. *V'cen-tay*.

"All right, all right, we both know Klaus is the real MV—" I yelp when a van pulls up beside my car. The side door opens and my heart is back to its rapid beats against my rib cage.

I pump the clutch and try to shift into first.

"What just happened?" Evie yells through the phone.

I let the gear slide out when reality crashes into me. They'll never stop.

Squeezing my eyes closed, my fingers find the buckle as I slowly unclick my seat belt. "Evie," I whisper, reaching beneath my chair, shoving my 21A Bobcat into the inside of my boot. "I need you to call the number that I have saved in your phone as 'Shit I forgot' and tell him that they have me."

"Who has you?" Evie screams this time, but it's too late. My door is ripped opened, and a hand is buried in my hair. Whoever it is drags me across the road as gravel bites into my flesh.

I don't scream. My mouth remains closed as I hold on to his arm until he yanks me up to my feet and throws me into the back of the van.

My eyes explode with pain when I land on the side of something hard, and my movements slow to a daze. Light flickers on above me, showing two others in the back. None I recognize. I don't think. The van jolts forward and I slam against the panel again, my head cracking against it, and I'm out.

"We can use her as our bargaining chip." Hushed whispers stir me to life.

"Why? When she's worth more! That's Bishop Vincent Hayes's daughter! She's worth an easy fifty million!"

"Because we don't have the means, dumbass! I wear a crucifix with a tie to you? Or a fucking skull, or Thorn of Armor tattoo? That's not our niche." I hear rustling, before a dust of warmth over my cheek. "She's waking. We need to decide what we're doing. I don't trust anyone back at the village," the dumb one announces.

"They got so many killed for this bitch. So many of us, man! The Kings might kill us too!" the dumber one blurts.

My chest cackles with fluid, and I roll to my back as blood dribbles down my cheek. "I can assure you, they will. And they'll find you. Within minutes. In fact, I would say they've already found you now."

A shadow casts over my body and I peer up at the man standing over the sofa. "What if I got her pregnant? That'd be a big fuck you to them all."

My lip curls. "You come near me, and I promise you, it'll be you the one who is pregnant, only not with a child." I swipe the blood from my mouth and glare back at the girl who is sitting on another old sofa in the center of the lounge. I don't know where we are, but it can't be far since we couldn't have been driving long. The blood is still wet on my face.

"You killed a lot of our people."

"Wrong!" My eyes widen on them. "We did something better… we gave them hope, made them chase their tails, made them think they had a future, and *then* we ripped their spleens out and watched them wither with time." My legs swing off the side of the bed. I don't even know who exactly it is they're talking about, but if they're going to blame me, I'll be theatrical about it.

But I do know why I'm here. "Where is he?"

The bones of my ribs ache and I wince, applying pressure to the side. Photographs line the fireplace and I study each one carefully. There's one taken near a lake, where fireflies glow through the night, and a large boulder in the middle of the water. Cute. It looks picturesque.

"I don't want to deal with you. Take me to him." Dust falls around my boots and I look over my shoulder. They're both staring back at me with open mouths.

"You know who we are?"

"Depends. Do you go by Bakers, or are you Candyman's bitches?" I raise a brow. "Of course, I fucking know. Jesus. Are you lot really that fucking stupid?" My head shakes from side to side, as I lift my hand to stop them. "Don't answer that."

My arms cross in front of myself, a satisfying smirk crawling over my mouth as they both shrink. I remember Dad talking about this. How people cower in your presence eventually, because they know what you're capable of.

"I'm tired and my best friend is waiting for me." My foot is in front of the other, as I make my way to the other side of the room, when the girl launches up from her chair and her palm flies toward my face.

The back of my hand whacks it away, as my other fist lands between her eyes. A loud crack splits the air before blood sprays over my cheek.

"Well, damn." War claps from the front door, a smirk wide and directed on me.

My teeth grind together as I swipe her cartilage from my knuckles. "Took you long enough. I could have died."

"What?" He spins around to follow me when I pass, and I ignore his persistent eyes. "You against these lot? Hell nah. They should be the ones scared."

"I'm not scared." I pin him with an icy stare.

He raises his hands in the air. "I know."

"I don't have time for this, War. Leave me alone." I head toward the front door when his hand catches my arm.

"Nah, fuck that. You're gonna tell me right now what you're talking about and why the fuck you had Evie call the emergency number." His eyes capture mine when he stares down at me. "Where were you going, hmm?"

I don't answer, but then his fingers slap my chin. "Answer me, Halen. Before your brother gets here with Vaden and we give them a front-row seat to yet another one of our fights."

"Yes, I was leaving, okay?" The words leave my mouth in a cruel whisper.

His face falls. "Why?"

I hate that I know he's disappointed.

"Because I can't—I can't breathe. Because I saw the fucking baby, War!"

His eyes narrow for a moment, and when he realizes what I'm talking about, he laughs, but it's sinister and ugly. "Oh, I see. Yeah, whatever, Halen. You go do whatever you've got to do to make yourself feel better instead of flat-out fucking asking me."

"I don't have to ask you!" I yell, my hands flying up. My anger feels rogue, but with every passing minute I stand here with him, my skin feels like a ticking time bomb.

"Whatever the fuck you guys do on Perdita, with all the games, torture, recruits, and the—sex!" I screech. "You managed to get her knocked up. Now she has your baby."

"That baby is four months old."

"And?" I snap. "How is that relevant?" I don't feel the tears as they fall down my cheeks. I don't feel anything but the resounding fracturing of my heart, because whether I like to admit it or not, he is *mine*. He always has been and always will be. Evie is my rock, but War has always been my world. It isn't that he came into my life during a time I needed him. No. It's that he is always there even when I don't need him. But now—now he's not. I've lost that. I've lost him. I've lost almost everything.

"Halo!" He forces my face to his by the squeeze of my cheeks. I melt in his grip because this is what he does. The only man walking this earth who can handle me, and he always lets me slip from his grip.

He rests his forehead against mine. "The kid. Ain't. Mine." My chest rises and falls as my heart continues to gallop. Silence pulses between us. Moments.

Clarity.

"Why would she—" I stop myself. She didn't. She just let me think it.

"Because she's fucking Katsia." His thumb skims the edge of my lip. "I haven't been with her for a while, baby."

My throat tightens around my sob, as he scans every inch of my face before resting on my mouth. "I haven't been with anyone else but you since this fucking started."

"But—"

"But nothing," he snaps, his fingers crawling to the back of my neck. "And yeah, I'm well aware that the same can't be said for you."

I wince.

"Oh, are we surprised that she's a slut?" the girl sings off in the background.

I sidestep War, taking purposeful strides to her.

"Halen..."

I ignore his pleas, picking her up by the throat and shoving her up against the wall. Decayed wallpaper crumbles from behind her head, and my grip tenses hard enough for the sharp tips of my nails to sink into the side of her skin. "I could tear your throat out right here and not bat an eye."

Her nails scratch at mine in a desperate attempt to get me off her. "But these shoes are expensive."

"You killed my boyfriend. He was—" she wheezes. "He was Candyman's son."

Her body falls to the floor with my parting words, "Call me a slut again, bitch, and I'll hang you from the ceiling by your tits while my brother records a porn with your corpse."

War snickers from behind me and I step backward until I'm crashing against the hardness of his chest.

With a grip around my forearm, he spins me around to face him. "We'll figure this out."

"I need everyone's attention."

I've fought it too long. Pop is right. Everyone is right. I can't do it on my own anymore, not even with Pop.

I need to turn around and take the other road.

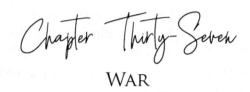

Chapter Thirty-Seven

WAR

I CAN SIT HERE AND THINK ABOUT ALL THE WAYS WE HAVE fucked things up in our lives, or I can do what she said. Even as she whispered those words into my ear, I can't trust her. I want to. Fuck but I want to, and I do. I trust her with my whole fucking life. I just don't trust her with her own.

Priest follows me through the front entrance of the Castle, and we drop the set of keys into the bowl near the front door.

"She all right?" Katsia asks from behind me, and the muscles in my shoulders stiffen.

Priest's eyes shift between the two of us, before he disappears down the hallway to the back wing of the house, also known as Bishop's office.

"Why the fuck did you say that to her?" I could kill her. Put everyone out of their misery. But then that would leave River in the firing line of Perdita, and, well…

"I didn't!" Her arms fold in front of herself, her cheeks reddening.

She sighs. "Okay, so I didn't correct her, but it wasn't to get her jealous. I thought if I had implied that poor, innocent child was ours she wouldn't run. That she'd, I don't know, fight me?"

I remain silent. I can't figure either of them out. They hate each other, I know that much, but there's something else there. Dare I say a level of respect from both sides…

"She's back, though, so that's all that matters. I'll be—" She jerks her head toward the kitchen, where Kyrin and Scarlet are. "—there when—if—she needs me."

I ignore her and push away from the table, making my way down the long corridor to Bishop's office. I open the door to everyone.

Bishop sits behind his desk, Priest parked up by the bay window with Vaden, and Nate and Brantley seated around the boardroom table near the back wall. Madison, Tillie, Lilith, Eli, and Saint are also there, with one more person. Tate. Madison's crazy best friend and mother to the baby out in the kitchen that Katsia tried to pass off as her own.

Hector's towering body rests on the edge of Bishop's desk, and right there, knees to chest on a satin wingback chair, is Halen. The hoodie she's wearing is pulled over her head, and her arms secure her knees to her chest.

"*Amica.*" Bishop is the first to break the tense silence. "We are your family. You know that anything you have done won't matter, baby."

Her body starts rocking a little, and I scrape one of the empty chairs up beside her. I need to give her space, not drag her onto my lap and swallow her whole.

For now.

"Do you want me to start?" Hector's voice is gentle. One I'd never imagine coming from a man born with the kind of savagery he has.

Halen's head bounces from beneath her hoodie.

Hector's fingers wrap around the bottle of whiskey that's on the table. "Before I start, what I'm about to tell you goes deeper than the people in this room right now. It involves others outside of it. We can handle them together. Agreed?"

A round of mumbles in agreement, and I raise a single finger to show my approval.

"Halen was fourteen years old. Three weeks before War's

birthday. A man came by the house and gave her a video. He threatened that if she didn't come to him, that she would live to regret it."

Fuck it.

My arms swoop around her body and I lift her onto my lap. Instead of fighting it like I thought she would, she curls into my chest.

My lips skim her forehead, bringing my arm out across her back to keep her locked against me.

"I can tell them." Her whispers scatter over my chest from the softness of her lips.

My hand lands on her head, forcing her further into my neck.

She wriggles and I know she needs space. A strangled groan leaves my throat as I spread my legs out, loosening my grip enough for her to be able to talk, but staying in the same position.

"First, I need to start by coming clean about the curse. I don't have it."

"We know," Priest's glare is hot from across the room. "Which is why we didn't give much of a fuck when you told us because we all knew you were lying."

"Priest…" Madison warns from the other side of the room. "Let your sister finish."

His mouth closes.

Halen continues, "I used it as an excuse after the night terrors and hallucinations started because the girls started asking questions. It grew from there. The only thing that would weaken them, if not rid them completely, was cold water immersion. A kind of—" She stiffens in my arms and I squeeze to reassure her. "—form of therapy for PTSD."

"PTSD?" Priest cuts in again, and I'm pretty sure I hear the growl of Madison at my back.

Halen ignores him. "It only worked for as long as I did it." She lifts her head from my shoulder, and I follow her line of sight to the girls. "I'm sorry I lied to you. When I got the booklet, it just kind of made it easy for me, because the truth was something I wasn't ready to talk about."

She rests her head back against my chest, her fingers wrapping around my wrist. "The video showed some kids around the same age as me, kneeling in front of the camera. They weren't beaten or malnourished. They just looked… sad. They had no life in them, as if they'd never known anything other than pain and torment. At that point, I thought he was crazy. Why would I care? They looked fine.

"He flipped the camera onto his face, and I was proven wrong. So wrong. He announced I had two days—" She stops, and the room falls silent.

Priest shuffles uncomfortably on his feet. "What kids, Halen?"

Madison kneels in front of us. "Honey. It's okay." When did she move? Why is my body trembling?

Halen shakes her head. "I'm just going to skip to the part where it started. Where I left with them…"

My body stiffens.

HALEN
14 years old

It's cold. Winter had come early, and the longer I stand out on this road, the more I'm going to freeze.

My hands work up and down my arms to keep them warm. The hoodie is thick, but still not enough to thaw the frost chilling over my skin.

Particles of snow fall to the ground around me, one melting against the tip of my nose.

My phone starts ringing in my pocket. Shit. I forgot to fucking leave it there. Mom's name flashes over the screen and I lose my balance when the world tilts, steadying myself with the street pole.

When the phone stops blaring, I open a new text message to Mom.

> **Mother. I have barely left the country. I told you I will be okay.**

I'd never had to lie to anyone before, and I already hated the way my stomach felt when I did.

> **I know. I know you said that it's a no-phone wellness camp—retreat—whatever—but please text me still every day?**

A smile touches my mouth, but I feel nothing but pain.

> **That wouldn't be very *cleanse thy soul of negativity* now, would it?**

> **You're a Hayes. You inflict pain! Come home. I miss you.**

A sob sticks to my throat.

> **I will be back before you know it. I love you. X**

I wouldn't be back. Maybe that isn't enough for a goodbye, but I can't bring myself to say any more. I never thought about the last words I'd ever say before I die, but I know she deserved more than that. They all did.

I close out her response and scroll through my contacts. Dad. Evie. The girls. My brother. Vaden.

My throat swells.

War.

My fingers fly over my phone to shut off the screen before I do something selfish.

Why is he taking so long?

My phone blares again, and this time, Lisa's name flashes over the screen. It's a photo of me when I was two years old, perched on her shoulders. She wouldn't call me if it wasn't important.

Unlike Mother, who would be calling to remind me that I didn't clean my room.

I sniffle back my tears, plaster a fake smile, and swipe to answer. "Hey! Everything okay?"

"Halie, I saw the video." Dread fills me. "Don't you dare do this. Where are you? I'll pick you up."

It feels like I swallowed sandpaper when I clear my throat. "I can't. I'm sorry, Lisa. I have to."

"No, you don't! You're not listening to me. Halen, these people… they won't let you go."

"It's okay—" I pause, her words catching up with me. "Wait, how do you know that?" My head swivels back to the road, even though I know there's no point. No one is here.

"Halen, I love you and your brother more than I could ever love anyone. I remember the first time I ever saw you not long after your mother gave birth. I knew then and there that I would do anything to protect you, that—" She stops mid-sentence, taking a deep breath. What's happening right now? "That my being put in your house to watch your father and the Elite Kings wasn't going to work for me."

My heart drops. I loved Lisa as if she was another mother to me. Why would she do this? "We love you. You betrayed us? Dad did everything for you!" I whisper-yell through the phone.

"No, Halie, listen—"

"Don't call me that!" I snap, the pillow of snow-covered trees blurring together from the tears in my eyes.

"I know you're angry with me. But I need to explain myself before you hang up."

Every Christmas. Every birthday. Every time she would cook for us, bake cookies, tell us stories and love both Priest and me with the kind of unconditional softness that you thought could only come from family.

I know she deserves grace. "Talk."

Turning back to the road, I lean against the streetlight once more. Whatever she says isn't going to stop me from doing what I need to do. *Nothing.* But she deserves a moment to explain. I owe her that much.

"My name is Nina Thorn, and my brother is Magnus Thorn."

I blink. "I don't know who those people are."

She sighs. "I know. Because unlike the Elite Kings, they very much keep to the other side of the spectrum. In the dark. I don't have time to go into explaining of the complexities of Thornhill, but Magnus put me in your life so that I could watch your father. Within the first year, they both came to a silent agreement that they'd stay out of each other's way. Neither of them addressed one another, but they stuck to their agreement. My family, Halen, are nothing like yours, but are in the sense that we don't follow a set of rules. It's more of a family business, than a society." I hear the faint sound of a car coming in the distance and I squeeze the phone in my hand. "Don't leave, Halen. These people, they are bad. He is a bad man. Magnus can help you. He has history with these people and knows what he's dealing with. Please let me help you get out of this."

I swipe the tears from my eyes as they fall. "It's not me who needs to be helped. You cannot tell Dad. You'll put people I care about in a dangerous position."

"I won't," she whispers. "I won't say a word to your father. I'm going to get you out."

I shake my head, my eyes flicking up to the van that's heading this way. "You can't help. Goodbye, Nina."

I toss my phone into the snow as a van pulls up to the curb. The doors slide open to an empty back seat. I take a deep breath and step inside, shutting the door behind myself. The driver's face is hidden behind a ski mask, as he turns the van around and drives off the same way he came.

"You have anything on you?"

I shake my head. "No."

"How'd you get here?"

"Taxi." I rest my head against the window and watch trees fly past my window.

"How do I know you're not lying?"

I glare at him in the rearview mirror. "I really don't care."

He doesn't speak again.

Hours later, my body jolts in my seat. I blink through the haze of my sleep.

In the van. On my way to be the sacrificial lamb.

The sliding door squeaks when it slides open onto the man who gave me the video.

He widens his arm out to the side. "Out of the car, Hayes."

My boots hit the cloud of snow when I follow his instruction. "Follow me."

Shivers break out over my body when I finally lift my head to take in my new surroundings, while maintaining a safe distance behind him. A scattering of office-size pods circle a larger building that sits right in the middle of the broad field. The ceilings are all low and flat, the style simplistic and kind of... weird. Like cubes that blend with the snow.

Blankets of sleet cover the crops and gardens, and there's a fenced-off corner that keeps in smaller animals.

I follow the small path behind him as he leads me to the main building. Stark white walls encase the mustard yellowing of the door. It opens, and his long arm gestures for me to enter.

I pause for a moment, my feet stuck to the ground. There's no second-guessing myself. I'd do it over and over again if it meant protecting the people I love.

My foot lands on the carpet inside around a bright flickering light that beams down from the ceiling. The space is empty, with nothing but a rectangular table that stretches down half the length of the room. Chairs are stacked and pushed against the far side wall, and my head tilts up to the enclosed box of glass that covers the entire size of the room.

"Do you like it?" he asks eagerly.

I tense. "I don't know what it is."

He makes his way to the other side of the room and opens yet another yellow door.

"You guys like yellow?"

His withered face twists, tracing his goatee with his leathered hand. "I didn't choose it."

I bristle. "Why am I important to you? Why am I here?"

His beady eyes flick to the door. "Follow me."

I trace his footsteps through the room and up the stairs. As soon as we reach the top, four people come into view, where they stand against a clear wall that displays the entirety of the room that hangs from the ceiling.

"This is Salem." He doesn't say her last name, but the girl's blonde hair hangs between her shoulders. He moves to the girl beside her. "This is Eloise Evans, or you might know her better as—" His smile widens. "Lala."

"Danny's daughter?" She keeps her head down, her fingers twisting in her lap. "I thought she died when we were young. I remember hearing my dad talk about it with my mom."

"Not dead." The man steps between the bodies of kids. "I just, well, took her." I'd never met her before, and our families were sworn enemies from beef that dates way back. We had to have a treaty between us and everything, but right now, I don't see an enemy. I see a girl who has had her soul ripped from her, left with nothing but the shell of who I'm sure she was.

"Now, this one, this one here is where you come in."

I follow his line of sight, down to another girl who is probably my age. She has washed-out ruby-colored hair that hangs down her back and a small, heart-shaped face. She's the only one I can get a good look at, because she's staring right at me. "Katsia Stuprum."

I also know who she is.

"Now, obviously, she is a little late to the party, since we only just managed to get her the night I gave you the video. Of course, once I found out that she isn't at all a Stuprum, well… I had to direct my attention elsewhere, and well—"

I swallow past the swell in my throat. "That's why you threatened to take River. Because she's a living Stuprum."

He lowers his body onto the sofa, crossing his legs at the ankles.

His head bends to the side as he studies me. "Yes. But you know, then I thought, hmmm… Was this set up? Did Mother Katsia know that I was going to do this and adopt this useless bag of bones as a decoy to protect someone else?"

He shrugs.

He was wrong. The old Katsia wasn't even of Stuprum blood. Good to know our classified files stay that way.

"I guess we'll never know now that she's dead, but I had a better idea. I use River to get to you. A Hayes. Not just any Hayes, but one who is also Venari. How is your grandfather, by the way? I must say, I've not seen him in a long time."

I clench my teeth. Of course, he knows Pop. Every bad man in this world knows him. But they always forget, Pop was nicknamed Hector "Mad King" Hayes, and whispers are fast swirling about Priest "Mad Prince" Hayes. Something I'll never get to see. The rise of my brother taking the gavel. As us Kings. It hurts too much to feel, so I squash it down with my anger.

My teeth grind together to stop myself from losing it. Waiting a few moments until I'm calm, I move to the final boy. "And him?"

"Well, this one right here is Deacon." The man's eyes flash with pride. "Deacon Hayes."

My heart stops as the boy lifts his head up to me. Forest green eyes that I'm sure will burn when given the chance, and soft sable hair. His chin is pointier than mine and Priest's, but he has the Hayes cheekbones.

"What?"

"Mhhmm. That's right. Your grandfather hasn't been as honest with you lot as you would have liked, and by 'you lot', I mean your father." Acid rises up my throat.

"Pop had another son?" My brows knit together. Not possible. "No."

My eyes fly to the aged piece of ham on the sofa.

"Your grandfather actually gave me this idea, so I should give him props. I bet not a single person knows this, not even your mother, but when your father and the Kings were, I don't know, around your age, Hector was still running around as the Mad King." His eyes widen as if reminiscing. "He ordered the three of them to give samples of their semen just in case, ya know—" He waves his hand. "Someone got someone pregnant and then the rest also needed to get pregnant within that birth window that you lot are wild about, or worse, none of them settled but they still needed another generation to carry."

"You're a liar." My nails dig their way into my palms. "How would you know this? No one is privy to King business."

"I know, Halen, because I was your grandfather's oldest friend." The wrinkles in his cheeks deepen when he smiles. "Think of you and Evie."

My blood turns cold. "Don't you ever say her name again."

"Noted." He pushes up from the sofa. "As I was saying, the samples were saved for a long time. When your father met your mother, and Nate and Brantley, and so on, they all ordered Hector to destroy them. Your pop did, because at that point, he was all *I'm a good father now.* Which is also around the time we stopped being friends." He stops a moment.

No one knows much about Pop's life, and I can bet that the mothers didn't know this happened either.

"He didn't destroy one. Bishop's. Because even though he was trying to be a good father, he was still, after all, the Mad King. I knew he wouldn't have discarded it. I knew Hector better than he knew himself." He moves to a small kitchen tucked in the corner of the room. I keep him in my peripheral, but I don't turn. My eyes stay on Deacon. "I had shared many things with Hector over the years. My ideas. What I thought the Kings needed to be stronger. One of them was breeding from the most powerful bloodlines known in the underworld. It was having generational power and, well, leverage. I cornered him one night. It was after your mother had you and your brother. He was outside, smoking a cigar, and looked the happiest he had ever been. I couldn't have that. He knew from the moment he saw me that I had been planning something. He noticed the gang of young boys across the street, and knew they worked for me. I told him that there would be a day that would come, where I'd take something from him, just as he did me. He knew he couldn't fight me. He knew he'd die a street rat. So, he gave me the one thing that would stop me from ever coming for you." He gestures out to Deacon with his glass. "Ta-da, the sperm!"

"What the fuck do you want with all of us?"

"Let me finish!" He scowls playfully. My skin crawls the closer he gets, until my body is a slab of ice.

His hand sprawls out on my hip. I swallow thickly, my head bent to the side and never straying from Deacon.

His stay on the man behind me.

"Or is that not how it happened? Did I use someone else to mother Deacon?" He blows out a breath, his hands clasping together with a loud clap. "Who knows. Anyway! I got a little agitated that Hector had a perfect life, and I needed to take more from him. So here I am, with the most precious thing Hector Hayes owns, and that's a man who shits diamonds, does he not?"

His fingers dig into my hip again. "Baker!" he barks loudly, and someone shuffles from behind.

"Yes, Candyman?"

"Get the pen ready."

Present

I didn't feel the tears fall as I replayed the story to everyone, until the wetness of War's chest slides over my cheek. He's stone beneath me. I'm almost too afraid to move.

Dad's tatted hand rests on my shoulder from behind, his thumb caressing me gently, and Mom's head is resting on my legs that hang off War's.

Pop's silence breaks with a shift of his weight.

"They, um—" My lips curl beneath my teeth as I push myself

up to sit. "It was every day. They would put us in the pen, and they would make us have sex with one another. Every night, when we would be in our beds, which were the single cube pods with five bunks stacked inside, he would come in. I thought—" I choke on my tears and my chest burns when I can't spit out the words. "I thought it was to everyone, but it wasn't." More tears fall and hit my hoodie, and War shuffles up, his arm tightening around my waist as he rests his forehead against my temple.

I clear my throat, annoyed with the power he still has over me. "He only came to me. He just made the rest of them watch. Every day and every night for fourteen days. I quickly found a way to cope with his visits. Some days I just took it, other days I imagined he was someone else—" I squeeze War's wrist. "—but every day I wanted to die. And I tried. I tried almost every night. I'd try to run through the forest to flee, I tried to jump from the ceiling of the main building, I tried to drown myself in a basin of water!" I shake my head with a sigh. "I tried everything but cutting my wrists because they kept sharp objects away from us."

The silence in the room only intensifies the tension of all the mixed emotions, but the more words I let out, the lighter the load becomes. I know it's selfish. That essentially, I'm giving my loved ones the heaviness of what I have been carrying for years, but I'm ready to release it now, and more than that, I know they're willing to hold it.

Fear grips around my heart. "And it's not Pop's fault. He didn't know right away."

"When did you find out?" Dad asks from behind, the anger rippling off him a contrast to the gentle caress of his touch.

"Dad..." I whisper. "Please. Pop helped. He helped me in ways that I'm not sure I would have survived through otherwise, had it not been for, well... the images of War."

"When did you find out?" Dad repeats as if I didn't say anything at all. Someone had just fucked with Bishop Vincent Hayes's daughter, and now it'll be a battle of who gets to take that retribution. I know his restraint is being tested, but I also know Dad. He's killed for much less.

Pop dips his head. "Two weeks after she got back. Nina found me at the chapel in town. She told me everything, down to how she got her out."

My eyes fly up to Pop's, clearing my throat. "They let me go. Was it because of her?"

Pop softens. "Yes, princess. It was her."

.

Past

My teeth catch dirt when a foot collides with my back, forcing me to the ground.

I no longer feel pain. Hurt. Sorrow.

It has been two weeks. Which means in exactly forty-eight hours, my mother will launch a search party if I'm not at the airport, waiting for her. It means that Halen Hayes will officially be a missing person.

"Katsia!" I cry out around the dribble of earth.

Katsia crawls over on her hands and knees, the nakedness of her body glowing beneath the moon.

She whimpers as she draws closer to me. The slashes on her back weep, dripping fluid around to her ribs.

Twigs and stones bite into my skin as I force myself to my knees, glaring up to the man beside Candyman.

I hate that name.

Katsia curls herself into a ball when she's beside me, her arms locked around her knees as tremors shiver through her frail body. She was in a bad way. Locked away for a week while they did whatever it was that they wanted, I'd be surprised if she made it through the night. That could have been River. My stomach forces bile up my throat when images of River being the one beside me right now flick through my head.

Better Katsia than her.

I touch her gently, her skin cold. "It's okay."

She shoves me away. "I—"

"Shh." I don't know what's happening. All I know is that there are three men towering over us, two clearly younger than the others, but still maybe five years older than me.

Candyman pops a lollipop in his mouth. "I will accept your offer for a trade, but only if you drop that one off on her island. Her job here is done." He flicks his wrist at Katsia before kneeling in front of me. "It has been swell, but would you believe, there is someone who is more important than even you? Never thought I'd see the day that happens."

He stands to his full height. "If you so happen to so much as breathe a word of this, I won't just come for River, I'll have Evie taken care of too. You know I have the means to do it." The glare he gives me is pure evil. "You know I will."

He's letting me leave?

It can't be.

He turns his back to me and disappears through the clearing of trees with one of the younger boys tucked beneath his arm.

No. No. No.

One of the men opposite lowers his height to me. "Let's get you home, our little leverage."

Now

I blow out a deep breath with the final memory. "That was Nina's family, wasn't it? The men who saved me? They were from Thornhill?"

Pop smiles, but it doesn't reach his eyes.

Dad gives me one last squeeze, before the shadow of his anger ripples its way back to his chair. "Halen." His voice breaks at the end. He's trying hard to conceal the pain in his eyes for me. "I love you, baby, but your pop—"

"No." My whole body tenses. "It wasn't him, Dad. Candyman."

"His name is Callihan Leon," Pop whispers through the ash-tray of his throat.

"He has *helped*. Not just me, but… Wait." I shake my head, peeling myself away from War, who hesitates. My eyes bounce around the room. The mixed emotions that have been weighing the tension in the room are displayed over everyone's face.

I straighten. "I don't want anyone's pity. This here, I don't want this. It happened, I got out, I dealt with it, and now we're fixing it! Do not shed a single fucking tear for me." I push away from War, finally wobbling to my feet and heading for the door.

I've told them what I needed to. I have no more to give.

I pull the door open and my eyes land on Eloise. She's curled into the corner of the hall, her frail arms struggling to keep her knees up to her chest.

Air rushes out of my lungs. "Come with me." I give her my hand and her eyes lighten when she sees it's me. Before I can say anything else, she pushes up from the ground and rushes for me.

I catch her in my arms. "Are you ready to go home? To your real home?"

She steps back, swiping the tears off her cheeks. "Yes."

I lean down to her eye level. "I have your journal."

Her mouth opens a little. "What journal?"

"You know, the letters?" I search the blues of her eyes. "I found them in the back of a car."

Her head tilts.

I take her by the hand and lead her down to the foyer before climbing the stairs. As soon as we're in the safety of my bedroom, I ruffle through the sheets of my bed until my fingers land on the familiar leather.

Eloise is beside me, her eyes wide when she sees what I'm holding. "That's not mine, but I know who it belongs to."

I slowly hand it to her. "Can you give it back to her?"

The corners of her mouth lift weakly. "Unfortunately, no, unless

I can go back in time." Her gaze never leaves the book, holding it in her hands as if it's the most precious thing in the world.

She notices me staring and clutches it to her chest. "I think it was my great-great-great-grandmother's. There were other pages in it that I had read, before they were torn out and it was taken from me, but some pages were already missing when I found it." She must see the confusion on my face, but she clears her throat. "It was left at the end of my bed my first night. I don't know who put it there. I quickly learned whose it was because I'd heard my father talk about the history of her."

"Of who?" I finally ask, the tone in my question gentle.

The corners of her eyes crinkle around the sadness of her smile. "Jeanne Van Hansen was her maiden name before she married into my family."

The words spin inside my head like a washing machine as I struggle to put the pieces together.

"Wait." There's no way. There's no way that the woman who wrote in that book is the very same… "You mean the woman who started the war between both of our families? You mean that's her writing?"

Eloise lowers her head. "Yes."

I take Eloise back to Dad and the boys, after she had said thank you one thousand times for returning the book of letters back to her. I still can't wrap my head around it being scarily similar to the setting of the Factory, and almost identical to how Eloise was picked up, if I'm going by Vaden and Priest's retellings of how they got her here. Coincidences don't happen in our world. Everything happens for a reason, and I'm not so sure I want to know what this one is.

After scrubbing up in the shower, I toss my damp towel into the wash basket. I don't know what they're all planning to do with the information. I'd been carrying it a long time; today was another Friday for me.

My door cracks open and War steps through, eating up the

space with his large body. I've never seen him look the way he does now. The hollow shadows of his cheeks, and the hardness of his eyes that refuse to soften until they're on me.

His jaw twitches, before he steps inside and closes the door quietly behind himself. "The girls told me I have ten minutes with you before they're all coming up." His arm snakes around my back when he pulls me in close. He bends and lifts me from below my ass, until my legs have no choice but to snap around his waist.

He walks us back to my bed, lowering down and resting his hands on my outer thighs. "I'm sorry, baby. I'm really fuckin—"

I press my finger to his lips. "Stop. I don't want that. I have been dealing with this for years, War. Years. Today is another day for me, only now, I don't know…" My eyes drift off before coming back to his. "I also feel weightless. I hate that in order for me to feel this way, I had to burden everyone—"

A growl rolls off his chest and my brow lifts as if to say, *really?* "If you ever, and I mean ever, think that you are a burden to anyone, I'll hurt you."

"Aw." I brush some of his short hair back. "And here I thought you were going to be gentle with me now."

"I will be." He winces, before darkness clouds his eyes. "But I have other ways I can punish you, all of which include you on my dick." He cusses. "Sorry. Fuck. Tactless."

I bend down and kiss him. "If you ever apologize for being anything other than your smartass self, I'll hurt you."

His lips spread in a half grin. "Oh, really?" He brushes my lips with his, biting at my bottom one. "Tell me how. Come on. We have to drop Katsia at Perdita and pick up some supplies. Give me some shit to work with."

I sigh, using my fingers to trace the tattoo on his neck. "She has been through horrible things, but when she purposely went after you knowing who you were to me—" I shake my head.

War shifts back. "How do you mean?"

My cheeks heat and I tuck my hair behind my ear. "Well, the

person I would imagine to get me through the nights that he would come in, was, well… you." His fingers bite into my thighs. "It was the only thing that got me through. She knew. She heard me whisper your name sometimes while it was happening."

I find War's face and the hardness is back. He bares his teeth before his hand finds the back of my neck and he pulls me into his mouth. "I'll meet you there, okay?" He's struggling, just like Dad was. He tries to blanket his anger with a soothing tone, but I know what lies beneath. Enough rage that he could take out an entire village with his bare hands.

He kisses me, leaving his lips against mine a moment longer. "Can't wait to see this island you and your pop have been fucking around with and filling with our enemies." So Pop had filled them in. Good.

I roll my eyes and kiss him harshly. "They're not our enemies. They're victims. We just can't have them near King territory."

"We promised Hector that we'd let it run its course. I mean, fuck, we could always use another place to branch out on anyway." He flashes me an innocent grin. "That's why we're all meeting you there tomorrow." He catches my chin with his thumb and finger. "I love you." The words hit me right in the heart as my breath hitches.

My eyes fall to the piercings on his nose, before returning. "I love you."

The door swings open from behind us.

"Ten minutes are up! It's our turn!"

War rolls his eyes, standing to his full height while using one hand to lift me, his lips never leaving mine. His tongue swipes over my own before he gently lowers my feet to the ground.

He kisses my forehead. "See you tomorrow."

Then he's gone.

Stella and River part, revealing Evie, her worried eyes on me. I shift to the person beside her.

Luna is dressed in casual yoga pants and a loose knit jersey. "I can leave! I was just coming to see if you guys were okay…"

"No!" I shake my head, waving her in. "I'd rather not tell this story ever again after today, so come in. Since you're, like—" My head cocks. "Half a King?"

Luna steps into the room as Evie closes the door behind herself. I can feel her. She already knows something is wrong and that what I'm about to tell her is going to upset her. I think the hardest part about sharing any kind of trauma with people is sometimes, we don't want to have to give the ones we love the pain that we've held on to.

This wouldn't usually be a problem, if your family wasn't an army of killers.

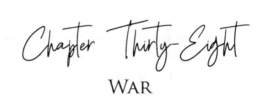

WAR

P RIEST BLAZES THE TIP OF HIS CIGARETTE. WE WERE
supposed to be in and out, but once we got here, there was
a new load waiting for us. The note read:

Your entrée for tomorrow night.
—Thorn

Then, well. We knew we had to see what it was. Even with tomorrow night looming in the background, whatever Archer Thorn
had sent here to Perdita had to be of importance.

I keep my eyes glued into the distance, as the *parcel* dances off
into the dark forest ahead. They're laughing, their smiles illuminating against the moonlight.

Vaden tosses back his drink, lowering the glass onto the steps
of the Perdita mansion. "Mom is working on the new translations
of what Halen gave her."

I freeze, my eyes flying to Priest who is already watching me.

"She got some of it last night. Turns out, the first translations
that we read of drinking the Carva during the ritual wasn't correct.
She's going to text us all once she's translated it."

"That's not good…" I taste the words in my mouth. Our parents had dragged their feet to hold off on the ritual for
years after Saint had translated the first booklet and it re-
vealed that upon the drinking process, there had
to be a sacrifice of one's soul. What

we had thought, up until right now, I'm guessing, was after we took the herb, the curse would find the soul most deserving of its pain.

We weren't to say which of us got it.

We weren't to speak of it upon waking from the slumber, and the only person who would remember what they saw while they were out, was the person it clung to. None of us believed in the bullshit and after we all woke, we all agree that none of us saw shit while we were out.

If it were true, pretty sure it's an obvious choice who it would go to.

Priest. We wouldn't even notice since he's already fucked up.

"Too late now," Priest shrugs his shoulders. "We've all already taken it."

Truth.

"Why are they dumb?" I blink at the two women, ignoring the boy. "You think they're Bakers?"

"Nah." Vaden regards them closely. "They're too... normal. They're annoying."

Their giggles ripple through the night as the whiskey burns my throat. None of us have said a word about Halen since we left. I think we've all silently agreed to leave it in the room, at least until tomorrow.

Priest winces. "It's like nails to a fucking chalkboard. You give them the right drug?"

Vaden quivers. "Don't know. I'll ask."

I kick off the wall and make my way to the group of idiots.

"I will kill you," Priest sings in an eerily quiet tone, insinuating that I'm about to fuck with one of the girls.

I pause, turning to face him. It's the elephant in the room and I'd rather just spit it out and tell him. "I'm with Halen, Priest. I've not fucked a single girl since I've been with her, and not a single pussy has been near me—"

"Errr, someone did suck your dick, though."

I glare at Vaden and he flashes me a menacing smirk.

I rest back on Priest. "I love her. You know I do, you've always known I have."

"It's not that I question if you love her. I know that. We all know you love her. It's in the *how* you love her."

I choke on my laugh. "Yeah, we ain't doing that. Not with you."

"What!" he calls out when I carry on. "I don't love anyone."

I flip him off. Asshole. That's precisely my point.

I stop when I reach them, and both women stop laughing, their dazed eyes lifting to mine. The boy is too fucked up to notice me as he traces the lines of his hand. "You look happy."

"I am." The older woman beams up at me as if I hold all the answers to every question she has ever had.

The younger one pales, her brunette hair glossy and her skin riddled with tattoos. "Oh no."

Oh yes.

The older one blinks up at me, her smile falling as if only just recognizing where she is. Her head swivels over her shoulder, before turning back to me. Panic looks good on her.

"Why are we here? Who are you?"

The boy trips to the ground. "You look awfully bitter for people of Candyman." I pretend to ponder. "Or should I say, Callihan Leon?"

I feel the air shift when they realize just how fucked they are. Katsia needs new drugs. This load is shit.

My eyes widen. "Run."

Vaden's footsteps stop beside me. "You figure out who they are?"

"They don't know Candyman," I say, watching as they disappear through the forest. "But they do know Callihan Leon."

I flip my cap backward after stripping out of my hoodie. "How can it be so fucking hot here but not far from Perdita?"

Vaden's tapping on his phone as the jet doors open. "Because it's closer to hell, no doubt. I mean, I get it. The need for a safe place that isn't going to bleed into EKC business and is kept away from Perdita, even though Perdita got hit by the fucking scum anyway."

I unclip my belt and we shuffle down the aisle. As soon as we hit the tarmac, we're in complete view of the spray of green hills and lush mountains. There's a building that looks almost the same as the White House, beehive included, only painted sable black.

Vaden's laugh is soft around the edges. "Well, shit. If it isn't the secrets we hide."

"What time does everyone arrive?" I ask Priest when I hear his hard footsteps over the metal.

"Eleven. Makes for a midnight slaughter."

We make our way toward the start of the path that leads to the… house? Building? Fucking whatever it's called, and I look over my shoulder just in time to see flight workers unloading a large wooden box.

Cargo is here.

"What are we gonna do with this place after tonight?" Vaden muses as long blades of grass whip our boots.

"Don't know. Pop has given it to us to do what we like." We climb the steps to the front door, and Priest pushes it open just as Halen makes her way down the hallway.

She comes straight for me, and my arms wrap around her back, pulling her in tight.

She kisses my arm. "Come. I want to show you guys something."

"Should I be scared?" I joke into her neck, lapping my tongue over the vein that bounces against her flesh but allowing her to lead me to whatever it is that she wants to show me.

"Always," she quips, before stopping.

I raise my head from her neck and my brows shoot up in surprise. "Okay. Now I see how you're your brother's twin."

"Don't be so dramatic."

I stare back out to the yard. Its flat green grass is clear of any excess shrubs or gardens, but to the left it looks to dip down over the cliff, as if you can walk it. I draw my eyes back to what Halen is gesturing to. There's a single clear cube front and center. You can see in, and they can see out.

"Archer and Danny didn't waste time after you got in contact with them last night. They kept to their agreement, that they would allow us Callihan, though I believe Archer gave you a gift, too?" Halen turns in my grip, peering up at us. "That is his wife, daughter, and son. I don't care for them personally, they did nothing to me. He kept them away from the Factory, from what I gather since I'd never seen them."

I keep my hand planted on her ass, forcing her in closer to me. "That's okay, baby, we're gonna kill them anyway." I use my other hand to tuck her hair behind her ear.

"Figured so." She winces. "There was a slight amendment to the agreement. And before you get angry, I agreed to it for us."

Priest steps closer to the window that overlooks the yard, resting his hand against the glass. "What is it?"

"They want to witness it."

Priest's head snaps to her. "What?"

She lifts her finger. "Priest, this man did bad things to Danny's daughter for almost ten years. Ten years. Archer? His father gave them his best friend in turn for me. He only just got out last night, when they blew up the compound and killed every one of the soldiers. Now, it's just the ones on the street, but they're kids selling drugs, coming from bad homes and all that. Most of them never met him because he'd just pay them off for what he'd get them to do, and they'd never ask questions."

Her eyes drift up to Vaden. "I'm sorry. I know I should have come to you—"

He shakes his head. "We can play nice for one night, I'm sure."

Halen smiles up at him. "Good. Come, I'll show you the armory."

HALEN

THE NIGHT FEELS YOUNG, EVEN THOUGH IT'S FIFTEEN minutes to twelve. The full moon hangs brightly in the sky as I lean over the concrete barrier that lines the mini-Italian-inspired Renaissance garden. I copied Mom, a little, but it was only for this part here, not her extravagant masterpiece. This is my favorite part of this island and one of the first places we designed. To get here, you walk down a pathway from the backyard, right where the clear cube is placed.

White pebbles direct you down until you're beneath a bridge that arches over your head from the slant of the cliff, to where the island ends, connecting to the articulately designed concrete barrier. Greenery and herbs grow over every inch of the concrete, camouflaging it with nature, and statues carved as skulls are placed evenly over the top. I threw in a Tuscan-style outdoor sitting area too, because I'm pretty sure I'll be spending more time out here than in there.

I peek over the rail at the man-made steps that slowly descend until they disappear into the angry waves of water.

I've thought about this night a lot over the years. How it would be done, what would happen when everyone found out. I didn't expect it to be like this. For what we have planned.

I rest the goblet glass against my chest, swirling the red wine around and losing focus on the endless abyss of the ocean. During the day, the sun is hot, but at night, the moon is cold.

Fitting. I don't even know if I'm dressed for the occasion. I kind of thought I'd be in Jimmy Choos.

Wearing flared denim-wash jeans, sneakers, a white crop top, and a beige mid-jacket with straps around the cuffs and hips, I don't know. The simpleness of it bothers me. This is the night I'd been dreaming about. I could have at least been in Jordans.

"How are you feeling, sweetheart?" Mom's voice lures the smile on my lips. She rests beside me, her hand next to mine.

"I'm okay."

"Wow. It's really pretty down here."

"Mhhmmm…"

"Nice designs." She jerks her head forward as if making a point.

"Yes, Mother, it's similar."

She laughs, snatching the glass of red off me. Her eyes close as she buries her nose in the bowl and inhales. Her head tips back as she takes a mouthful, wiping the edge of her lip.

"I've never told you this, but when I was young, something happened to me, too."

My heart drops. She must know my question because her head shakes from side to side.

"I don't want to talk about it much today, but I just want you to know that you're not alone." She rests her hand on mine. "Okay?"

I squeeze her hand as a silent agreement. I want to, though. I want to ask her how, what, and fucking *who*. But I don't, because I know how it feels to have someone force words out of your mouth.

She swallows more wine, remaining fixed on the ocean. Even at this age—not that she's old, she's beautiful. She has grown into an elegant kind of beauty that reminds me of Nanna Scarlet, more than her own mother.

The pain in her words cut deep. "I'm just really sorry, baby. Your father and I, we—" She shakes her head. "I don't want to make this about me and him, because it's not." She turns to me, and I reach up to wipe her tears. "I just need you to know that I am always here.

We are always here, and it doesn't matter what you do, your father and I will always love both you and your brother."

I roll my lips behind my teeth. "What about Deacon?"

"We'll take that day by day. He's your father's son, so he's mine. I'll be whatever he needs me to be."

My lips stain red when I sip on my wine. "He's not a bad person. He's a pain in my ass and really fucking annoying, but he's not a bad person. He tried, you know, to get me out of there. One of the nights that I tried to take my life, I fell from the rooftop of one of the buildings." Another gulp. "He caught me."

She pats my hand just as we both hear footsteps from the side.

Priest and War stare back at me and Mom. "Ready?"

I nod as Mom takes my hand with hers. We walk slightly behind the boys, back up the path that leads to the yard as "I Need You" by Jelly Roll plays from the surround system. I move in slow motion as I feel everyone's eyes on us. Trust my family to make an event out of murder.

War turns to the side where the cube is set up, baring his teeth with untamed rage, and my eyes swing up to the large alfresco patio that sweeps out onto the vast size of the yard to see seven hand-carved, satin black thrones. That isn't what catches my eye first. It's the men sitting on them.

From the left is Brantley, Nate, Dad—I hold my breath when my eyes find Archer Thorn, but he's already looking right at me. *Holy shit.* He doesn't look anything like his father. With wide-set shoulders that stretch out his suit shirt, and a body built like a beast. His brown skin is flawless, except for the faded scar that cuts across his neck in a way that I know someone had slit his throat.

And succeeded. That's a death cut, not a battle scar.

He eyes me carefully as I examine him with unease. A hard, angular jaw, ebony hair that's shaved on the sides in a fade cut, keeping it a little longer on the top. He embodies carnal masculinity as he follows me with dark eyes.

Jesus. I get it now. If he represents Thornhill, that would be a hard *no* from me, and I've been surrounded by dangerous men all my life. Very often do I recognize one outside of our own fold.

I break eye contact and settle on the man beside him. He has similar dark hair, only styled differently. He's not quite as big as Archer, but he's lean and strong. Even from here, I can see the edges of his classical features. Unlike Archer, he has tattoos that cover every inch of skin that peeps out of his obsidian suit. His eyes are on someone to the left, and I follow what he's looking at.

I bite back a laugh when I see he's been staring at a certain raven-haired vixen talking with Luna, before going back to studying him from a distance. I almost lose my footing when I find him now staring right at me.

His eyelashes are so thick, it almost looks as though he's wearing liner, but his eyes, even from here, are so blue they almost seem white. Jesus. He's… creepy. I'm guessing he's Archer Thorn's notorious right-hand, also known as Belial.

I quickly shift to the man beside Belial.

Danny Dale. The Gentlemen. Our enemy in the flesh. He's dressed in a dapper gray suit that's paired with a vest, as he lights the end of the Cuban cigar that hangs from his beard-covered lips. The tattoos on his hands and face only add to his rugged looks, and as if feeling my gaze, his eyes land on me, before further bouncing over Mom and Priest. They settle on Vaden.

Danny Dale and our dads are the first generation to even be able to settle with a treaty instead of a war. Danny's great-grandfather and Vaden's were legendary foes back in their day. Actually, they all equally hated each other. From what Dad has said, their reasoning for peace was simple, since they all had children around the same time. They collectively decided no blood was worth spilling when it could stain your kids. The treaty was then born.

Beside Danny is—I roll my eyes, skipping him. Moses Dale, aka Danny's firstborn. I've never met him personally, but I've heard whispers about him over time.

We stop near the patio and Mom places a kiss on my head, nodding at War and my brother.

War's hand covers mine, the fingers of his other curling beneath my chin, lifting my head up to his. "We'll be down here. They'll be up there, spectating. This won't be easy to watch, baby. You sure you don't want to go inside?"

I rest my hand over his, taking a quick peek over his shoulder in time to catch Stella, River, and Luna sitting on lawn chairs that surround a small bonfire. They're shoving marshmallows onto sticks and laughing. It takes me a moment to realize that they're making s'mores.

Luna says something and Stella's head tilts back, flashing her sharp natural fangs as her infectious giggles fill the air.

Sociopaths. All of them.

I shake my head. "I'm good. Where's Pop?"

War's eyes fly over my me. "Referee, I guess…"

I pat his shoulder a few times, as the music continues to fill the air. Leaning up on my tippy-toes, my lips meet his for a second, before I grab my brother's hand and squeeze it in passing.

I'm making my way over to where the girls are, when Stella curves her hands around her mouth like a speakerphone and chuckles. "Sic 'em, boys!"

WAR

I F I COULD EXPLAIN A MIDNIGHT SLAUGHTER IN ANY WAY, it would be this. Under a full moon, music playing, and adrenaline pulsing so fast through my veins I feel dizzy.

The clear box is a holding cell. Similar to the one I'm sure they used at the perverted fucking village.

Priest unlocks the door to the cube and the hostages stumble their naked bodies out, with tears rolling down their cheeks. Metal collars are latched around their necks, with chains linked to the back, where Priest grips onto with one hand.

The older woman with sandy blonde hair wails, "What do you want?"

The young girl with tattoos gives nothing, until Priest's heavy combat boot slams against the backs of her knees and she falls to the ground. The boy that's with them screams, launching at Priest with pathetic juvenility, when he's met with a fist straight in face.

Crack! The sound of cartilage splitting merges with Jelly Roll.

The boy crawls over the ground with blood spilling from his face, as smoke rings drift out from between my lips. I have to calm the fuck down or it'll be over too fast.

The distinct squeaking of rubber wheels becomes louder the closer Vaden gets, as he drags the wooden table that Callihan is strapped down to.

Callihan's arms are stretched

wide, his feet too, and his naked body glows against the moon-light as he hangs upside down from the tilt of the plank.

His wife screams again, her body flying forward.

I roll my eyes and flick my cigarette to the ground, stomping on it with my boot.

Vaden regards me with a silent question, and I jerk my head to the patch of grass right in front of the patio, allowing everyone a clear view. "Face him this way first—" I point to where Priest is. "This won't take long."

Vaden turns over his shoulder, looking right at Danny Dale. Time stops a moment, before he opens his mouth. "Moses. Care to play with Priest?"

Moses lifts his chin, rolling the sleeves of his shirt up. Danny has three sons and two daughters. Eloise is his eldest daughter and was born the same year as us, but he has a younger one too. Same age as Stella. Juliette Dale doesn't see the light of day, from what we hear. No one has even seen the girl. Danny lost one daughter, so when he finally got another after breeding a line of boys, he locked her ass up.

Moses grabs his father's hand and lifts it to his lips, before taking the steps down while placing a single kiss on the crucifix that hangs off his neck.

He tucks it beneath his suit, nodding at Vaden in silent appreciation. For tonight, we're not enemies.

For tonight only.

He crosses the small distance to Priest, going straight for the wife.

"No!" Callihan howls loudly, tugging on the metal clamps around his wrists. "Please. Just not—not her!"

I circle the table he hangs from, tracing every line of his skeletal body. "I just have to know." I tap my head with the sharp side of my knife. "Did you really think that you could get away with what you did?"

His angry eyes narrow. He really is an ugly motherfucker.

His refusal to answer has Hector emerging out of the shadows. Even in this light, he looks like a bad motherfucker. Inked from head to toe, Hector Hayes is not the man you want beef with. And this idiot did it more than once. Finishing in the worst way you ever could.

"Answer." He remains passive, but I know he's anything but.

"We did." Callihan releases a laugh, and my teeth crack from how hard my jaw snaps tight. "For years. You can't take that away." His bushy brows curve inward when he smirks. "What we did to her? She has to live with for years."

I nod slowly, lifting my shoulders in a shrug. "Point well made." The blood coursing through my veins is all I can hear for a brief moment.

His next words stop me, and my eyes fly straight to him. "You think she doesn't hate you, War? She will hate that you weren't the one who saved her. She would whisper it in my ear every night I'd take her pussy. For fourteen days. She whispered your name as I drove my cock through her ripe cunt, listening to her prayers that you would come. You didn't. You failed her more than anyone else—" My knife leaves my hand and with a loud thud, the sharp end pins the base of his cock to the wooden board.

His pain rips through his mouth with a scream. That's nothing. Barely a warm-up.

I blink past the empty ache that his words left behind. Fuck. "Moses, you have four minutes to make her hurt."

"I set the timer!" Stella calls from behind us with a giggle.

Priest bares his teeth around a smirk. "Four minutes?"

"Wait!" Callihan groans. "I didn't kill her! I didn't kill any of your worthless children! Even though I'm sure she killed one of mine..." *We know she killed one of yours.* Fucker.

Vaden clucks his tongue at him, circling the board. "Wrong thing to say."

"Please," he whispers. "Please don't kill her. I didn't kill Halen! I just—"

"You just what?" The rage of my anger roars so close to his face that he cowers. His cheeks pale. "Raped her?" I lower my voice to a sarcastic whisper. "Stuck your dick inside of her so many times that you made her want to kill herself? Made them all fuck each other in front of your group of little fucking clowns?"

Eli clears his throat from the patio.

I step back once more, not surprised at the way I lost my shit. "An eye for an eye, maybe?"

My head turns to where Moses has her wriggling in his grip.

The begging starts, before tears stream down her cheeks and smudge what was left of her makeup. Her age is fixed into the leather of her skin, but even then, she doesn't look as old as sore dick here.

My head bends as I follow the lines of her body. "You ever been fucked by a King?"

Another throat clear and I spin around to see Halen glaring right at me, a burnt marshmallow hovering an inch from her lips.

"Huh." I turn back to Callihan. "Well, aren't you lucky that my girl is the jealous kind. Moses." I keep my eyes on the piece of shit in front of me, relishing in the sound of flesh being ripped open. There's a short pause, before what I'm guessing are chunks of organs and bodily fluids that splatter to the ground.

Callihan's mouth falls open as shock spreads over his face. But just like the calm to a storm, his screams are loud enough for the veins on the side of his neck to pop.

I blaze another cigarette. "Priest. The kid."

Callihan wails, his head bowing between his shoulders. "I don't give a shit about her."

I nod once more, squinting around the smoke. "Cool."

He spits. "Kill her. I don't care. It was my Tricia who I cared for. Nothing else."

I share a look with Vaden. The question we both want to ask ourselves seems ridiculous, but it could be true.

My fingers are around the handle of my blade as I pull it out of Callihan's limp dick with a spray of blood. I don't want him to pass out.

I flick the end of my knife toward the girl. "What's your name?"

With tattoos marked over her skin and bloodstained brunette hair, her bottom lip quivers.

"Zadie. My name is Zadie, and that monster—" She coughs loudly, but blood cackles from her lungs. "Is *not* my father."

"Is that true?" I ask, staring between the two.

"By blood, maybe. But I have—" She hiccups. "—not seen him in years. He has hunted me for as long as I can remember. I've bounced around the country to get away from him."

Priest shifts to the boy beside her. "But that's not true for him, though, is it? Because I know for a fact that he participated in the events at the compound." It's news to me. I assumed he didn't know shit.

Zadie lifts her shoulders. "I don't care about him. I didn't even know I had a damn brother. I just knew that piece of shit and the bitch who birthed me!"

Priest waves his hand out and blood splatters over us all from the machete he's holding. Moses spins the metal cuff around his fingers and back into his palm, as he makes his way back to his chair.

My blade finds the base of Callihan's chin as I use it to lift his eyes to mine. "Vaden. See if she's lying."

Vaden shuffles around in the background, and I don't have to turn around to know his fingers will be resting against her neck. He refuses to embrace his mother's witchy side and tries to play it off as if he can tell someone is lying by how fast their pulse quickens. It's bullshit. He's intuitive by nature.

"Have you always been running from your father?" he asks coldly.

"Yes." Her words are exhausted. "Ask the old man who grabbed me. I was in Spokane. Killing him will be doing me a favor."

"Truth," Vaden says from behind. "But I think we should still kill her. You know. To be poetic."

Ignoring the out-of-pocket comment from the pure King, I trace the end of my knife over the angry lines of Callihan's throat. "Priest, finish the boy."

Priest's eyes fly up to someone near the girls, and I shift over my shoulder to see Deacon now between River and Luna.

His head bows at Priest, and my brows lift in surprise. Well, shit. Nothing like murder for brotherly bonding.

Priest releases the leash that's connected to the girl, dragging the boy up beside his father.

I give a swift nod to Vaden, who flips the table back upside down, before it swings down again, now with Callihan facing the patio. Pride holds the smirk to his face.

So much for 'I love my wife.' Sick fuck.

Something hard lands on the grass. I turn to catch Priest stabbing a long metal pole into the earth.

His eyes widen. "What are you doing? Just kill me!" Callihan doesn't even bat an eye. In fact, I'm betting the only real reason why Priest is being theatrical with it, is because he did some shit to Deacon.

The metal stick protrudes out from the grass, and someone on the patio clears their throat.

Priest cracks his neck, tugging on the chain to his leash.

"Please. No," the boy pleads. It's pathetic.

Priest yanks it again until it's wrapping around his wrist, and his feet push him up to stand on one of the concrete stools.

Priest widens his legs on the base to steady his balance, before his hand is at the boy's throat and he's slowly lifting him from the ground with ease.

Priest is strong, and the guy in his hand is fucking skinny as shit, but goddamn. That would still take wrist strength.

He tries to swing at Priest, but Priest whacks his hand out of the way before bringing both of his to his neck, lining the wrangling rapist up with the pole.

Priest's lip curls up in a snarl, as the familiar shadows of evil swallow the color of his eyes. "See you in hell."

He lets go, releasing his full weight. Metal and bone grate through the air, mixed with the distinct slush of pulped human organs. Shuffle from the patio catches the corner of my eye, but I stay fixed on the pole that's sticking out of the guy's mouth. The tubes of his large intestines coil around what little metal is now showing, as blood spills from his lips like lava.

"You fucking missed, dickhead…" Vaden taps his shoulder with his.

"Fuck off I did." Priest examines his work proudly.

"You did," Belial says from the patio with a shrug. "Can't always get it perfect."

I suck down enough marijuana to blow out Snoop Dogg, before exhaling and keeping my eyes on Callihan.

His grin deepens when his eyes lift to mine.

My eyes squint around smoke. "Ever heard of a blood eagle?"

His smirk falls as fast as his son's ass did over that pole.

Someone whistles from behind me. "Damn."

"Jesus. You're right. They're worse." I hear Dad shuffle back in his chair.

"Flip him to his stomach."

I grab my hoodie from the back collar, pulling it over my head. I turn around to toss it onto the patio, when Halen's hand comes to mine.

She blinks up at me, taking it and folding it over her arm before slowly placing it onto the step. I think I hold my breath, waiting to follow her lead and afraid I'll do something to fuck it up.

Her fingers flex at the hem of my white T-shirt, tugging it over my body until my arms fall to my sides. She places a gentle kiss over my chest, before lowering down onto the step that meets the grass. I don't know if I want her this close, but I know she's not to be argued with.

All noise in the background ceases to exist as I stare at Callihan's bare back. Hair sprouts from his skin, and I tap the wooden pump with my foot, lowering his body to my level.

He tugs on the chains again around his wrists, lifting his face from the wood, but I press the sharp end of my blade against the nape of his neck, just enough to break the skin.

Blood trickles over my arm as I continue with the incision, trailing all the way down until I hit the bottom of his tailbone.

Show. Fucking. Time.

Using the knife, I make a four-point cut from across his shoulders, and to the lower level of his back. When it looks like a capital I, I bite down on the bloody handle of my knife as I bury my fingers beneath his skin. Lumps of fat get in the way, but I manage to separate his skin enough to start.

Once I'm sure I have enough of a grip, I give one forceful tug, and the skin on his back rips open, tearing away from the meat of his muscles.

His head bends at an unnatural angle, as the convulses start vibrating through him and his pale body goes limp.

I stagger backward, sucking in a deep breath as the adrenaline bounces around inside my body like a damn ping-pong ball. I can feel the erratic beating of my heart slow to an exhausted thud. As if all of the rage and anger that I harnessed over time has finally beaten down a door and used it as an outlet.

"Bravo! Just—" Belial stands from his chair, clapping his hands loudly with a wide grin. "That's—" He gestures to the display. "Art! Both of them!"

"Jesus," Bishop cusses, standing to his full height. I still haven't leveled back out when he pulls me into his arms, slapping my back.

"You good?" I don't miss the worry lines between his brows, but there's something more there.

Pride.

We've killed people before. Many times. Most of them personally, enemies of ours. I don't take a life lightly, it's always personal. If you've touched, tried to claim, or threatened what's mine, I'd put a bullet between your eyes faster than your neurons can signal your next thought process. But this is different. The weight of emotion hardens on my shoulders the more time passes.

This kill wasn't senseless.

It wasn't because of some dumb shit our enemies had done, or wandered into in the middle of a game that no one should know about.

This was personal. Not because they touched what's mine, but because they fucking touched *her*. The weight of her torment is heavy, but I'll fucking carry it for the rest of my life if it means that she never has to.

Dad ruffles my hair playfully, but I can't find it in me to smile. I don't feel fucking proud. I don't even feel good. Because this doesn't take away the fact that they did this to her. They hurt her.

My jaw tenses as I feel that same anger temper down my arms and fizzle through my fingertips. This isn't good. I need to collect myself.

Before I can conjure up a plan, Hector pulls me in by the back of my neck until my forehead rests against his. "Proud of you, son. You took care of family. You did what needed to be done." I did everything but what mattered. Protect her at the time.

My chest swells and my skin dampens from the beads of sweat, but I nod, before dipping out from beneath him without being obvious. I don't want anyone, much less her, to see how fucked up I am. This is a weakness. I hate hard, fuck hard, love hard, but rage? Pain? I feel that shit just as hard.

Champagne corks pop off in the background and the backs of my eyes turn hot. Every second that I'm here, I feel the penetration of those parting words sink further and further into my flesh. It's only a matter of time before they get all the way in. Then I'll detonate.

I can't stay.

I fucking need to. For her. I can do it for her. But she deserves softness when it comes to this. Halen is both leather and velvet, and I'm a fucking craftsman when it comes to her. I've not only seen every inch that there is to see of her, felt every fucking scar and wound, but I've existed within her. We are one. We always have been and always will be. But for right now, I know that this is something she doesn't need to see. She doesn't need to see that I am slowly being consumed by my own guilt. She doesn't need to witness my penitence shrivel and die at my feet on a night that should be celebrated by her.

I hate myself for feeling this way.

Right now, she needs peace. Not war.

My body turns to leave, when the laughter of the group near the bonfire stops me. They all blur together, and I rub my eyes with the base of my palm.

As soon as my vision clears, I catch Stella snapping selfies with the leftover corpses still in their resting positions. Her leg lifts against the side of the one with the stick, as she grabs at one of her tits with her free hand, resting her tongue against its jaw. *Snap. Snap. Snap.*

River shakes her head at Stella but doesn't stop her, as Vaden's heavy footsteps land in front of his sister. I can hear him going on about evidence and using her head for something other than sex and murder for once. Her response is hostile, throwing back in his face how not everyone can be the perfect child, and that it's a Polaroid so no one else will see. Her arm swings over to Priest, who meets her with a raised brow, either in challenge or pride, before yapping about adding the photos onto the wall with Priest's victims.

There's a reason why Stella and Priest are never allowed around each other alone. This is a prime example.

For once, not even my family's antics are enough to pull myself out of the emotional sludge I've found myself in, and I can feel myself sinking deeper and deeper.

My feet carry me back through the way I came, while ignoring everyone in sight, when I bang into a little five-foot-something body.

I catch her by the waist with a steady hand, and the ground tilts beneath us.

She's safe. She's here. *Mine.*

Both of our eyes slide to where I've caught her. With one hand on her waist, and the other on her upper arm. When I release her arm from my grip, blood stains her cardigan like a cruel reminder.

I fucking manifested this shit.

"You okay?" Her voice lulls me back to the moment.

I brush the back of my finger over the silk of her cheek, ignoring the way the dagger that burns in my pocket feels more like it's lodged in my heart. "Yeah, baby. I'm good. You?"

I have to be smart. As in tune as I am to her, she is to me. Bonded from before birth, our souls were forged together by a fucking firestorm of chaos, one that will burn eternally, and turn everything in its path to ash.

The corners of her eyes slant, but it's not because she's suspicious. It's that she's... free. She's been snatched of so much—I'll fucking die before I let the teeth of my guilt so much as graze her.

Her fingers twist behind my neck, and she pulls me down until I'm almost level to her. Almost.

Her lips brush over mine and I fight a groan that strangles me. "I love you. Thank you."

Fuck it. Like the sadistic prick that I am, I grab her by the face and force her lips onto mine, swiping my tongue over hers as she feeds me the soft little moans that I've been ravishing since the second her mouth had first landed on mine.

I pull back, resting my forehead against hers while massaging her temples with my thumbs. "I'll be back, okay?"

"Okay," she whispers, and it's that velvet side that she only ever allows me to touch.

"Say it." I kiss her once, before allowing our lips to sail over each other's. "Tell me you know that I'll be back. That I'll never leave you."

Her eyes search mine, and I can almost hear her pleading with me.

She reaches up until her hand rests against the side of my neck, skimming the tattoo there. "I know you'll always be back—" When I go to step away, she forces me back against her lips, and out of instinct, I bite at the bottom one before she kisses me again. "—and

I'll always be here waiting. You're mine, War. All of you. Especially the parts that you think I can't handle. They're all *mine*."

"I love you, baby," I whisper against her forehead, my throat swelling around the words.

She leans up once more and plants a gentle kiss below my jaw. "I love you, War. Thank you for always catching me. Even with blood on your hands."

And I always would. I just hadn't realized that one day, it was going to be her blood that was on my hands.

I wait until she dances off near the bonfire, swiping the bottle of whatever it is Deacon is drinking as he examines the photos Stella just shot. Seeing Halen smile is a reminder of all the years I robbed the earth of seeing it. She should have been like this all along. Never touched. *Never fucking touched.* That same rage bubbles beneath my skin and I tear my eyes from her, implanting that smile inside my head as if she doesn't exist in there already. Before anyone can catch me, I slip beneath the shadows of the trees and with every step I take, I feel myself fall deeper and deeper into the abyss of my own condemnation.

Fifteen minutes later, I'm nestled between our jet and the sleek ivory pearl of the Gentlemen's. It's a complete contrast to our satin black.

The distant sound of propellers chopping against the wind gets closer, but it is still five minutes or so out.

Five minutes I don't have.

The knife continues to burn against me, and my fingers flex in the palm of my hand. The urge to use it to cut myself open and release the shit inside of me is strong.

The blood of an enemy washes off, but the blood of the woman you love stains. It'll decay in the rot of your bones. Nothing washes that shit off. As it shouldn't. I want to feel it. I want it to remind me exactly what the fuck I had failed at. Just not while she is around.

"Where are you going?" My muscles lock at the sound of Dad's voice from behind.

Fuck. I don't have time for this.

His hand squeezes my shoulder from behind. "You did well tonight, son. Real well." I don't bother to turn, afraid that if I do, he'll see the torment eating me alive.

"It shouldn't have happened to her." My anger finally pools in the corners of my eyes. I brush the tears away, spinning around to unleash even just a little on to him, when I come face-to-face with not just Dad, but Bishop, Brantley, Madison, Mom, and Saint.

My legs buckle and my eyes blur as thunder roars through my body in a round of uncontrollable tremors. Arms catch me and it's not until I'm back on my feet that I see Dad, Bishop, and Brantley surrounding me.

"War, baby…" Mom whispers from behind the wall of muscle.

"I'm fine, Mom." I bare my teeth, scrubbing the tears away even though more trail close behind. "I'll be fine."

Dad searches my eyes, turning over his shoulder to the mothers. He shakes his head slightly, but I don't care to think into it.

"Son, look at me." Bishop is in my face now, with his thick but well-trimmed beard and deep-set eyes that look so much like Priest's it's uncanny. "You do whatever you got to do to unleash what the fuck is eating you in here—" He stabs his finger into my chest. His eyes never leave mine as his hand snakes behind my neck and holds me in place. The tears continue to fall. "—then you come the fuck back to our girl, you hear me?" He rests his forehead against mine, and fuck if I didn't hear his breath catch. "You killed her demons. Now take care of your own. You know she'll be there when you're ready. We all are here, son. We're a family. But I also know you, Warren fucking Malum. We all fucking do. Her included."

Bishop pulls me back and my eyes bounce around the parents. All of them. They've always parented each of us the same way. We don't have one mother, we have three. We don't have one father, we have three.

Brantley's head bows, and Saint pushes her body between Dad and Bishop, leaning up and kissing me on the cheek.

When she disappears, Madison takes her place, swiping my tears away. "I love you."

My heart squeezes in my chest as I nod at her.

In a flurry of pink hair, Mom doesn't waste time when her arms fling around my neck. She steps back, placing a gentle kiss on both of sides of my face and then lifts her chin slightly.

"Go. Not too far, War." Mom pats my chest. "We will be spending some time with Halen over the next couple days." Her eyes narrow, but then soften. "Not too far." The shadows of the night swallow her as she leaves.

The sound of the chopper whipping violently through the air slows, as it lowers to the ground with a powerful pulse of air.

Dad tugs me in again, his mouth at my ear. "Don't take too fucking long. If she's anything like your mother, and we all know she's her auntie's girl, she'll be busting down your door before you know it." Then he releases me, and they're gone.

The days move slowly. Passing minutes turn into hours, and then days. Throughout that time, all of the parents have come through every night to check I'm still breathing. They thought I was asleep, but I don't think I fucking slept at all. I'd stare down at that same blade every fucking hour of every day as I drowned myself in alcohol, in hopes to numb every-fucking-thing.

The new tattoo artist came on the third day, spent six hours on my neck until the angel of death was permanently inked into my skin, with the words *IACY EWBOMH* beneath it. She was quiet. Probably terrified.

On the fourth day, my door swung open and in a flurry of fire and sass stood Evie Paige. She grumbled around the room, complaining about how much she hated how the last episode of some bullshit show she was watching ended, and then sat with me all day as I helped her choose the color of her new ride. We settled on satin black like the rest of us. She was practically a King; the closest you'd ever find an outsider to our group is Evie. When night came, she shoved me into the bathroom, ordered food, and made sure I slid into bed. I didn't remember a lot of this, since I could barely walk through the waft of alcohol I'd been poisoning myself with.

On the sixth day, both Priest and Vaden came and didn't leave. They'd been around a lot, but they knew to keep their distance. I think everyone was making sure that I hadn't tried to really tear out the pain and accidentally kill myself in the process. Because there were times between day one and day seven where I wanted to. I wanted to cut myself open to rummage through the torment and tear it out with my bare fucking hands.

But something held me stationary. Suspended in the air by whatever was left of my decaying soul. I knew what that something was. And I wanted to move for her. Even if the said moving was my hand, around a bottle, and lifting it to my mouth. It was movement. It was time. *It was numb.*

That first week passed.

And then came the second.

The movements were a little different. I could feel my heart beating in my chest instead of it thrashing against my rib cage. I could stand to look myself in the mirror, if only for a second. Which is where I am now, squeezing the bathroom sink with my hands and wondering how long I can maintain this grip before it turns to dust in my hands.

There's a faint knock, and then my bedroom door swings open, but I don't move. It'll be someone. Hopefully Evie. Wouldn't mind seeing that new ride.

Running my hand over my face, I catch Mom in the mirror, her eyes moving around the room. The knife I used that night still lays on the floor, around the mess and empty bottles of alcohol.

Shit. Maybe I'm not doing as good as I'd just thought.

I feel a pang of emptiness in the pit of my gut.

She steps farther into my bedroom, making her way to the other side and spreading the curtains wide until the sun blinds my retinas.

"Shit, Mom. Really?" I shade my eyes from the sun before turning on the tap and wetting my toothbrush. I pause when my eyes land on the half-empty bottle of bourbon in the washing basket, and the three lines of coke that blend with the porcelain.

Mom leans against the modern archway that separates the bathroom and my room. She looks down at the counter, before finding my eyes in the mirror again. "Halen is throwing a party tonight. You should go. It's their final one before they move into the old frat house."

Doubtful. About the me going to a party, and her living anywhere that isn't with me part.

"War." Mom's voice is closer. She rests her hand on my arm with the kind of warmth only a mother can offer.

I lean over and spit out the toothpaste, grabbing at a towel to wipe my mouth. I dip down and kiss her on the forehead. "I'm okay now, Mom."

I could have blacked out for those two weeks and I still would have woken up today feeling the same way that I did the minute I got off that chopper two weeks ago. But through these torturous days, I've realized something that I should have before, had I not been caught up in the emotions of the night.

I blow out a breath. "It'll never happen again." My jaw hardens. "To any of our girls."

There's a bang on the door, pulling me from Mom's gaze.

"This is me knocking!"

My heart beats against my ribs. Fuck. Shit. I kind of thought I'd have a few hours to sort out my hundredth apology.

Halen's body fills the bathroom, and I forget how to breathe. Mom disappears out of sight, and Halen takes her place.

"War. Look at me, dammit." Fuck. I don't want her to know that I've been a major fuckup and let my feelings eat me for the first time.

My eyes peel open, and a hiss escapes my teeth when her fingers wrap around my chin, forcing me to look down at her.

"I gave you two weeks. I had no idea how you were feeling that night until I noticed you were gone when the mothers and fathers came back. I tried to chase you, but one of the dads caught me and reminded me that it wasn't about me. I was upset with myself that I had to be reminded, that I didn't see it in your eyes that night. The torment of guilt that I never wanted you to feel, and how you've always protected me, War—"

I try to force myself out of her grip when those words leave her mouth, but she's stronger, pulling me back into her. Well, fuck. If it isn't *mine*.

"—and how you feel." She rests the palm of her hand over my heart, her eyes falling to the new ink on my neck. Her eyes widen to a veil of glass. "How you always feel to such an intensity that it consumes you." She lifts her other hand and her fingertip skims the fresh ink. "Rage, jealousy, anger, love, pain." She swallows roughly and I trace the way her throat contracts before her eyes collide with mine. "Guilt. Don't ever try to hide your feelings from me again."

A tear glides over her cheek and I bend own, catching it with my tongue.

"Or I'll shoot you." It's a promise, not a threat. For the first time in two weeks, the corner of my mouth curves up.

My arm snakes around her back as my hands land on her ass, lifting her up onto the counter. "Fuck." I rest my forehead on hers. "I'm sorry, baby."

I feel her relax in my arms. My heart twists against the cavity of my chest as my lips skim hers. "I'm both the worst part of myself and the best when I'm with you."

She kisses me gently. "And I love them both the same. Even if one side thinks I can't handle the intensity of its love."

My hand finds the back of her neck, my thumb circling the tender flesh there.

I bite back a laugh and it rustles over the ghost of kisses. "There isn't a version of me that has ever existed where I didn't fucking love you. This—" My other hand trails up her back, burying into the nest of her dark chocolate curls. "—was never about love. This was about me dealing with my own guilt while not wanting it to touch you."

She shakes her head, her hands resting on both sides of my throat. "I knew you'd be back. I was just sad that deep down, the best thing I could do for you at that time was to let you go. You'll always be back. I'll always be here." She leans up until her lips touch my chin. "If only you did fuck me that first time I asked, huh, we could have started this earlier. Maybe then Ba—" My hand flies to her throat. The corner of her mouth lifts in a wicked smirk as her legs find their home around my waist.

I mirror her grin, but my eyes dance with warning. "Halo? You ever think of saying his name again and I'm not responsible for what happens to you, baby, you hear me?"

I catch her lower lip between my teeth, and her nails drag down my arms as goosebumps rise over my skin.

"Shut up and fuck me." Her kisses trail down until her tongue touches the edge of my jaw. She nibbles at my earlobe as her smirk curves against my cheek. "Hard enough to break me."

I shove her up against the mirror and her head flies back as spiderwebs split through the glass.

"Yeah?"

Her hands fumble with my sweats as she forces them down, before sliding off the counter and falling to her knees.

The pillow of her lips wrap around the crown of my cock, as I bury my hands in her hair and direct her over my length. "Promise I won't almost kill you with my cock like the last—"

Her teeth lock around me, setting off a ripple of sharp bites of pain.

My grip in her hair tightens, the deep groan in my chest turning into a chuckle. "Fuck, okay. Shit. I'm sorry. Damn."

Epilogue

HALEN

WAR WRAPS HIS ARMS AROUND MY SHOULDERS, AND I duck my mouth behind them. The buildings burn like a blaze of inferno, as he uses the strength of his arms to pull me farther up the hood of his car.

"You okay?" I ask from behind the sweet taste of his skin.

All of our cars are curved in a crescent moon as we watch the tongue of flames flare through the night. All of us rode out to watch this hellhole burn tonight. Soon, it will be nothing but a pile of ash.

I bend my head back when he doesn't answer, and he stares down at me from above. "Yeah. Fuck, I am."

Evie bumps us at the side, swirling her water bottle at us both. "Just so you know, I get her on Saturdays." We both laugh as my eyes drift off to the side, where Priest is watching the carnage burn to the ground.

She's being dramatic. Evie is not only my best friend, but everyone else's too. I think I've realized that more this month than I ever have. She's the rock of the family. The foothold we have to the outside world. She keeps us all grounded. I wonder, now that I'm older, if that's why Dad and Mr. Paige had become so close. He was Dad's foothold.

River and Stella both lean against their RX7 and NSX, and Stella's head jerks back to laugh at something River said, just as Deacon saunters toward them, flashing two bottles of tequila.

Stella shoves him away

playfully with another laugh. Deacon is obviously new to them, but he isn't to me.

As if sensing my thoughts, his eyes come to mine. A weak smile falls on his lips as he bows at me, lifting the bottle in the air.

Everything is right in the world in this moment.

War drowns kisses on the top of my head again, and my hand finds his neck, where his new tattoo is inked into his skin. An angel with a skull as her face, and her wings rippling into bone. Creepy.

But perfect. So fucking perfect. My heart explodes inside my chest as his hand slips between my thighs—

The sound of all our phones alerting us interrupts our night and I groan, reaching into my pocket with an eye roll. It's never a good thing when the parents hit us with a text at the same time. Maybe I should start a damn group chat with them too.

The light of all our phones beam around us, as I read over the same text I'm sure they are.

I've completed enough of the translation of the booklet to be able to shed some light. It seems we had it wrong. The initial translations were correct, in the way of the steps you take during the ritual. But the herbs that you took does in fact trigger the curse, just not in the way that we assumed.

We were right in the fact that it takes one soul, but we were wrong in assuming that you would know when you woke from the daze.

The person it chooses won't know straight away. It comes in the subtle changes of yourself. It starts small. No one knows what they see because it was never documented, implementing the "rule" upon completing the ritual of becoming a King.

It won't touch the girls, as the witchcraft they used is from a coven of witches that settled near Scandinavia.

It seems the scorned lover of a King pursued this witch and made a deal to put a curse on the land of Riverside, as a way of punishing every generation that came after them. Although your fathers took the gavel the same way, as did Hector's generation, regardless of them not residing in Riverside itself, it seems that the curse did not exist within their generation. I haven't figured out why yet. This will come in time.

Although it may not happen with you all, there's also a very, very high chance that it could. The triggering of it, appears to be in the consumption of the herbs that burned around you, as we had earlier suspected.

The land it's taken inhaled on, and the blood age of who inhales it.

To keep the curse a secret, somehow, someone worked in the rule of silence to stop the Kings from talking about it with each other. I'm sure it's why there was always one King who was worse than the rest of them. They were none the wiser, except for the one it touched, who was sworn to silence under the false guise of a clause that didn't exist with the EKC. This was a spiteful, but intelligent woman—he no doubt did awful things to her for her to go this far. She knew to use the herb, the one thing that cannot be supplemented during a ritual to become a King to lace her magic with.

I'll continue working on the rest of the translations. It's hard because of the language that is used. It's not only a dead language, but it seems it had never been spoken outside of their coven. Keep an eye on one another. Take care of each other. Watch for the signs. This is a cruel taking of evil. One myself and the mothers personally fought for you all to not partake in, but we had run out of time. You're all Kings. You're strong. Resilient. We

will get through it when it happens together. If you come across any more Recipes from the Damned, don't hesitate to bring them straight to me.

Love, Saint

The pounding of my heart doesn't let up, and I fight with myself to not reread over her text. Recipes from the Damned? That's what they're called? Why the hell did I get one sent to me?

Before I can analyze my own King to look for warning signs that he's the unholy marked one, Priest's silence is finally broken.

He's ignored her the whole time that she's been back, but something tells me he's about to break. Probably the snarl on his mouth.

His jaw tenses. "What the fuck are you doing here?"

Jesus. What the fuck happened between them all those years ago?

Priest and His Anarchist
Book Two in the Carpe Noctem series.

The rules of the Concordat

1) Friendships made do not leave the grounds of Escolar dels morts
2) Disciples do not speak of the blood that runs through their veins.
3) When your time is up, you will be called upon.
4) You accept the oath of silence.
5) Accepting contracts in your year group is forbidden.

Within signing this agreement, you agree to abide by the five rules on the Concordat of Escolar dels morts, with the final seal of your blood. Breaking these rules upon departure or during your cycle, will see to you being eliminated, and a proposition will then be submitted to your organization for a replacement disciple.

Escolar dels morts does not hold the responsibility of any disciples, and those who do not wish to participate, will be neutralised according to the laws of tacet a mortuis, enforced by the forefathers of Malum.

Signed:
Luna Nox Rebellis
Dated:
03/04/17

To stay up to date with my latest releases, be sure to follow me on social media.
Instagram: www.instagram.com/darkromancemommy
TikTok: www.tiktok.com/@darkromancemommy
Or subscribe to my newsletter:
www.amojonesbooks.com/newsletter
(that I always forget to send out so I won't spam)

Looking for a standalone from me? Start *Sicko* now...

Want to dive into a completed twisted, eight book series? Start The Elite Kings Club now!

Want something a little less committal with all the power of a completed series? Start Midnight Mayhem series now. A dark, adult circus where the mystery is as hot as the spice...

Don't forget to join my Facebook group too.
www.facebook.com/groups/1011419462242293
They find out everything first! From next releases, sneak peaks into current WIP's, and they're just a general bunch of good vibing people.

More books by
AMO JONES

All can be purchased here through Amazon (link)

The Elite kings Club
The Silver Swan
The Broken Pupet
Tacet a Mortuis
Malum 1
Malum 2
Sancte Diaboli 1
Sancte Diaboli 2
Ruined Castles

Midnight Mayhem
In Peace Lies Havoc
In Fury Lies mischief
In Silence She Screams
In Chaos We Reign

Wolf Pack Duo
Sicko
Wicked

The Crowned Duet
Crowned by Hate
Crowned by Fate

www.ingramcontent.com/pod-product-compliance
Lightning Source LLC
Chambersburg PA
CBHW061403310325
24357CB00027B/578